The Dandelion Killer

Sometimes blood runs yellow

WANDA LUTTRELL

BARBOUR
PUBLISHING

The Dandelion Killer

ISBN 1-58660-753-7

Acquisitions Editor: Mike Nappa
Editor: David Lindstedt
Art Director: Robyn Martins

Published by Barbour Publishing, Inc., P.O. Box 719, Uhrichsville, Ohio 44683, www.barbourbooks.com

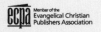 Member of the
Evangelical Christian
Publishers Association

Printed in the United States of America
5 4 3 2 1

For Johnny

Thanks for the memories—
and the turnips!

My special thanks to:

The Army Corps of Engineers for technical information about the Kentucky River;

Officer William Riley of the City of Frankfort Police Department for advice concerning police procedure;

Randall N. Baer for insights into the New Age Movement from his book *Inside the New Age Nightmare* (Huntington House, Inc., 1989);

Frances McGill and the Tuesday Morning Women's Prayer Group at Frankfort First Assembly of God for their prayers;

Leah, Becky, Cara, Jennifer, and Brad for their encouragement and support;

Ana Victoria and Lidia Leigh for their patience.

God bless you all!

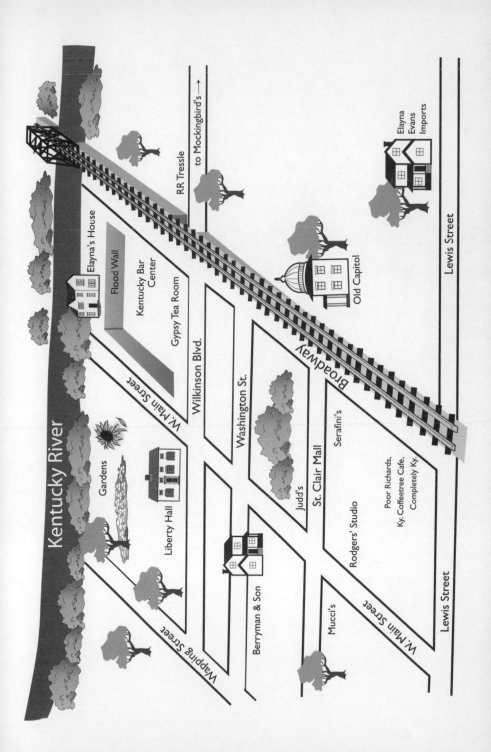

Chapter 1

Jayboy Calvin watched the fog rising from the luminous green surface of the river. It swirled and thickened, reaching greedy fingers toward the bank where he stood. Within the fog was the blackness. He knew it was out there. Waiting. As it had waited for him for more than fifty years.

Jayboy shivered and turned toward the small brick cottage behind him, comforted by the warm glow that fell from the upstairs window onto the lawn below. Knowing 'Layna was up there, working on one of her projects.

As his gaze moved idly across the grassy expanse, he murmured, " 'Layna'll want me to mow one more time." She hated stubble sticking up through the snow. Even if it was just the stems of a few late-blooming dandelions.

"I won't do it!" he vowed. The rebellious thought trembled in his mind. He always did whatever 'Layna asked of him. But she knew how he felt about dandelions. She was the Princess of Dandelion! Surely she wouldn't ask her trusty knight to mow until the dandelions all blew away! Or until the killing frost came and turned them black.

He hated black! He never let Doris buy him anything black. Shoes, pants, jackets, caps—none of his were black. And when Doris bought him a new box of crayons, he always broke the

9

black one and threw it in the trash. Before they left the store. Before it had a chance to spread.

The blackness was out there tonight, though. He jerked around to face the river again. He could feel it out there. Hidden in the fog. Tugging at its restraints. Eager for the time when it would be turned loose to seep into the moonless, starless night. To slip inside his slender body. To fill his emptiness with its evil darkness.

Jayboy whimpered and half turned toward the cottage. Could he outrun it? Could he get to his safe place before it caught him? He began to run. He could feel it behind him. Reaching for him. He forced his legs to move faster.

He hit the lattice with a thump, pulled up the loose piece, and scuttled under the porch.

Breathing hard, he crouched against the stone foundation of the house, his head touching the wooden floor joists. Willing his heart to stop pounding. Willing his burning lungs to work quietly. Searching his mind for a weapon against the blackness. Knowing it would come.

Chapter 2

Elayna Evans proofed the last paragraph of the catalog paste-up that was spread across the walnut teacher's desk in the study tucked between the sloping eaves.

Stretching her cramped back muscles, she took a deep breath, catching a whiff of the carnation-scented powder her grandmother had worn, mingled with the hint of hay and horse sweat that seemed to haunt the ancient stable-turned-cottage.

She pushed back her chair and walked over to the gable window at the far end of the long room that spanned the narrow space between the eaves of the steep roof—the space that had been her bedroom as a child. Pulling aside the heavy curtain, she noticed the fog that had crept up from the river while she worked, making it a perfect night for hauntings—as if she believed in such things.

Despite the mist, squares of light spilled through the small panes onto the back patio and surrounding lawn. A few unseasonable dandelions were blooming and the lawn would need mowing at least one more time before winter. She knew that Jayboy would resist mowing until the yellow blossoms turned to white seed and scattered everywhere.

Sometimes she wished she were more like Jayboy, a perpetual member of the "Dandelion Kingdom" they had created as children—a kingdom of eternal youth reached by following secret paths all the way to spring, where the dandelions bloomed and time stood still.

She sighed and glanced at her watch. *One of the disappointments of becoming an adult is the realization that time does not stand still—although Court doesn't seem to understand that.* He was late again. He had promised to arrive no later than ten o'clock to finish the copy for the voters' questionnaire he ran in each Sunday's edition of the *State Journal*. *Courtney Evans is a good brother-in-law and a good city commissioner, but he has absolutely no sense of time!*

Elayna went back to the desk, pulled open the top right drawer, and took out a sheet of stationery. No doubt Court was still down at City Hall, embroiled in the commissioners' meeting. She might as well complete the handwritten cover letter with which she began each new catalog. Then the project would be done for another season.

She paused, absently running the tip of one unpainted, manicured fingernail across the embossed silver logo that spanned the top of the gray-blue paper. The color had become a part of her trademark, the color Hunt had liked seeing her wear because it matched her eyes.

Her time with Hunt had become a little out of focus, like Streisand's "misty watercolor memories," but tonight it was unusually vivid. She supposed it was due to their imminent anniversary. Tomorrow would make it twenty-five years she had spent as Mrs. Hunter Evans, although the last ten years she'd been alone. Was Hunt out there somewhere tonight thinking of her on the eve of their anniversary? Was he even still alive?

She turned her concentration to the logo on the letterhead. The sight of "Elayna Evans Imports," with its silver ribbon forming the first E and circling under the name and back up to cross the T, usually thrilled her. It was an elegant logo for an elite import mail-order company she had created from nothing. She carried nothing but the best merchandise—hand-blown Italian glass, delicate Chinese porcelain, silk screen prints from Japan, a few quaint pottery and wooden items, some marble, terra cotta, brass, leather—each exquisitely executed by the finest craftsmen.

Tonight, somehow, it doesn't seem important, Elayna thought, running her fingers through her short, dark hair tinged with its own occasional ribbon of silver.

The phone on the desk rang, and she grabbed it, glad for a reprieve from her morbid thoughts. "Elayna Evans," she said.

"Elayna, it's Whit. I'm going to be out of town the end of the week, so I was wondering if we could have dinner tomorrow night. There's a new restaurant. . . ."

"Oh, Whit, tomorrow?" she said, buying time as she collected her thoughts. Whit Yancey was the state senate's most eligible bachelor, and Elayna had from time to time accompanied him to dinner, a play, or a concert. But she had deliberately kept their relationship casual, and Whit had always respected that. Still, she didn't know how to tell him that tomorrow was her anniversary and she still felt very much married to Dr. Hunter Evans.

"I'll have to take a rain check, Whit," she began. "I've got—"

"—a report to finish, a meeting to attend, and/or a new catalog to complete," he finished her sentence for her, an uncharacteristic coldness in his voice. "This is the third time in nine days, Elayna," he reminded her. "If ever you find you have a moment to spare, give me a call." He hung up without saying good-bye.

Elayna stood holding the dead receiver in her hand, debating whether or not to call him back and apologize, to say she would very much like to go out with him tomorrow night.

Whit was a man of impeccable taste—from the clothes he chose to outfit his trim body to the delightful restaurants and events he found for them to enjoy. His dark eyes sparkled intriguingly, and there was just enough gray in his dark hair to complete the air of sophistication he wore so well.

And he's pleasant company, she thought, regretfully replacing the receiver. She hoped she had not offended him beyond repair.

Leaving the blank piece of stationery on the desk, Elayna moved restlessly to the dormer window at the front of the room. Again, she pushed aside the heavy curtain and peered into the fog. Though only a few yards separated her cottage from Liberty Hall, the three-story Georgian mansion of Kentucky's first U.S. senator, all she could distinguish in the fog-shrouded gardens was the white picket fence and a shadowy outline of the brick house.

A perfect night for hauntings, she thought again. Did Paul Sawyier touch a ghostly brush to canvas on a phantom boat down on the river? Was the legendary "Gray Lady" astir next door, spreading covers over Senator John Brown's long-dead guests? Did the spirit of his young wife, Margaretta, pace the lonely corridors or peer with dark, soulful eyes from the tall upper-story windows, wondering about the inhabitant of this cottage that had once been the neighboring estate's stable?

"Nonsense!" Elayna scoffed. Never had she encountered anything remotely supernatural here, despite her childish fantasies that the Gray Lady beckoned from Liberty Hall's third-floor window, or that old Mrs. Hoge passed her in a cold stirring of air on her eternal death-walk from the cottage next door into the river.

Anything could be out there tonight, though. Or anybody. That shadowy outline by the elm tree, for instance, could be Hunt, standing there watching the house, gathering the nerve to ring the doorbell.

She sighed. It wasn't likely, but, then, this *was* the eve of their twenty-fifth anniversary.

The mist shifted, exposing a portion of black sky, and Elayna shivered. *There's just something about this night, something electric and spine-tingling.*

Chapter 3

It was dark under the porch. Pitch black. Musty. Friendly. So long as he kept near the opening. Jayboy didn't like to be shut in where he couldn't get out. He peered through the lattice. It was nearly as dark out there. No stars. No moon. And the fog wrapping itself around everything.

He wasn't afraid of the fog. He could see through it. Like looking through the worn spots in his blanket when he woke up scared and covered up his head. The fog was friendly. Like the dark. They both hid him from things.

The blackness, though, was different. It was out there. Wrapped up in the fog. Waiting for its chance to slip inside him. To fill him up. To make him a part of it.

Jayboy shivered and began putting his things back into the coffee can, identifying them by touch. His ball of shiny foil. The brass button from Mac's old army coat. The silver belt buckle he had found in the mud. Doris's old high school ring she thought she had lost. Candles from his last birthday cake. The glass doorknob that 'Layna had thrown out when she got the new brass one. A piece of a glass paperweight that had arrived at the shop broken.

He shifted his position. He couldn't hear 'Layna in her office upstairs. But it made him feel good knowing she was up there. She had been his special friend for a long, long time.

Since that day when he and Mac and Doris had moved here. Years and years ago. From that tall building right on the street to their house on the street behind 'Layna's. With the big tree by the back porch. The grass. And the golden flowers scattered all around, like jewels bestrowed by some fairy godmother.

"Why, thank you, son," Doris had said when he brought her that first tight bouquet. But she had a funny look on her face. Later, he had found the golden flowers in the garbage can. Mac hated dandelions. He gouged them up with his pocketknife and piled them by the curb for the garbage men to take away. Only 'Layna had understood how he felt about the dandelions.

He would never forget the first time he'd seen her. She had come through the back yard. With her granny carrying that big jam cake with caramel icing. "Hi, I'm 'Layna," she had said. "I'm in the third grade. What grade are you in?"

And he had hidden behind Doris. He couldn't go through all that again. The stammering and getting his words all tangled up. And the other kids laughing. And yelling, "You don't know? Hey, kids, this dummy don't know what grade he's in!"

But 'Layna had just looked at him. Out of those quiet gray eyes. From under all that black hair with sparkles where the sun struck it. Then she had smiled. Not to mock him. But in a way that let him know it was all right that he didn't go to school.

"What's your name?" she had asked. Like she really wanted to know. And he had been able to answer her.

The next morning, he had gone out early and picked a tight bouquet of dandelions. And he had left them on 'Layna's back porch. When he saw her pick up the wilted flowers and put them in a glass of water, he knew. And he had loved her from that moment on.

When the dandelions turned white and blew away that year, he had cried. But 'Layna had told him the dandelion seeds had gone traveling on the wind. To spread the magic Dandelion Kingdom far and wide.

Then she had reminded him how his red balloon from her birthday party had exploded when he squeezed it too tightly. And how the cotton candy Doris had bought him at the carnival had melted into a sticky mess when he grasped it in his hand.

"We just have to enjoy the dandelions, Jayboy, while they're here," she had said. "And not try to hold on to them. Next spring, the wind will whisper. The sun will beckon. And they will appear again. Like magic." She had promised. And she had been right.

Jayboy sighed. How he longed for those precious days of the Dandelion Kingdom! Sitting under the boxwood with 'Layna in the gardens at Liberty Hall. Listening to her soft voice. Watching her gray eyes picture the words as she told him her stories.

Rapunzel. Peter Pan. Robin Hood. Lockinvar. Daniel Boone. Richard the Lion Hearted. He had kept the names and the bright images locked up inside him, like the treasures in his coffee can.

He wished he had a dandelion he could keep in the coffee can. A dandelion that would never blow away. He wished those days of the Dandelion Kingdom could have lasted. Forever. But he guessed he had held on to them too tightly. For they had melted away, leaving a big hole inside him. And the blackness waited to fill it up.

It was worse since Mac went away. He felt a sharp thrust of longing. For Mac's strong arms holding him close. For his soothing voice murmuring in his ear, "It's all right, son. It's all right." Until the blackness crept away, and he could breathe again.

Mac was gone, though. Buried in the ground. Rotting by now. Jayboy shivered and quickly turned his thoughts away from the dark, smothery thought. He needed to do what 'Layna said. Think of something he liked. Something that brought him pleasure. Like 'Layna telling him he could climb just like Spider-Man. Or that he was doing a good job.

He had heard them talking when 'Layna wanted him to come to work for her down at the shop. Her mother had said, "He's retarded!" And even Doris had reminded her, "He can't read and write." But 'Layna hadn't listened. "He can load and unload boxes. He can sweep floors and wash windows," she had told them. "Jay and I understand each other. We will get along fine."

They had, too. He had tried very hard to do a good job for 'Layna. For his Princess. And just this week, she had told him, "You are more than just a good employee, Jay. You're my special friend."

He loved 'Layna. She would always be his Princess of Dandelion. And he would always be her trusty Knight of the Golden Scepter.

He could feel the blackness begin to retreat. Pushed back into the fog by the happy thoughts. He knew it would crouch there. Waiting. But he would be safe for awhile.

Chapter 4

Elayna finished the introductory letter for the winter catalog and placed it on the stack of proofed copy to go to the printer. She sighed with satisfaction at the completion of another exciting catalog for her tenth pre-Christmas issue.

Had it really been ten years since that bleak November night when she had sat at the kitchen table paying bills with the last of the money Hunt had left in their joint account, knowing her grandmother's stroke made it necessary for her to resign her state government job and stay home with her, wondering how she could make a living if she did?

Then, as she had leafed idly through a stack of cheap catalogs looking for inexpensive gifts for the few people she simply could not cut off her Christmas list, the idea for Elayna Evans Imports had come to her. Her company would be different, she had vowed, offering selections not available through the major chains or the myriad junk catalogs she had just deposited in the trash can, yet without the outrageous price tags displayed in the few elite catalogs she received. "Exquisite gifts for the elite taste at an affordable price" had become her mission statement, and it had paid off, far better than she'd dared to hope.

The tinny sound of the old-fashioned manual doorbell at her front door brought Elayna out of her reverie with a start. Laughing at her jumpiness, she ran lightly down the steep stairs, automatically skipping the squeaky second step from the top, the doorbell's continued shrilling accompanying her all the way.

"Congratulations!" she called sarcastically as she flicked on the outside light, turned the big brass key, and swung open the heavy walnut door. "You're only forty-five minutes late!"

"Late? You didn't even know I was coming. How could I be late?"

"Oh, hello, Shirleene," Elayna said. "I thought you were Court. I should have known he isn't late enough yet!"

"He's not here then?" Shirleene swore under her breath.

Elayna hid her surprise at her sister-in-law's obvious disappointment. "I suppose he's still at the commission meeting. I didn't hear the car," she said, her gaze falling on the candy-apple red Porsche gleaming softly in the feeble glow from the fogged-in security light. "But it's impossible to hear anything through these thick walls and doors," she added.

"Let me in, Elayna!" Shirleene begged, glancing to either side of the stoop. "It's creepy out here with all this fog and no moon or stars!"

Elayna unlocked the storm door and held it open. "Sorry," she apologized, as puzzled by Shirleene's apparent fear as she was by her eagerness to see her husband.

Shirleene headed down the hall toward the back of the house, trailing some heavy musk perfume. Elayna glanced once more into the mist surrounding the stoop, then quickly shut and locked the storm door, closed the inside door, and turned the key. Then, realizing she was letting her sister-in-law's melodramatic entrance get to her, she laughed and walked casually down the hall.

Shirleene was helping herself to a cup of coffee when Elayna reached the keeping room/kitchen that spanned the back of the house.

"Just closed the tearoom?" she asked, wondering what had earned her this rare visit. The two of them never had been close, though they had an easy tolerance for each other that served them well when they were thrown together on family occasions.

Shirleene nodded. "You wouldn't believe the crowd that was in there tonight!" She reached for her inevitable cigarette and lit it. "You'd have thought it was Friday or Saturday night, instead of just Thursday."

Positioning herself on one of the stools at the work bar that separated the kitchen from the living area, Shirleene automatically arranged her voluptuous figure so that it was displayed to its best advantage. Even sitting still, Elayna noted, she exuded an electric energy.

"Where's your car?" Shirleene asked. "When I saw it wasn't parked out front, I was afraid you might not be home."

"It's in the shop," Elayna explained. "It runs awhile, then quits. Frank hasn't found the trouble yet."

"You did say you're expecting Court?" Shirleene interrupted, blowing a stream of smoke toward the dark overhead beams.

Elayna nodded. "He's late, but annexation was on the agenda again, and Cy Ames gets so wound up over the cost of sewer lines, water service, police and fire protection. And Court says Martin Jamison is just as determined the Bald Knob Road area will be—"

"I've gotta talk to him, Elayna!" Shirleene broke in. "It's. . . urgent." She slipped from the stool and began to pace, the bright reds, blues, and purples of her full skirt swaying exotically around her shapely legs.

Elayna noticed that Shirleene's low-cut blouse, the same cobalt blue as her three-inch-high heels, was pinned at the top with a replica of the dandelion Elayna had designed as a logo for

Court's first political campaign. It had been meant to represent his humble identification with the common man.

Shirleene's anything-but-humble version had petals formed of a delicate gold filigree supported by a slender thread of stem adorned with two gold leaves. A diamond dewdrop—at least a carat—clung to one petal, reflecting a rainbow of colors in the light from the mock candle flames of the electric chandelier overhead. *Not exactly what the logo was meant to convey,* she thought.

Shirleene went to the telephone, removing one gold hoop earring and laying it on the counter. She picked up the receiver, punched in the seven numbers, listened for a moment, then hung up and replaced her earring. Elayna noticed the diamonds that formed a unique design on the lower part of the hoop. At least, they looked like diamonds to her.

"You're welcome to wait for him, Shirleene," she said. *Why is she so anxious to see Court tonight, when she hasn't given him the time of day—or night—lately?* Even the red Porsche out front belonged to another man. *I wonder if she's aware that I know that?*

Shirleene continued to pace, puffing furiously on her cigarette. She lit another from the stub of the first and waved the smoke away from her eyes with a practiced but impatient hand.

"That's Mannington's top-of-the-line Williamsburg Plank inlaid linoleum you're wearing a path in, Shirleene," Elayna joked, but the pacing seared her nerves as much as the smoke affected her lungs.

Shirleene paused, momentarily distracted. "I thought the floors in this place were all two-foot-wide planks that came over on the Mayflower or something."

"Not quite two feet wide in the front part of the house," Elayna said, "but all original poplar, put down when my great-grandfather converted the stables from the old Harmon mansion into living quarters. But Granddad added this room and the back porch. Then, after I moved back here. . ." She let the words trail off, realizing that Shirleene wasn't listening.

At the sudden silence, Shirleene looked up. Elayna again noticed the striking contrast between the dark eyes and the shoulder-length platinum hair. "Court's blonde out of a bottle," Hunt had called her. But she was fifty-two years old and still a beauty, despite a little too much makeup and the clothes that clung just a little too closely in places.

"What can be keeping him, Elayna?" Shirleene asked. Then she smiled. "They say the wife is always the last to know!"

"Shirleene, you know that, wherever he is, Court is not doing anything wrong!"

Shirleene laughed, but Elayna noticed that the laughter never reached her eyes. "Sometimes I wish he would," she said. "Go out and get roaring drunk—or have a wild, crazy affair. I get so sick of his holier-than-thou attitude."

"He's put up with a lot out of you, Shirleene, and you know it!" Elayna snapped. Then she stared in amazement as tears welled up in the other woman's eyes.

"I realize he should have kicked me out years ago, Elayna," she admitted, "but I guess he loves me." A tear trickled down her cheek, leaving a trail for the next to follow.

"Shirleene, I. . . ," Elayna began, then stopped helplessly as her sister-in-law began to sob. She hadn't seen her cry since that day when Shirleene, or Shirley Ann as she was called then, had come into the school restroom with those other junior girls, her face red and puffy from crying, and unmistakable greenish-purple bruises underneath her smeared makeup.

"I'm never going back home!" she had vowed. "My daddy's hit me his last time!"

Everything about her had seemed so glamorous to Elayna and the other freshmen girls—the job at Woolworth's, the room and kitchenette downtown over Mrs. Watson's Hat Shop, changing her name to Shirleene. Then, soon afterward, she had married the town's most eligible young law student, who had swept her away to a cozy cottage on the edge of Frankfort.

The story should have had a fairy-tale ending, Elayna thought sadly. *What had turned the promise of happily-ever-after into a series of sordid affairs and endless conflict?* She put an arm around Shirleene's quaking shoulders, reaching with her other hand for a tissue. "Is there anything I can do?" she asked as she handed her the tissue.

"I wish I'd never met C. J. Berryman!" Shirleene choked out.

Not knowing how to respond to the unexpected reference to Berryman, Elayna patted Shirleene's shoulder and let her cry until her sobbing gradually eased and she perched on the edge of the stool again, daubing futilely at the tears that wouldn't completely stop now that the dam had broken.

A thump near the back door brought Shirleene to her feet with a small scream. Then she shared Elayna's laugh and sank back down on the stool. "That Jayboy!" she said, her lips curling in distaste. "Still hiding his treasures under your back porch like an eight year old, I guess."

Elayna frowned. "It's awfully late. Of course, Jay can see like a cat at night, and he's never been afraid of the dark. But he's been acting strangely ever since Mac died. His mother can't seem to do anything with him."

"Doris never could do anything with him, and losing his father had nothing to do with it," Shirleene said. "Jayboy Calvin's always been as nutty as a fruitcake!"

"That's not true, Shirleene. Jay just never acquired that veneer of cynical sophistication most of us apply to hide the bewildered, vulnerable children we still are inside."

"Oh, you and your amateur psychology!" Shirleene scoffed.

"I still say he's nuts. He gives me the green, galloping creeps! He's over fifty years old, Elayna, and he still hasn't got enough sense to walk around and chew gum!"

"Shirleene!"

Shirleene quickly held up one hand in apology. "I'm sorry," she said. "I keep forgetting how little sense of humor you've always had where Jayboy is concerned. What a bleeding heart you are, Elayna!" She smiled then, as though at some fond memory. "You and Jimmy O'Brien," she added softly.

Elayna couldn't remember having heard the name before. *Was he a frequenter of the tearoom, or one of Berryman's crowd?* She waited for Shirleene to offer enlightenment, then asked, "Who's Jimmy O'Brien?"

"Oh, he's this preacher I know," Shirleene answered.

"Preacher!" Elayna blurted in astonishment. "I thought the last time you were in church was when Court insisted you say your wedding vows there!"

Shirleene laughed huskily, sat back down on the stool, and reached for another cigarette. "I didn't meet Brother Jimmy in church," she explained. "He drove A. C. home from a party one night awhile back. She'd had a little too much to drink and. . ." Shirleene laughed again. "She was bombed! And she's so funny. . ."

"Anne Courtney is sixteen years old, Shirleene!" Elayna interrupted. "How can you be amused at her drunken antics? Your own daughter!"

Shirleene's expression sobered. "Yeah, I guess you're right, Elayna." She held up one hand, as though to fend off further attack. "I know you're right. You and Jimmy O'Brien and Court. Always in agreement. Always right."

"I don't know this partying preacher of yours, Shirleene, but I do know Anne Courtney is running wild, and as long as you encourage her, there's not much Court can do, short of locking her in her room and barring the windows."

"Aw, A. C.'s okay, Elayna. She's turning into a real looker," Shirleene said with a smile that mingled fondness and pride. "You should be down at the tearoom sometime when I let her sing. The guys go crazy! I really think she could make it in the big clubs—you know, New York, Chicago, Miami."

"Shirleene, Anne Courtney's only sixteen years old!" Elayna repeated, knowing she wasn't getting through, that there was nothing she could do to protect sweet little Annie from growing up in her mother's sordid world. "Doesn't it worry you to see 'the guys go crazy' over her, Shirleene?" she finished helplessly.

"A. C. can take care of herself," Shirleene said. "She's my kid all the way. I don't worry about her half as much as I did when she was little and always wanting to hang out over here, playing with that creepy old Jayboy under the bushes in Liberty Hall's garden."

"That was all innocent fun, Shirleene!" Elayna protested indignantly. "I played with Jay myself when we were little, remember? He's just a big kid whose mind did not mature with his body. There's absolutely no harm in him!"

Shirleene shivered. "I never could understand what you saw in that idiot!"

"Jay's not an idiot, Shirleene! He's emotionally disturbed. And you and your friends probably are the cause of part of his emotional problems."

Shirleene laughed. "He used to get so scared! We'd catch him down by the river and. . ." She swore and jumped down off the stool. "I gotta go back to the tearoom, Elayna. I forgot. . . something. Tell Court—"

She swore again. "Just tell him I'll see him at home. Please don't keep him too late, Elayna. I really do need to talk to him—for the good of all of us!"

Something really is bothering her, Elayna thought, as she followed Shirleene's clicking heels down the polished hallway and unlocked the front door for her.

Shirleene eased the storm door open and looked to both sides of the stoop. "Watch me into the car?" she said. Then she turned to look straight into Elayna's eyes. "If anything should happen to me," she said seriously, "tell Court the evidence is—" She stopped and bit her lip. "Oh, never mind. I'll see him tonight."

"Evidence? Shirleene, what are you talking about?"

Shirleene hugged her quickly, pushed the storm door open, and ran out. Elayna watched her unlock the car door, look into the space behind the seat, climb in, slam the door, and lock it. She started the engine, threw the car into reverse, backed onto the grass, and was down the drive and out of sight beyond the Bar Center's wall before Elayna could collect her thoughts.

At least she's going to tell Court about it tonight, she comforted herself. *But what on earth was she. . . ?*

Elayna gasped as a shadow edged along the wall and melted in the wake of Shirleene's red taillights. She hesitated a moment, then slammed the door, turned the key, and shot the bolt into place.

Chapter 5

Jayboy brought his legs up close to his body, wrapped his arms around his knees, and began to rock from side to side, his head just clearing the floor joists above him.

"Nutty," she had called him. He had heard her up there talking to 'Layna. He had heard her crying, too. And 'Layna trying to make her feel better. But he knew 'Layna didn't like her, either. It was just her way to try to make people feel better.

Shirleene wasn't nice like 'Layna. Always telling him—her and her friends—that they would tie him to a stake and burn him up. Or put a rock in his pants and throw him into the river. Or turn him over to the police—who would cut off his ears. Then his nose. Then his fingers, one by one. Then. . .

Jayboy squeezed his eyes tight shut. He pounded his fist against his thigh. "I want her to feel bad!" he whispered. "Like she has made me feel all these years. Like I still feel when I meet her in the street and she looks at me like she's smelling something nasty. Then she grins. Like she'd do it all again if she had the chance."

He whimpered, drawing his knees up tighter against his chest. He could feel the blackness creeping up behind him. Reaching its sinister arms out for him. If it ever got inside him, he would do something terrible! He knew he would! He wouldn't be able to stop himself.

Quick! He had to do like 'Layna said. Picture something he liked. Put an image between him and the blackness. Something that would bring him pleasure.

He pictured Shirleene. Afraid. Her heart beating against her ribs. Like that little bird that fell down the chimney and beat its wings against the windowpane. He pictured her hands. Wet and cold like one of Doris's dishtowels after he had dried the supper dishes on a cold winter night. He imagined her mouth. Dry and bitter inside like when he tried to swallow aspirin for his headache in church without anything to wash them down. He pictured tears running down her face. And everybody pointing at her and laughing. The way she and her friends had laughed at him.

Suddenly he remembered the sacrifice. He had been right here the day he had discovered it. Under 'Layna's porch. Her granny's porch, it was then. The day he had fed Hunt to the blackness.

He had liked Hunt when he first started coming around. He had told 'Layna once that he thought he and Hunt were a lot alike. With their sandy-colored hair and blue eyes and that sunburnt kind of skin. Hunt was taller. But he was just as skinny. "Scrawny," Doris called it.

Hunt liked him, too. He could tell. Letting him come with him and 'Layna on the boat. Tying up at the landing at his farm. Sitting on the deck. Eating watermelon. Spitting the seeds into the river. Watching the sun sink behind the hills. Listening to them talk. Just as he had listened to 'Layna all their lives. Then Hunt would untie the boat from the willow limb. And let him back it out into the current. And steer it all the way home.

He hugged himself. Feeling again the warm, happy feeling of being together. Of being a part of their lives. Even after little Carrie Hunter was born. Like he was part of the family, with a new little sister.

But those days had ended. Just like the balloon had popped. And the cotton candy had melted. And the dandelions had blown away.

He had been here under the porch when 'Layna came to visit her granny, not long after little Carrie died. He had lain in the murky, musty shadows, holding the can with his treasures inside. Listening to 'Layna's voice above him telling her granny that Hunt had gone off down the river in his boat. Alone. He had listened to 'Layna sobbing like her heart would break. And he had felt the hot hate spread through him. Hatred for Hunt. The one who had made her cry.

He had felt the blackness creeping up behind him. Then, all at once, he had whirled around and thrown Hunt into its path. Flat on his back in the grass. Right in front of the blackness. And it had crept over Hunt and swallowed him. And they never had seen him again.

If Shirleene got gobbled up by the blackness, he would never see her again. The thought spread through Jayboy like a sip of hot chocolate on a snowy day. But he pushed it away. He knew he was to blame for Hunt never coming back. For 'Layna's grief all these years. He never had told her. But he'd never sacrificed anybody to the blackness again. Not even now that Mac was gone and it had crept closer.

Jayboy heard footsteps above him. Leaving the kitchen. Going down the hall. He heard the front door open.

The blackness waited. There in the shadows. *Hovering over Shirleene now!* Jayboy smiled. Then he began to wriggle out of his hiding place.

Chapter 6

Elayna stood uncertainly with one hand on the telephone receiver. Court should be here any minute. According to the custodian, the meeting had adjourned ten minutes ago, and everybody had left the building. Of course, Court could have been waylaid by the politicians who were urging him to run for Whit's senate seat when Whit sought the gubernatorial nomination next May.

Should I call someone else? The police? She definitely had seen that furtive shadow follow Shirleene's car out of sight. He probably couldn't keep up with her on foot, but he might see the car pull in at the tearoom and follow her there.

Why would anyone be following Shirleene? She *had* been jumpy tonight, though. It was highly possible that Court's impulsive wife had gotten herself involved with something or someone she couldn't handle. Elayna bit her lip. The breath of Shirleene's obvious fear chilled the base of her neck.

Suddenly, an eerie wail from the direction of the river sent the chill racing down her spine. She gasped before she recognized the cry of the 11:35 freight, heading up Benson Valley toward the railroad bridge. Glancing at her watch, she saw that the train's reputation was safe. And so was Court's—for being unbelievably late! She couldn't wait any longer.

She dialed the number of the city police station, asked for

Detective Myers, a long-time friend, and related what she had seen. "It probably was just a vagrant," she added apologetically, "but I'd feel better if you'd have someone check it out, Dave."

She hung up, feeling somewhat better now that she had Dave's promise to follow up on it. Surely the shadow she had seen was that of a vagrant, and it was merely coincidence that he had slunk around the wall just as Shirleene left the driveway.

Still, the area was fairly isolated. Except for a scattering of stately old homes and four or five rental houses down near the railroad trestle, the neighborhood consisted of historical shrines, the Presbyterian church, a few law offices, and a couple of antique shops, all closed for the night.

The security light at the wall that separated her house from the Georgian-style law library of the Kentucky Bar Center cast a feeble glow that was quickly swallowed by the fog.

She couldn't see any lights on in the "strangers' rooms," once used to extend hospitality to travelers not well-enough known by Senator Brown to be welcomed into the main house and now rented by an attractive young state government employee named Laura something.

Is there any other human being awake in the area tonight? Elayna wondered, feeling the need for company. With vagrants afoot and. . .

Suddenly she laughed shakily and sank down on a bar stool. *Jayboy!* Of course, that's who she had seen! His visit under her porch completed, he must have headed home just as Shirleene pulled out. He usually catapulted over the wall like his hero, Spider-Man, cut across the Bar Center grounds, and through the hedge into his own back yard. But if he had been playing one of his cops and robbers games, he might have followed Shirleene.

She got up and poured herself a cup of coffee, embarrassed at the state of nerves she had allowed her imagination to create.

How Shirleene would laugh if she knew that Elayna had feared for her because Jayboy Calvin had followed her! She and her friends had tormented the poor fellow most of his life, and he had always been too scared to fight back.

Elayna jumped at the sound of the doorbell, then ran down the hall, relieved that Court surely was here at last. Pulling open the door, she saw that it was indeed her brother-in-law. She unlatched the storm door.

"Sorry I'm late," he said, reaching for the door handle.

Elayna was sure the apology was sincere, though she doubted he'd given the time a thought until now—if he even realized how late he was.

"Come in, Court," she said. "I learned long ago that it is useless to fight City Hall. So, was it a long commission meeting or other politics?"

"Both," he answered over his shoulder as his long legs carried him with easy familiarity down the hall to the keeping room. He turned at the doorway. "They're up to something, Elayna. I just wish I could figure out what it is!" He ran his square, blunt fingers through his hair, hardly disturbing its thick, natural waves. A frown creased his suntanned face and underscored the laugh lines at the corners of his deep-blue eyes.

He's still a very good-looking man, Elayna thought. *Shirleene definitely has been going out for hamburger when she has steak at home!* There was no comparison between the weaselly C. J. Berryman and Courtney Evans, no matter how rich Berryman might be.

"Shirleene was here earlier, Court, but she went back to the tearoom. Said she forgot something, and to tell you she'd see you at home." She didn't mention the shadow.

"She promised to be in early tonight," Court said. "She hinted at some 'big secret' she had to tell me. I'm sure it has something to do with Berryman and company." His mouth registered the bitter taste of the realtor's name.

He poured himself a cup of coffee and carried it to the table, where he removed his suit coat and hung it over the back of a ladderback chair. He sat down, stretched his feet under the small, round table, and pushed out the chair opposite him. Elayna took it.

"They had Grady Enroe bring up annexation of the Bald Knob Road area tonight," he said. "But Cy Ames got the vote postponed."

"Why do they want that area annexed so badly, Court?"

"I don't know, but I've been doing a little homework down at the courthouse. There's been a significant change of ownership of property all around the rim of the river basin. And something's going on down at the locks, too," he added. "Whit says, now that the Army Corps of Engineers has turned them over to Kentucky, the state is strengthening and enlarging them to hold more water. I suppose it has to do with the floodwall."

He sighed, pushed back his chair, and walked over to the window. Pulling the curtains aside, he peered out. "The political currents under the surface of this innocent-looking little state capital are as treacherous as those in the river down there," he said.

Elayna pictured the s-shaped curves of the Kentucky River, wondering what her brother-in-law was leading up to.

"You know, Frankfort is the only county seat of the only county in the Commonwealth that dared to vote heavily against our dear ex-governor," he said, coming back to the table and taking his seat. "What if Sheldon is plotting some sort of revenge?"

"Oh, Court, that's so childish!"

"And who's any more childish than Amos Sheldon?"

"I've always thought he was just a poor little rich boy looking for new toys," she said.

"He is that," Court agreed. "He's always been prone to follow whims, determined to have his own way. But lately he's acting almost irrational."

"And you think he's openly buying up property around Frankfort with some kind of revenge in mind?"

"I don't know, Elayna. He's not buying it openly. But my friend Debbie down at the courthouse has been doing a little research for me in the deed books, and—"

"Is that the pretty girl with all that wonderful curly hair?" Elayna interrupted with a sly grin.

He nodded seriously, ignoring her teasing. "Debbie found that Thornhill practically belongs to James Binford," he continued. "Crestwood is Arland McDee's. Bob Arness has Glens Creek Road. Tanglewood is Sheldon's, and River Bend is Berryman's. Bellepoint and the top of the cliff above Bald Knob Road is Martin Jamison. Lou Gasparo owns most of Buttimer's Hill."

"All members of the Sheldon consortium," she breathed, beginning to believe it. "But what could they want with it? Some of that property is valuable, but much of it is strictly low-rent district." She turned the idea over in her mind, then said, "Is Sheldon going to run for governor again?"

"Whit thinks he has somebody handpicked to run, some fair-haired boy who has no taint of scandal, no federal investigations or media-exposed graft. We just haven't figured out who it is."

"Whit's going to run for governor and you're going to run for the state senate, aren't you, Court?" she said quietly, more a statement than a question.

"It all depends on what the consortium has up its sleeve," he answered evasively.

"Maybe they just know something about Frankfort that means property values are going to rise all around town and they're buying up all the options."

He shook his head. "I'm convinced they're up to no good, Elayna. I'd stake my life on it, even without the hints that Shirleene has been dropping lately. You know she's seeing Berryman?"

Elayna hesitated, then nodded. There was no use trying to pretend that Shirleene was faithful to her husband. Berryman was just the latest in a long line, and everybody knew it.

"She doesn't love him, Court," she offered, for want of something better to say.

He looked up at her, and the miserable confession in his eyes took her by surprise. She hadn't suspected that Court still loved Shirleene so deeply, despite her infidelity. But was that so hard to believe? Didn't she still love Hunt, so much so that just to sit across from his brother and look into those Evans-blue eyes knifed her with pain?

Court handed her a sheet of paper filled with his illegible scrawl. "I've got to go, Elayna," he said. "If you can't read the questionnaire or if you think it should be changed in places, give me a call."

He picked up his coat, and she followed him to the front door. With his hand on the knob, he paused, looking up at the watercolor of Sawyier's boat on the river that Elayna had given Hunt soon after he had bought his boat.

"You haven't been on the *Elayna* lately, have you?" he asked.

She shook her head. She knew Court kept the boat in shape and sometimes took it out, but the few times she had been on the boat in the past ten years, she had found it too haunted by memories. "I. . .I don't enjoy it anymore," she said.

He nodded with understanding, then gave a short, mirthless laugh. "Aren't we a pair? You with a hermit husband with his medical degrees probably hanging from the wall of some bachelor houseboat, and me with a. . ." Tears filled his eyes. "Why couldn't it have been you and me, Elayna?" he asked sadly.

She patted his arm. "We have too good a friendship for us ever to be lovers, Court."

He smiled and bent to kiss her cheek. "And I'm too old for you, though you haven't thrown that up to me since you were a freshman cheerleader."

She laughed. "Well, at fourteen, twenty-one seemed pretty ancient. Now, seven years is less significant," she admitted.

"See you around, kid," he said with an exaggerated Bogart lisp. He opened the door and stepped outside.

"See you around," she echoed, laughing again as she pulled the storm door shut and locked it. She stood in the doorway, watching him maneuver his dark gray Chrysler into the street. *The car suits him—dignified, dependable, handsome—just like the flashy red Porsche suits Shirleene,* she thought, as she watched the car's red taillights disappear around the wall.

She closed the heavy door and locked it, listening as the bells of the Presbyterian church down the street struck the half hour. She glanced at her watch. *Is it only 12:30?* She dreaded the long, lonely night that stretched before her.

Chapter 7

There was blood on his right sneaker. He stared at the widening stain under the beam of Mac's flashlight. Spreading like water running upstream, from the dirty white rubber sole into the faded orange canvas. He flicked off the flashlight and laid it down. He could feel the blackness behind him. Reaching.

He dropped the gold pin beside the coffee can and he rolled away. He wriggled through the hole in the lattice, sat up, and jerked off the shoe. Throwing it into the darkness, he scrambled back under the porch.

Jayboy shut his eyes. Still, he could see her. Lying on her back. Yellow hair spread out. Brown eyes staring. Her bright blue blouse turning an ugly purple. Thick, dark puddles on the floor.

His stomach heaved, but there was nothing left to come up.

He dumped the contents of the coffee can on the ground. He fingered the buttons, the buckle, the ring. It was too dark to see and he didn't want to turn on the light again. Someone might see. He knew his treasures all by heart, anyway. He unwrapped the blue tissue paper from around the candles that had been on his last birthday cake. The paper had wrapped 'Layna's gift of the new Spider-Man T-shirt.

He picked up the pin and pictured it in his mind. Gold. Shiny. Slim gold stem and two gold leaves. And on the fringed petals, a dewdrop sparkled. A dandelion that would never blow away. It would be his forever. He had known the first time he'd seen it. It was meant to be his.

Jayboy wrapped the pin in the blue tissue paper and placed it inside the can. He replaced the other things on top of it, put the lid on, and set the can back against the foundation of the house.

He took off his left sneaker and set it beside the can. His favorite shoes. He could never wear them again. Because of Shirleene's blood.

What would he tell Doris? That he had lost them? That he had dropped them into the river crossing the railroad bridge? But he wasn't supposed to walk on the bridge.

Would Doris notice if he wore his Sunday shoes every day? He knew she would. She knew he never took off his sneakers. Except to take a bath or to go to bed. Or when she insisted that he wear his Sunday shoes to church.

Besides, he didn't think he could stand to wear them every day. He thought about how his feet felt on Sunday mornings as he walked to church. How they felt all through the service, all cramped up and tingly. Then he thought about how good his feet felt when he got home and took off the hard leather shoes

He wouldn't get another pair of sneakers till next August. When all the other kids started back to school. A tear spilled out of the corner of his eye and trickled down his cheek. How could he bear it without his sneakers? Until August!

He wished he could talk to 'Layna. She always knew how to make him feel better. She might even buy him a new pair of sneakers. She could pay for them out of the salary she always gave Doris for him. But he knew he couldn't tell 'Layna about the blood on his shoe.

He couldn't tell her about the dandelion pin, either. Couldn't show it to her. Not because he couldn't trust her. She knew he kept things under her porch. She knew how much he loved shiny things. And she understood how he felt about dandelions. That was why he loved her so much. She was so different from those other girls. From Shirleene.

A grin started in Jayboy's mind and spread down over his face. He wouldn't ever have to be afraid of Shirleene again.

Chapter 8

Elayna walked over to the hall table and sorted through a stack of books she had brought home from the library. The new one by Bodie Thoene. A much-loved Helen MacInnis. A Mary Higgins Clark. Catherine Sheets's latest tale of romantic suspense. She chose the latter and headed back to the keeping room.

"I wish Court could have stayed awhile longer," she said aloud, fingering the book. She really liked her brother-in-law, always had. He had the makings of a real statesman, too. To most people, including her mother, Court was the more attractive of the Evans brothers. But Hunter was the one she had wanted, from the first day she had met him in junior high.

Hunt would be fifty-one in July. Had time been gentle with him? Or had his trim body developed a paunch and the unruly sandy hair given way to a bald spot?

She couldn't imagine him any way but lean and strong, with a smile beginning in the blue depths of his eyes and tugging unevenly at the corners of his mouth. A mouth that surely was made for smiling. *And for kissing.* She closed her eyes, remembering. Amazingly, after ten years, she still could feel those lips against hers, could feel the strong, well-scrubbed surgeon's hands that always smelled faintly of disinfectant, gently caressing her face, her neck.

Dashing tears from her eyes with her fingertips, she walked to the kitchen window and stood gazing without seeing at the small brick patio and the white iron lawn furniture that the unseasonably warm weather had coaxed her into leaving outside.

In her mind's eye, she could see Hunt and Granny seated at the small round table, eating fresh-baked cookies and drinking Granny's favorite Earl Grey tea from dainty cups that suited her small hands and looked totally out of place in his. They would talk seriously for awhile, then Granny would say, "Would you like another cookie, kind sir?" And Hunt would reply, "Yes, thank you, mi'lady." Then he would go over to the lilac bush to pick a bloom for—

Elayna gasped as a chunk of the lilac bush separated, moved, and then melted back into the shadows. She closed her eyes, then looked again. Nothing moved. She studied the bush, wishing Court were still there. Had she imagined the whole thing? Or was that, too, some leftover from the vanished past that haunted this place?

"What I saw was a human form," she said aloud, "purposely dressed to blend with the dark night." He had stood where he— or she?—could watch the house. *But why?*

She tried to dismiss her concern as she had when she'd first thought she'd seen Jayboy following Shirleene's car. *Probably just another vagrant who jumped off one of those freight trains passing through town.* The tracks were just a couple of blocks away. *Someone looking for a handout? or perhaps an easy burglary?*

She shivered, crossing her arms and trying to rub in some warmth with her hands. She had no real valuables. Her mother had sold everything as soon as the will was probated, even the land where the Bar Center now stood. Then she'd gone off on a tour of the world that continued to this day, leaving nothing behind except her daughter, the cottage, and a few antique furnishings that had been willed specifically to Elayna.

The watcher might not know there're no valuables here, though, she realized. *He or she might think there's something here worth stealing.*

Suddenly, her heart skipped a beat. Could it have been Hunt out there, keeping a lonely vigil, as she had done so many nights since he had left, waiting for the appropriate moment to approach the house on the eve of their twenty-fifth anniversary? She stared at the lilac bush with longing, willing Hunt to be out there, wondering how they would react to each other after all this time.

Eagerly her eyes searched the yard beyond the patio, impatient with the fog as it shifted and swirled. At one point, she could see the rising river, lapping now at the dark decoupage of the lawn's edge, framed by the overhanging willow branches against the black velvet mat of sky. Even with the fog, she could see the green luminescence of the house lights and shore lights that hovered over the water, evoking an ethereal, Sawyieresque scene.

A faint creaking, then a thump sounded under her feet. Jayboy again, lifting the loose section of lattice and bumping against the porch floor as he entered the crawl space beneath it. Had it been Jay she had seen by the lilac? *Most likely,* she thought with disappointment. For a moment, she had almost believed it was Hunt.

Something must be wrong, she thought. *Why would Jayboy be going to his "safe place" again so late at night? Maybe I'd better go have a talk with him.* But before she could reach the back door, the phone rang.

"Aunt 'Layna, have you seen Shirleene?"

"Hello, Anne Courtney," Elayna said. Shirleene insisted that her daughter call her by her first name now, since she wasn't ready to admit she was old enough to have a sixteen-year-old daughter.

"Aunt 'Layna?" the girl repeated, and Elayna realized that

she hadn't answered her question.

"Your mother was here earlier, Annie, but she went on home, I think. She said she wanted to see your father."

Anne Courtney snorted. "That's a switch!"

Elayna said nothing.

"Well, anyway," Anne Courtney continued, "I need. . .uh. . .I need to talk with her. But I guess it can wait."

"Your dad was here earlier, too, Annie. I think he also was headed home. You might reach him there. . . ."

The girl's giggle cut her off. "I don't think I want to talk to Dad right now."

Elayna could hear party sounds in the background. Maybe she needed a ride home. "Can I help, Annie?" she asked. Even without her car, Elayna knew she would find a way to help her errant niece. "Where are you?"

The girl giggled again. "Oh, I don't know, Auntie Em, but I don't think I'm in Kansas anymore!"

Elayna's heart sank at the slurred tone in her niece's voice. "Annie, where—?"

The phone went dead. Anne Courtney had hung up.

Elayna hung up the phone, then grabbed the receiver again and began punching in Court's home number. The phone rang several times before the answering machine clicked on. She waited for the tone, then hung up. What could she say? She didn't even know where Annie was.

The little brat! she thought angrily. *Court doesn't deserve this, after all he's put up with from her mother.* Her anger softened as her favorite memory of Annie came to mind—the time when her five-year-old niece brought in a broken and bleeding tomcat for "Uncle Doc" to repair.

"He wasn't even in the road!" she had sobbed. "He was just lying by the curb, and that man ran over him on purpose! Oh,

Uncle Doc, please make him better!"

Elayna had thought the girl might grow up to be a veterinarian, with the love she had for animals and the admiration she had for Hunt and his healing profession. *Well, maybe she will yet,* she thought hopefully, *once she's sown her wild oats, if she doesn't get destroyed in the process.*

She smiled again at the memory of Annie and her orange-striped cat. She had named him Lazarus, because her Uncle Doc had raised him from the dead, just like in the story she'd heard in Sunday school.

"Whoa, there, sweetheart!" Hunt had protested. "You're giving your old Uncle Doc powers he doesn't possess. Old Lazarus here wasn't quite dead, unlike the original Lazarus."

That had made no difference to Annie, though, and she and the "resurrected" Lazarus had been constant companions for five or six years, until the beat-up old tomcat finally used up his last life and an older and wiser Annie buried him sadly in the back yard.

She sighed. What a delightful child Annie had been. How sad that she wasn't "in Kansas" anymore. *Well, maybe after she visits "Oz," whatever that might be, she'll find her way home again, like Dorothy.* Shirleene would certainly be no help. She was trying to relive her own troubled adolescence through her daughter. *Poor Court!* she thought. If only she had the power to patch up his splintered family like Hunt had patched up Annie's stray cat!

She picked up the phone and dialed Court's number again. This time, she got a busy signal. *Maybe Annie wised up and called home,* she thought. If she knew Court, he would be on his way as soon as he got off the phone.

Then the thought hit her: *But what if Annie got the answering machine instead of getting through? Should I try Court again?*

Her indecision was interrupted by the approaching wail of

an ambulance that sheared the silence outside the house. Close behind came the demanding *whup, whup, whup* of a police cruiser and the throaty braying of several fire engines.

There must have been an awful wreck somewhere, she thought, opening the back door and peering futilely into the blackness and the fog. Across the bridge beyond the railroad trestle, the parade of flashing lights turned south on Wilkinson Boulevard, and began heading toward her. *Probably not a wreck then,* she reasoned. *Traffic's sparse this side of the trestle, especially at night.*

As she watched, a tongue of orange-red flame shot up between her and the trestle. *Too far east to be Jayboy's and Doris's place. Is it the tearoom?* It was either the Gypsy Tearoom or something dangerously close to it! But surely Court and Shirleene were both home by now.

Elayna grabbed her jacket from the hook by the door and ran out into the blackness.

Chapter 9

Jayboy gasped. *Sirens!*
The police are coming! His heart was like a trapped bird inside his
ribs. Just like he would be trapped when they found his sneaker
with the blood on it. They would take him away. Just like he
had taken the pin. They'd lock him up. Just like on Doris's
police shows.

He had spent a lot of time with 'Layna and her granny
watching their black-and-white TV. He preferred the shows
they watched to Mac's cowboy shows with all the shooting and
dying, and Doris's police shows with all that Technicolor blood.
And all those people being locked up behind bars.

He whimpered. The sirens were closer now. They would find
his shoe. Out there in the grass. Then they would find him.
Drag him out. Put handcuffs on him. Throw him in the back of
a police car and haul him off to jail.

He had to find that shoe before the police found it! He
crawled out of his hiding place and scuttled back and forth over
the grass, like a giant crawfish, searching with his hands.

His left hand closed on rubber. The sole of his sneaker. Sticky.
He shuddered and swallowed the bitter taste that rose in his
throat. He lifted the shoe by its laces and carried it over to the
faucet where 'Layna hooked up her garden hose. He twisted the
knob and water gushed out. He washed and scrubbed. Washed

and scrubbed. Washed and scrubbed. Washed and scrubbed.

Jayboy held the shoe up to the narrow stream of light from the kitchen window. The outline of a stain still clung to the orange canvas. He grabbed a stick and scrubbed some more. The sole had long since come clean, but the canvas held a shadow of the rusty stain. Barely noticeable. But he knew it was there.

He looked around. Where could he put it? He couldn't wear it. Never again. He didn't want it under the porch with his treasures. Where could he hide it? Where he wouldn't have to look at it. Where the police wouldn't find it.

He walked around the house, carrying the dripping shoe by its laces. He pictured bright red drops falling onto his bare foot. He swallowed a scream as he rubbed the top of his foot on the grass. He held the shoe at arm's length. Still the drops fell onto the grass with the thunder of a pounding heart.

Then he saw it. *'Layna's garbage can!* It was standing by the curb for the next morning's pickup. He ran to the large, plastic barrel, removed the top, and pulled out a crumpled sheet of newspaper. After dumping chicken bones back into the trashcan, he wrapped the soggy paper carefully around the shoe and pushed the hard bundle down into the mound of garbage. Under the bottles and cans. Almost to the bottom.

With a furtive glance over his shoulder, he scuttled back under the porch, panting for breath. He listened to the sirens as they came closer and closer. The sneaker was buried now. The police would never find it. And they would never find him. Not here.

Jayboy smiled, picked up his can, and cuddled it against his chest. The Knight of the Golden Scepter was safe—and so was his dandelion.

Chapter 10

Elayna pulled the gray, all-weather jacket over her arms as she ran around the side of the house. Stepping over the low wall, she cut across the lawn of the Bar Center and through the hedge onto Sutterlin Lane.

The fire seemed to be at the corner of West Broadway and Wilkinson, two blocks away. *It has to be the Gypsy Tearoom!* she thought as she hurried across the lane and onto the uneven brick pavement of Nash Street. Shirleene had closed the tearoom around 10:30, so there were no patrons inside. *But Shirleene went back there,* she remembered. Had she left something burning that had caused the fire—a stove burner, one of her ever-present cigarettes?

Her heart skipped a beat and she almost lost her footing. Had someone set fire to the tearoom? Perhaps the "someone" Shirleene had been afraid of tonight?

She could see the flames clearly now, as she came out of the alley onto Wilkinson Boulevard and turned left. Above the dying whine of sirens, she heard the furious roaring of the fire. The acrid scent of burnt wood stung her nostrils.

"I'm sorry, ma'am, you can't go any farther." The black sleeve of a city policeman blocked her way. She saw other dark figures outlined against the glow of the fire, blocking off the area with yellow crime-scene tape.

"But it's the tearoom!" she protested.

"Sorry, Miz Evans," the young policeman apologized. "I didn't recognize you in this fog."

It's the Butler boy, she now realized, a rookie that Court had helped to get a position on the force. "Danny, if Court and Shirleene aren't here yet, I may be of some use down there. Let me through," she ordered.

He avoided her eyes. "You don't want to go down there, Miz Evans," he said firmly.

"Danny, please. I won't get in the way," she promised. "But until Court or Shirleene gets here. . ."

"Miz Evans," Officer Butler said gently, "Shirleene's not. . . she's. . ." He looked away, swallowed hard, then forced himself to look her straight in the eye, his own eyes filled with some unexplained misery. "She's dead!" he blurted.

"Dead?" Elayna echoed. "But the fire just started. She can't. . ."

"She was dead before the fire was set," he said. "Believe me, Miz Evans, you don't want to go down there."

"Tell me, Danny," she demanded, certain now that whatever she was going to hear would be horrible. Yet she had to know. "Tell me!" she repeated, shaking his arm.

"She was murdered," he answered reluctantly. Then, the dam breached, the words tumbled out. "Stabbed six or eight times with a carving knife from the tearoom kitchen. The place is a wreck, and the blood. . ."

Elayna felt her knees go weak. She clutched the policeman's arm for support. *Her eyes were so scared, so dark as she begged me to watch her into the car.* Elayna drew the thin jacket closer around her, shivering in the black autumn night, the haunting memory of Shirleene's fear imprinted forever on her mind.

"I'm sorry, Miz Evans," Danny said from what seemed a long way off. "But you had to. . .I'm sorry!"

Elayna swallowed the nausea rising in her throat. "Danny, do they have any idea who could have done it? And why? I know Shirleene is. . .was. . ." She swallowed again. "She never really hurt anybody but herself," she finished weakly. *And her husband,* she added silently.

"I know," Danny agreed. "I knew her. . .pretty well," he said, avoiding her eyes again. Elayna tried to identify the emotion that choked his voice. Grief? Embarrassment? Then she knew. *Even this child has been corrupted by the frivolous Shirleene,* she thought wearily.

Danny coughed and stumbled suddenly toward the adjacent parking lot. Elayna heard him gag. She swallowed hard again. Then her attention was drawn to a city police car that pulled in under the railroad trestle and stopped. The door opened, and she saw Court get out. He stopped the white-coated attendants carrying a sheet-covered stretcher. She could see him arguing with the men. Then one of them pulled back the sheet, and she saw Court sag. The chief of police came up and took Court's arm, steadying him.

Elayna stepped over the yellow tape and ran, dodging the outstretched hands of another policeman, ignoring his command to stop. She reached Court just as the attendant pulled the sheet back over Shirleene's white face, but she glimpsed the wide brown eyes, frozen now in a stare of perpetual horror.

She put an arm around her brother-in-law. "Court, I'm so sorry!" she murmured, longing for some magic salve to soothe the pain in his bewildered gaze. He leaned against her as a silent sob recoiled through his body. Then he stiffened his back and gathered his composure.

"Are there any leads, Chief?" he asked. Elayna was relieved to see that he was in control again. He would reserve his personal grief for a private time.

The chief shook his head no. "The fire hadn't reached the spot where we found her. The scene of the crime was intact, though I assume the fire was set to obliterate it. Dave Myers took a call about a vagrant and sent Danny Butler down here to check it out. Lucky he did, too, or there might not have been—"

"Was it robbery?" Court cut him off.

Again the chief shook his head. "Robbery doesn't appear to be the motive. The money bag with the night's receipts was in her purse, and she still was wearing her diamond wedding band and engagement ring, her watch, and one gold earring. The other hasn't been found, but I'm sure it's around here somewhere. There was no tear in her earlobe. It probably came off during the struggle. Nothing else seems to be missing, but you'll know more about that than we do."

A memory stirred in Elayna's mind. She remembered the gold-and-diamond hoop earrings Shirleene had been wearing earlier, but something was wrong with the picture the Chief had painted. In the numbness of shock, her brain would not allow the memory to focus.

She followed Court and the chief into the tearoom, then stopped, appalled at the shambles and the blood. A chalk outline marked where the body had lain. She saw Court pick up something from the top of the telephone.

"Hey, Chief!" Elayna turned toward the shout and saw Dave Myers holding a flashlight aimed at the street near the corner where Sutterlin Lane intersected with Broadway. She supposed Danny had called the detective, once the murder was discovered.

She followed Court and the chief, watching the beam of light trace a trail of faded red footprints across the lane and down Broadway to where the railroad trestle ran headlong into the floodwall along the riverbank.

The tracks grew steadily fainter, fading from a bright red

back near the tearoom to a dark, rusty brown at the intersection. She realized with a fresh shock that the trail had been made of Shirleene's lifeblood, obscenely tracked down a dirty street.

"A right athletic shoe, sir, about a size eight-and-a-half or nine. Man's," Myers guessed. "Distinct sole pattern. Left one's clean. It made no trail." The beam of light followed the tracks across the sidewalk and onto the grass between the pavement and the floodwall. There they ended.

Suddenly the beam of light shot up and across the wall. One faded half-print was outlined clearly about halfway up. *As if someone ran straight up the wall,* Elayna thought.

The detective pulled himself up onto the wall. "They're here, sir, along the top, but very faint." He ran lightly along the top of the narrow wall, following the light. "He jumped off here, Chief!" he called back.

Elayna gasped. The murderer had jumped from the wall into her back yard! That must have been the shadow she had seen by the lilac bush just before she left the house. Had it been the murderer she had seen following Shirleene's car earlier, and not Jayboy? If she had not hesitated but had called the police immediately, would Shirleene still be alive?

Her thoughts shifted to why? Why had he attacked Shirleene? Nothing had been taken from the tearoom. What had he wanted? And why had he come back to her house afterward? Wouldn't it have been easier to escape by slipping away down the river in one of the boats moored along the bank? Or to disappear into the dark recesses of the Capital Plaza area a few blocks away? And why had he been in her yard in the first place? Had he followed Shirleene when she left the tearoom earlier?

The footprints, though, must have been made later, because Shirleene had still been alive when Elayna had seen the first shadow. Had he returned to her place after the murder while she and Court were talking inside the house?

Suddenly she remembered that, in the urgency of flames and sirens, she had neglected to lock her back door. Was the murderer, even now, hiding there, awaiting her return?

Elayna shuddered at the thought that she might have brushed past Shirleene's killer in the dark after he had leapt like Spider-Man from the wall into her yard.

"Spider-Man!" she breathed. "Oh no." A picture formed in her mind of Jayboy running along the top of the floodwall, laughing at her fear of heights, playfully calling dares down to her. She had given him a T-shirt one Christmas with a picture of Spider-Man on it, and he had worn it constantly. For his birthday, she had given him another one exactly like it, so Doris wouldn't have to wait until he went to sleep to wash the first one.

Her heart began to pound. *Jayboy couldn't have done such a thing!* she told herself. He was horrified of blood, even on TV. He was a sweet, gentle person, a fifty-five-year-old child who pilfered bright pictures out of her magazines and brass buttons from his mother's button box and kept them in a coffee can under her porch. He was a lover of dandelions and shiny things.

Then the missing piece of the police chief's picture clicked into place. Shirleene had worn the gold dandelion pin with the diamond dewdrop earlier tonight, but she hadn't been wearing it when her body was discovered. The chief had mentioned all of her jewelry except the pin.

"Not Jayboy!" she breathed. "It can't be Jayboy!" But the evidence pounded through her head. Jayboy hated Shirleene. Shirleene had been murdered. And the only thing missing was a shiny dandelion pin.

Elayna felt panic rising as she remembered something else: Jayboy wore size nine sneakers, and his "safe place" was behind the floodwall under her back porch.

Chapter 11

Jayboy peeled off his dew-wet socks and threw them into the corner where the roof sloped so low he couldn't stand up under it.

Downstairs, he could hear a car chase and gunshots from one of Doris's police shows. He felt sure she had not heard him come up the back stairs.

Quickly, he stripped to his underwear, tossed his jeans after the socks, and hung his T-shirt neatly over the back of the rocking chair where he could see the picture of Spider-Man on the front of it.

He turned back the yellow woven bedspread. He had begged Doris to buy it because the design reminded him of fluffy white dandelions just before they blew away. He lay down on his back and pulled up the covers, sticking out his right foot to make sure he wouldn't smother, to make sure he could get out.

He was so tired! His bones felt like they might melt right into the mattress. Breathing was difficult on his back, though, with his sinus trouble, and he turned to his right side. In the dim light from the streetlight outside, his gaze met Spider-Man's, staring at him from the back of the rocking chair.

Jayboy couldn't quite decide what Spider-Man was thinking under his mask. He might be laughing at some secret joke he had heard. Or maybe he had played a joke on somebody. Spider-Man was nice, though. He never did things to hurt people. Not even in a joke. Not like that Shirleene and her friends.

'Layna called him Spider-Man sometimes. When she watched him run up the wall the lawyers had built in front of her granny's house. Or when he teased her from way up in a tree. She wouldn't even climb the tulip poplar, and it had limbs almost to the ground. Like the rungs of one of Mac's ladders.

Jayboy stretched. It made him feel good inside to know there was something he could do that 'Layna couldn't. He shared a secret smile with Spider-Man.

Suddenly his heart flopped over in his chest. Was that a spot of blood on Spider-Man's chest? He had been so careful not to get any on his clothes. He hadn't even known he had stepped in it until he was under the porch and the beam of Mac's flashlight fell on his shoe.

Jayboy sat up. The spot on Spider-Man's chest was getting bigger! It was turning bright red. Like a bullet hole. Right through Spider-Man's heart.

He could feel the blackness swirling around him. He tried to focus his blurring vision on the spot on his shirt. A huge red eye. Watching. Mocking. Accusing. He tore his eyes away. Then looked back. The spot was gone! He was sure it had been right over Spider-Man's heart. But there was nothing there now.

Sweat popped out all over him. He sank back into the pillow. He concentrated on the crack in his ceiling. Running his gaze along the jagged line that ran like a crooked road from the corner over his clothes to the window by his bed. Then he twisted back to look at Spider-Man.

There! He had caught it. Staring back at him. A fierce red eye. Glowing in the swirling blackness.

He jumped up and grabbed the shirt, wadding the picture inside it. What could he do with it? Hide it in his shirt drawer?

No! He couldn't stand to think about wearing any shirts that had touched it. He yanked open the closet door. But he couldn't hang it there with his other clothes. And he didn't want it on the shelf with his magazines and games.

Finally, he stuffed the shirt into the right corner on the floor. Behind his Sunday shoes and the Lego blocks he used to build his forts and castles. Just till he could think of some way to get rid of it.

Jayboy shut the closet door. He pushed against it to make sure it was shut tight. Then he lay back down on the bed. His heart pounded against his ribs. Like he had pictured Shirleene's. But Shirleene's heart was still now. And empty. All the blood had drained out.

He pictured her bright yellow hair. Spread out all around her head. The wide brown eyes full of fear. Like he had wanted her to feel. But he felt a little sorry for her now. Dying with the hot fear in her. Turning cold inside. Never to leave her again.

Then he smiled. Shirleene could never make him afraid again. Still smiling, he turned on his side and drifted into sleep.

Chapter 17

Elayna refilled Court's coffee mug, then her own, and set the pot back on the warmer.

"Who could have hated Shirleene enough to kill her—and in such a brutal way?" she said, finally voicing the question she had sidestepped all night.

Court's hand trembled as he raised the mug to his lips. He set it down. "I've wrestled that question all night," he said, massaging weary eyes with the tips of his fingers. "Shirleene made enemies—jilted lovers, jealous spouses. But, mostly, she just hurt herself. And me." He sat staring at the wall across the kitchen. Then he added, "Her latest fling, C. J. Berryman, is single. No outraged spouse there."

Except you, Elayna thought. Then she pushed the ridiculous idea away. She knew Court hadn't committed this terrible crime. But the police had called it a "murder of passion, of intense hatred or vengeance."

Either motive could point to C. J. Berryman, she thought. She never had liked C. J., not even when they were children and her father and his had been partners in a real estate business. At one time he had wanted Shirleene badly enough to buy the red Porsche for her to drive. But his desire could have turned to hatred as Shirleene became more and more possessive or demanding. Or he could have attacked her in a fit of jealous rage over one of the many sordid little affairs that were so much a part of Shirleene.

She studied her grieving brother-in-law, sitting at the table with his head in his hands. He was attractive, intelligent, successful, well-liked. He was, as the old poem said, "steel true and blade straight," a decent man who had, perhaps, tolerated his wife's infidelities because he knew about the abuse she had suffered as a child and how hard it was for her to trust in the love of a man. Still, tolerance usually had its limits, and Shirleene surely had tried his. Why had he put up with her all these years?

She had made no attempt to hide her involvements with other men, from Court or the world, which Elayna knew was doubly humiliating to him. On the other hand, these flings never seemed to mean much to Shirleene. She would fan a flame until it blazed, flit around it like a moth, then leave it to fizzle and die, without so much as a singed wing. Her escapades were more like games she played to amuse herself until she found another, more exciting game to play. Her affair with C. J. had lasted longer than most, yet just tonight she had said she wished she'd never met him.

Court got up and went again to the telephone on the wall beside the hall doorway. He punched some numbers and waited. "Annie, this is Dad. Call me at Elayna's as soon as you get in." He paused for a moment and then added, "Baby, please call no matter what time it is. I have something extremely important to tell you."

He hung up, took a couple of turns around the room, then came back and dropped into his chair at the kitchen table. "She's supposed to be in by one o'clock on Fridays," he explained wearily, "but Shirleene thinks I'm too strict on Annie. She encourages her to do as she pleases and then lie about it to me. Sometimes I just want to turn both of them over my knee and. . ."

Elayna saw the shock of realization hit his eyes. He dropped his head into his hands, supported by his elbows propped on the table, as if it had suddenly grown heavy. She reached over and laid her hand on the back of his neck, wishing there were something she could say to comfort him.

He raised his head. "You know what bothers me the most, Elayna?" he asked, his eyes filled with misery.

She searched for an answer: The loss of his wife? The horror of her murder?

"I'm afraid she's. . ." He swallowed, and Elayna leaned toward him to catch the whispered last word. "Lost."

He got up and began to pace the room. "I know Shirleene has gone into eternity unprepared, Elayna." His voice grew stronger with agitation. "There's no hope for her. She is doomed to spend eternity without hope, separated from God, in that awful place prepared for Satan and his angels, and for all those like Shirleene who reject the salvation He has provided."

"Oh, Court," Elayna broke into his anguish, "Shirleene didn't 'reject' anything. She had no choice. It wasn't her fault she was murdered before she had a chance to make things right with her Creator. Surely the loving God we were taught to believe in as children would not send someone like that to hell."

Court drew a shaky breath and wiped his eyes with a tissue from the box Elayna offered. Was it really only hours ago—it seemed like eons—since she had offered Shirleene a tissue from the same box as she had perched there at the bar, wanting to see her husband, babbling about some mysterious "evidence"?

"God doesn't send people to hell, Elayna," Court said. It was the old Court, completely in control again. "The choice is ours. But not to make a choice is to reject Him. You know that. You went to the same Vacation Bible Schools that Hunt and I did, every summer. I even remember you accepting Jesus as your Savior at one of them," he recalled with a tender smile. "We all did, at one time or another—you, Hunt, and me."

Elayna's memory went back to that time when she and some of her friends had walked down the aisle of the big church, taken the hand of the preacher, and nodded their heads in answer to his questions about their faith in Jesus. Later that week, they had been baptized.

"To my knowledge, Shirleene never did," Court was saying. "Time after time, I begged her to make that confession of faith, to admit she was a sinner in need of the grace of God that paid for our sins through the blood of Jesus. Sometimes she would get angry with me and tell me to mind my own business. More often, she'd laugh at me." His voice caught on a sob. "Her mockery of me doesn't matter, but God will not be mocked, Elayna."

"Oh, Court, Shirleene surely didn't mock God! She just never got around to. . ." She stopped, uncomfortable under the intense scrutiny of his sharp blue eyes. She dropped her gaze to her hands and noticed she was holding a mug of now lukewarm coffee.

"This coffee is cold," she said, getting up from the table. She shifted the mug to her left hand and reached for Court's mug with her right.

He grabbed her hand. "Elayna, there is no more time for Shirleene! She's. . ."

"I can understand about the lack of time," she broke in, easing her hand from his grasp and taking his mug. "I go to church when I can—most Sunday mornings and religious holidays. Other than that, I haven't had much time for religion myself." She laughed shakily, emptying the contents of both mugs down the sink. "As Whit says, I always have a report to finish, a meeting to attend, or a new catalog to—"

"I'm not talking about religion, Elayna," Court interrupted. "I'm talking about a personal relationship with Jesus Christ, the Son of the living God. Without that, religion is just so much pomp and circumstance."

"This pot is nearly empty again," she said, reaching up to the cupboard and taking out a coffee canister and a pack of filters. "How much caffeine have we consumed tonight?" She busied herself with emptying, rinsing, and refilling the pot, then arranging the filter and measuring the coffee into it.

"Elayna, you do know what I'm talking about, don't you?" Court insisted.

She searched for some way to answer him. Before she'd lost Carrie and Hunt, she had been too wrapped up in her family to feel the need for any deep involvement in religion. Afterward, though she had sought comfort and meaning, she had not been able to find in it the solace her grandmother found. For the past ten years, she had made her business her religion. Now she wished her faith were more vital, more like Court's or Granny's. She wished she had something to offer Court right now.

Suddenly, the image of his parents flashed into her mind—her mother-in-law, petite and silver-haired with eyes as blue as Hunt's and Court's, and her father-in-law, built like a small bear, with Hunt's sandy hair and eyebrows. Their calm, wise support certainly had been a blessing to her as she had dealt with her losses. She had missed them dreadfully since they moved to Florida three years ago.

"Have you called your parents, Court?" she asked, glad for a distraction from his probing questions, wishing they were here already. She could use a bear hug and some down-to-earth common sense right now, and she was sure Court could, too.

Court shook his head. "They're on a cruise down around the Keys. Won't be back 'til Sunday morning. I guess I could have the state police track them down, but there's nothing they can do here. Of course, they'll want to be here for the funeral."

The word hung heavily in the air between them. She knew

arrangements would have to be made soon.

"Can I help, Court?" she asked. "With Granny sick and Mother. . .well, Mother, you, and Cliff and Vivian were the rocks I leaned on in those bleak days after Hunt disappeared. I'd do anything to help you and Annie through this. I hope you know that."

He patted her hand, unable to speak, his eyes shiny with unshed tears. "I'll let you know, once I talk with Annie, and once the autopsy is over and they release the—" He swallowed hard.

The phone rang, and Elayna jumped for it, glad for the reprieve. When she heard it was Annie, she handed the receiver quickly to Court. She glanced at her watch. It was four A.M.

"Where have you been, Anne Courtney?" she heard Court say. "I've been trying to reach you all night!" He listened a moment, then responded angrily, "One o'clock, my foot! I've called every half hour since midnight!" Then his voice softened. "Listen, Annie, stay put until I get there. I have something to tell you that I don't want to say over the phone."

He hung up and stood with his eyes tightly shut for a moment, one fist clenching and unclenching. Then he walked over to the couch, retrieved the suit coat he had flung there, and put it on. He reached into the right pocket and pulled out a key. For a moment, he stood looking at it, his shoulders sagging. Then he straightened and handed the key to Elayna.

"It's my key to the tearoom. The police have Shirleene's, but who knows what. . . ?" He let the words trail off, turned, and walked down the hallway. She heard the front door open and shut, and seconds later his car pulled out of the driveway.

She went to the door, locked it with the key, and shoved the deadbolt into place.

Poor Court! I don't envy him the chore of telling Anne Courtney about her mother, she thought, as she crawled into bed to sleep the weary sleep of exhaustion for a couple of hours.

Chapter 13

Jayboy sat up. It was still dark outside. With his feet he groped for his sneakers. Then he remembered and his heart sank. What would he do without them? Except for Sunday mornings, he had worn those orange sneakers every day since Doris had bought them for him. On their last "school" shopping trip.

He smiled, remembering how 'Layna and her granny had invited him and Doris to go along when they went shopping for school supplies that first year. And how, ever since then, Doris had bought him a new pair of shoes each fall when the other boys and girls started school. And new blue jeans. And a new pencil box. And new, sharp crayons. And he would break the black one and throw it in the trash. Right there in the store.

After their shopping was done, he and Doris and 'Layna and her granny would go to Mucci's for lunch. He closed his eyes, hearing in his memory the important click of their heels on the black and white tile floor and the pleasant hum of the paddle fans overhead. They would find a table or a booth where they would be cozy and together in that special way.

Even after little Carrie Hunter came along, they still had their trips. But after she died, 'Layna wouldn't go any more. Doris had said he couldn't mention it to her.

This year he and Doris had caught the bus out to Wal-Mart

and had eaten lunch there after they finished shopping. But it just wasn't the same. Even though she had bought him new jeans and socks and underwear. And those wonderful orange sneakers.

Jayboy sighed. Why couldn't good things last forever? Mucci's. Little Carrie. His favorite shoes. All gone. Like fluffy white dandelions at the first puff of wind.

He remembered his Spider-Man shirt. Hidden in the closet. With that awful spot of blood on it! Now it would be gone, too. Thank goodness, he had another one. 'Layna had given it to him for his birthday. But Doris would want to know what had happened to this one. Or she might even find it. Back in the closet behind the Legos. And she would see the blood.

He pictured the spot on Spider-Man's chest. Spreading over the shirt. Spilling onto the closet floor. Oozing under the door. He sat up and looked. There was no blood that he could see. But he knew it was there. Behind the door. In the corner. Spreading. . .

Jayboy got up. He had to get rid of that shirt! But what could he do with it? Flush it down the commode? No, it would stop up and Doris would find it. Burn it? Yes, but where? Doris was always cautioning him about fire. And the city wouldn't let you burn things.

Then he remembered the grill in 'Layna's back yard. Down at the edge of the river. Where she and her granny had cooked hamburgers and hotdogs and steaks. And sometimes they had invited him and Doris over to eat with them on warm summer nights when Mac was on the night shift out at the distillery.

The grill burned good. If he could get some matches from the kitchen. Without Doris hearing him. . .

Jayboy opened the closet door, grabbed his Sunday shoes, and stuffed his bare feet into them. He stood there, looking at the shirt, barely visible above the Lego box. He couldn't touch it! But he had to get it out of there!

He picked up a shoe box and dumped a pile of Matchbox cars onto the closet floor. He stuffed the shirt into the box and put the top on it. Then, with the box under his arm, he headed for the stairs.

Chapter 14

It's like I'm groping through a thick fog. I can't find my way any more. I'm lost! Don't you understand, Elayna? I'm lost!"

Elayna awoke with a start and threw off the covers. She was drenched in sweat, from her nightgown to her hair. She knew what had triggered the dream, though. Hunt had been on her mind so heavily last night, and today was their anniversary.

She lay there a moment, thinking about Hunt, seeing again the bitterness and confusion that had been in those blue eyes the last time she had seen him. He simply had been unable to cope with losing his beloved child to what he called "a whim of fate."

Elayna sat up and groped with her feet for her slippers. The first lines of a poem about dandelions that she used to read to Jayboy came into her mind:

> Balloon tugging at its string,
> Cotton candy on a cone,
> Serendipity appears—
> Is gone. . .

Little Carrie had come and gone, a serendipity child, a dandelion that bloomed briefly and blew away, a balloon that had tugged its string from their feeble grasp and soared far above any experience her earthbound parents could understand. But she didn't believe it was "fate" or even a cruel, calculated act of God. It was just one of those things that happened to people, and no one could explain why.

Her thoughts went to Leslie Marsh, her assistant down at the gift shop, whose husband and only child had been killed three years ago in a car accident. When she had interviewed the young African-American widow for the job, Elayna had tried to express her sympathy.

"The Lord gives and the Lord takes away," Leslie had responded. "Bob and Robbie are with Him. My grief is for myself, and I'll just have to cope with it until I can be with them." She had met Elayna's gaze out of grief-scarred brown eyes under a heavy fall of dark hair, then changed the subject to her need to sell her house and find a smaller place to live.

Elayna had found nothing to say to this woman who had grieved but accepted her loss and moved on—except to offer her the job and the partially furnished apartment above the shop to live in until she could get her financial affairs in order.

Hunt's reaction to the loss of their child had been just the opposite of Leslie's. "If God didn't cause Carrie's death, He let it happen, Elayna," he had agonized. "If He's all-powerful, He could have prevented it."

She had known, even then, that Hunt's bitter words were inspired by his own feelings of guilt that he was unable to stop the terrible attack of meningitis that had taken little Carrie's life. Instead, he lashed out at Elayna and at God.

"Why did God allow it, Elayna?" he had cried. "What did our little girl do to deserve death? Or was Mark Twain right when he pictured a heartless God playing chess with our lives?"

Elayna put both hands over her ears as if to shut out those awful questions, for which she had never found adequate answers—for Hunt or for herself.

"Carrie is safe and happy with the Lord, Hunt," her granny had tried to comfort him. "We grieve for our loss, not for her."

"How can you be so sure she's happy? How do you know she even still exists?" he had lashed out, his pain unbearably exposed in the new bitter lines etched around his wide mouth.

Not even Granny, with all her wisdom, had had answers for those questions. Still, she believed her precious namesake was safe in the presence of Jesus, whom she had taught little Carrie to love. Somehow, Elayna had taken comfort from that.

She went over to the window and pulled aside the white ruffled curtains. The house floated in a thick, white cloud world of its own, totally disconnected from anything earthly. Did Carrie's sweet soul inhabit such a cloud world now? She could see her daughter's little face turned skyward, hands cupped around her mouth to "help God 'n' Jesus hear better" as her clear young voice called loudly, "I love You, God! I love You, Jesus!"

It was difficult to imagine Carrie as anything but a sturdy, tow-headed four year old, jumping up and down in her excitement about going out to the Game Farm to see the "manimals" and then to lunch at "Happy Donald's," as she called it, combining her favorite restaurant with her favorite meal.

Elayna's breath caught on a sob and she closed her mind to the memory. It had been more than ten years ago, but she still could not eat at McDonald's.

If she and Hunt could have shared their loss, it might have made a difference. But he had shut himself off behind an iron curtain of grief that no one had been able to penetrate. Finally, he had left physically, too, and she, doubly bereaved, had moved in to take care of Granny, who suffered a stroke soon after Hunt's disappearance.

Elayna dropped the curtain, turned wearily to pick up her

light robe, and pulled it on as she groped her way down the dim hall to the keeping room. She switched on the kitchen lights, took a glass from the cupboard, and filled it with orange juice.

She raised her glass. "Happy anniversary, Hunt," she toasted, "wherever you are."

Putting the past behind her for the moment, she turned her thoughts to the current tragedy. It was inconceivable that her sister-in-law now lay still and cold a few blocks away. She couldn't imagine Shirleene not moving. An aura of energy had surrounded her like an electric field.

Where is Shirleene now? she wondered. *Does she float, disembodied, in some foggy limbo, without form or purpose, waiting for the final judgment? Is there any hope for someone like Shirleene?* Court's tortured comments the night before made it clear that he didn't think so. *Is there any hope for me?*

Suddenly, she was nine years old again, sitting idly in the rope swing her grandfather had hung from a limb of the elm tree shortly after she and her mother had come to live with her grandparents. It was one of those endless childhood summer days, not long after the Vacation Bible School where she had been baptized. Her mother was off somewhere on one of the trips she had begun to take soon after Elayna's father had dropped dead of a heart attack in his office. She remembered feeling alone and sorry for herself.

Then she had become aware of a warmth filling the lonely, empty space inside her, much like the summer sun that caressed her shoulders through the thin material of her one-piece shorts outfit. For several moments, she had experienced an indescribable awareness of the presence of God, enveloping her, letting her know everything was going to be all right.

Tears came to her eyes as she recalled the breathless ecstasy, the conviction that her skin surely would burst with joy and her spirit would float away on the summer breeze like an overripe dandelion. She impatiently brushed away the tears, amazed at the longing she felt to know that feeling again.

No part of childhood revisited as an adult is ever the same, she told herself, *just as summer days are no longer endless and Granny's famous pork and red gravy is just another meal, no matter how carefully I follow the recipe.*

Still, she had known that never-to-be-forgotten joy. Had Shirleene ever known anything but a wild and savage pleasure seeking that apparently had not satisfied, that seemed only to inspire an increasingly frantic search?

The ringing of the phone broke into her morbid thoughts, and Elayna reached for the receiver.

"Hello, darling," her mother's voice crackled over the wire from Paris. It was uncanny how she always seemed to sense news.

"Hello, Mother," Elayna answered. "I'm glad you called. I have something to tell you." She stopped, unable to put the terrible events of last night into words.

"You've decided to divorce Hunt," her mother cut in breathlessly. "You should have done it a long time ago, dear, or declared him dead. How many times have I told you that?"

"Don't start that again, Mother," Elayna begged, feeling a familiar throbbing begin at her temples. "I'm neither divorcing Hunt nor declaring him dead."

"You never should have married him," her mother cut in again. "I always said you should have married Court. He wouldn't have deserted you like that irresponsible—"

"I loved Hunt, Mother! Can't you understand that?"

"Loved?"

Elayna had been unaware of her use of the past tense until her mother's fine-tuned perception picked it up. Was her love for Hunt a thing of the past? she wondered as her mother rattled on about Court's finer qualities and his brother's lack of them.

"I did not love Court, Mother," she cut in wearily. "And he loved Shirleene." *The past tense is accurate there,* she thought sadly.

Her mother's snort was clear, all the way from France. "Shirleene! If you had shown one speck of interest in him. . ."

"Mother, please," Elayna said. "That simply isn't true. Court always loved Shirleene. And, anyway, she's dead. That's what I had to tell you."

She heard her mother's sharp intake of breath, then her laugh. "What did you say, Elayna? I thought for a moment you said Shirleene was dead. These international phone connections!"

"That's what I said, Mother. She's dead. Murdered. Last night at the tearoom." She bit back unexpected tears at the memory of Shirleene pacing the floor in her blue silk blouse and gypsy skirt.

"Murdered, you say?" her mother asked. "Well, I suppose there are many candidates for the job. Was it an irate wife, or. . . Elayna, it wasn't Court?"

"Don't be ridiculous, Mother! We don't know who did it. . . ."

Her mother's voice rose. "Elayna, that tearoom is only two blocks from your place, and you're alone down there behind that wall."

"Really, Mother, I'm fine."

"But you don't know who or where the murderer is? I'm coming home, Elayna. As soon as I make flight arrangements, I'll let you know when to meet me."

"No, Mother, please," Elayna cut in firmly. "I'm okay. And you never liked Shirleene. There's no reason for you to cut your trip short."

When they hung up, Elayna breathed a sigh of relief. Her mother seemed convinced that there was no reason for her to come home immediately, though she had made Elayna promise to call her every night.

Elayna glanced at the clock, then dialed the number of the shop. "I guess you've heard about Shirleene. I won't be in until after the funeral, Les," she said. "I'm taking the new catalog to the printer this morning, and the sales brochure should be ready for proofing," she continued. "If you need me. . ."

"Don't worry. I'll take care of things here," Leslie assured her. "I'm so sorry about Shirleene. She wasn't one of my favorite people," she added, with her usual honesty, "but no one deserves to die like that. If there's anything I can do, let me know."

Elayna thanked her and hung up, grateful that Leslie had answered her ad for help two years ago. She couldn't imagine what she would do without her.

She hurried into the bathroom to shower and put on jeans and a favorite gray-blue sweater. She pulled on socks and rubber-soled walking shoes, then ran upstairs to get the catalog paste-up she had finished proofing last night, before Shirleene had come ringing her doorbell for the last time.

With the catalog under her arm, Elayna locked the heavy front door behind her and dropped the outsized key into her purse.

The air held a distinct scent of burnt cloth, probably from the charred furnishings of the tearoom, she reasoned, as she turned and groped her way east on West Main Street, through the dense, persistent fog that all but obliterated sign posts, buildings, even people.

Chapter 15

Somebody was in the house. Jayboy could hear the stealthy footsteps as they crossed the back room. And drawers and doors being opened. And things being dumped on the floor. Then the noises were not so loud. And he knew they had gone upstairs to 'Layna's office.

It wasn't 'Layna. He had seen her leave the house a few minutes ago, just as he had come up from the grill by the riverbank where he had burned his Spider-Man shirt. She had locked the front door with that big old key and gone down the street with a thick package under her arm. She hadn't seen him. He had been hidden by the trees.

A door slammed above him. Could it be Court up there? No, he didn't think so. Court's big gray car wasn't out front. Neither was the senator's black one. Who could it be? Did 'Layna know they were here? Had she hired somebody to do something for her? Paint, maybe? Or clean house?

It wasn't likely. 'Layna always cleaned her own house. She'd let it get all cluttered up when she was hard at work on some project. Then, when the project was finished, she would light into cleaning. Like that white tornado he used to see on Doris's TV. And everything would shine and smell like lemon. 'Layna was a good cleaner.

He was a good cleaner, too. If 'Layna had been going to hire somebody to do something, she would have hired him. She bragged on him all the time for the way he kept the shop. The floors waxed and shiny. The display cases clean. She said she could hardly tell there was glass in them! He kept the dust off everything. The shelves around the wall. The pretty things Leslie put on them.

He liked Leslie. She was nice. Like 'Layna. He had gone to church with her once. To that big church across town. They'd had a party. With lots of food and games and music. And lots of people. All laughing and talking and moving around. He had eaten the food Leslie brought him. But he hadn't wanted to play the games. He didn't like doing things in front of people he didn't know. And he had just sat there beside Leslie. With his head down listening to the music. He had liked the music. It was church music. The words were about God and Jesus and the Holy Spirit. But it was loud. With drums and guitars and a piano. It was fast and happy. He liked Leslie's church. If only there weren't so many people.

Something fell and broke. Jayboy jumped. What would 'Layna say when she came home and found the mess somebody was making up there? And stuff broken?

He was careful down at the shop. He never broke anything. Well, he had once. That big glass bowl had slipped right out of his hands when he had unpacked it. It was from somewhere across the ocean. And it fell on the floor and broke into lots of pieces. But 'Layna hadn't been angry. She had understood. She had given him a hug. And one of those Scooby Doo Band-Aids that Leslie always kept, to put on the cut he had made in his finger when he picked up the pieces.

Would she be mad at him now for not stopping whoever was upstairs? Should he go up there? He didn't know what to do. He had gone into the Gypsy Tearoom. And that had caused all kinds of trouble. He had to throw away his sneaker. And burn his Spider-Man shirt.

He had the dandelion pin, though. Right here under the porch. Sparkling in the darkness inside his coffee can. A dandelion that would never blow away. Just the thought of it made Jayboy smile.

Chapter 16

As she crossed St. Clair Street, Elayna glanced to her right, down toward the Singing Bridge. The bridge, the stately old courthouse midway down the block, and the war memorial in front of it were mere shadowy outlines etched in the fog. To her left, at the north end of the St. Clair Mall, the Old Capitol was totally lost in the mist. It seemed an appropriate setting for her feelings of unreality this morning.

She carefully mounted the curb in front of her and covered the remaining half block to the print shop. *The things one does to make a living!* she thought as she groped for the door handle and pushed against it. But getting the new catalog to the printer today would give Walter a head start. At least he could get the camera work well under way so that he could get an early start in the morning. He had told her he was saving time for it.

"Hi, Betty," she greeted the blonde who was busy at a computer across the room. "How are you?"

Betty groaned and rolled her eyes. "Snowed under!" She waved a hand at the piles of paper on her desk. "We've hired some temporary typesetting help, but we're still behind. I won't be able to get to your brochure for a day or two, Elayna."

"Uh-oh, I knew I smelled trouble!" Walter said from the doorway to the work rooms behind the office.

Elayna laughed, then dropped the thick envelope bearing

her logo on Betty's desk. "It's your baby now, Walter!" she said, the familiar banter beginning to replace her feelings of unreality with a comforting sense of time and place.

She smiled briefly at a customer who entered the shop and noticed how his smile in return caused freckles to slide into crevices on a boyish face that belied the gray scattered through his red hair.

"I'm so sorry about Shirleene," Betty broke into Elayna's idle scrutiny of the stranger. "What a terrible thing to happen!"

Elayna turned back to Betty. "It's awful!" she agreed. "Court's heartbroken, and. . ."

Betty's gaze met hers briefly, then dropped to the papers on her desk. Elayna glanced around, catching the same look of disbelief on Walter's face before he turned and disappeared into the back room.

The stranger was staring raptly at the envelope Elayna had placed on the desk. His freckled face held the strained, white look of shock.

Suddenly she understood. All of them—even this stranger—had their doubts about Court's grief. *They think he killed Shirleene!*

Elayna's thoughts were as murky as the fog that drifted viscously around her as she left the print shop and headed west down Main Street. Was Court really a suspect? Even her mother, who adored Court, had mentioned such a possibility.

"That's ridiculous!" she said aloud. "Court could no more have done that terrible thing to Shirleene than I could have done it to Hunt!" The crime had been one of intense passion, though—violent hatred, insane jealousy. Either of those emotions could overtake a husband pushed beyond endurance by his wife's infidelities.

Feelings of guilt assaulted her as she slowly walked toward home. She knew Court was innocent. And surely he could prove it. He had been at the commission meeting, then with her working on the questionnaire, possibly even while the murder was being committed. Or had he? Had there been time for Court to visit the tearoom between the meeting and his very late arrival at her house? But there had been no blood on his clothes, as surely there must have been on the murderer's, and he had shown no emotional upheaval, which she knew he would have been unable to hide had he just murdered his wife.

After he left her place, then, while she was trying to reach him about Annie, had he driven by the tearoom on his way home, seen Berryman's red Porsche parked outside, and stormed in to confront Shirleene? Had he, in a fit of uncontrollable jealousy, killed his faithless wife?

Elayna forced herself to picture the scene: Court grabbing the knife from the counter, plunging it—

But the image would not focus. It was all wrong. *Court simply is not capable of such an act*, she thought. It was absolutely impossible.

Neither was it possible that Jayboy had committed the terrible act. Although it was true that Shirleene and her friends had tormented him mercilessly most of his life, they never had physically harmed him. Still, their threats and taunts, along with his fear of the blackness that he thought was waiting for him, had made his life miserable.

Nevertheless, she knew that the childlike Jayboy was not capable of the vicious attack Shirleene had suffered at the hands of her murderer. *With his horror of blood—of violence of any kind— no matter how much he may have feared or hated her, Jayboy did not kill Shirleene*, she thought firmly. As she reached her front door, she pulled the oversized key from her purse.

The scent of burnt cloth was still strong as she stepped up onto the brick stoop, pulled the storm door open, and reached to insert the old-fashioned key in the lock. At her touch, the door swung slightly open. Elayna froze, sandwiched between the glass of one door and the dark wood of the other, willing her ears to pick up any sound above the suddenly erratic pounding of the blood through her veins.

The deep silence of the hallway and the house beyond was broken only by the calm, reassuring ticking of her grandmother's Seth Thomas clock from the mantel in the living room. It was a normal, everyday sound, reinforced by the forceful hum of the ancient refrigerator rumbling in the kitchen.

Surely she simply had forgotten to lock the door when she left less than an hour ago. But she distinctly remembered using the big old key and dropping it into her purse.

Elayna studied the door. It was as solid as a bank vault, put on the house back when wood was real and doors were built to keep a house and its occupants secure. She bent to examine the lock. Were those fresh scratches around it, or had they been there all along? She couldn't be sure.

A thud from somewhere deep inside the thick walls alerted all her senses. She stood poised to run yet desperately wanting to identify the sound. Had it come from back in the keeping room? or from the bedroom? or from her office upstairs?

Then she heard the unmistakable creak of the second step at the top of the stairs. Heart pounding, she slipped out from between the doors and eased the storm door shut. She left the stoop and crept down the walk to the driveway, grateful that her footsteps in the rubber-soled shoes made barely a whisper against the concrete.

She paused at the Bar Center wall and looked back at the house. Amid the drifting fog, the overhanging eaves and weathered brick walls promised the cozy security she always had known there. Had it all been her imagination? Were the threatening sounds, the unlocked door, products of the strain of the last incredible hours? Or were they evidence that someone—possibly the murderer!—was in her house?

She rounded the wall and was relieved to see Laura's mauve Honda parked in its usual spot across from Liberty Hall. That meant there was at least a chance that she was home and Elayna could use her telephone. Should she call the police? Was she letting her imagination run wild?

She looked back at the house again. As she watched, a persistent ray of sunlight broke through the mist, touching the small window panes with a golden light that promised warmth inside. It was impossible to believe that anything evil lurked inside the empty house.

Was the house empty, though? Was someone, even at this moment, watching her movements from one of those front windows, silently awaiting her return, perhaps with a kitchen knife. . . .

Elayna swallowed hard. She began to walk, then to run.

Chapter 17

Jayboy hesitated. He could hear footsteps crossing the kitchen again. Going into the hall. Then he couldn't hear them anymore. Had whoever it was left the house by the front door?

Suddenly he remembered the black figure he had seen through the tearoom window. He had thought it was the blackness come to swallow him up. Only it had found Shirleene first. He had sacrificed her to it!

Then he had known it wasn't the blackness. It was somebody dressed all in black. And he had hurt Shirleene. Again and again. And she had died. Right there in front of his eyes.

He had seen the man's face. He didn't know his name, but he knew who he was. He could identify him. Like they did on Doris's police shows on TV. The police could line him up with five or six other men. And old Jayboy Calvin could identify him. Yesiree!

Suddenly a new thought hit him. Had the man seen him looking in through the glass door? Did he know he could identify him? Maybe that man was upstairs in 'Layna's house. Maybe he was looking for him right now! Jayboy felt the blackness creeping up behind him. The man would come for him with that big old knife. Or maybe with a gun. If he didn't find him at 'Layna's, he would come to his house. Jayboy shivered. He must not think about it or the man would know!

Then he smiled. The man would never find him here under the porch. He reached out to touch his can with the dandelion pin inside. It was meant to be his! A dandelion he could keep. Always.

He couldn't understand why some people didn't like dandelions. They were so beautiful spread all through the grass like golden jewels. And they were so full of magic. Springing up. Flying away. Coming back again. Mac had hated them, though. Wouldn't allow one to grow in his yard. Doris didn't like them much better. 'Layna was the only person he knew who did. But then, she was the Princess of the Kingdom of Dandelion. No wonder she loved them! Just like he did.

His stomach growled, reminding him it had been a long time since he had eaten. It had been barely daylight when he got back from burning the T-shirt in 'Layna's grill. And as soon as he had climbed back into his room, he had smelled sausage cooking. And scrambled eggs. And biscuits. Then Doris had called him to come eat breakfast.

He had come back over to 'Layna's after breakfast and had gone down by the river to see if the shirt had burnt up in 'Layna's grill. Then he had seen her leave the house, and he had gone to his safe place under the porch. That was when he'd discovered that someone was up in the house.

His stomach growled again. It must be nearly noon. What was Doris fixing for lunch? Or would she just wait until he got there and ask him what he wanted? Maybe he'd have something quick to fix. He was too hungry to wait long. Maybe he would have a microwave pizza. Or a cold bologna sandwich with cheese and lots of mustard on it.

There was a muffled crash above him. Then he heard a low curse. The man was still up there. Should he call the police? He knew how to dial 9-1-1. Doris had shown him. In case of emergency. But he would have to leave his safe place under the porch. He would have to go home to use the phone.

Then he gasped at a horrible thought. What if 'Layna came home while the man was in the house? What if he hurt her like he had hurt Shirleene? The police wouldn't be able to get here in time.

Chapter 18

Elayna stopped at the gate to Liberty Hall's gardens and glanced over her shoulder. No one was following. Had she simply let her imagination and the fearful events of the past couple of days get the best of her?

"Better to be safe than sorry, as Granny used to say." She took the stepping-stones to the brick sidewalk that ran alongside the old mansion.

If someone was in her house, they might not have known she had come home. The element of surprise could still be in her favor, or in the favor of the police, if she could reach them soon enough.

She hurried along the uneven brick walk. Instinctively, she glanced down the stone steps leading to the cellar and was relieved to see that no one crouched there waiting to pounce on her. Next, her eyes followed the wooden steps leading up to the old laundry room. No place for anybody to hide there. She laughed weakly at the shambles her nerves had become.

She wondered if Liberty Hall's Margaretta Brown had examined every hiding place when she came into the gardens in the dusk or early morning hours. Had she felt the threat of Indians who might have glided down the river, left their canoes at the bottom of the gardens, and slipped up through the trees and shrubbery to ambush the unwary? Had she lived in constant fear, or had the threat of attack become commonplace after awhile?

The heavy wooden shutters on the outside of the mansion's long lower windows were mute testimony that protection against attack in the frontier town had been a necessity. There had been no police to call in those days. People survived by their own wits and skills. And when the men were away, it was often the women who defended the homesteads.

There were things about those days I would have enjoyed, she thought. *The uncomplicated lifestyle, the slower pace, the elegant clothing—but Indian warfare was not one of them!*

She climbed the wooden steps to the old mansion's back porch and turned to the left. Her footsteps, even in the soft-soled shoes, echoed as she crossed the wooden floor to the small attic-like door that led to Laura's apartment.

She pulled on the latch, but the door was locked. She knocked but then noticed that the door was locked with a small, new-looking round brass lock on the outside. Obviously, Laura was out.

She looked for a doorbell but didn't see one. She'd have to go around to the front where visitors to the mansion were admitted for tours and ask the curator if she could use the phone.

As she turned to leave the porch, she saw the red-haired Laura and a friend coming around the back corner of the house.

"Hi!" Laura said, a welcoming smile lighting her green eyes. "Did you finally decide to come visit me?" Before Elayna could answer, she rushed on, "This is my friend, Toni." She shifted her sack of groceries to the other arm. "Toni's been staying with me," she ex-plained, as the other girl extended her right hand and murmured a greeting.

Elayna shook Toni's hand, looking up into wide blue eyes in a pretty face framed by a sweep of light hair.

"You haven't been staying down there behind that wall alone, have you?" Laura asked, her eyes widening. "Aren't you terrified?

I heard you saw the murderer! In your own yard!"

"Actually, all I saw was a shadow. Twice," she answered. "Laura, I need to use your phone. May I?"

"Yours out? Sure, come on up." Laura handed Toni the groceries to hold while she unlocked the door, then retrieved the sack and motioned for Elayna and Toni to precede her up the narrow stairs. At the top, she opened a second door and led the way into a long hallway.

"The phone's there in the bedroom," she said, pointing to the first doorway on their right. "The book's beside it. Help yourself." She carried the groceries down the hall and disappeared, followed by Toni.

Elayna went to the phone, looked up the number of the police station, and dialed. She asked for Detective Myers, believing he would be more tolerant of her nervous imaginings if it turned out to be a false alarm. When they had left the murder scene Thursday night, he had checked her house thoroughly and had ordered her to call him "any time, day or night, if you need me."

"Dave," she said when he came on the phone, "I think there's someone in my house." She answered his terse questions, then said, "Thanks, Dave. I'll wait for you at Liberty Hall's back gate." Before he could protest, she hung up.

She wandered down the hallway in search of Laura to thank her for the use of the phone.

"Is your phone out?" Laura asked again, looking up from the couch, where she and Toni were sharing a fashion magazine. "That's not good, with all that's been going on around here!"

"Well, no, I thought I heard someone inside the house when I came back from the print shop a few minutes ago," Elayna answered, and found two pairs of eyes suddenly riveted to her face. "I was just too chicken to go in alone, after what happened to Shirleene," she added apologetically.

Both girls nodded. Finally, Toni found her voice. "I told you, Laura. Didn't I tell you? Instead of me coming here, you should have come home with me! And until this madman is caught, that's exactly what you're going to do! We're not staying one more night down here!"

Laura laughed shakily. "I really thought he would be several states away by now. I didn't dream he would still be here, stalking his next victim. Or whatever he's doing."

"Wait, girls!" Elayna held up both hands to stop the excited babbling. "I'm not even sure I didn't imagine the whole thing! Certainly, all our nerves have been on edge. Let's wait until the police check things out. I'll let you know what happens."

Laura and Toni looked at each other, then back at her. "Okay," Laura answered, following her to the door. "But be careful! Don't go down there until the police get here. Promise?" She grabbed Elayna's forearm and held on until she nodded agreement to the promise.

"And if you need us, you just yell," Toni added.

Elayna had to smile. As scared as Toni had seemed a moment ago, Elayna had the feeling that one yelp would bring her running to the rescue. It was a good feeling, after all the years she had spent on her own, to know that someone was genuinely concerned about what happened to her—even though she had just met Toni and she and Laura had only exchanged casual pleasantries on the street or when they happened upon each other in the gardens surrounding Liberty Hall, where Elayna still walked occasionally.

She ran down the stairs. As she left the shelter of Laura's stairwell, she scrutinized the yard for any possible hiding places. Pausing to peer into the recess formed by the cellar steps, she rounded the corner of the house just as a blue and white patrol car bearing the legend Capital City Police Department eased to the curb.

Detective Dave Myers stepped from the passenger seat as Officer Danny Butler put the vehicle in park and spoke briefly into the two-way radio. When he had joined the detective at the curb, the two men turned to walk toward Elayna's house.

"Dave!" Elayna called as she jogged toward the two men. "I'm over here."

"Elayna, this is police business," Detective Myers said. "I'm going to have to ask you to sit tight while we check out your house."

Ignoring his admonition, she followed the two men over to the house and watched as they separated, guns drawn. Danny Butler headed for the front door while Dave Myers ran around back. Elayna was right behind Detective Myers as he reached for the doorknob, turned it quietly, and found it locked. She handed him the key. "See, you needed me here after all," she whispered.

"Stay back!" he mouthed to her. Unlocking the door, he eased it open before slamming it back against the wall. Crouching, with his gun held in front of him with both hands, he slipped into the house and across the room.

Chapter 19

Jayboy lay down on his stomach and began to wriggle out from under the porch. He had to warn 'Layna about the man in her house! He couldn't just let her walk in on him! He might hurt her! Kill her! She was the Princess of Dandelion. And he was her trusty knight. It was his duty to protect her. He had sworn an oath saying he would always protect her. Whenever she needed him.

He stopped. What if the man in black saw him waiting to warn 'Layna? What if he knew he had seen him that night? What if he attacked him? What could he do against a knife? And the man was strong. Shirleene had fought like a tiger, but the man had overpowered her. Jayboy knew he wasn't strong enough to fight him off.

He tried to think. What would 'Layna do? She was the Princess. And the Princess always knew what to do. She probably would call the police. She always tried to make him believe that the police were their friends. Once, when they got lost from Doris and 'Layna's granny, she had gone right up to a policeman and told him they were lost. And he had helped them. That time.

He knew, though, that the police did terrible things to people. Shirleene and her friends had told him. The police would take him away. Lock him up. Beat him. Make his nose bleed. Cut off his ears. And his fingers. One by one. Then they would. . .

Suddenly Jayboy had a new thought. What if it was the police up there in 'Layna's house? What if his Spider-Man shirt hadn't burned completely? When he had gone back to look at it, scraps still were smoldering. What if the police had found it? or his blood-stained sneaker? Way down in 'Layna's garbage can. Beneath the chicken bones and the trash. What if they knew about the dandelion pin? What if they believed he had killed Shirleene? Not just thrown her in the path of the blackness, but killed her himself with that big knife. What if they were looking for him right now?

They would take him away. Lock him up in a cold, dark cell, where he couldn't breathe. And they would beat him. With a rubber hose so it wouldn't leave bruises or scars. Shirleene had said so. Shirleene was mean. But she knew about those things. And he had seen some of it—on TV. He tried not to watch those shows. Most of the time, he watched cartoons on the little TV in his room. But he had seen enough to know Shirleene was right.

He could feel the blackness creeping up behind him. Reaching for him. He could hear the footsteps overhead coming his way. Fear rose into his mouth. Sour. Sickening. He whimpered and hid his face in his hands.

Chapter 20

Elayna gasped as she peered over Dave Myers's shoulder. Cupboard doors gaped open, with dishes, boxes, and cans exposed or spilling out. The contents of drawers hung over the edges or lay scattered on the floor. Chairs and stools lay on their sides amid the strewn contents of the trash can. Even an unburned log had been pulled from the fireplace onto the hearth.

She heard the front door slam open, and Danny Butler appeared in the hallway—crouching, coiled, alert. The two policemen met in the hallway, nodded, and began moving from room to room, guns ready. Elayna heard closet doors open and shut, heavy footsteps, and furniture being moved. Then the two men reappeared and headed upstairs.

The telltale creak of the second step from the top signaled their arrival at the landing, and Elayna relived the fear she had felt less than an hour ago as she had stood outside her front door, knowing that her house should be empty, knowing it was not.

Brushing aside the memory, she went to the refrigerator and opened the door. Reaching to the back of the bottom shelf, she took out a cardboard orange juice carton. She opened the spout, thrust her hand inside, and pulled out a small plastic bag with a wad of money inside. She counted it quickly. The two-hundred dollars she kept for extra change at the shop was all there.

She heard the scrape of furniture and a curse from one of the men upstairs. Then she heard their footsteps descending the stairs. Hurriedly, she thrust the money back into the carton, replaced it on the bottom shelf of the refrigerator, and shut the door.

"All clear, Miz Evans," Butler reported, coming into the keeping room ahead of Myers. "But the whole place has been ransacked."

"The scoundrel's torn up everything, Elayna," Myers added. "Your office. . ." He stopped and shook his head, apparently at a loss for words to describe the mess they had found up there. "But whoever did it is long gone," he assured her.

"It was Shirleene's killer, wasn't it?" she asked. Who else could it be?

"It seems likely that the two crimes are related," Myers answered reluctantly.

"But why?" Elayna cried. "Why did he come here? What was he looking for?"

"You tell me," Myers said. "Do you keep any cash in the house? Is anything missing?"

She glanced around at the mess, then raised both hands in a gesture of futility. "It's hard to say what's missing. But, no, I don't keep cash lying around."

"Check your other valuables," Butler advised.

"Jewelry," Myers suggested. "It's always the first to go. Easy to carry, easy to fence."

"I've never really been into jewelry," Elayna said. "The most valuable pieces I own are this wedding set on my left hand and this opal birthstone ring Hunt gave me." She held out her right hand. "But I'll check what few good pieces I have." She started toward the bedroom and the jewelry box in her dresser drawer.

"Danny, get an officer down here with a fingerprint kit," she heard Myers say. Danny relayed the detective's orders on his radio.

When Elayna walked into her bedroom, she winced at the disarray of clothes and books, the open dresser drawers, the gaping closet. She hesitated, feeling violated, dirty, before plunging her hands into the tangle of silk scarves and underwear in the top dresser drawer. Pulling out her jewelry case, she opened it to find the contents seemingly intact—the keepsake pieces from Granny; her father's diamond ring, which her mother had thought too valuable to be buried with him; and a few special things Hunt had given her over the years.

Next, Elayna raced upstairs, automatically skipping the second to last step, and stopped in dismay at the door to her study. The room was covered with papers and books, the contents from her files and desk drawers dumped in piles and scrambled in a hopeless jumble. Feeling sick, she turned and retraced her steps to the kitchen.

"I can't determine that anything is missing, Dave," she said. "Though I probably won't know for sure until I sort through this mess." She sighed. It would take days to get everything back in order, even if she got Doris and Jay to help. *Thank goodness I took the catalog to the print shop!* she thought. "I really don't keep any valuables here," she added.

The detective pushed back his hat and scratched his head. Elayna was reminded of all the stereotypical detectives she had seen on TV. Then she noticed, with surprise, that Dave's curly hair—once brown—had turned almost completely gray. He had been in a class somewhere between Hunt and Court. Involuntarily, she reached up to touch her own hair, and her thoughts went to Hunt. *How has he withstood the pillage of time?*

"He sure was after something, Elayna," Myers said. "Apparently he thought you had it. If he didn't find it. . ." He let the words trail off.

Officer Butler glanced up from the notes he was making

in a small notebook. "You think he might come back, sir?"

Elayna felt an iron band of fear tighten around her chest. Shirleene's killer had been here looking for something he thought she had, and he might be back!

Suddenly she remembered the shadows she had seen the night Shirleene was murdered. While she had toyed with fantasies of Hunt coming home on their anniversary, hiding in the shrubbery while he built up the courage to face her after ten years, it likely had been the killer watching her in the darkness.

She reminded Detective Myers of her phone call before the murder had been discovered, then said, "Dave, I saw a second shadow that night, hiding in the lilac bush out back, just before the sirens began and we all were embroiled in the horror of Shirleene's death. I thought it was a vagrant making his way from the railroad to the river."

"Our perpetrator likely followed Shirleene here, saw her come in, waited, and followed her back to the tearoom," Myers reconstructed. "He killed her, and then, not finding whatever he was after there, he came back here, thinking she might have given it to you. He waited again, probably because you've been here, and we've been watching the area pretty closely at night. Then, today, when you left the house, and we weren't around, he took his chance."

Elayna shivered. She had been alone in this house all night last night while a killer possibly watched from the shadows? Worse, he might still be out there somewhere, waiting for the policemen to leave. She shivered again.

"You got anywhere you can stay for a few days?" Myers asked. "I'm going to put a guard back here, but I'd feel a lot better if you were somewhere else."

Elayna looked at the mess around her, wanting to start in right now to set it to rights, wanting to scrub, to disinfect, to wash everything that had been touched by the intruder's filthy, prying hands. She'd have to wait until the fingerprinting was done, but she knew she couldn't live with this mess any longer than necessary.

"Dave, I just can't leave this—" she began, but her words were cut off by a shout.

"Freeze!" Danny Butler yelled as he ran out the back door, leveling his gun at a figure trying frantically to scale the wall to the Bar Center grounds.

Chapter 21

Jayboy's hands clawed at the wall. His feet in the slick Sunday shoes could find no hold. He slid to the ground. His scraped fingers burned. He licked them and tasted blood. He gagged. Gagged again.

He could hear them back there. Cheering for him. "You can do it! You can do it!" they yelled. Just like at the football games Mac had taken him to sometimes. "Come on, Jayboy! You can do it! Old Spider-Man can do it!" Mac. Doris. 'Layna. Leslie. Cheering him on.

But he couldn't do it! Not in these slick Sunday shoes. Not without his sneakers!

He risked one glance over his shoulder. The blackness was closing in! Reaching for him! Yelling, "Freeze!"

Fear gurgled in his throat. His heart jarred his body. He gathered all his strength and leapt for the wall again. His fingers clutched the top and held. His feet scrambled. Slipped. *Hold on!* Fingers burning. Shoulders and arms aching. Feet scrambling.

He felt fingers close around his right ankle. His fingers slipped to the edge. He kicked back and heard a grunt as his foot hit something. But the blackness held on. Dragging him down. Stripping skin from his fingers.

He fell. And lay there. Gasping for air.

He felt something grab his right shoulder. Slide down his

arm. Twist it behind him. Circle it with cold metal. He could hear the thing that held him panting. He whimpered. His head began to jerk. He couldn't stop it.

The black thing pulled his left arm back. Forced it into metal. Locked it to his right. Jayboy could feel the cold metal moving from his hands up to his chest. Tightening. Squeezing. He gasped for breath. Struggled to scream. The smothering blackness swallowed him.

Chapter 22

"Dave, please listen to me!" Elayna begged, looking up from her crouched position beside the whimpering man handcuffed to the porch railing. "I've known Jayboy practically all my life. He's totally harmless!"

Myers's look was cynical. "Elayna, psychopaths often seem harmless—until they suddenly go berserk."

"We caught him red-handed, Miz Evans!" Butler said. "I saw him wiggle out from under your porch and go for the wall. There's no doubt he's the one who trashed your house."

"And more than likely he's our killer," Myers added. "All the evidence points to him. We found a black sweat suit in the city's trash collection this morning. It's covered with Shirleene's blood, and it's about Calvin's size."

Elayna shook her head. "No, Dave. Jay's no killer. I've never seen him kill anything. Just the sight of blood terrifies him!" Then something Myers had said registered. "Did you say the sweat suit is black?" she asked. At Myers's nod, she went on excitedly, "It can't be Jay's! He hates black! He won't wear anything black. He won't even color with a black crayon!" She stopped, aware that the detective wasn't listening.

"Now, Elayna, be reasonable," Myers said. "I know you've been a lifelong friend to the Calvins, you and your granny. But these things happen. Jayboy's always had something missing in the upper story, but he's been downright weird since his daddy died. A real nut case!"

Elayna put her arms around Jayboy's thin body and could feel his trembling. They talked about him like he wasn't there, like he couldn't hear or had no feelings. "You're wrong, Dave," she said stubbornly. "Jayboy's just a kid who never grew up, who plays childish games and hides his treasures under my porch. I'd stake my life on. . ."

She saw the policemen exchange looks. Myers motioned to Officer Butler, who immediately left the porch, lay down on his stomach, and examined the lattice. He lifted the loose section and shone his flashlight inside. Then crawling by elbow power, he disappeared under the floor.

Jayboy whimpered, and Elayna smoothed back the hair that had fallen over his damp forehead. "It's all right, Jay," she whispered, as she had heard Mac do when his son was scared or upset. Jayboy laid his head on her shoulder, and she could feel his body quiver.

Danny reappeared, backing out through the opening, carrying a coffee can in one hand and an orange sneaker in the other. Elayna recognized the can as Jayboy's treasure chest and the shoe as one of a pair he had worn daily since last fall. She glanced at his feet and was surprised to see that he was wearing brown leather oxfords.

Setting the shoe and the can on the porch, Danny attempted to brush the dust from his black uniform. "That's it, sir," he said. "That's all there was under there."

Myers picked up the sneaker and examined it closely. "Size 9," he said ominously, his lips drawing a tight, straight line across his face. "No blood stains, though," he admitted—*reluctantly,* Elayna thought. He set the shoe down and picked up the can.

"They're just his playthings, Dave," she said, dreading the

exposure of her friend's pathetic "treasures" to mocking eyes. She glanced at Jayboy, then moved to block his vision with her body as Myers pried off the can's plastic lid. She motioned to him to take the can inside before he examined its contents.

With a somewhat exasperated but determined-to-humor look, Myers moved into the kitchen. Butler followed, taking a stance beside the kitchen table where he could still see their prisoner.

Elayna watched as the detective turned the can upside down and dumped its contents on the table. She could see him pawing through the things she knew Jayboy kept there—buttons, a ring, a doorknob, birthday candles. She turned away, suffering the pain Jayboy would feel if he hadn't been hiding against her shoulder.

"Crim-i-nin-ity!" she heard Danny Butler exclaim. She looked back to see him holding Shirleene's golden dandelion pin between his thumb and forefinger. Even from here, she could see prisms of light reflecting from the diamond dewdrop.

Myers whistled. "Is it real?"

"It's real, all right," Butler said. "Shirleene told me it was a gift from. . ." He glanced Elayna's way, then lowered his voice, but she clearly heard him say, ". . .C. J. Berryman. She said it was a joke on her husband. I have no idea what she meant by that, other than that she was messing around with Berryman behind Mr. Evans's back."

Elayna knew what Shirleene had meant. The ostentatious pin had been made to mock the logo that portrayed her husband's humble ties to the common man. C. J. had been furious with Court over a couple of his votes on the city commission that had stopped some real estate developments that would have made C. J. extremely rich but hurt the surrounding property.

She had thought Shirleene's involvement with C. J. was just another in the long line of sordid little affairs with which her sister-in-law had amused herself. Now she wondered if C. J.'s affair with Court's wife, flaunted by her driving his red Porsche, had been calculated on his part to humiliate Court before the community he served as a city commissioner and to cause embarrassment to his campaign for state senator. She certainly wouldn't put it past C. J. to seek revenge that way. And Shirleene, convinced of her ability to charm any man, would have seen the pin and the affair simply as a grand joke on her long-suffering husband.

"You mean this pin belonged to Shirleene?" Myers asked excitedly. At the officer's nod, he slapped one hand down hard on the table. "Then we've got him! The blouse Shirleene was wearing when she was killed had a tear in it, like a pin or something had been ripped off."

Elayna's thoughts flew back to that night. Yes, Shirleene had been wearing the pin, a dandelion that would never blow away. "Oh, Jay!" she breathed.

"Step back, Elayna," Myers said, releasing Jayboy from the railing and handcuffing his hands behind him again. "Go get the cruiser, Danny," he ordered.

Jayboy's eyes pleaded with Elayna, but the sounds that came from his grotesquely moving mouth were gibberish. Suddenly he began to scream hysterically, and Myers slapped him across the face. The screams stopped abruptly, but Elayna saw Jay's body begin to jerk convulsively.

"No, Elayna, that's not police brutality," Myers explained before she could protest. "It's the best cure I know for hysteria."

She went to Jayboy and put one arm around his shaking shoulders. With the other hand, she tried to raise his chin so she could look into his eyes. "Look at me, Jay!" she commanded. "It will be all right. I will help you." She turned to Myers. "Dave, please! There has to be some explanation!"

"Yeah!" Myers said gruffly. "He murdered Shirleene and

stole her pin. And that's the only explanation there is. Of course, since we didn't catch him in the act or at the scene, I can't put him in jail as a murder suspect until we get an indictment. But I can take him in for criminal trespass. We did practically catch him in the act here today."

"Dave, why would Jayboy wreck my house? I've been his best friend for years! And you said yourself that whoever did this was looking for something. What would Jay be looking for?"

"You tell me, Elayna," Myers countered. "Maybe he's gone completely off the deep end. Maybe he's just suddenly turned violent and destructive. All I know is, I'm booking him for criminal trespass. That's a misdemeanor. You probably can bail him out in a couple of hours for about a hundred dollars. But if you really want to help him, get him a good lawyer to defend him in a murder trial, because I'm convinced he's as guilty as sin, and I intend to do everything I can to see that he's indicted."

It's impossible, she thought. *Jayboy couldn't have killed Shirleene!* It just wasn't in him. He couldn't even watch a TV show that had blood in it. But how had he acquired the dandelion pin? Had he ripped it from her blouse as she lay dead on the floor? Had he found it where it had fallen during the struggle with her killer? She didn't know. She only knew that Jayboy was no murderer.

"Dave. . . ," she began.

"Elayna, I understand how you feel," he said patiently, "but, believe me, this man has suddenly become dangerous. A good lawyer can get him into an institution where he can get the help he needs, instead of going to prison, but he should not be left free to kill again."

Elayna realized she was fighting a losing battle. "Do me one favor, then, Dave," she begged. "Don't cuff him. He panics when he's tied down or closely confined. That's why he screams."

103

Myers considered this, then reached over, unlocked the cuffs, and removed them. "I reckon the two of us can handle him," he said with a grin.

"Thank you, Dave," she said, as the detective took Jay by the arm, led him off the porch, and propelled him around the house. She could hear the cruiser pulling into the driveway out front. Suddenly, Jayboy began to scream again, and she knew they were forcing him into the cruiser. Then the screams stopped abruptly, and she wondered if Myers had slapped Jay again. The car door slammed, and she heard the cruiser pull away.

She had to help Jay! But what should she do? *Maybe I could tell the police about how Shirleene and her friends have tormented the poor man all his life, and how scared of them he always has been,* she thought. But that might help convince them he had killed her. "A crime of passion," the chief had called it. Hatred and revenge were very strong passions and could be motives for murder.

And the evidence was mounting—the tracks in blood along the wall made by a size nine athletic shoe; the shoe under her porch, size nine; Shirleene's one-of-a-kind dandelion pin and the torn spot on her blouse where the pin had been the night she was killed.

"But he didn't do it!" she said aloud. "He didn't wreck my house, and he didn't kill Shirleene. I know he didn't!" How could she prove it, though? Jay had been out that night. She heard him under the porch twice. Surely the footprints were his. He had the pin. "But he didn't wear a black suit!" she said with surety.

Since they had arrested Jay, she knew the police—at least Myers and Danny—were satisfied that they had caught the killer. She supposed that let Court off the hook, but her mind would no more let her accept Jayboy as the killer than it would Court. And what about the real killer—where was he? Was he, at this moment, watching the house, waiting for the opportunity to sneak back inside?

Chapter 23

Jayboy huddled in the back corner of the police car. His throat hurt from screaming. His body had stopped jerking, but he felt clammy. And cold. Clear down to his bones. He wished he had his blanket to wrap around him.

Did 'Layna know where they were taking him? He whimpered, wishing she would come and get him. Or Doris. He wished Mac were here. To hold him. To make the fear go away. To shield him from the police in their black uniforms.

They hadn't hurt him much. Yet. Except for slapping him to stop the screaming. But that was nothing. Shirleene and her friends had told him all the bad things the cops would do to him. Like on TV. In their black uniforms. With pieces of rubber hose in their hairy hands. With meanness in their beady eyes. And they would hit him. And cut him. Make him bleed. And hurt. Make him scream. So they could hit him again.

Then they would put him in a cell. A smothery, cramped-up little room with bars. And a big bald, fat man with a bunch of jingling keys would lock him inside. Just like on that TV show Doris liked so much. There would be no way out. And he would smother. There in that awful room with the cracks in the ceiling and the pockmarks in the floor. He would die. And nobody would find him until he rotted and began to stink.

The car stopped in the parking lot beside the flat brown building that Doris had told him used to hold the Kroger store. Now it was the police station.

"You alert the photographer, Danny, and get the paper work started," Myers said, "and I'll take Calvin here to the interrogation room."

The interrogation room! That's where they do the beating and the cutting! Jayboy's breath hung in his throat.

The driver turned off the car and got out. He went inside the building. The older one—'Layna's friend that wouldn't listen to her—got out and opened the back door of the cruiser. He was motioning for him to get out. Reaching for his arm. He couldn't let him take him in there! He couldn't!

Suddenly, Jayboy lurched forward and butted the cop in the stomach with his head. The cop fell. And Jayboy heard his head crack against the pavement.

Then he was running. Crying. Trying not to make any noise. Trying to figure out where to go. He looked around frantically. The floodwall was high. Way higher than his head. With no footholds for his slippery Sunday shoes.

Then he saw an opening and raced through it into another parking lot. With the river lapping at its edges. He veered left and jumped the low guardrail. He scrambled along at the base of the wall. Slipping in the mud and the wet leaves. Falling. Sliding. The toe of his shoe went into the muddy water. He grabbed for a bush and pulled himself back up. He stood for a moment catching his breath. Trying to make his heart stop pounding.

Then he was crossing the big rocks they had spread below the floodwall. Below Second Street School. Where he had gone when he was little. And the kids had made fun of him because he couldn't read or write or tell them what grade he was supposed to be in. Nobody but 'Layna had ever understood how he felt. The kids had made him feel so bad. And he had never hurt anybody. No matter what the police thought about Shirleene.

Then he remembered knocking the cop down. And his head hitting the parking lot with that awful cracking sound. He hoped he wasn't dead. Then he really would be what they thought he was. A killer!

Jayboy's breath caught in his throat. He could feel the blackness creeping closer. There was no place to hide here. He had to find a way across the river—where all his hiding places were—before they found the cop.

Chapter 24

Elayna stood looking out the keeping room window into the back yard. The fog had lifted some, and she could see the river, lapping at the edges of the lawn down below the trees. It seemed strange to be able to see the *Elayna* from here, bobbing up and down on the river current, fighting its rope like an untamed horse.

She wanted to go post bond and get Jayboy home. He must be terrified. She knew she would have to wait, though, until the fingerprinting expert had come and gone.

She had tried to call Whit to represent Jay, but his secretary had informed her that he would be in Washington until Monday. She didn't want to get another attorney. Whitley Yancey was the best defense attorney in the area. He was honest and direct. Juries believed him. Judges respected him. He rarely lost a case. His reputation across the state was solid, and he even had gained national attention with the legislation he had sponsored on behalf of the rights of crime victims.

Whit's a good man and a very special friend, she thought. He certainly had helped her fill some lonely hours these past years, and she hated to admit how glad she would be when he was back in town. *Is there more to my feelings for Whit than friendship?* she wondered suddenly.

"I'm not going there!" she told herself firmly. "I'm still married to Dr. Hunter Evans, wherever he is, and there is no room in my life for anything more than friendship."

Elayna glanced at the clock, then sighed. *Speaking of friendship, who can I call to get Jay out of jail? Doris doesn't drive, and even if I had a car, I can't leave here until the fingerprint expert has come and gone.* Then, she thought of Leslie, who was probably just closing the shop for the evening.

Quickly, she dialed the number and explained her dilemma. "Take a hundred dollars or so out of the cash drawer, Leslie," she said. "No, take two hundred, just in case. And if you'll drive Jay home afterward, I'll be eternally grateful."

Satisfied that Jay was in good hands, she went to the bedroom and began sorting her scattered clothing from the dresser and chest into baskets to wash, careful not to touch anything that might bear incriminating fingerprints, reluctant to touch her own things now that he had defiled them. After dumping a load of clothes into the washer and adding a double portion of detergent, Elayna turned on the radio to take the edge off being alone in the house.

When a female officer came with the fingerprinting kit, she introduced herself as Officer Hunley and went to work without another word. After efficiently and thoroughly photographing and fingerprinting everything that could possibly be evidence, she packed up her kit and left.

When she was gone, Elayna realized that she might have time to rescue Jayboy, after all. She was reaching for the phone to call Leslie when a news bulletin came over the radio.

"Jayboy Calvin, arrested early this evening for criminal trespass at the home of local business woman Elayna Evans, escaped from police custody and is still at large," the announcer reported. "Calvin, also an alleged suspect in the vicious murder of nightclub owner Shirleene Evans, wife of city commissioner Courtney

Evans, was being taken into the Frankfort Police Department for photographing when he knocked Detective Dave Myers to the pavement. The unconscious Myers was discovered moments later by Officer Daniel Butler and transported by ambulance to the Blue Grass Regional Medical Center, where he is being held for observation."

"Oh, Jay!" Elayna said aloud. "You've made things worse! What are we going to do now?" She hoped Dave Myers was not seriously injured, and she knew that Jay must be terrified, alone and confused by all that had happened.

"When apprehended, Calvin had in his possession a gold pin the victim was wearing at the time of the murder," the voice continued. "Rings, earrings, and a watch were found on the body, and a money bag containing the night's receipts was nearby. The pin, a golden dandelion with a diamond dewdrop on its petals, has led the press to dub the murderer the Dandelion Killer."

How ironic! Elayna thought. Jay wouldn't even mow the lawn while the dandelions were blooming for fear of killing one.

"Calvin is not believed to be armed, but is considered dangerous," the announcer said. "If you have information concerning his whereabouts, please call Crime Stoppers at eight-seven-five—"

Elayna clicked off the radio. It was impossible to believe that Jay—this fifty-five-year-old child who had hated any kind of violence all his life, who could not even watch TV shows in color if there was any chance there might be blood—had suddenly turned violent. She knew he must have panicked when he struck down Dave Myers. He was so terrified of being locked up that he had completely lost control. She understood that.

Where has he gone? If he had gone home, Doris surely would have called her. He did not have a key to the shop or to the empty apartment above it. She had not heard him enter his hiding place under her porch. Anyway, she doubted he would go there now, since that was where the police had found him in the first place. *Where has he holed up?*

The phone rang. When she answered, Leslie said, "He wasn't there, Elayna. I took the money and went to the jail, but they said he had not been brought in. They wouldn't give me any more information. I didn't know what else to do, so I put the money back in the cash box. Is there anything more I can do?"

"I just heard on the radio that he has escaped, Les. Apparently, as Dave Myers was taking him into the police station, he knocked him down and ran. He's in a lot of trouble, but I don't suppose there's anything anybody can do until he's found," Elayna answered. "Thanks for trying. I really appreciate it."

"Poor Jay!" Leslie said. "He must be so scared! I'll be praying for him, Elayna, and I'll let you know if he shows up here. Let me know if I can do anything else."

Elayna said good-bye and hung up the phone, knowing she had to find Jay, to help him some way. She had been his friend since the first day she'd met him, when he had hidden behind his mother and been afraid to tell her his name, and she had felt such empathy for this poor boy who had been ridiculed and ostracized all his life.

From that time on, though she was younger than he was, she had been his self-appointed guardian and mentor. She had played with him, taught him, stood up for him against Shirleene and her friends. She would fight the world for him. But where should she begin to look for him? And when and if she found him, what should she do? Turning him in to the police would put them right back where they were before his escape.

She wished she could talk with Court about it, but she just couldn't bother him with this now. If only Whit were here! If only she had some new facts that would refute the mounting evidence against Jay.

With the bloody footprints—if they could match them to his sneakers—and the dandelion pin found in his possession, the police weren't going to be impressed with her testimony about his gentleness toward dandelions or his not being able to kill anything because of his horror of blood.

She heard her grandmother's clock in the living room strike six o'clock, followed by the bells from the Presbyterian church down the street. Outside, a preliminary darkness already was claiming the sky. At this time of year, it would be completely dark in another hour or so.

If I had a car, Elayna thought, *I would take some supper out to Court and Annie.* She was sure they wouldn't even think to eat unless somebody insisted on it. *Well, I can fix it and invite them down here to eat. Or I can call Court to come and get it and take it home.*

She dialed the number and let the phone ring several times. As she was about to hang up, she heard Court's cautious, "Hello? Elayna? I wasn't going to answer, but then I saw it was you on the caller ID." No doubt he had been harassed by calls—from the media, from well-meaning friends, from not-so-well-meaning busybodies.

"Oh, don't bother with supper, Elayna," he responded when she had explained what she wanted to do. "People have brought food all day. We've got casseroles and salads and desserts in every available space, and some stacked on top of each other. I've totally run out of space in the refrigerator, and I've started putting some of it in the freezer.

"You're welcome to come over," he added. "But I must warn you that Shirleene's family is on the way—*en masse.* They sort of invited themselves over for supper, with the excuse that they are bringing food, which Annie and I will not touch, I assure you. Have you ever been in any of their houses?"

"Court, I am so sorry!" Elayna blurted. "About the family, I mean. I can imagine what an ordeal that will be, and neither you nor Annie need that right now."

"Annie escaped with some of her friends as soon as she heard her grandparents and aunts, uncles, and cousins were coming," he explained, with a rueful laugh. "I didn't have the heart to argue with her about it."

"No, I guess we can't blame her," Elayna said. "Do you need me to help you, Court?"

"Oh, I'll just set out some of this food, give them paper plates and cups, and get them out of here as soon as I decently can," he answered. "Shirleene fed them often, you know," he added.

"I know," Elayna said, wincing at the pain in his voice. "Court, you would have to come get me, but I'll be glad to help, if you need me."

"As I said, you are welcome, but there's no need to put yourself through this. After fending off the police and the media all afternoon, I guess I can handle Shirleene's parents and siblings. I've already told Mallie and her other daughters that there will be no dividing up of Shirleene's things until after the funeral."

"You mean they've mentioned it?" Elayna gasped. "That's incredible!"

"Oh, well, consider the source, Elayna," he reminded her. "They are all the things the media have taught the world to expect of Kentuckians, only they have shoes," he added wearily. "Shirleene saw to that."

Elayna laughed. "I'll see you at nine A.M. tomorrow at the funeral home, then."

"Thanks, Elayna," he said. "I really appreciate your being willing to help me make the arrangements. Annie won't even talk about it. She acts as if none of this has happened."

"It's her way of handling the shock, Court," she assured him. "She's in denial. Sooner or later, she will face her loss, and grief will run its natural course. Right now, she's like the proverbial ostrich, hiding her head in the sand, hoping that if she doesn't acknowledge this awful thing, it will go away."

"Yeah," he agreed. "I know the feeling. It just doesn't work that way."

"Call me, if you need me," she repeated, and hung up, wishing there was something more she could do to help him.

He had been her accountant, her attorney, her moral support, and often her lone tie to sanity in those early days following Hunt's disappearance. Sometimes she had found money in odd places after he had been there, though he never would admit it had come from him. She wanted to be there for him in that same caring, empathetic way.

I'll have to admit, though, that I'm glad he didn't feel the need for my assistance this evening. She couldn't think of a group of people she'd rather avoid than Shirleene's pathetic family.

She and Shirleene had never been close. The only thing they had in common, she had often thought, was the fact that they had married brothers. Still, she knew she wouldn't be able to handle the blatant covetousness of Shirleene's family with the diplomacy that Court would display.

I'd probably end up telling her greedy mother and sisters how self-centered they have always been with Shirleene, she thought, *and her brutish father and brothers that it was their abuse of her as a child that made her unable to believe in the love of a man like Court, that made her seek affirmation of her worth and desirability again and again in tawdry little affairs.*

Elayna sighed and walked over to the window. The yard was nearly dark now under the trees. *Where is Jay?* Her heart ached for him. *Where will he go to hide? Where will he sleep? What will he eat? What will he do when he feels "the blackness" stalking him?*

Chapter 25

Jayboy knew the police would be looking for him. How could he get across the river? They would be watching. And it wasn't quite dark yet. He could not cross the Singing Bridge or the one that led to the capitol. They would be watching the bridges. He would have to go all the way around. *Below that street where Doris's friend Mattie lives.*

He could see there wasn't much room between the water and the street. But he had to stay below the road. Down where no one would see him. And keep above the water.

He scuttled along the bank. His heart pounded. His feet slipped again and again into the edge of the angry water. Before long, his shoes were squishy and the legs of his jeans were soggy. And cold.

It made him dizzy to look down at the river racing along below him. Making whirlpools. Carrying limbs and trash. If he fell into it, he would be carried away. Buried in the deep, dark water. Like Mac was buried in the ground. He would be fish food. Until he washed up somewhere far away. Rotten and stinking.

He never would see Doris again. Or 'Layna. Or Leslie. He never would go back to work down at the shop. Where 'Layna vowed he kept the floors so shiny she could skate on them. And where Leslie bragged on how clean he kept the windows.

One time, he remembered, a bird flew right into that big

window in the front and knocked itself out. Jayboy had thought it was killed. But, after a few minutes, it had come to and flown away, weaving a little, like a drunk man. Leslie said the windows were so clean, the bird had thought he was flying through air.

He worked hard at the shop. Nobody but 'Layna had ever trusted him with a job. He had helped Mac sometimes. Holding things or carrying things. But Mac never let him do anything important. Nothing like he did now.

He had worked for 'Layna—he counted on his fingers—all of one hand and three fingers on the other. It took all the fingers on one hand to show how many years he had worked in 'Layna's warehouse in the back rooms of the tall gray-blue house on Lewis Street. Sweeping up. Carrying boxes.

Then she had opened the shop in the front rooms. And Leslie had come to work with them. For three years he had worked in the shop. Using the sharp box cutter to open boxes that came from across the ocean full of beautiful things. Packing things in that plastic with the bubbles that made a loud popping noise if he burst one. Cleaning and waxing. Taking out the trash. Going with Leslie or 'Layna to the post office to carry the heavy boxes inside.

Sirens! He heard them now, wailing in the distance. He saw a blinking red light going up Louisville Hill. He guessed they were taking the policeman to the hospital. He prayed to God that he wouldn't die! He didn't want to be a murderer!

He knew he was in a lot of trouble, anyway. Even if the cop lived. He had knocked down a policeman! Soon he would hear the *whup, whup, whup* of the police cars with their whirling blue lights. Coming after him. He could feel the blackness breathing down his neck. He scrambled faster.

Across the river, he could see 'Layna's boat tied up at the landing. Pulling against its rope. Trying to get away. Like he was. If he could swim across the river, he could climb up the bank and be right there at her house. But he couldn't swim. Even if the river had not been moving so fast. Then he remembered. He couldn't go to 'Layna's house. The police knew about his safe place under her porch.

If I can just get to the railroad bridge! Most of the time, the gate to the other bridge was locked. But he could walk the railroad ties to the floodwall in front of his house. He had walked them many times. Only when Doris found out, she had told him never to do it again.

"I have to, Doris!" he whispered. "I have to!"

Chapter 26

As she followed Court and Annie out the side door of the funeral home into the parking lot, Elayna stopped for a moment to let her eyes adjust from the dim interior of the building to the bright morning sunlight. Then she saw a man in a tan trench coat shove a microphone in Court's face. Just beyond, a cameraman, his video equipment bearing the logo of a Louisville TV station, took aim on Court.

"Mr. Evans, you have our sympathy in the loss of your wife," the interviewer began unctuously. Then his demeanor changed. "Our audience would like to know your opinion of the motive for the murder," he probed, "and do you think the police have the right suspect in Jayboy Calvin?"

"No comment," she heard Court mutter as he pushed the microphone out of his face and strode across the parking lot toward his car, keeping Anne Courtney in tow with a firm hand on her elbow. The cameraman quickly moved out of his way but never stopped filming.

"But, Mr. Evans, the public has—" the interviewer began again.

"I said, 'No comment!' " Court repeated, escorting Annie into the car and going around to get in on the driver's side.

Elayna tried to follow Court, but the reporter had turned and now blocked her way.

"Ms. Evans, I understand you were the last person to see the murder victim alive, except for the killer, of course," he said, with a demure smile for the cameras on this solemn occasion. "Can you tell us—?"

"Let me pass!" she demanded through gritted teeth. "I have nothing to say." She glared at the man, but he appeared unfazed.

Actually, she thought, staring into the man's avid brown eyes, *I have a lot I'd like to say!* She wanted to tell him how callous she thought he was, to point out how little respect he was showing for a man whose wife had just been murdered; who, in fact, had just spent the morning picking out her casket and grave clothes. For Court's sake, and for Annie's, she held her tongue.

The reporter stood his ground, but she brushed past him and the cameraman and got into the back seat of the gray Chrysler. Instantly, she heard Court lock the doors. The reporter was still talking into his microphone as Court started the engine and drove out of the parking lot, nearly running down the cameraman as he tried to shoot one last scene of the departing vehicle.

As they turned right onto Washington Street, Elayna saw a TV news van from a Lexington station careen into the funeral home parking lot.

"How did they know we were here?" she exclaimed, as they turned right onto West Main and headed toward her house. "They're like vultures!"

"They're just doing their job," Court said tersely, looking into the rearview mirror. He relaxed a little then, and she assumed they were not being followed.

"I've been fending off reporters ever since yesterday morning. This is just a different crew," he said. "I'm surprised they haven't been camping on your doorstep, too, since you were 'the last person to see the victim alive.' "

"Other than a brief interview with a very understanding reporter from the *State Journal*, and one call from a Lexington radio station, I've been blessedly media free," she said. "Of course, it helps not to answer the phone when the caller ID indicates the call is from the media."

"I don't know what part of 'no comment' they don't understand," Court said. He sighed. "I can't seem to get it through to them that I am not going to talk about my wife's murder. Even if I wanted to, the case against her killer could be jeopardized by some careless remark. And I want him—," he said fervently, "signed, sealed, and delivered."

Elayna felt the depth of his uncharacteristic emotion. "We'll probably be on the evening news, looking surly and uncooperative," Elayna said.

Court glanced in the rearview mirror. "Does it bother you what the reporters say, Elayna?" he asked.

"Not really. And I do understand that they are just doing their job, Court. They just seem so unfeeling."

Annie said nothing, as she had all morning, staring vacantly out the side window. Elayna wondered what was going through the girl's mind.

She was wearing a cobalt blue pants outfit that made her eyes appear almost black, and her dark auburn hair fell neatly to her shoulders, held out of her face by a matching blue ribbon. Elayna didn't know if Court had suggested her outfit, or if Annie had chosen it on her own. She didn't answer when Elayna got out of the car and said good-bye.

"Please don't be offended, Elayna," Court begged, as he walked her inside the house and took a quick look around. "Annie's. . ."

"I understand, Court. I really do." She waved away his excuses. "I'll see you tomorrow night." She held the door as Court stepped out onto the stoop. "Call me, if you need me before then," she added.

The private family viewing of Shirleene's body was planned for Sunday at six P.M., and Elayna had promised to be there with Court and Annie. Except for Court's mother and father, who would be flying in tomorrow night from St. Petersburg, he really had no other family. She knew she could be of some comfort to Court, but she didn't know what to do for Annie. She would be glad when the girl's grandparents arrived. *Of course, Anne Courtney has all those relatives on her mother's side. . . .*

Shirleene's family would have their viewing at 6:30. She had suggested that Court plan it that way, so he and Annie could have some quiet time before the others descended on the place. Shirleene's mother would probably scream and faint, and her father would play the pious and bereaved, if he were sober enough. The rest of them would be their usual rowdy, gaudy selves.

I dread the whole affair, she thought wearily, going to the bedroom to change into jeans and a sweatshirt.

"I must get this house back into some semblance of order." When she looked at the mess the intruder had made, and was reminded of his having been there, she felt sick. "First, though, I need to call the hospital and find out about Dave."

When she called, she was relieved to hear that the detective had been released that morning. "Good," she said aloud after hanging up the phone. "I'm happy for Dave that he wasn't seriously hurt, and it may mean less trouble for Jay." She walked into the kitchen, stuck a potato into the microwave, and fixed a small salad of lettuce, tomato, and green peppers. She washed it all down with a glass of Pepsi.

After lunch, she set to work straightening and cleaning the house. By evening, the front hallway and the keeping room, where she spent most of her time when she wasn't upstairs in the office, were neat and orderly again. She drew in a deep breath, relishing the fresh, clean smell of floor wax, window cleaner, and furniture polish. *There's no hint of the intruder now, at least in this part of the house,* she thought with satisfaction.

She looked out the window into the deepening dusk. Suddenly, she caught her breath. The furtive image she saw outlined against Liberty Hall's white plank fence was more than a shadow. It was a human being, dressed to blend with the night. At the end of the fence, he disappeared.

Had he gone down the steep path to the boat landing on the river below? Or had he melted around the end of the fence into Liberty Hall's back gardens? Would he be back, to hide in the shadows, watching for his next chance to steal or kill? Was she now the intended victim?

Suddenly, Elayna felt a hot surge of anger sweep over her. "I refuse to cower here waiting for him to strike!"

Grabbing her gray all-weather jacket from the hook beside the kitchen door, she stuffed a flashlight into the right pocket, her cell phone into the left, and headed for the front door.

Chapter 27

Elayna pushed the storm door shut and stood on the front step, peering into the corner of the yard by the fence. The sun had set. No moon or stars had yet appeared. The black shapes of trees and bushes and possible murderers blurred together in the gathering darkness.

Knowing she was outlined like a target in the light from the open door behind her, she moved down the walk to where the path of light ended. Had the furtive figure she had seen slipped around the end of the fence into Liberty Hall's gardens, or had he gone down the path toward the river? She had no idea. She strained to pick up any sound. A couple of streets over, a dog barked. Below her, the river rushed past. Otherwise, the silence was deep and unbroken. What she could see of the gardens beyond the fence looked alien, unfriendly, certainly not like the pleasant place where she and Jay had spent so many childhood hours.

She turned toward the riverbank. The feeble illumination from the house and shore lights rose in an eerie greenish glow against the now black sky hovering over the water. Where golden sunflowers and purple lady's bonnets bloomed in summer, where tangled vinca spread across the ground on both sides of the path and twined around tree trunks and fallen logs, she could see only dark water. The river had climbed the winding path nearly to the top of the bank, where it gurgled and sucked at the land, reaching greedily for more.

She could see the dark outline of the *Elayna,* almost at the edge of the yard, bobbing on the current, tugging against its tether like a rebellious teenager determined to follow the destructive flow of temptation.

There was little room for anyone to walk along the bank above the water. Surely her fugitive had not gone there. She turned back to the gardens, took another step, then stopped.

Have you lost your mind? she asked herself silently. *What are you doing out here in the dark, armed with only a flashlight and a cell phone, following a stealthy figure that, at best, is a vagrant and, at worst, a murderer?*

She looked back toward the front of the house, just as the door closed, cutting off the path of light. Fear slid down her spine. Was the murderer now in her house, waiting for her to come home?

It must have been the wind. Some stray breeze pushed that door shut. But she knew there was no breeze inside the house, with the other doors and windows locked and the storm door shut at the front. It had to have been a human hand that shut the door. Had he locked it, too? She had come out without the key.

What does that matter? she thought, amazed at her own stupidity. *If the murderer is waiting in my house, why would I want to get inside?*

She reached for the cell phone in her pocket and quickly dialed 9-1-1. As she waited for someone to answer, the thought came to her that it might have been Jayboy who had entered her house, seeking help with the terrible mess he was in, seeking comfort from the only one he trusted.

If the police came and it was Jayboy, wouldn't she be throwing him to the wolves? She needed time to find some evidence that would clear him of Shirleene's murder, and then Whit could defend him against the other charges that had resulted from his fear and confusion. Just as the 9-1-1 operator came on the line, Elayna broke the connection.

What should I do now? Should I try to reach Court? But he has Shirleene's family at his house. And what would he do if he found Jayboy at her house? Does he think Jay killed Shirleene? Would he just turn him over to the police?

She studied the house. The yellow light seeping out from the edges of the curtains promised warmth and security inside. But could she trust that promise? What really was concealed behind the heavy wooden door, beyond the welcoming facade? She had to know before she called for help. But would help come too late? Would they find her mutilated body lying on the floor in a pool of blood, as they had Shirleene's?

It has to be Jayboy in the house! she reassured herself. He was in more trouble than he surely had ever dreamed in his worst nightmares. It was logical that he would come to her, to the only true friend he had known.

If it was Jayboy inside her house, though, who had she seen leaving the yard a few minutes ago? Or was that just Jay going some roundabout way of his own through the gardens to get to her front door? If he had come through the gardens, though, she surely would have heard him move the chain on the side gate. She had heard nothing.

What should I do? She crept around the side of the house to the keeping room window. The light inside would shield her from view, while illuminating the room like a stage. She tiptoed to peer through the window. The room was empty. Unlike the last time her house had been invaded, nothing appeared to have been disturbed. That added to her belief that it was Jayboy. But where was he? He rarely went into any part of the house except the keeping room. Maybe he was in the bathroom. He probably needed some freshening up, after all he'd been through. But she didn't hear the sound of any water running or the commode being flushed.

A dog barked down in River View Park, somewhere down along the floodwall. The dog was soon answered by the one that lived two streets over. There still was no sound from inside the house.

She had to find out who was inside her house. If it was not Jayboy, she could call the police. Dave had said they could not make an arrest for murder without first getting an indictment, but they could arrest someone for criminal trespass, as they had with Jay.

She knew she could not get in through the back door. She always kept it locked. She retraced her steps to the front, mounted the step, and eased open the storm door. Silently, she turned the knob of the wooden door and pushed against it. It was locked! Whoever was in her house had locked her out! That surely meant it wasn't Jayboy.

A throbbing ache began behind her temples. As she absently reached up to massage them with her fingertips, she let the storm door slip from her grasp. It shut with a bang. From somewhere inside the house she heard a splintering of wood and a loud crash.

Switching on the flashlight as she ran, Elayna came around the house to find the back door wide open, yellow light spilling across the empty porch. She swung the beam of the flashlight across the backyard, but no black figure was captured in its light. Turning back toward the doorway, she gasped. The back door hung from the lock, ripped completely off its hinges!

A chill slid down her spine. What kind of strength had it taken to tear that heavy door from its solid oak frame? If the intruder had been Shirleene's murderer, what kind of man was he?

Certainly, neither Court nor Jayboy had that kind of strength. There was no one among her acquaintances who could have done it! Did the intruder have some superhuman strength?

Elayna leaned up against the side of the house to steady her rubbery knees and quickly dialed 9-1-1. This time, she asked to be connected with Dave Myers. She didn't think he would be back on duty so soon after his release from the hospital, but it was worth a try.

"I'm sorry, ma'am, but this is the 9-1-1 dispatch center," the operator said. "Would you like to report an emergency?"

"Well. . .yes." Elayna knew she couldn't wait until morning. "I'd like to report a. . ." she began, then stopped. Could she call it a "break-in" when she had left the door open for him? "I'd like to report a criminal trespass." It was certainly that, even if she had all but invited him into her house.

"Okay, ma'am. If you'll give me the address, I'll dispatch a patrol car."

Elayna supplied the requested information as she entered the house through the gaping back door and locked the storm door behind her.

"Now if you'll just stay on the line until. . ." the operator was saying, but Elayna didn't hear her. She had already broken the connection and slipped the cell phone back into her pocket so she could push the wooden door back onto its splintered frame with both hands, though she knew it provided no security.

Cautiously, she checked the rest of the house, but nothing appeared to have been disturbed. *Why did he come back? What was he after? And what kind of man could tear a solid door from its hinges, apparently with his bare hands?*

Just then she heard the doorbell. When she opened the front door, she found two young police officers standing on her front doorstep. They stared at her with wide, unbelieving eyes as she told them, sheepishly, about running out of the house after a murder suspect, with only a flashlight and cell phone, and leaving the front door wide open.

"Ma'am," the first officer said, "you're either the bravest woman I've ever met, or you're—"

"I know," she finished for him, "the most foolish. But, suddenly, I was just so angry, so tired of living in fear while he called all the shots. I ran out without really thinking it through, and by then, he was in the house."

"Well, we'll check the house," the other officer said. "But it sounds like you're pretty certain the suspect is gone."

When the officers saw the damage to the back door, one of them let out a low whistle. "Looks like a grizzly bear got ahold of that door, ma'am. Maybe we should move that big cupboard there over across the doorway until you can get it repaired. It won't be as good as a locked door, but it might give you some warning if someone tries to break in again."

"Yes, please," she said, feeling better once the officers had shoved the heavy piece of furniture over the useless door.

"We will make a thorough search of the grounds and surrounding areas before we leave," the first officer said. "We'll let you know, ma'am, when we catch him."

"It may be a comfort to you, ma'am, to know that, since our murder suspect has escaped, Detective Myers has asked for an extension of the extra patrols of the area," the other one added.

Oh, can't any of you understand that it's not Jayboy? she wanted to scream. "Thanks, officers," she said instead. "I appreciate your coming so quickly."

She wanted to ask them not to tell Dave Myers how stupid she had been, running out alone into the night after a murder suspect, but she knew it would do no good. They were bound to make a report. And since it involved a case he was working, he was bound to read it.

As the police cruiser pulled away, she closed and locked the front door. Then, feeling exposed and vulnerable in the lighted rooms, she walked through the house turning off lights. She peered out the darkened living room window toward Liberty Hall's gardens, but the darkness was thick, impenetrable.

Suddenly, she saw a light flicker deep inside the gardens. It was soon joined by several others.

It's too late in the year for fireflies, she thought. The lights she saw were too large for fireflies, anyway. They looked more like candles. But who would be carrying candles around over there, especially at this time of year?

Sometimes weddings and other special events were held in the gardens, but usually in the daytime. The museum was closed, so there was no way to find out if anything was scheduled for tonight. Should she call the police again?

Surely it's just some sort of celebration—and a celebration means people. At least for awhile, she would not be alone down here on the river behind the wall. Whatever was going on over there, she welcomed its company.

Chapter 28

Jayboy stood up and stretched. He shook the chain link gate again. It still was locked, just like it had been last night when he first got to the bridge. There was no room to squeeze around it. No way to get over it. No way onto the bridge that cars used to cross—or onto the walkway along its side.

He hadn't been able to walk the railroad bridge last night. It was too dark. Instead, he had slept underneath it, curled up on the rocks. Cold. Scared. But the police hadn't come.

In the murky early dawn, he stepped gingerly onto the ties of the railroad bridge. For a moment he stood looking down through the cracks at the dark water rushing by below. He could feel himself drawn toward the unfenced edge, beyond the rails where the train wheels rolled. Something was urging him to jump into the swirling, muddy river, to become part of some messy clump of tree limbs, twigs, and trash. To float with them under the bridges. Through the locks. Way off downstream. To wash up on some shore far from here.

The force was drawing him closer to the edge. He could feel himself beginning to fall. . . .

Jayboy jerked himself upright and threw himself sideways. He fell onto all fours between the iron rails. His knees and hands cried out with pain. His heart pounded. He gasped for breath.

He had almost been a goner!

Slowly, he stood up, wiped the sweat from his forehead, steadied himself.

The railroad ties were slippery with dew. He wished he had his orange sneakers so he could get some traction. Carefully, he placed one hard-soled shoe onto the next tie. He took another deep breath and pulled his other foot up even. He eased his way from tie to tie.

The pounding of the current against the pier supports of the bridge caught his attention and he peeked at the deep, dark water rushing by below. "Don't look down!" he whispered. "Don't look!"

He shook his head and focused once again on the tracks ahead. A few steps later, the bridge seem to shudder slightly and the timbers creaked, causing Jayboy to glance over his shoulder to where the tracks disappeared around the bend down Benson Valley. Suddenly he realized that if a train came, there was no place for him to go. He would be run over. Cut to pieces. Like that hobo they had found scattered over the tracks last year.

Jayboy swallowed hard. He took a deep breath. He stepped to the next tie. And the next. Willing the train not to come.

After what seemed like an eternity, he reached the end of the trestle and jumped to the top of the floodwall. It was too high along here to jump to the ground, so he'd have to run along the top until he reached a lower part.

He could see his house on the little branch of Broadway that ran to a dead end at the wall. Doris was there. She would be watching that talk show she always watched on Saturday mornings.

He wanted to see Doris! He wanted to go into the house. Eat breakfast. Go to his room. Sleep in his own bed.

He couldn't go home, though. Not now. Not after he had hurt the policeman. Doris would make him go back.

He jumped down into the Bar Center's parking lot. He couldn't go back to his safe place under 'Layna's porch, either. It wasn't safe anymore. The police knew. They would look there.

Jayboy ran through the empty parking lot and onto the bricks of Nash Street. He stopped where it ran into Wilkinson and looked both ways. No one was in sight. But where could he go? He looked both ways again. Turned to the right. Ran crouched over. To the corner of West Main.

Then he saw the wall. Walling in shrubbery and flower beds and small trees that bloomed in the spring when the dandelions came back. He remembered that beyond the wall was a porch— the covered porch ran in front of the chapel. He could hide there.

Chapter 29

Jayboy heard the door of the chapel open. From the corner of his eyes, he saw a woman in a red-brown coat come in. She had a flowered scarf tied over her head and shoes like Doris wore. Dr. Scholl's. Only these were black ones. He shivered.

Doris always wanted to get the black ones so they wouldn't show the dirt. But he had talked her into getting the white ones. Like the nurses wore at the doctor's office. She knew how he felt about black.

The woman didn't look his way. She walked down front, knelt and bowed her head, and began to speak softly. Jay guessed she was praying. Like 'Layna used to do here after little Carrie died. And after Hunt disappeared.

Doris came here, too. Not to pray. To clean. But she wouldn't come today. She always cleaned on Monday and Friday mornings. He was pretty sure this was Saturday.

Suddenly Jayboy realized that the woman was bound to see him when she turned around to leave. Quickly, he turned and knelt in front of his seat, like he was praying. Like he and Doris always did over their food.

He was hungry! But there was no food in the church. Doris said that was why they always said, "Poor as a church mouse." There was nothing here for even a mouse to eat. And any mouse

that lived here would be very poor. Unless the congregation had
had a big dinner. Or a wedding reception with cake and punch.
Then there might be something in the kitchen. Sealed up in little plastic bags. Or in the refrigerator. Or in the trash cans. But
the door to the church from the chapel was locked. He had tried
it. Doris said they always kept that door locked because they
didn't always lock the chapel.

The homeless men slept here in the chapel when the
weather was really cold. Doris sometimes found their blankets
rolled up in the back corner. Waiting for the next night. She said
the preacher didn't have the heart to lock them out. When it was
cold enough outside to freeze your nostrils together when you
breathed in. And when your breath came out of your mouth and
hung in the air like cigarette smoke.

Thank goodness it wasn't that cold now. This was October.
'Layna's birthday month. When the leaves changed and fell. And
a few dandelions bloomed when they weren't supposed to. He
liked October. It was all colors. Like the pictures in the colored
glass windows of the church. And it smelled good. Like wood
smoke and mellow leaves. Like that perfume 'Layna wore. The
nights might be cool, but the days were warm. Unless the fog hid
the sun. Or it rained.

He didn't think it was raining now, though. He hoped not.
He had to find some food. Somewhere. If only his empty stomach wouldn't growl while that woman was here. She surely
would hear it!

The woman turned and came back down the aisle. Jayboy
put his hands over his face and laid his head down on the bench.
He heard the chapel door open and close. When he peeked out
around his left hand, the woman was gone.

He eased the chapel door open and peered around it. There
was no one in sight, except the woman in the red-brown coat.

But she had her back to him. Hurrying downtown.

The sunlight was bright outside. How could he hunt for food without being seen?

Chapter 30

Elayna worked frantically all Sunday morning, trying to finish cleaning her downstairs rooms before she had to get ready to go to the funeral home.

She had reached a carpenter at home, and he had assured her he would repair her door first thing Monday morning. She tried not to look at the splintered door frame, or to think of the brute strength that had ripped the door from it.

She hadn't been out of the house all day. She didn't know if Court had gone to church or not, but she would be surprised if he hadn't. He was there every time the doors were open. Most of his married life, he had gone alone.

Well, so have I, she thought. Hunt hadn't been a regular churchgoer. He had been so busy at the hospital, and when he did get a day off, he liked to lounge around the house in sweatpants and a T-shirt, reading the paper. Or he would go off down the river on the boat. If he was in a lounging mood, sometimes she would get ready and go to church. If he was in a boating mood, she usually went with him.

She knew it was time to get out of her jeans, take a shower, and dress for the ordeal to come at the funeral home. Still, she stood at the window, sipping at a half-cold cup of black coffee, looking at the untimely dandelions "bestrowed," as Jayboy called it, over the back yard.

I don't know if that is a word, but it ought to be, she thought. It conjured up such an image of benevolence, of a kindly deity lavishing beauty on his subjects. She smiled, recalling how excited Jay always got when the dandelions appeared and how he grieved when they blew away. She wondered if he remembered the stories she had told him of the magic Kingdom of the Dandelions.

How beautiful life was back then. So carefree and uncomplicated. It had been beautiful in the early days with Hunt, too. But those happy days together in the little stone house they had bought on the south side of the river had been brief and seemed light years removed from her present existence.

She and Hunt had gone back to the house alone after Carrie's funeral, but its five average-size rooms had seemed as big and as empty as the nearby state capitol on a holiday. Finally, Hunt had gone out one Sunday morning, supposedly to buy a newspaper, and never returned. She and Court had found the boat tied up at the landing on the farm, with a note telling her good-bye. She had no idea how he had traveled from there or where he had gone. Ten long years had passed. She hadn't heard a word from him since.

When it had become apparent that he was not coming back, and when Granny's stroke had made it necessary for Elayna to move in to take care of her, she had sold the stone house. She had no desire to go back there. The place would forever be haunted by the bittersweet shadow of a four-year-old child and her father. It had been a relief to see it sold, along with most of its furnishings.

She still could see little Carrie's room as plainly as if she were standing in it this moment—the pale lavender walls trimmed with a border of white geese and little girls in lavender dresses; the matching bedspread, curtains, and lamp; Bandit, the raccoon, and Pot Belly Bear on the bed.

Elayna wiped the memories away by imagining a chalkboard

eraser sweeping over her mind, as she had been taught to do in the counseling sessions soon after Carrie's burial. Sometimes she felt the mental trick was the only thing that saved her sanity. She wished Hunt had gone for the counseling. It hadn't taken away the terrible hurt, but it had helped her to cope with it, and with Hunt's disappearance later.

Where was Hunt? she wondered again. What was he doing with those square fingers that could so gently examine a sick child or reach out to touch the side of his wife's face? Did those beautiful blue eyes still mirror such pain that she would not be able to look into them? Did he ever think of her?

A sudden longing to see her husband, to feel his strong arms around her, shook her with such force that her hand jerked, sloshing black coffee onto the floor. She dabbed at it with a napkin, then reached the corner of the napkin to her eyes to head off threatening tears.

"Will I never stop missing him, loving him?" she asked aloud. She set the cup in the sink and threw the soggy napkin into the trash. It might have been different had he left her for another woman; but so far as she knew, Hunt had no "other woman," unless you counted the river, his longtime love.

Again she used the mental eraser to cleanse her thoughts of the painful memories, as she walked down the hall to her bedroom. Opening the closet, she deliberately focused her mind on what to wear to the funeral home.

The charcoal gray, light wool suit would do nicely, she decided. Not the severe black of heavy mourning, but demure and respectful. Her freshly washed teal blouse would keep the outfit from being too austere and would lend color to the pale face she saw peering back at her from the full-length mirror inside the closet door. Gray shoes and purse. . .

On second thought, perhaps I should save the gray outfit for the funeral. If so, what can I wear tonight? She started moving hangers to the right, then to the left, riffling through her assortment of dresses, suits, and coats.

A memory swept over her—of cramming her things in beside Hunt's in the little stone house with too little closet space, of catching the scent of aftershave and masculine cologne when she moved his sports coats and slacks to get to her own things.

"Stop it!" she ordered aloud. Grabbing her robe from the hook on the closet door and clean underwear from the dresser drawer, she headed for the bathroom.

When she turned off the water and stepped from the shower, she heard the phone ringing on the nightstand. Clutching her bath towel around her, she ran into the bedroom and grabbed the receiver. Her "hello" was a bit terse.

"Elayna?" a masculine voice asked. "I just called my secretary, and she told me about Shirleene. I'm so sorry!"

"Oh, Whit!" she said, glad that he could not see the quickening of her pulse. "How good of you to call!"

"I can't get a flight out until seven o'clock this evening," he went on. "I'll be too late to come to the funeral home tonight, but I'll be there tomorrow for the funeral. Is there anything I can do from here? How's Court?"

"He's. . .well, you know Court. He's handling it."

"I'm sure he is, but it can't be easy. What a terrible thing to happen! Well, I'll see you tomorrow. And Elayna, please take care. I understand the murderer has not been caught?"

She hesitated, then decided not to mention Jayboy's arrest and escape until she could talk with Whit in person. "No," she answered truthfully, "he has not been caught."

After Whit said good-bye, Elayna stood holding the receiver for several seconds. How good it had felt to hear his voice, and how alone she felt now that the connection had been broken.

Finally, she replaced the receiver and retraced her wet footprints to the bathroom, a little disconcerted to realize how eagerly she looked forward to seeing Whit tomorrow.

Forty-five minutes later, wearing a powder blue light wool suit and black sling pumps, Elayna adjusted the strap of her black shoulder bag and stepped out onto her front stoop just as a Riverview Florist van pulled into her driveway. *On Sunday?* she thought.

The driver got out and handed her a vase containing a dozen yellow roses. The card read, "Thinking of you. Whit."

I guess the senator can get flowers delivered any time he wants to, she thought as a smile spread across her face.

Still smiling, she carried the roses inside and set them on the kitchen table. Whit was good about things like that. He always sent her flowers after their evenings out, often the yellow roses that he knew were her favorites. Tonight, since he could not be here, he had sent the roses to let her know he was with her in thought. She felt a warmth spread through her at this evidence of his caring, of his very special friendship. She needed a friend right now.

With a last appreciative glance, she left the flowers and the house, and walked briskly toward the funeral home a few blocks away.

Chapter 31

Jayboy shivered in the shadows of the little courtyard. His clothes were dry now and his shoes were just a little damp. But the night air was cool.

He had left the chapel early this morning before Sunday school started. He knew a Sunday school class met there now. He had wandered behind the houses in back of the church looking for food. But there just wasn't any that was fit to eat. Then he had hidden inside an unlocked shed. When he had dared to come back to the chapel after all the cars had driven away from the church, he had found it locked. There was nowhere to hide except the porch and the little courtyard.

He was glad it was dark. The lights in the bell tower and at the side of the church had not yet come on. He knew they worked on a timer. He had watched Mac do the wiring. But he didn't know what time they were supposed to come on. Or even what time it was now. He had to get away. Before the timer flooded the courtyard with light. Before they came looking for him.

He wanted to talk to 'Layna. But maybe he shouldn't. Maybe she couldn't help him anymore. She had tried to stop them from taking him away. But they had taken him anyway.

The courtyard was a good place to hide for awhile. But it was small. Once the lights came on, there would be no place to hide. Unless he went back inside the chapel.

He had spent last night in the chapel, sleeping on the hard bench at the back. Wishing for his soft bed and his warm gray blanket. He couldn't keep staying here, though. It was warmer in the chapel, but it was locked now. And he needed a blanket. And warmer clothes. And something to eat! He hadn't had anything since yesterday afternoon when he had found a half bag of stale potato chips and a piece of birthday cake wrapped up in foil, in a garbage can behind a house down the street.

And what if someone who knew him came to the chapel to pray? Doris and he came to church here since Mac died. Before that, they had gone to another church in the car. A big red brick Baptist church. But Doris didn't drive. She had sold the car. So they came here now.

He liked coming here. Especially on Christmas Eve, when candles flickered on the altar and on the windowsills. Or on Good Friday. When the sunlight fell through the colored glass windows in all the colors in his crayon box. And the church always was full of people, but nobody paid any attention to him. He liked the way the preacher shook his hand. And the way he smiled at him. Not like Shirleene. Making fun of him. But like he was somebody. It made him feel good.

Maybe he could talk to the preacher, tell him everything. About Shirleene and her friends. About the Dandelion Kingdom. And the dandelion pin. About the blood on his shoe. And his Spider-Man shirt. But he knew the preacher would say, "Give yourself up, Jayboy, and I'll see what I can do to help you."

He couldn't go to jail! He would smother! He couldn't stand it! But he had been arrested. And he had escaped. He was a criminal now. Maybe even a killer. If the cop had died. He had seen enough of Doris's police shows to know that. There was no help for him. He had to get away. Before the lights came on. Before they found him. But where could he go?

Chapter 32

Elayna turned the knob of one of the big double doors and stepped inside the funeral parlor onto a thick carpet that muffled the sound of her heels. The scent of dying flowers assaulted her, and she reeled with the impact of memory.

Clutching the back of a folding chair in the last row, she steadied herself for the walk to the front of the nearly empty room, where Shirleene's body lay in the rich cherrywood coffin that Elayna and Court had chosen.

She had been so full of boundless energy, of the innocent joy of being alive. And she had been cut down like the flowers around her, cut off from the life source before she really had a chance to bloom.

Elayna realized her morbid thoughts of her sister-in-law had somehow metamorphosed into those she had endured when it had been her four-year-old child lying in a coffin across the river at Rogers Funeral Home. A different place, a different still white form, but the smothering panic she felt rising inside her was the same.

Carefully, she stripped the cloying memories from her mind and took a deep breath. Then, steeling herself, she let go of the chair and walked quickly down the aisle to where Court and Anne Courtney awaited her on a small loveseat in front of the coffin.

Court looked up as she stopped beside him, and for an instant, incredible pain darkened his blue eyes to nearly black. She leaned down to put her arm around his shoulders, then kissed him on the cheek. For a moment, he leaned against her. Then he straightened, and when he again looked into her eyes, his emotions were neatly tucked away beneath his usual iron control. Elayna patted his shoulder and turned to Anne Courtney.

The girl sat staring at a spot above the coffin, her face frozen into an emotionless mask. She looked down at Elayna as she knelt in front of her and put her arms around her, but her expression did not change, and she did not yield to her aunt's embrace.

"Annie, I wish there was something I could do to make it better!" Elayna whispered, removing her arms from the girl's stiff waist to take her cold hands in both of hers.

"Thank you," Anne Courtney said politely. The blankness in her eyes frightened Elayna.

Elayna turned away, and her gaze fell on the still form resting stiffly against the satin pillows. The coffin was lined in a soft gray fabric that created a perfect backdrop for Shirleene's bright hair and rose-colored silk dress. The carefully made-up face resembled her sister-in-law, but there was nothing left of the restless energy that had been Shirleene. This image in front of her might have been a wax replica.

Elayna stood up and began to examine the floral arrangements that already had arrived, her own basket of fall flowers among them. Next to the pink rose arrangement Court had chosen for the coffin itself, the largest was a basket of mums and daisies bearing a card that read, "I'm so sorry. Whit."

She wandered around the room, reading cards, admiring unusual designs, until Shirleene's family noisily descended upon the funeral home. She persuaded Court to retire to a back room for a cup of coffee while the relatives played out their melodrama.

Then the crowds came. Before the interminable evening of

receiving condolences was over, it was all Elayna could do to keep from shouting at well-meaning visitors, "No, she doesn't look natural! She looks dead! And Shirleene never looked dead a day in her life!"

It was with great relief that she slipped out of the funeral home after the last caller had gone and stood on the porch, inhaling deep breaths of fresh air to replace the stale taste and scent of death.

The light from the porch did little to alleviate the fog that had crept back, turning the deserted street into a perfect setting for an old English mystery. Elayna expected, at any moment, to see Vincent Price swirling his cape around him as he stalked his next victim. She shivered, knowing that Shirleene's killer was still on the loose.

Elayna gasped as a man appeared suddenly out of the fog and started up the steps toward her. She half turned to run back inside. Then the feeble light fell on his open, friendly face under an unruly mop of dark red hair, and he smiled, causing freckles to slide into unsuspected crevices. She paused, sure that here was no threat to her safety.

"Jimmy O'Brien," he introduced himself, extending his hand.

She shook his hand briefly, then drew her own back to fold it securely under her other arm, trying to remember where she had heard the name.

"I've been asked to preach the funeral," he supplied. "I'm a friend of the daughter, Anne Courtney. Is she here? I'm sorry to be so late, but there was an emergency. One of my congregation was rushed to the hospital with what appeared to be a heart attack. Turned out to be the gallbladder, thank God!"

"Anne Courtney left about twenty minutes ago with some of her friends," Elayna replied. She hadn't known the four teenagers with whom her niece had left after Court had gone back to talk with them about the inappropriateness of their loud laughter. She was worried about Annie, though. As close as she and

Shirleene had become lately, the girl hadn't shed a tear tonight.

"I'm Annie's aunt by marriage," she explained. "Elayna Evans."

He nodded. "I know." He stared at her, studying her features in the dim light. Then, "Pardon me for staring," he said. "I once knew someone who. . ." He made a visible effort to gather his thoughts. "I know who you are because I saw your name on the materials you left at the print shop this morning," he said instead. "It's an unusual spelling."

"The Spanish spell it E-L-E-N-A, I believe," she said, "but my mother always had a mind of her own." She smiled.

"I've only seen it spelled your way once before," he said seriously. "It. . .it's beautiful." Then, murmuring something about needing to discuss details of the funeral with Court, he excused himself and went inside.

Strange man! Elayna thought, bemused by his reaction to her name, but too tired to try to solve that puzzle tonight.

She knew she should wait for Court to finish last-minute arrangements and let him drive her home, but she was exhausted, totally drained both physically and emotionally. All she wanted was to be home and in bed with a book to take her mind off the events of the evening. And it was such a short walk home.

She descended the few steps to the street and turned right into the parking lot next door. She crossed the lot and stopped to look to her right, then to her left down the dark expanse of Long Lane, noting the black recesses that could easily hide an assailant.

Surely the murderer is far away from here by now! she reassured herself. Now that he knew she did not have whatever he thought Shirleene had left with her, he must have moved on to some isolated hideout or to the anonymity of a big city.

She set off at a brisk walk down the alley, glancing only briefly into doorways and breaks between buildings. At the corner, she stopped and looked both ways up and down West Main Street and across into Petticoat Lane. So far as she could see in the fog, the whole area appeared deserted.

She turned right onto West Main and stepped up on the curb, where she stood uncertainly, peering into the mistiness ahead. From this angle, she couldn't tell if there was light behind any of Laura's second-story windows. She could see a distant fuzzy glow around the light by the Bar Center, and she could distinguish the small lights that lit the footpaths at Liberty Hall. None of them did anything to illumine the dark cavern created by the buildings on either side of her.

Two blocks and her driveway and she would be home. "Am I such a scaredy-cat I can't walk home by myself?" she scoffed. She had done it literally thousands of times over the years. Of course, there had been no murderer on the loose, but there was no reason why anybody should be after her, she told herself, taking half a dozen steps and stopping again.

What was that sound? It seemed to come from the miniature courtyard on her right that normally was lit invitingly by lights from the bell tower of First Presbyterian Church. But tonight, had she not known the charming little courtyard so well, she could not have made out the flowering tree and shrubs, the tulip bed edged in brick in the shape of a cross, and the sign that proclaimed, "Chapel open for prayer."

What else is hidden there by the fog? she wondered, trying desperately to see into the courtyard and across it into the hacienda-style porch that joined the very old sanctuary of the church to the new education building. Her heart had begun to beat so hard she couldn't be sure what she had heard, if anything.

There it was again! A stealthy movement. A kind of rustling.

Suddenly the fog was pierced by light as a car roared around the corner behind her and screeched to a halt at the curb. A scream on her lips, she whirled around as the driver's door opened and shut. Then she began to shake as she recognized the car and the man coming toward her.

Chapter 33

Jayboy crouched inside the porch, tears of frustration stinging his eyes. She had been so close! He could have run out and touched her. In a moment, he would have. But the car had come roaring around the corner and stopped in front of the church. He had been forced to take refuge behind one of the pillars of the porch.

He had heard a car door open and shut. Then again. And again. Like somebody had put someone in on the passenger's side and gone around to get in on the driver's side. And the car had pulled away. Had someone taken 'Layna away? Hiding here in the dark, he couldn't tell which way the car had turned at the corner.

He'd like to tell 'Layna good-bye. She was the only friend he'd ever had. His Princess of Dandelion. He would like to tell her "thanks." For the stories. For the Dandelion Kingdom. For being his friend. For treating him just like regular people. For letting him work with her and Leslie down at the shop. For telling him he did a good job. For trying to save him from the police. Even though they wouldn't listen to her.

He wanted to see Doris one more time. He thought of her arms around him. Her soft voice saying, "It's all right, baby. It's all right." Making him feel warm and safe. Not as safe as he had felt with Mac. But safe. She would make him go back, though. Just like she had when he had taken the glass doorknob from

'Layna's trash can. Or the magazines with the bright pictures from the doctor's office. She said it was always better to "face the music." No, he couldn't let Doris know.

Most likely she was still up, though. Watching one of her police shows or some love story. When she was watching TV, she never heard him climb up the drainpipe and onto the back porch roof. She never heard him push his window open and drop silently to the floor of his room.

He needed some clean clothes. And a warmer jacket. And some food! He was so hungry!

He wondered what Doris had fixed for supper. Maybe she would have fried some chicken. In that heavy black skillet with the lid on it. And made white gravy with milk and chicken crumbs in it. And a big old bowl of mashed potatoes with butter puddling in that low place in the middle. Or she might have fixed pork chops with barbeque sauce on them. And fried apples with sugar and nutmeg and cinnamon. And peas with sugar and butter, but no milk. He didn't like milk in his peas. Doris knew that.

He knew he had to do it. He had to go home. Get some clothes. Maybe a blanket. And sneak down the back stairs and get some food.

Jayboy stood up. He peered out from behind the pillar. The lights still had not come on. He stepped around the pillar and into the garden.

Chapter 34

I've checked the entire house, Elayna, and there's nobody in it. But I still don't like leaving you alone down here behind that wall, especially with that back door hanging open," Whit said as he rejoined her in the keeping room.

"Oh, I'll be all right," she assured him. "But I appreciate your rescuing me from my childish panic when I heard those noises back there in the church courtyard. You don't know how glad I was to see that it was you coming toward me in the fog."

"Well, I could stay. . . ." he offered, a hopeful gleam in his dark eyes.

She laughed. "That won't be necessary, Senator," she said firmly. "But you are welcome to a piece of homemade poppyseed cake before you go."

He sighed. "You can't blame a guy for trying, Elayna. You're an attractive lady."

Her pulse quickened. He certainly knew how to make her *feel* attractive, though this was the first time in all the evenings they had spent together that he had even hinted at anything more than a few pleasant hours of companionship. She had been sure he understood that she wasn't interested in a sordid little affair, but she decided to keep it light.

"Flattery will get you everywhere, sir," she said with a mock curtsy. "I'll even throw in a cup of coffee."

He shrugged and threw up both hands. "Cake and coffee, it is," he conceded. "Black." He took a chair at the kitchen table. "Do you have any of that special coffee you served me last time? Remember? The night we played Monopoly until two A.M.?"

"The John Conti Irish Creme," she recalled. "I believe I do." She went to the cupboard, took down a tin, filled the coffeemaker, and plugged it into the wall socket.

Suddenly, from behind her, she felt his arms go around her waist. He brushed her hair with his lips.

"Whit—" she began, turning to face him.

"Marry me, Elayna," he broke in. "We are good together. And I have such plans."

"You're going to run for governor," she supplied.

He didn't deny it. "You'd enjoy the role of First Lady of the Commonwealth, Elayna," he said seriously. "And you're perfect for the part."

She laughed softly and moved out of his embrace. "And you need a 'perfect-for-the-part' mate to complete your image as the 'perfect-for-the-part' candidate. I wasn't born late last night, Senator! Thanks, but 'no thanks.' I was twenty-five years old when I married Hunt. I married strictly for love. If I ever re-married, it would be the same. I wouldn't settle for anything less, Whit."

He shook his head. "You misunderstand me, Elayna. I believe we have a spark here that could be fanned into a first-class romance. Won't you give us a chance? I know we could be happy."

"Whit, I'm still married to Hunt," she reminded him.

"It's time you either divorced him or had him declared legally dead, Elayna," he said. "He's been gone ten years, for Pete's sake! Let him go! Get on with your life! We're not getting any younger, you and I. Let's not waste any more time."

Completely at a loss for words, she busied herself with slicing the cake and placing it on two small plates, laying out forks and napkins, taking down cups and saucers, and pouring coffee.

"I've always thought there was some powerful chemistry between us, Elayna. Don't you feel anything for me at all?" he asked softly.

"Oh, Whit, of course I do! You're. . .well, as you say, 'perfect for the part.' It's just that. . ." She groped for the right words. Then she realized that she didn't know what she wanted to say. Could she love Whit? Was it time she put Hunt behind her and moved on? Apparently he had put her behind him and gone on with whatever he wanted to do.

"Don't answer me now," Whit broke into her thoughts. "I realize I've taken you by surprise. I've waited all this time, wanting to be sure you were ready to put the past behind you. I can wait awhile longer. All I ask is that you give the idea a fair chance. I still believe we'd be good together, in every way."

She nodded, unable to meet his eyes, afraid he would read things in hers that she wasn't ready to share.

Share? I don't even know what I feel—except total and utter confusion. Whit was a very attractive man, but she couldn't imagine being married to anyone but Hunt. If only she knew what had happened to him, if he was still alive!

"This is delicious!" Whit said, deliberately bridging the awkwardness that had suddenly arisen between them. "What did you call it?"

"Poppyseed cake. It was my grandmother's recipe. But nothing ever tastes as good to me as it did when she made it."

"I remember Mrs. Luther," he said. "She was a real lady, and as bright as they come, an enlightened thinker far ahead of her generation. I never could understand why she was so hard-shelled about her religion. It was her only blind spot."

Hard-shelled? Elayna thought. *Granny?* "She was very ecumenical for her day," she said defensively. "She didn't care what church you attended, so long as you attended. She sent me to every Vacation Bible School in the county. Every summer."

"But I'll bet they were all fundamentalist Christian churches," he said. "You're not like her, though, Elayna. I've never heard you mention your religion—but, for her, everything seemed to revolve around it."

Granny's life had revolved around her faith, Elayna knew. Once, when she was trying to deal with her double loss, she had confessed to her grandmother that she envied her the peace that seemed to be rooted so deeply within her that no earthly troubles could touch it. And Granny had replied, "You can find that peace the same way I did, honey. I just gave it all to Him a long time ago." When Elayna had responded that her faith just wasn't as big as hers, Granny had laughed. "My faith is just the plain old garden variety, honey. I've just got a great big God!"

If anybody had a faith I envy, it was Granny, Elayna thought. "She had the most incredible peace about her, Whit," she said wistfully. "It undergirded her entire life."

He nodded. "It's just that there was no room in her thinking for other faiths, other cultures. Christians are like that. They are the only ones who won't join in with the New World Order."

"What do you mean, Whit?"

"There are many faiths, Elayna, all basically seeking the same thing. Why can't we just work together to make our world the best it can be, to realize our cosmic human potential?"

Again, Elayna was at a loss for words. They never had discussed religion, but she had assumed he believed all the traditional basics. She had to admit that her own beliefs had been more abstract, less personal than her grandmother's. *But if I had a personal kind of faith, it would be like Granny's,* she thought firmly.

"The seminar I was attending in Washington this week was fantastic," he went on. "You'll have to go with me next time. There are so many exciting things going on—holistic health, training for consciousness-raising. And the time is rapidly accelerating. It can't be long now before. . ." He checked the flow of words, but his gaze still magnetized hers over the coffee cups. "We are all seeking the same thing, Elayna," he said finally. "We all want to grow toward godhood."

"We do?" she murmured.

"Of course we do!" he insisted. "We are all on a quest to become one with the cosmic god force. I am a part of God, Elayna. You are a part of God. Therefore, we are one, you and I, whether you agree to marry me or not!" He was smiling, but his dark eyes, still boring into hers, were completely serious.

"But, Whit, I . . ."

He took her hand. "After you have thought over and—I hope—accepted my proposal, I will share something very beautiful with you, Elayna," he promised.

He got up and came around the table to stand over her. Quickly, he bent and kissed her lightly on the forehead. "Sleep well, my love," he said. Almost before she knew it, he was gone, leaving her with her thoughts and emotions in a whirl.

Could she bring herself to accept Whit's proposal? she wondered, as she locked the house and prepared for bed. The idea was tempting. She really liked Whit, and she had been alone—and lonely—for a very long time.

Chapter 35

Jayboy climbed from the drainpipe to the porch roof. He pushed the window open and climbed over the low sill into his bedroom.

He could hear the TV downstairs. Cars racing. Tires squealing. Guns cracking. He hated police shows! The noise was good, though. Maybe Doris wouldn't hear him moving around up here.

If he had his sneakers, he could walk as quiet as a shadow. But these hard-soled Sunday shoes made lots of noise. He slipped them off and walked barefoot over to the dresser. He eased open the middle drawer and took out a pair of heavy white socks. He pulled them on. They would make his shoes fit tight. But they would keep his feet warm. It was getting cold outside.

Jayboy pushed the drawer shut and opened the bottom onc. He took out his yellow sweater. His favorite. He pulled it over his head, over his other Spider-Man shirt. Then he remembered that the bright yellow would make it easier for the police to spot him. He pulled the sweater off and stuffed it back in the drawer. He pushed the drawer shut.

He tiptoed over to the closet and opened the door. Slowly. So it wouldn't squeak. He slipped his gray sweat jacket off the hanger and pulled it on over his T-shirt. With the hood hanging down his back.

He started back to the window to get his shoes. Then he

turned and crossed over to the bed, pulled off the dandelion bed-spread, and laid it on the chair. He took the faded gray blanket underneath, rolled it up, and tucked it under his left arm.

Picking up his shoes in his left hand, he opened the door to the back stairs with his right and began to ease down the stairs. One step. Stop to listen. Next step. Listen. Finally, he reached the kitchen.

He pulled open a cabinet door and took out the peanut butter. Peter Pan. Creamy. The only kind he would let Doris buy. There wasn't much left in the jar, though. He stuffed it into his jacket pocket. Then he added the last package of crackers.

He was afraid to open the refrigerator to get something to drink. He could open it silently, but, from where she was sitting, Doris would see the light come on.

He took a can of pineapple juice from the cabinet. He stuffed it into his other jacket pocket. He eased open the drawer next to the sink and took a small can opener and stuffed it into his left jeans pocket. He had his Scout knife for the peanut butter. In the other pocket.

A commercial came on TV. He heard Doris get up. She would head for the kitchen!

He wished he could tell her good-bye. He felt tears gathering in his eyes and throat. He would miss her. He hoped she knew that. But he knew she would make him give himself up to the police. He couldn't let her know he was here. Instead, he saluted in Doris's direction. The salute of the Knight of the Kingdom of Dandelion.

Then, silently, he eased open the back door and left the house.

Chapter 36

Elayna sat at the kitchen table in a comfortable faded blue sweatsuit, sipping hot tea, listening to the comforting sounds of the carpenter's saw and hammer, and watching a bright red cardinal and his drab little mate argue over a sunflower seed from the feeder in the crabapple tree.

"Cardinals mate for life," she remembered her grandfather telling her. "Seems to me they've got a lot more sense than some people."

She smiled, thinking that the birds' bickering was much like the needle-sharp exchanges between her feisty Granny and her hardheaded Grandad. Strangely enough, it was those arguments that had securely stitched together the pleasant patchwork days of her childhood.

Her father had been wrapped up in his real estate business. Her mother had been absorbed by her looks, her clothes, her social life, and Elayna's appearance. Her father had provided her clothes. Her mother had seen to it that they were the best brands and the latest fashion. It had been Granny and Grandad who had provided the loving companionship and the undergirding stability she needed.

Elayna sighed and took a sip from her cup. It had been a long time since she had felt that secure. Maybe if Hunt were here. . . But, to be honest, she hadn't even felt it with him, especially during those last months before he had gone away.

She had tasted briefly of a kind of security last night when she had recognized Whit coming toward her in the fog, when she had sunk gratefully into the leather seat of his Mercedes and let him drive her the short distance home. She hated to admit how terrified she had been when she had heard the furtive noises in the church courtyard, how glad she had been to accept Whit's offer to see her safely inside the house.

Can I accept his subsequent offer as readily? she wondered. *Could I truly cut my ties to Hunt and build a new life with another man?* If so, Whit was the logical choice. He was intelligent, attractive, fun to be with, and he was considerate of her feelings. He had accepted the role in which she had cast him—escort, friend, casual companion—without ever encroaching on the protective space she had built around her private self. Until last night.

She felt a warmth spread through her at the memory of Whit's arms around her as he had proposed. Then she became aware of the "golden oldie" playing on the radio, the Frank Sinatra ballad she and Hunt had chosen for "their song" back when they first had begun to get serious about each other.

She could feel Hunt's arms around her as he crooned his own off-key version of "When somebody loves you, it's no good unless he loves you, all the way! Through the good or lean years and all the in-between years, all the way! Taller than the tallest tree is—that's how it's got to feel. . . ."

And that's how it had felt, she remembered. At least for her. She was sure it had been that way for Hunt, too. And deep down, beneath all the hurt and the bitterness, she never had believed that he had stopped loving her. Why, then, had he stayed away all these years? They could have healed their hurt over little Carrie together. After his first frantic running from the pain, why hadn't he recognized that and come back?

He hadn't, though, so why couldn't she forget him and get on with her life? Why couldn't she find that treetop feeling with someone else—Whit, for instance? But, as attracted as she was to the handsome senator, she knew she did not feel about him the way she had about Hunt.

From that day in eighth grade when she had looked up and there he stood, asking to borrow a pencil, smiling at her with that crooked grin, swallowing her up with those fathomless blue eyes. . .

Though they had dated others in between—theirs had been a love that had to be. She had thought it would last forever, "through the good or lean years, and all the in-between years," as the song said. And, for her, it had.

She didn't know if she could ever feel that way about Whit, about any other man. But maybe she expected too much. Maybe a love like that was only meant for the first time around. Should she settle for a comfortable companionship now? Should she accept the role Whit had offered her as the candidate's "perfect-for-the-part" mate?

Could she have Hunt declared dead? Legally, she could, but it seemed, somehow, like she would be killing him. She didn't think she could do it. She supposed she could divorce him. After all, he had deserted her. He had left her alone for ten long years. Was it time for her to cut all ties to Hunt?

"Deeper than the deep blue sea is, that's how deep it goes, if it's real," Sinatra crooned.

" 'What is real?' the Velveteen Rabbit asked the Skin Horse one day, when they were lying side by side near the nursery fender."

The words came to her from out of the past. She had read Margery Williams's little book to Carrie Hunter so many times that they both had been able to recite it from memory. She could still see Carrie, P. B. Bear in her lap and the dog-eared favorite book spread out on the patio table before her, earnestly "reading" the story aloud to the bear.

" 'Real isn't how you are made,' the Skin Horse replied. 'It's a thing that happens to you. When a child loves you for a long, long time, not just to play with, but REALLY loves you, then you become Real.'

" 'Does it hurt?' asked the Rabbit."

Suddenly, tears stung her eyes. "Yes, it hurts!" she whispered. "It never stops hurting!"

" 'But once you are Real,' " the Skin Horse said unfeelingly, " 'you can't become unreal again. It lasts for always.' "

The realness lasts, she thought, *long after the love that made you Real is gone.* She guessed her problem was that she hadn't been loved, REALLY loved—by a child or anybody—for a very long time.

That brought her back to Whit. But not yet ready to deal with Whit and his unexpected proposal, she discarded the troubling thoughts with the dregs of her tea, rinsed the cup, and turned it upside down in the drainer.

Forget Whit! she thought. *Forget Hunt! There are more urgent matters to address here.*

Resolutely, she turned her mind to Jayboy. She had to find him, to help him some way. She walked down the hall to the front door, pulled the door shut behind her, and stood on the front stoop, not knowing what to do next.

The raucous sound of a chain saw sliced through the morning, and she saw that the wide back gate to Liberty Hall's compost bins was open, apparently to admit the tan pickup truck she could glimpse through the slats of the fence.

Gasoline-powered engines from the hectic modern world seemed out of sync with the heavy sense of peaceful timelessness that pervaded the eighteenth-century estate. But she knew that Senator Brown had incorporated many labor-saving devices into the design of his home. It was likely he would have welcomed the convenience of power tools to fend off the ever-encroaching wilderness, she thought, heading for Liberty Hall's side gate in the white picket fence between the back corner of the mansion on her left and the wellbox and toolhouse on her right.

She pushed through the gate, always open to the public, and walked slowly down the brick walk. At the place where the walk branched, she struck out across the lawn and stood looking down upon the green patina of an ancient sundial, feeling the inevitable sense of timelessness begin to erode her urgency to find Jayboy.

The place had changed so little over the past two centuries. She could have been Margaretta Brown standing here breathing the pungent, horsey odor of boxwood, soaking up the pleasant warmth of the autumn sun to carry her through the long, hard winter to come, when she would be cooped up within the brick walls behind her for endless weeks.

She traced the Roman numerals of the sundial with her forefinger. Had the senator's young wife spent long summer days here in the gardens, as Elayna had, dreaming of riding the river below to far-off adventures? Or had she longed to follow it back to more civilized places? Had she accepted the fact that, as a lady, she would never know the delight of cool, green waters on bare white skin? Or after her household was safely asleep, had she risked Indian capture for a stolen moonlight swim in its satiny depths?

Despite the demure pose of her portrait in the museum next door and the stories of her gathering the neighborhood children for Sunday school right here in these gardens, there was a fire of independence banked in those dark eyes that made Elayna sad that their moments of time and place would never coincide. For—pretend as she and Jay had that time stood still in the magic Kingdom of Dandelion—the sundial silently, relentlessly marked off the hours, carrying her generation farther and farther away from Margaretta's.

She sighed. The hours she and Jayboy had spent here, playing their childish games! But this was no pleasant interlude of hide-and-seek or kick the can. No one would sing out, "Allie, allie, all in free!" so that Jay could come in without penalty when the game was over. By his escape, he had set in motion events that, like time, would move relentlessly to their conclusion.

Again, she felt the urgency gnawing at her, and she crossed the lawn to pace between Margaretta's ancient flower beds. She had to find Jay before someone else did. She had to find a way to prove his innocence.

But where do I start?

Chapter 37

Jayboy breathed in the cloying scent of old horse sweat. Like it used to smell in his grand-daddy's barn. Only there were no horses here. It was the scent of the boxwood leaves in the hot sun. Overlapping above him like a cave of branches. So thick the gardener could not see him.

'Layna would know where to find him if she thought about it. They had spent whole days here under the boxwood. Making up stories about the Princess of Dandelion and her trusty knight.

He wished 'Layna would come and find him. But would she make him go back? He knew she would. 'Layna and Doris always did what was right. No matter how much it hurt.

He sighed and changed positions. The ground under his blanket was damp. There had been frost last night. And now it was melting in the sun.

He picked up the peanut butter jar. It was empty. He had scraped it clean last night. He ate the last two crackers, which made him thirsty. He had finished the can of pineapple juice last night, too.

What was he going to do? He couldn't stay here. He had been cold last night in spite of the blanket. And now his food was all gone. Tonight he would be cold and hungry. He was hungry now.

What he wouldn't give to be sitting at Mucci's with Doris and 'Layna. Eating a big old roast beef sandwich and real mashed potatoes with brown gravy dripping down over all of it.

Then, after they had eaten every bite and sopped up the gravy, he and 'Layna would order black and white Bostons. He could feel saliva forming in his mouth at the thought of the smooth vanilla ice cream mixed with thick chocolate syrup sliding over his tongue and down his throat. And there would be a gob of whipped cream on top with nuts sprinkled over it. And one shiny red cherry stuck right in the middle of it. 'Layna always ate the cherry first because she didn't like cherries much. But he always saved his to crunch into the very last spoonful of ice cream and chocolate.

What I wouldn't give for a B and W. He had ordered one at that new ice cream place once. But they never had heard of it. They had tried to give him a plain old chocolate sundae. He felt tears gathering in his eyes at the memory. He had tried so hard to make them understand. Then he had heard them laughing back there behind the counter. And he had run out of the store. He made Doris order their ice cream after that.

He grieved for black and white Bostons. For Mucci's. For the days when they had all been together. And happy.

Jayboy whimpered. Where could he go tonight when the warm sun sank behind the hills and the cold, pale moon shone down? When the thick, white fog crept up from the river with the greedy blackness inside it. He could feel it out there. Waiting for him. Licking its lips.

Suddenly, he remembered. The boat! Tied up at the dock just below 'Layna's house. Warm and dry. Stocked with canned food. And Kool-Aid. And blankets. He knew the key would be under that loose board on deck. If only he could get past the gardener without being seen.

Jayboy picked up the can opener and slipped it into his left jacket pocket. He picked up his knife and slipped it into the right pocket where he could reach it with his best hand. Then he crouched and peered through the boxwood to where the gardener was working. Right between Jayboy and his only hope of escape.

Chapter 38

Elayna paced the middle path between the flower beds in Liberty Hall's gardens, then turned right into a tangle of boxwoods that arched far above her head. Here she and Jayboy had hidden from the world, creating the intricate rules and legends of their Dandelion Kingdom.

She gasped. Could this be where Jay had gone to hide? It would seem a sanctuary to him. Had he spent last night out here under the boxwoods, cold and hungry? Had he lain there shivering, fighting the psychological blackness that had stalked the troubled man ever since he was a child? Was he cowering there even now?

She pushed aside the spreading branches and entered the cave-like room beneath. The sense of timelessness here did not go back two hundred years, but to her childhood, when she sat here spinning tales of adventure for Jayboy, about the Princess of Dandelion and the strongest and bravest knight of the kingdom.

In memory, she could see Jay, wearing the funny-looking foil-covered helmet she had made for him, holding up his foil-wrapped cardboard sword, as he repeated the oath of allegiance to the Princess of Dandelion. And, over her shorts and halter, she would be wearing the long yellow wrap-around skirt Granny had made her, with her own foil-wrapped tiara on her head, as she dubbed him Sir Jay, the Knight of the Golden Scepter.

Then she would lead the way, with Jay carrying his sword protectively behind her, on a search through the paths of the garden for the dreaded enemy. The gardener, blissfully unaware of the danger he faced as the leader of the Warriors of the Scythe and Sickle, would salute them playfully and go on about his business of pruning and mowing. The siege might last for days, or at least until noon, when they would stop to eat the sack lunches Granny had packed for them.

Her tongue vividly recalled the taste of sausage and grape jelly on flaky biscuits, baked ham on little buns, grape or orange Kool-aid in blue Mason jars, and the little fried apple pies Granny sometimes added to their lunch.

A glimpse of something in a second, more secluded boxwood room pulled Elayna's thoughts from the past. She pushed her way through the branches and discovered a faded gray blanket in a heap beside an empty peanut butter jar and a crumpled package that might have contained crackers.

Obviously, someone was camping out here. It was quite likely that someone was Jayboy. Apparently, he had gone home to get some supplies and planned to stay here in the boxwood hideout.

She returned to the path. What should she do? Should she call the police? Should she wait for Jay and try to persuade him to surrender? What would the police do with him? He had assaulted an officer, and they were convinced that he was Shirleene's killer.

She was sure Jay had not killed Shirleene, even though she and her friends had tormented the poor man unmercifully for most of his life.

Once, he had become so traumatized from the things they told him and their threats of what they would do to him that it had been necessary for him to go away for a few weeks for treatment. He had become so fearful that he simply could not function in the normal world, and he would not tell his parents or his doctors why. He was too afraid of what the girls would do in retaliation.

He had gotten better, somehow, and come home. By then, Shirleene and her friends had moved on to more mature entertainment and left Jayboy in peace. Years later, he had told her all about it.

Still, she knew that Jay simply was not capable of the violent act that had ended Shirleene's life. She realized he had been there that night, that he had taken the golden dandelion pin. But he couldn't have killed her.

How could she convince the police of all that, though? She was tempted just to leave the gardens and pretend she had not found his hiding place.

Suddenly a new thought stopped her pacing. What if it wasn't Jayboy who had been hiding in the gardens? What if it were the murderer who lay here wrapped in his blanket under the boxwoods night after night, munching his crackers and peanut butter, watching Laura and Toni as they came and went, watching her own front door only a stone's throw away?

Why would he still be around here, though? Was he simply a homicidal maniac stalking his next victim? Or was he waiting for another chance to try to find whatever he thought Shirleene had given Elayna? Had whatever he sought been the "evidence" that Shirleene had gone back to the tearoom for that night? And, if so, why hadn't he found it? Surely the murderer had searched there already, either before or after he had killed Shirleene. Perhaps she had been killed because she had surprised him at his search when she went back to the nightclub unexpectedly that night.

The police had said, though, that the door had not been forced, so whoever killed Shirleene had come in after her. Or had a key, a clue that pointed straight to Court. But she also was convinced that Court was innocent.

She recalled the shadow that had slunk around the wall behind Shirleene's disappearing taillights. Surely he had deliberately stalked Shirleene, as even now he might be stalking her.

She had to find whatever it was everybody thought she had. Most likely it still lay hidden at the tearoom, if it had not been destroyed by the fire.

As she started toward the gate, a motor coughed down on the river, stuttered, and died. It coughed again, then began a steady chugging. Elayna gasped as she recognized the miss in the engine that Court said indicated a need for new spark plugs.

The boat was moving now, apparently away from the dock, picking up speed as someone took the *Elayna* rapidly downstream.

She would have to call the police, the Coast Guard, somebody who could find out who had her boat and where he or she was taking it. *It is likely that the killer has hidden here, awaiting— whatever he was awaiting,* she thought. *Then he either gave up, or found what he was looking for, and decided to make his escape.*

Elayna heard the boat sputter downriver, then smooth out and continue its journey. Suddenly she knew who had her boat. Jayboy always had trouble regulating the engine when Hunt had let him take the wheel.

Hunt had shown endless patience with him, though, putting his captain's cap on Jayboy's head, working with him to teach him how to handle the boat, calling him Captain Jayboy, saluting him with an "Aye, aye, Captain!"

She laughed weakly. Jay was all right. She knew where he was. And, if she knew Jay, she knew where he was headed—to the landing on Hunt's grandfather's farm at the mouth of the creek, where they always had tied the boat while they enjoyed the lazy summer days.

With the boat gone, she couldn't follow Jay down the river. But she had to reach him. She would just have to go the long way around, down the winding country road to the farm. They hadn't driven it often, but she thought she could find the way.

"I don't need the police," she said aloud. "What I need is a car."

Chapter 39

Jayboy threw his fist into the air in triumph. He had done it! All by himself! He had slipped past the gardener and onto the boat. He had started the engine. He had backed the boat into the middle of the rising river. He was steering it downstream. Just like Hunt used to do. Just like Court!

The river was up. Running very fast. Trees flew by on his left. Tall cliffs on the right. It might not be easy getting the boat out of the current and over to the bank. But he could do it. He knew he could!

The warm sun felt good on his shoulders. He spread his feet wide. Planted them solidly on the deck. He could handle this. He could take the *'Layna* all the way to the landing.

He was sure he would recognize the landing. It was on a farm that Hunt and Court had inherited from their grandfather. Now it was Court's. But he knew Court wouldn't mind him using it. Court always had been good to him. Hunt had, too. But he had hurt 'Layna. He had made her cry. For days and days. And Jayboy had been glad when he had fed him to the blackness.

Sometimes, he wished he hadn't done it. 'Layna had cried so much when he didn't come back. And she had wondered what had happened to him. He wished he could tell 'Layna what he had done. But it was too late now. Hunt had been gone for years and years. The blackness had swallowed him. And the blackness never gave anything back.

Suddenly, he felt the hair rise on the back of his neck. Something was wrong. He could feel it. The way he could feel the blackness. There behind him. Hovering. Snuffing out the sunlight.

Jayboy stared straight ahead. Carefully holding the boat in the middle of the river. If he didn't look, maybe it would go away. Maybe he could outrun it. Maybe it wasn't the blackness. Maybe it was just that smothery feeling he always got when he thought about deep water closing over his head. Like dirt on a grave.

He loved being on the boat. On top of the smooth green water. He even liked swimming. With the cool water lapping around him. But not over his chest. Then he couldn't breathe. And somebody would have to get him out. Like 'Layna did the day he fell off the boat. And she had jumped right into the water, grabbed him by the wrist, and whirled him around before he could grab her around the neck. Like she had learned in that Red Cross life saving course she had tried to get him to take with her at the YMCA.

He had been too afraid to take the course. But he was glad 'Layna had. She had saved his life. He had been so scared. He hadn't stopped shaking until they were back home.

There wasn't any reason to be afraid now, though. He was on the boat. He was in control. He was Captain Jayboy Calvin. Skipper of the 'Layna.

Another shiver ran up the back of his neck. It wasn't the water. It was the blackness, all right. He could feel it back there. Gathering. Waiting. Reaching for him.

Chapter 40

Back in the keeping room, Elayna reached for the phone to call Frank to check on her car. She jumped when the phone rang before she could lift the receiver from its base. She picked it up and said, "Elayna Evans."

"Ms. Evans," a husky female voice said in her ear, "this is Jamie Madison. I know this is going to sound silly, but I believe you have something that belongs to me." She laughed nervously. "You see, Shirleene. . .uh. . .well. . .surprised C. J. and me one evening by paying him an unexpected visit. And, to make a long story short, to spite me, she took some drawings I had done for engineering class. I've been told she left them with you the night she was killed."

"I have no idea what you are talking about, Miss Madison," Elayna managed to get out before the girl started in again.

"Please, Ms. Evans. My project is due tomorrow. I can't possibly redo it—all that figuring and measuring. And it was all in color. Well, you've probably noticed. I spent weeks on it. Without that project, I fail the class. And that means I lose my scholarship. Without that scholarship, I can't go to school!"

"I'm sorry. I haven't seen your project—" Elayna began.

Again, the girl cut her off. "Sure you have!" The husky voice rose roughly, then smoothed. "I realize you had no way of knowing it was mine. Or maybe Shirleene put it in an envelope or

171

something and you haven't opened it yet."

"Miss Madison, you're not listening to me. I have nothing that belongs to you," Elayna repeated. "Contrary to what everyone seems to think, Shirleene left nothing with me. I'd be happy to return your project, but I simply do not have it."

"Hold on a minute," the girl commanded, and Elayna could hear her talking with someone, apparently with her hand over the phone. "Don't hang up," the woman said and put the phone on hold. Elayna was subjected to a couple minutes of twangy country music. She was about to hang up when the girl came back on the line.

"Ms. Evans, those drawings can't mean anything to you, but they're extremely important to me! I'll be happy to come after them."

"Let me make this perfectly clear," Elayna broke in, "I do not have your drawings!"

With a curse, the girl slammed the receiver down in Elayna's ear.

Elayna hung up the phone with an exasperated sigh. Why did everybody assume that, because Shirleene had visited her the night she was killed, she had left something with her? She almost wished she had whatever it was they wanted so she could give it to them and get them off her back.

If the missing papers had been at the tearoom that night and the killer had not found them, it was likely they had burned in the fire. Or. . .

All at once, Elayna knew where she would find Shirleene's missing "evidence," whatever it was. She knew the killer hadn't found it and that it hadn't burned.

She still had Court's key to the tearoom, but she wasn't sure she could go there alone. She couldn't ask Court to accompany her to the scene of his wife's gruesome death, but she remembered that Whit had offered to help in any way he could.

"Of course, I'll go with you," he said instantly when she got him on the phone and explained what she wanted. "I'll be there in fifteen minutes." He was ringing her doorbell in two minutes less than that.

They walked together to the tearoom, Whit talking casually about the new supper club down the street. "They say the food is excellent. We'll have to try it soon," he said.

"I'd like that," she replied, stepping over the now drooping yellow tape that still roped off the crime scene. She handed him the key and watched as he unlocked the tearoom door.

The door swung open, and the acrid smell of charred wood assaulted her nostrils and lungs as she stepped across the threshold. She stopped as her eyes took in the incredible disorder— overturned tables and chairs, broken glass, mutilated furnishings. The cover of a Queen Anne loveseat hung in shreds. The saddle of the wooden rocking horse that had been Annie's as a child lay beside its rockers that had been broken from their posts. The Spanish moss bird's nest that had filled the open door of an antique iron mailbox was missing, a burned black spot marking the place where it must have fallen to the floor.

She walked over to the wooden bar that filled the back of the room to the right of the kitchen doorway. Piles of shattered bottles and glasses from the shelves behind it littered the floor, some melted together from the heat of the fire. Pictures hung askew or lay amid the shards of glass and broken frames on the floor.

It is obvious that the murderer thoroughly searched the place, she thought grimly, turning back toward Whit.

He was studying the chalked outline that still marked the spot where Shirleene's body had been found. He took a notebook from his inside jacket pocket and quickly sketched the layout of the room. He looked up and saw her watching. "This is the first time I've been at the crime scene," he explained.

"Jay didn't do it, Whit," Elayna said. "You will represent him, won't you? I'll pay. . ."

He held up one hand. "That won't be necessary, Elayna. Of course I'll represent him, if that's what he and his mother want." He added the chalked outline to his sketch.

Elayna turned away from the grisly reminder and carefully made her way through the debris to the kitchen. She went to the fire-blackened refrigerator and opened the door. The odor of sour milk and rotten hamburger assailed her as she reached for a half-gallon orange juice carton at the back of the bottom shelf. She opened the carton's flap and peered inside. The usual wad of money was not there, only a cardboard tube containing some rolled-up papers.

Had she discovered Jamie Madison's missing engineering project? she wondered, carefully removing the tube. She replaced the empty carton and shut the refrigerator door.

"There you are!" Whit said from the doorway. "I didn't know where you had gone."

She waved the papers she had taken from the tube. "I think I've found something." She unrolled the papers and stared in surprise at the top one. It *was* an engineer's drawing. That much was obvious, even in the dim illumination that filtered in from outside.

Whit walked over and raised the window shade above the sink as Elayna spread the papers out on the counter.

Several colors had been used to represent various streets, buildings, and landmarks, with a blue-green swath running through it that Elayna assumed was the river. Measurements in miles and feet, as well as what looked like a surveyor's markings, were scattered over the page. The street names—West Main, St. Clair, Ann, Wilkinson, Broadway, High, Washington—made it clear that the drawing was of Frankfort's downtown area.

She peeled the second sheet from behind the first and heard Whit swear softly as she spread out an artist's delicate watercolor rendition of the engineer's prosaic graphics. This one showed the river swollen into a lake from a gobbling up of the entire downtown area and part of the south side of town. There were no houses or streets, nothing but blue-green water, from one cliff to another, with the capitol rising majestically from the emerald velvet of lawns studded with vivid beds of flowers. Atop the cliffs were what appeared to be office buildings and apartment complexes, even a couple of parks, with the Frankfort cemetery to the east.

"Well, I guess I misjudged Miss Madison," Elayna said uncertainly. She began carefully to re-roll the papers. "I didn't get her phone number. I hope she calls back."

"I know Jamie, Elayna. She works at the capitol. I'll take care of it for you," Whit offered, holding out his hand for the papers.

Something isn't right here, Elayna thought, as she struggled to reinsert the papers into the cardboard tube. The drawings were awfully good to be the work of a student. "Shouldn't we turn these over to the police, Whit?" she suggested. "With Shirleene's hints about 'evidence,' and her hiding these drawings in the safest place she knew. . ."

Whit shook his head, a knowing smile on his lips. "The circumstances under which Shirleene acquired these papers could be embarrassing—to Court and to several other people." Again, he held out his hand. "I'll take care of them."

Elayna stubbornly held on to the tube. "Whit, if someone wanted these drawings so badly that he risked ransacking my house after the murder, they must be extremely important, though I don't understand why. Maybe we should show them to Court and let him decide."

Whit studied her out of unreadable dark eyes. Finally, he shrugged. "Whatever you say, Elayna," he said quietly.

Suddenly, Elayna felt "a goose walk over her grave," as Granny would have described the chill that pimpled her skin. "Let's get out of here, Whit," she urged. "I'm getting the creeps! And it's getting late. We've got to get ready to go to the funeral."

Whit followed her out of the building, locked the door, and handed her the key.

Chapter 41

Jayboy couldn't stand it any longer. He had to look behind him! To see the horrible black thing back there. Blocking out the sun's light. Shutting off its warmth. Making him shiver.

He whirled around. There! In the doorway of the boat's cabin. He had caught it! Looking right at him. With pale, cold eyes. He whipped back around. He couldn't look at it!

He had looked at it, though. What would happen now? Now that he had looked into its terrible eyes? His heart began to pound. He gasped for breath. There was nothing he could do. He had nothing to sacrifice to it. Nothing to throw in its path. Like he had done with Hunt. And with Shirleene. Nothing to keep it from coming closer.

Was it coming closer? He had to see! He whirled around again. It was still there. In the doorway. Watching him with an evil smile. But it hadn't moved.

Then he knew. It wasn't the blackness! It was a man. And he had seen him before. At the tearoom the night Shirleene was killed. He was sure of it. He was the one who had torn up everything. He had seen him through the glass in the door. Then the man had gone out the back. Leaving Shirleene lying there on the floor. And he had seen the dandelion on Shirleene's shirt. He had known it was meant to be his. And he had gone in after it.

Why was the man on 'Layna's boat? Had he been hiding here ever since he killed Shirleene? Planning to use the boat to get away? Yes, the man needed this boat. But he didn't need Jayboy. He had no reason to keep him alive. And he was pointing a gun right at his back!

Jayboy recognized the landing on his left. Out of the strong current. Safe against the bank. Where he and 'Layna and Hunt always tied the boat. He thought he could get the boat over there. He had done it before. But did he dare to try?

He could feel the gun behind him. The cold, pale eyes watching. Waiting for him to make a wrong move. To slam a bullet into him. Just like on Doris's police shows. And his blood would pour out. Like Shirleene's.

His hands began to sweat. He took one off the wheel. Wiped it on his pants. Then he wiped the other. He gripped the wheel. All he had to do was jerk it to the left. Then. . .

"Don't even think about it!" the man growled.

Jayboy jerked the wheel involuntarily. Back toward the middle of the river. The boat swerved. Then straightened. He heard the man swear. But the gun was silent.

He watched the landing slide by. Tears stung his eyes.

Chapter 42

It's a perfect day for a funeral, Elayna thought, folding her umbrella and placing it in the stand by the entrance to the funeral home. It had started raining just after she and Whit had returned from the tearoom.

"If this rain keeps up, Frankfort's in for a flood," she heard a man say as she waited to get through a clump of early arrivers so she could join the family down front.

"Well, that depends more on the amount of rain upriver and whether or not they decide to open the floodgates at Dix's Dam," a woman answered.

"They say there's a crack in it and they have to ease the strain or it'll bust."

"The selfish yahoos don't care a hoot about what it does to Frankfort!" someone said.

Elayna inched her way toward the front, knowing the dire predictions about a flood were likely true. This morning she had been able to see the river from her kitchen window, surging heavily past the top of its banks, filled with mud and debris. She hoped Jayboy had reached the landing and had tied the *Elayna* securely. Better still, she hoped he had left the boat for a safer hiding place.

Anne Courtney was sitting on the loveseat in the front row, twisting a tissue between her fingers. She didn't answer when

Elayna spoke to her.

Court was receiving sympathizers up by the coffin, and she started toward him. Then she saw a handsome, dignified couple come in from the back room and ran to greet Court's parents.

"Vivian! Cliff!" she cried. "You look wonderful! So suntanned and trim—like models for an article in *Modern Maturity!*"

"Thanks, I think!" her petite, silver-haired mother-in-law responded in the throaty voice that Elayna had always found so attractive. The vivid blue eyes she had bequeathed to Court and Hunt sparkled as she reached to give Elayna a kiss on the cheek.

Her father-in-law bent to catch her in a bear hug. "How's my girl?" he asked, his hazel eyes under sandy brows, so much like Hunt's, conveyed his genuine interest in her welfare.

The lump in Elayna's throat, as they walked together to the family chairs, told her how much she had missed the two of them. As they sat beside Anne Courtney, Elayna slipped into the row behind them, glad they would have a chance to visit at Court's after the funeral, which was about to begin. The funeral director had just seated the red-haired preacher in one of the chairs to the left of the coffin, facing the crowd.

She looked around. The place was packed with people. *How Shirleene would have loved the attention.* She glanced at the coffin and was relieved to see that it was now closed. It would be easier to say good-bye to her sister-in-law without the interference of the artificial image she had seen last night.

You were so alive, so vibrant only days ago! Where are you now, Shirleene? she asked silently. *Do you still exist? Can you see this crowd gathered to pay you homage? Are you aware of the genuine sorrow many people feel for your untimely death, of the excruciating grief your husband and daughter feel at your loss?*

She could feel the lump in her throat swelling as tears stung her eyes. *Little girl lost, do you finally know that someone loves you,*

REALLY loves you? she thought. *Can you put aside all your playacting now and become Real?*

"We don't know a lot about the real Shirleene Evans," Jimmy O'Brien began, his words meshing eerily with Elayna's thoughts. "We know of her generosity in providing a free lunch or dinner at her tearoom for the down-and-out, of her eagerness to contribute to any community need. We know of her unlimited kindness to her mother and father and to her siblings and their families."

Elayna heard loud sniffling from the rows behind her, and one wild outburst of sobbing, but she had little sympathy for these who had done so little for Shirleene, even as a child, and had taken so much from her.

"We know of her pride in her lovely young daughter," the preacher continued, "and her deep admiration for her husband."

Elayna considered the preacher's carefully chosen words and had to agree. Shirleene had been faithless, but she had known her husband's worth. Hadn't she commented the night she was killed that she knew Court loved her, that he was always right, that he was "holier" than she was?

"We know little about her relationship with her Creator," Jimmy O'Brien said, again uncannily in sync with Elayna's thoughts. "We don't know if she ever accepted the salvation provided through the death of His Son, Jesus Christ. It is likely that she believed Jesus of Nazareth was crucified one dreary Friday outside Jerusalem. Most of us do. But so do the demons—and tremble. Will it be better for them than for us on the day of judgment? How shall we escape if we neglect so great a salvation?"

Elayna glanced quickly at Court to see how the preacher's bluntness was affecting him, but she could see only the back of his head, appropriately erect and focused on the speaker. She saw his mother reach over and take his hand.

"But I believe," Jimmy O'Brien was saying, "that no one who

would be saved, given one more chance, would be denied that chance. Or why would God—who quickly wrote off Saul, Ahab, and Judas—have extended that all-important opportunity to Nebuchadnezzar, David, and Peter? Because He arbitrarily chose to save some and to condemn others? No, it was because He knew each of their hearts and what their ultimate decision would be.

"No one knows exactly what took place in the last moments of Shirleene's life," he went on. "Perhaps, like the thief on the cross, in her dying moments, she cried out to Jesus Christ—as we all must—for forgiveness and restoration to the family of God. Let us not attempt to speculate. Let us simply commit Shirleene into the hands of the God who made her and loved her and who knew what her eternal choice would be long before she was born."

Elayna found that she was clutching the back of the chair in front of her so tightly the knuckles of her hands were white. She forced herself to let go, to sit back in her chair, hoping no one had noticed her reaction to this strange funeral oration.

The preacher was reading some Scripture now: "The eternal God is your refuge, and underneath are the everlasting arms," he concluded, looking earnestly into first Court's, then Annie's, then Elayna's eyes.

The verse was from Deuteronomy. She had heard Granny quote it many times. Jimmy O'Brien said it with authority, though, as if he knew God personally and could vouch for the promise.

All through the drive to the gravesite and the brief service that followed, even as she and Vivian served the family and friends who gathered at Court's for the traditional Southern social affair afterward, Elayna found her thoughts on Jimmy O'Brien's gripping words.

When she looked up from pouring iced tea for a guest and saw the preacher standing beside her, she jumped and dropped the glass, watching in dismay as it shattered, spilling tea across the kitchen floor.

"I'm sorry," he said, grabbing paper towels and stooping to clean up the mess. "Why don't people use paper cups for these affairs?" he asked, as he dumped soggy towels full of broken glass in the trash can.

Elayna brought more towels and knelt to help him. "Some people do," she answered, "but my mother-in-law wouldn't dream of it. And now I've broken one of those priceless Evans family heirlooms."

"I'm so sorry," he repeated. "I didn't mean to startle you. I was just going to invite you to our little country church."

"Oh, well, I doubt that I could find it. . . ," she hedged.

"You can't miss her if you take Flat Creek Road to the river," he insisted. "She's a slender, regal lady, dressed in faded rose, presiding over a small congregation of gray and white gravestones. And you'd be more than welcome to bring a little life to the place," he finished, looking directly into her eyes.

He stood up, discarded the remaining wet towels, and slipped away before she could concoct an answer.

That Jimmy O'Brien is a strange one, she thought, *and he has a strange way of saying things.* She liked the lilting poetry of his speech, though. She supposed it was the Irish in him. When she had Jayboy's situation under control, she mused, she just might look up the red-haired preacher and his "regal lady."

She vaguely recalled such a church on the road to the farm, though she and Hunt usually had taken the boat downriver, avoiding the winding roads. She needed to drive it now, though. She felt sure Jayboy was down there at the landing. If only she had a car!

Chapter 43

Jayboy's hands ached. But he couldn't turn loose of the wheel and let the boat go spinning out of control. To crash into the limestone rocks on the right. Or into the muddy riverbank on the left. They would be just another tangle of rubbish carried along by the current. Like the swirling piles of trees and limbs and dead animals he had seen along the way.

The trees and the cliffs whizzed by. Reaching out to him through the rain. Pleading with him to stop.

I want to! he shouted silently. He wanted to pull in to the bank, to get out of the current, where he could tie the boat to a willow limb. But the racing brown water carried them on.

Behind him, he could feel the ugly black bore of the gun pointing right at him. He knew the man would kill him. Would shoot him right in the back. How bad would it hurt? How long did it take to die from a gunshot? It had taken Shirleene a long time from the knife. And she had screamed and screamed. Then there had been a gurgling sound in her throat. Like the sound he made when he gargled mouthwash after he brushed his teeth.

Jayboy whimpered. Any minute now he would feel the bullet slamming into him. Knocking him to the deck with its force. And the blood would flow out of him. Like on TV. When the sheriff shot the robbers. Or the cop shot the killers. Or the bad guy shot somebody else. Blood would cover the deck. His blood. And the man would step in it. Like he had stepped in Shirleene's that night at the tearoom. It would stain his shoes. And leave tracks when he came to push Jayboy's body into the river. Where the deep, dark water would close over his head like a grave.

Suddenly, he threw both arms around his head. Dropped to the deck. Rolled into a ball. And lay there. Whimpering.

The boat lurched as the wheel spun out of control. It veered to the right. Then to the left. Whirled around. A captive to the whim of the merciless current.

Jayboy felt the man step over him. He heard him swearing. The blackness closed in. Wrapping its arms around him. Squeezing out his breath.

Chapter 44

Elayna walked down the hall to the bathroom, ran a comb through her hair, and washed her hands.

When she started back down the hall, she heard a low, angry voice coming from Anne Courtney's room. She reached for the doorknob, then hesitated, flinching at the graphic obscenities she was now able to discern. She wasn't happy with Annie's choice of language, but she knew the girl needed to release some of her pent-up grief. So far as Elayna knew, Annie hadn't cried once during the visitation or the funeral.

At the next outburst of anger, Elayna turned the knob and pushed the door open. "It's me, Annie," she announced. They had been close once. As a child, Anne Courtney had spent many weekends at Elayna's while Shirleene pursued her own activities.

Annie lay face down across the bed, her bare feet sticking out of skin-tight jeans under an oversized sweatshirt. She peeked under one arm to confirm her aunt's voice, then let her long, dark hair fall back to cover her face. She struck the palm of her hand on the bed beside her, and Elayna took the gesture as an invitation.

As she moved toward the bed, Elayna noted that the room, decorated in Disney characters the last time she had seen it, now displayed impressionist-patterned fabrics and Monet prints interspersed with posters of grungy-looking rock stars. Yet over on the window seat sat a well-worn Raggedy Ann and Andy, and an old-fashioned rocking chair in the corner held a collection of stuffed bears, rabbits, and dogs from a more innocent time.

Elayna sat down gingerly on the edge of the waterbed and was relieved to find it relatively stable. She laid her hand on her niece's back and felt the effort she was making at self-control. *Like father like daughter,* she thought.

"It's okay to cry, honey," she said. "Crying is a natural part of—"

"I'm not crying, Aunt 'Layna," she said, rolling over and pulling her knees up into the circle of her arms. "I'm just so angry! At God. And at whoever did it. It's just so awful! Mama. . .uh, Shirleene didn't deserve that!"

"I know," Elayna agreed. "It is awful, and I want whoever did it caught and punished."

"I want him to suffer like she did!" Annie said with a child-like insistence. Elayna wished she had some salve to soothe the raw pain she saw exposed in her niece's dark eyes, which were so much like Shirleene's.

"I know," she repeated, unable to think of anything more comforting.

"Jayboy didn't do it, Aunt 'Layna," Annie said then. "You've got to make them believe that! It wasn't Jay! They want to lock up an innocent man in that filthy jail, while the real murderer walks around free and gloating!"

Annie had spent her time in the gardens with Jay. She knew, as well as Elayna did, that this horrible act could not have been committed by the gentle man with the simple mind of an eight-year-old child.

"I'll do everything I can, Annie," she promised.

"Aunt 'Layna?" Her voice dropped to a whisper, and Elayna bent closer to hear her question. "You don't think Daddy. . . ?"

"Of course not!" Elayna cut off the tortured words. "Your father could no more do such a thing than you or I could!" But she remembered that same question crossing her own mind earlier.

"He got awfully angry at her sometimes," Annie said. "I've heard him threaten to divorce her. Several times. This last time, at least, I think he really meant it."

"Your mother hurt him deeply, many, many times, Annie. Most people wouldn't have blamed him, no matter what he did."

"I know," the girl said, so softly Elayna could barely hear her. "I loved her, though, Aunt 'Layna. She was good to me. And I think Daddy loved her, too. In spite of what she did."

"I know he did," Elayna said firmly. "Your father is a very understanding man, Annie. He knew what your mother went through as a child, and he tried to make it up to her, but, you know, our childhood experiences shape our adult lives more than we'd like to admit."

"I've heard about the abuse she suffered," Annie said. "That's why I can't stand my grandfather and my uncles. Mama never would let me be with them without her or Dad around."

"Good for her!" Elayna said fervently.

"As far as all of us were concerned, I only had one set of grand-parents, and one uncle, and that was Uncle Doc." She looked up with a smile. "I really loved my Uncle Doc, Aunt 'Layna. He was so rad!"

"Rad?"

"Oh, you know, Aunt 'Layna. Radical! Cool!" she explained impatiently.

Elayna knew "radical" had been a buzzword among the teen-agers for awhile, but she thought it would be out of fashion by now. She guessed if any uncle could fit that description, though, Hunt was the likely candidate. *He was so...well, radical!* Again, she wondered where her errant husband was while his only brother buried his wife and his niece remembered him with fondness.

"Do you ever wonder where he is, Aunt 'Layna? What he's doing?" Annie echoed her thoughts. "What beat-up old tomcat he might be resurrecting at the moment? Remember Lazarus?"

Elayna leaned over and hugged her. "Of course, I do, Annie." She answered both questions at once. "I was there for old Lazarus's funeral, remember? I think I sang—or maybe I should say 'croaked'—a solo." She shared a laugh with Annie, then added seriously, "And I think about your Uncle Doc every day of my life."

The girl didn't answer, her eyes fixed blankly on something outside the window.

There was a soft knock at the door. "Annie? Are you in there, punkin?" Elayna recognized Vivian's voice.

"Come on in, Gram," Annie invited, with an amused grimace for her grandmother's old pet name for her.

Elayna watched her mother-in-law cross the room gracefully and take a seat between the rag dolls on the loveseat.

"Granddad and I will be going back to St. Petersburg in the morning," she said. "Your dad is driving us back, and we were wondering if you'd like to come with us, maybe stay for awhile."

Annie didn't answer, her eyes again focused on the window.

Vivian reached over and brushed her granddaughter's hair out of her face. "We'd love to have you with us, sweetheart," she assured her gently. "And you know how you love the beach and all that sun! You could work on your tan, and there are some nice young people who have moved in up the shore."

Annie rolled her eyes, which Elayna interpreted to mean, "What do I want with some boring, nice young people?"

She patted the girl's arm and stood up. "Listen to your grandmother, Annie," she advised. "It will do you good to get away from here. And I promise to do everything I can to help Jayboy," she added, as she left the two of them together.

Elayna hoped that Anne Courtney would go with Vivian and Cliff. *Their firm common sense will be good for her, and it certainly won't hurt her to make some new friends,* she thought as she went to the phone and dialed Frank's number. Her car still wasn't ready, and she went in search of her brother-in-law and a ride home.

As Court turned the Chrysler down West Main Street, Elayna saw Toni and Laura crossing the street toward their cars, and suddenly she knew how she could get out to the farm without worrying Court about where she was going and why. She hadn't even bothered him with the drawings she had found in Shirleene's refrigerator. They would just have to wait until he returned from St. Petersburg. Right now she had a more urgent errand.

Ten minutes later, she was maneuvering Toni's white Cadillac around another of the hair-raising curves for which U.S. 421 North was famous. *"Infamous" might be the better word for it!* she thought grimly, easing on the brakes as the car began to pick up speed down a long, winding hill. The car was an older model but handled beautifully. Afraid she might damage it in some way, she almost wished the response had not been so generous when she had told Toni and Laura about her car still being in the shop and her need for transportation.

"Here, take my car," Toni had offered instantly, handing her the keys. "We're on our way to a wedding, but we were going to drive Laura's Honda, anyway."

Normally, Elayna wouldn't have dreamed of asking a casual acquaintance such a favor. *But nothing about these past few days has been normal,* she thought, setting the wheels for another challenging curve.

It had been years since she had been out this way. The road had been widened, a curve or two taken out; but, except for a scattered handful of new houses and the inevitable trailer deposited here and there, the tall cliffs and deep valleys had protected the area from the suburban sprawl that had afflicted other roads around the capital city.

The rain had stopped, and a bright autumn sun seemed to set the red and gold leaves of the trees aflame. *It's a beautiful day for a drive in the country,* she thought as she left the highway and turned right onto Harvieland Road. Soon closely spaced houses gave way to isolated farmhouses and trailers perched atop the hills or hunched into the cliffs beside a meandering creek.

The road suddenly ended at an intersection with another road. Again, she turned right, and the road wound steadily downward. The tangled wooded hills closed in around her with an encroaching loneliness that made her wish for company.

A tall, narrow brick church appeared below her, towering over an unfenced conglomeration of gray and white gravestones in a picture-postcard setting of red oaks and orange maples. There was no sign visible, but the name on the roadside mailbox hanging from a white post read JAMES T. O'BRIEN, PASTOR.

She lifted her foot from the accelerator. Should she stop by today, while she had transportation? *Who knows when I'll get back out this way, and I do want to talk with him about Annie,* she thought. *He seemed to have a rapport with her.*

"Or do you just want an excuse to talk with that strange, red-haired Irishman again?" she scolded herself aloud. "You know Annie's agreed to go home with her grandparents for awhile."

She pressed her foot on the accelerator. First, she had to find the *Elayna* and Jayboy. She had to talk with him, find some way to help him.

After several more minutes and countless curves, she pulled up at the entrance to the rutted farm road. Leaving the car, she walked down to the riverbank.

The water lapped at the rotting remains of the wooden steps Hunt and Court had built to the landing, but Elayna's heart sank as she saw that there was no boat tugging against its moorings where the river tides slapped against the shore below. She had been so sure she would find Jay here! Had the boat gotten away from him? He never had handled it alone, and the water certainly was higher than he'd ever experienced it.

The coffee-colored water raced by, flecked with dirty white foam, like cream. As she watched, an eddy whirled a piece of driftwood around, then spit it into the air. It came back down and was buried momentarily in the murky water. She shuddered. Had Jay and the boat suffered such a fate at the whim of the angry water?

Jay always had been too afraid of the water to learn to swim, but even a strong swimmer would have trouble with that current!

Maybe he decided to take the boat on downstream to some other hiding place, she reassured herself. *But where? And what should I do now?*

Finally, she turned and made her way back to the car. *There's no use standing here watching driftwood and debris float by, dreading what I might see.*

Chapter 45

Jayboy shivered. He reached for the scratchy blanket with his free hand. The damp river air came right through the broken window pane. The one the man had broken to get into the cabin, back at the landing below 'Layna's house.

He pulled the blanket up to his chin and over his shoulder. He couldn't cover the other hand and arm, because it was hooked to the rail of the bunk above him with a chain.

He was hungry. His stomach echoed with emptiness. He hadn't had anything to eat since the two crackers early that morning. He was sure there was canned food in the cupboard. But he couldn't reach it from here.

'Layna always used to keep food on the boat. Sardines and crackers. Meatballs and spaghetti. Beef stew. Canned fruit. Then, when they were going to spend the day on the river, she would bring a picnic basket with all kinds of goodies in it. Fried chicken. Spice cake with caramel frosting. Like the one she and her granny had brought when he and Mac and Doris had moved into the neighborhood. The day he had first met 'Layna.

She had stood there in their new yard. With the grass and the dandelions, her black hair shining in the sunlight, smiling at him. Not to make fun like the kids at school, but letting him know it was all right that he couldn't tell people what grade he was in.

Because he wasn't in a grade. And it was all right with 'Layna.

He had given her the bouquet of dandelions, and she hadn't thrown them away like Doris did. She had put them in a glass of water. He had known right then he would always love her. And he had loved their days together on the boat. First, the three of them. 'Layna. Hunt. Jayboy. Then little Carrie came. And they had been just like a family. With a mother and a father and two kids.

After Carrie Hunter died and he had fed Hunt to the blackness, 'Layna had gone on the boat a few times with him and Court and Annie. Then she said the boat was "too crowded." He didn't know what she meant by that. There weren't any more people on it than before. But she never went on the boat anymore.

Maybe she had let the food run out! He hadn't thought of that. But Court used the boat sometimes. He might have stocked the cupboards with food. He'd bet it was up there.

It didn't matter, though. He was chained like a dog to a post. He couldn't get to the food. He couldn't go to the bathroom. He couldn't get away.

The man was gone. He had talked to somebody on a telephone that he kept in his pocket. Ordered someone to pick him up at the end of the road. He had given directions. Then he had chained Jayboy to the bunk, put the key to the padlock in his pocket, and left the boat. Jay had watched him climb the hill and disappear into the trees.

He didn't know why the man hadn't killed him. He had to know that Jayboy knew he had followed Shirleene to the tearoom. And Shirleene had opened the door and let him inside. He had been angry. He had kept saying, "I want those papers, Shirleene!" But Shirleene had laughed at him. Then he had yelled and called her names, and grabbed the knife, and hurt her, and kept hurting her.

Jayboy's empty stomach heaved.

Chapter 46

On impulse, Elayna pulled into the gravel parking lot, stopped the car, and sat absorbing the scene before her. The bricks of the church and the small, steep-roofed cottage behind it had faded to a soft rose color, marked with the graffiti of many passing seasons. There was no bell tower, but a cross topped the small white cupola that, along with the door and window trim, seemed freshly painted. The grass, even around the gravestones, was neatly trimmed.

She took the keys from the ignition and dropped them into the jacket pocket of her gray wool suit. Locking the car, she followed a series of wide, somewhat crumbling brick steps, feeling an aura of timeless tranquility begin to envelop her as she approached the double front doors of the church.

"A house of God, Estab. 1868," a small white sign beside the doors proclaimed simply. It claimed no affiliation with any domination.

She pressed the latch of one of the tall doors, and it swung open silently on well-oiled hinges. She stepped into a small foyer that opened immediately into the cool dimness of a tall-ceilinged sanctuary.

Sunlight filtered through stained glass onto the polished planks of golden wood that formed the floor and the pews that marched in two straight rows to a pulpit of the same wood, fenced in by a polished brass altar rail.

Elayna took a deep breath, feeling almost smothered by the weight of time. How many christenings and weddings, how many funerals had the more-than-a-century-old structure witnessed? What tales of lives well-spent—or misspent—could these ancient walls relate if they had the power of speech? How many petitioners had knelt on the carpeted space before the altar? How many had reached out to God in this quiet sanctuary?

She made a deliberate effort to shake off the heavy sense of endless, futile repetition that was subtly replacing the peace she had felt as she approached the church.

There was no choir stall or organ, she noted. There wasn't even a piano. *What kind of church is this?* she wondered. What kind of preacher was Shirleene's "Brother Jimmy"?

Elayna jumped as a voice behind her said, "Hello! I saw you come in from my office window back in the parsonage. Welcome to our house of God, Elayna Evans. I didn't expect to see you quite so soon!"

"Brother O'Brien, you nearly scared me out of my wits!" she gasped. "I thought you were a relic from the past!"

"Sometimes even I think that, especially when my arthritis acts up!" He laughed, and again she noted how his freckles slid into suddenly exposed crevices across his boyish face. "This place has a way of doing that to folks," he admitted. "It's just so. . .old!" he finished, laughing again at his inadequacy to put the atmosphere into words. "Some people are disturbed by that, others find peace in it." His smoky Irish eyes held her gaze.

Elayna shifted uncomfortably. Then she extended her right hand. "I want to compliment you on your remarks at the funeral. It was a difficult situation, and you handled it well."

"Thank you, Elayna," he said, taking her hand. Again his gaze locked with hers. "Do you mind if I call you Elayna?" he asked.

She shook her head. "Of course not."

"It's such a beautiful name," he said softly. "Elayna."

The way he said it made it beautiful, she thought, much the way Hunt had said it—drawling the middle syllable, *"E-laaay-nuh."*

"A soldier I once knew in Afghanistan had a wife named Elayna. He talked about her in such glowing terms, I always felt I could see her—soft gray-blue eyes alight with the joy of living; black hair reflecting the sunlight like a mirror; small, delicate bone-structure, with slender, graceful hands." A blush joined freckles to freckles, and he seemed at a loss for words. "A lot like you, I suppose," he said, his voice deep with some emotion that Elayna could not identify.

Finally, he laughed softly. "I guess I fell in love long ago with another man's wife, or with the image his words created. But I've never before found anyone who fit the description." He stared at her, still holding her hand until Elayna eased it from his grasp, changing the subject by remarking about the church's architecture.

The pastor grasped eagerly at the diversion. "The church was built three years after the end of the Civil War," he said. "It's been in operation continuously ever since, though once it came close to dying. It seems that when the congregation became affluent enough to purchase an organ, there were some among them who did not believe in instrumental music, who said the New Testament church had not had it and so it was not scriptural."

"So that explains the lack of a musical instrument," Elayna said.

"The organ ended up outside a number of times," O'Brien continued, "until the congregation split up, and those who wanted the organ moved on. The church here was kept alive by three old ladies who led the singing, served communion every Sunday, and prayed for a preacher and men to lead and build up the church once more."

197

"And. . . ?" Elayna prompted, fascinated.

"Oh, eventually their prayers were answered. I'm just the latest in a long line of pastors since then, none of whom have had the courage—or the audacity—to restore instrumental music to the services—though lately I have sneaked in a guitar or two for special occasions," he confessed, freckles disappearing as he grinned at her.

"What denomination is it now?" she asked, her curiosity piqued by his colorful tale.

"It is simply, as the sign says, 'A house of God.' We worship here with a fundamental faith in the virgin birth, the sinless life, the sacrificial death, and the triumphant resurrection of Jesus Christ, the Son of the living God, our Creator. Our doctrine is very simple. It consists of John 3:16: 'God so loved the world that he gave his one and only Son, that whosoever believes in him shall not perish, but have eternal life,' " he finished seriously. Then his boyish grin transformed his face again.

Elayna could not help grinning back. "Well, I asked!" she admitted.

He was staring at her again. "You are so like her," he murmured. "Or like I always pictured her. It's uncanny that there could be two of you, and with the same first name!"

"Is that the parsonage I saw behind the church?" Elayna blurted, seeking relief from his intense gaze. "That charming brick cottage with woodbine climbing the chimney?"

Again, he grasped the conversational rope she threw him. "Yes. Well, it once belonged to the church. I bought it from them when I first came here, to help them through a lean financial time. They were determined to sell it, and I took a liking to it. Would you like to see it? It's very quaint."

"Some other time, perhaps," she answered, still unnerved by his reaction to her. "The reason I stopped by was. . ." It was her turn to stop in confusion. Why had she come?

"Annie!" she said, seizing gratefully upon the returning memory. "I'm worried about Anne Courtney, Brother O'Brien. She's been so mixed up lately, even before her mother's death."

"My friends call me Jimmy," he said. "And, yes, I know Anne Courtney's confused. And rebellious. And feeling the rising of the sap of youth."

"She was such a sweet child," Elayna recalled sadly. "She was constantly dragging in stray animals to be patched up by her 'Uncle Doc.' That's what she called my husband." She sighed. "She's been a different person lately, Shirleene's child all the way."

That's not completely true, she thought. *I caught a glimpse of the old Annie during our talk earlier today. Surely there's still hope for this rebellious child!*

"Deep down she's a good kid, Elayna. That's why I've tried to keep an eye on her, tried to talk her out of drinking, and driven her home when she hasn't listened to me." He patted her arm. "I'll talk with her when she gets back from Florida. I understand she has agreed to visit her grandparents for awhile."

Elayna nodded. "I'm glad. Vivian and Cliff will be good for her. They are so wholesome. And I think Annie needs to get away from that wild, uncouth set of friends she has here. And thank you, Brother. . .uh, Jimmy," she said, "for your concern. I guess I'd better be going."

"I hope you will come again soon," he answered. "Perhaps to services. Sunday school is at ten, worship is at eleven, and Sunday and Wednesday night services are at seven. Or I'd love to show you my house, to sit by the fireplace and chat with you over a cup of. . .tea?"

She nodded, and he went on, "I knew you'd be a tea drinker. I drink a lot of coffee when I'm out, but at home I keep the teapot on and Earl Grey ready on the shelf."

"Earl Grey?" she repeated, holding tightly to the present, refusing to let her mind go reeling back into the past.

"Yes, have you tried it?" he asked. "There's no other tea quite like it—fresh and brisk with just a hint of the minty flavor of bergamot."

She smiled weakly, feeling as if she were living out a weird sequence of déjà vu. "Well, it's been. . .interesting," she said, holding out her hand to end the encounter. "I'll take a rain check on that Earl Grey, if I may. It's a favorite of mine, too, but it's nearly dusk, and I don't relish these winding country roads after dark, especially in a borrowed vehicle."

His handshake was firm and strong. "You have a standing invitation, Elayna."

She broke the magnetic pull of his eyes and turned toward the parking lot. She was almost running when she reached the car. Quickly, she unlocked the door, jerked it open, slipped inside, and locked the doors.

She looked back as she turned the ignition key, and found Jimmy O'Brien watching her. He raised one hand in a half salute, and she waved back, convinced that he was much older than his boyish, freckled face would have her believe.

She put the car in gear and pulled out onto the roadway, eager to get away from the uncanny feeling that, though she had just met Jimmy O'Brien, he had known her for a very long time.

Chapter 47

Jayboy turned away from looking inside his head at the awful Technicolor memory of Shirleene's murder. He looked out the window instead. Cold air came through the broken pane, but it was dark now and he could not see anything.

He wished 'Layna would find him. He wished he knew where he was so he could tell her. If he ever got the chance. He knew how to dial her number. But the man kept the phone in his pocket.

The boat was tied up at a landing somewhere below Hunt's and 'Layna's, just above where a creek poured out into the river. The man had ordered him to pull in there. Then the man had jumped out with the rope and tied the boat to a river willow. Just like Hunt used to tell him to do. Then they would get out the fishing poles and the fishing worms. And they would fish off the back of the boat until 'Layna called them to lunch.

They would eat around the little table over there. All the good things 'Layna had brought in her picnic basket. Then they might stretch out for a nap on the shady side of the deck, feeling the gentle rocking of the boat beneath them, and the cooling breezes that blew through the trailing branches of the river willows. Listening to the hotbugs singing.

Soon it would begin to get dark. The evening star would

come out. And he and 'Layna would make a wish on it. And Carrie Hunter. When she was still alive. Then they would eat supper. Whatever was left in the basket. And 'Layna would tell stories. And the crickets would begin to sing.

It was quiet out there now. Except for an old screech owl calling back in the woods. He thought it might be starting to rain. He could hear a soft pattering on the roof. And he could hear the greedy water sucking mud from the bank. Lapping at the sides of the boat. He could hear the creaking of the rope as the boat tugged to be free. To go with the swollen river.

He knew how the boat felt. He couldn't stand being tied, either. He thrashed around in the narrow bunk, jerking at the chain. He had to get free! But the chain was strong. He couldn't break it. He was going to smother! He had to think about something else!

He wondered what was out there in the darkness. All along the riverbank he could see glowing yellow eyes. Under the rocks. Back in the trees. Watching. Waiting for him to go to sleep.

He shivered and reached for the blanket. Then he pulled it all the way over his head.

Chapter 48

The phone rang, and she picked up the receiver. "Good morning. Elayna Evans," she said automatically.

"Good morning, Elayna Evans," a deep voice answered. "If I remember correctly, you took a rain check on a cup of tea with me. And, ma'am, if you'll kindly look out your window, you'll see that it's lovely weather for ducks or a cup of Earl Grey."

She laughed, glad for the cheerful distraction from her morbid thoughts. "Hello, Jimmy O'Brien," she said. "You have an excellent memory. But I'm not about to walk ten miles in this downpour. Or even in the sunlight. I like to walk, but not that much." She laughed again. "My car's still in the shop," she explained.

"In that case, the mountain shall come to Mohammed. See you in about thirty minutes." He hung up before she could think of a reason why he should not come to visit.

Elayna sighed, carried her coffee cup and toast saucer to the sink, and went to the bedroom to pull on a pair of jeans and a sweatshirt, clothes she might have hesitated to wear had it been Whit Yancey on his way over instead of Jimmy O'Brien. Somehow, though, she felt that the red-haired preacher was a comfortable, old-jeans and leather patches kind of man. And, if he wasn't, she really didn't care, she decided, as she went back to the kitchen to light a fire in the fireplace to take the chill and dampness from the room.

That done, she looked around and, finding the place a bit too "comfortable," began plumping pillows and putting away magazines and papers. The fire was burning cheerily, and the room looked cozy and inviting by the time the doorbell announced the preacher's arrival.

She opened the door and found him grinning at her from the stoop, a fat yellow Thermos in one hand and a green-paper-wrapped autumn bouquet in the other. An ancient black pickup truck sat in the driveway.

"You'll have to furnish the cups and the vase," he said. "I put a little cream and sugar in the tea. I hope you don't mind."

She shook her head weakly, again experiencing the giddy feeling of déjà vu. She could see Hunt and Granny sitting at the table on the patio out back, sipping tea laced with cream and sugar from the delicate moss-rose china cups, playing their little games of make-believe.

"May I come in?" Jimmy O'Brien asked.

"Oh, I'm sorry!" she apologized, returning to the present and unlocking the storm door. She held it open. "My mind suddenly went back about fifteen years. Earl Grey with cream and sugar was a favorite of my grandmother and my husband," she explained, leading the way back to the kitchen.

He set the Thermos on the table. "Where is your husband?" he asked, handing her the flowers.

"I wish I knew," she said. She took the flowers, got a blue Mason jar from the cupboard, and busied herself arranging the flowers in it. "He disappeared ten years ago," she added, as she set the flowers in the middle of the table and went back to the cupboard for two of Granny's china cups and saucers.

"And you haven't heard from him since?" he prompted, pouring tea from the Thermos into the cups.

She shook her head. "No. He just disappeared into thin air, as they say. Our little girl died, and he couldn't cope with the guilt, though it wasn't his fault. There was nothing anyone could have done to save her," she said softly, the old pain finding its way back into her voice. "He left a note propped up on the table in his houseboat. And I haven't seen hide nor hair of him since," she finished, trying to lighten the mood.

She looked directly at her visitor then, and was surprised to see that his face had grown grave and still.

"Elayna, what was his name?" Something about the way he said it made her heart stop, then start again with a thump. She reached out to steady herself against the back of a ladderback chair.

"Dr. Hunter Evans," she answered. "He was a first-class surgeon. And a first-class husband and father until he pulled his disappearing act."

He nodded absently. "Hunter Evans. Hunter Aimes," he murmured. "I should have put it all together before now!" He looked up at her. "I think I knew your husband, in my days as a mercenary in Afghanistan, back when the Russians were the villains."

Elayna sank down into the chair. "What do you mean?" she whispered. "Afghanistan? Hunt wasn't. . .didn't. . ." But how did she know what Hunt had done, where he had gone after he left Frankfort? She hadn't heard from him since that day.

"I knew him as Hunter Aimes," he explained, "a paramedic who knew more about medicine than any surgeon I've ever known. He could patch wounds we thought were beyond patching, save the lives we thought were gone, work medical miracles without supplies or instruments. We called him Doc, but he never admitted to being a full-fledged doctor, and he had no license, at least not in the name of Hunter Aimes."

Elayna shook her head slowly. It couldn't be. It was totally unbelievable. It was. . .

"It was he who introduced me to Earl Grey tea with cream and sugar. And he was eaten up with grief over the death of his little girl." He paused for a moment before finishing, "And it was he who had the wife named Elayna."

"Where did you last see him?" Elayna asked, but the words were silent, frozen in her throat. She cleared it and repeated the question, this time aloud.

He leaned forward and placed one freckled hand over hers. "You're cold," he said. "Sip that hot tea, Elayna. It's been eight years since I last saw your husband. He—"

"He's dead, isn't he?" she said quietly, suddenly knowing it was true and that she had known it for a long time. He nodded, avoiding her eyes.

"How?" she managed to whisper.

"A child came out of a cave, crying. Her head was bleeding. Doc knew better, but something in him would never let him turn away from pain, especially the pain of a child. He went to her, picked her up in his arms, and they both just disintegrated into the sky." He put his hands over his eyes, as though to shut out the unbearable memory. Elayna found herself placing her hand on his arm to comfort him.

He rubbed his face hard, ran one hand through his hair, and looked across at her, his eyes still filled with pain. "I'm sorry, Elayna."

"I knew he was dead," she said. "I've known it for a long time. I just could not admit it. I loved him, Jimmy. We had some good years together. But when our little girl developed meningitis, he blamed himself for not being able to cure her. He thought I blamed him, too. I tried to convince him otherwise, but he wouldn't listen."

"He loved you very much," he said. Again, he placed his hand over hers. "He talked about his wife incessantly, so much that I literally fell in love with her myself, sight unseen! After I got back to the States, I tried to find her—to find you. I drove an eighteen-wheeler for two years, all over the country, and everywhere I went, I searched for Elayna Aimes. I know now I was searching for the wrong surname."

He sat staring into space, apparently reliving those days. Finally, he sighed. "His death had a profound effect on me. In fact, it was the reason I ended up as a minister, once I got it all sorted out. So, you see, Doc is still helping people, even though it's by proxy."

His smile was contagious, but she barely noticed. He touched her hand. "Only God could have brought the two of us together, Elayna. We were meant to sit here sipping Earl Grey tea." He gestured toward her still full cup. "It's probably cold by now," he said. He took the cup, carried it to the sink, and dumped it out. Then he returned to the table, picked up the Thermos, refilled the cup, and placed it in her hand.

She picked it up and sipped the hot tea absently, her mind struggling to absorb the things she had just heard. *Hunt is dead,* she told herself. *He's been dead for eight years. He was dead when Granny died, when I tried so desperately to find him. He was dead. . . .*

"I realize all this has been a terrible shock to you," Jimmy O'Brien said. "I'm sorry to be the one to tell you, but it must be better to know than to wonder."

Elayna nodded. "Thank you. I've searched for answers for so long. You're right. It is better to know for sure." Or she thought it was. It all seemed so unreal. "Oh, no! Once you're Real, you can't become unreal again," the skin horse said cruelly. Suddenly, she had to be alone. "Can you excuse me?" she asked. "I need. . ."

"Some time to bury your dead," he finished for her. He patted her hand, got up, picked up the Thermos, and walked down the hall to the front door. She heard him let himself out before the long overdue tears took over.

Chapter 49

Jayboy opened his eyes. Someone was coming down the hill above the riverbank. He could hear the footsteps sliding in the wet leaves.

He peered out the broken window. He must have slept. It was light outside. Even though it was raining. Cats and dogs, Doris would say. But there never were any. It was always just water falling from the sky.

He couldn't feel his left arm or his left hand, but he could still see them. Chained to the bunk above. He tried to wiggle his fingers, but they wouldn't move. They were dead!

Was that the way Mac's arm and leg had felt after he had his stroke? When he had to pick them up with his good hand and put them where he wanted them? Sometimes his hand would flop off the tray. Or his foot would slide off the footrest. Then he would have to start all over. Picking them up with his good hand. Placing them where he wanted them. He had felt so sorry for Mac. Would his own arm and hand always be like Mac's? It was an awful feeling! Tears gathered behind his eyes.

Jayboy turned and looked out the window across the cabin. Over the table and benches that Hunt had built and fastened to the wall. Usually he would see the yellow sunlight spreading slowly across the sky, spilling down onto the cliffs and over the treetops. Like butter melting over hot biscuits. This morning, though, the sky was gray. Like a lid set down on top of the river valley.

He turned back to the window by the bunk. He could see the man now. Sliding down the steep hill above the bank. Cursing when he fell. He didn't see the gun. But he knew the man had it. He probably was coming back to shoot him. To make sure he could not identify him as Shirleene's killer.

Jayboy threw himself against the chain. It rattled, but it held him. Fastened like a dog to the bunk above. Waiting to be executed. Like on those war shows Mac had watched. Where they lined men up against the wall and blindfolded them. Then the soldiers shot at them and they all fell down. Dead.

Would the man blindfold him before he shot him? He didn't think so. He hadn't blindfolded Shirleene. He had just killed her. With her biting and scratching and trying to get away from him. Like he was trying to get away from the chain. Only it hadn't worked for Shirleene. And it wasn't working for him.

The boat was throwing itself against its rope, too. As frantic as he was to escape. It looked like it floated now in the tops of the river willows that grew nearest the water. It was higher up the bank than it had been last night. The river must have risen.

He could hear footsteps on the gangplank, then crossing the deck. He saw the door to the cabin fly open. Jayboy cringed and covered his head with his free arm.

Chapter 50

Elayna opened the storm door for Whit. "I was just thinking about lunch," she said. "You're welcome to stay." She led the way back to the keeping room. "I make a mean tuna casserole in the microwave in about fifteen minutes."

Whit shook his head. "I only have a minute, Elayna. I'd like to examine those papers again. It occurred to me that they may relate to some research Court's been doing that I've found extremely interesting."

She took the tube from her purse, removed the drawings, and spread them out on the table, holding down the curling edges with her hands.

He gave them a cursory glance. "Don't you want me to take them off your hands, Elayna?" he asked. "For some reason, someone wants these papers very badly. You could be in danger."

"Actually, Whit, I still think they should be turned over to the police. I just want to show them to Court first."

He looked directly into her eyes for several seconds. "Of course, Elayna. I understand," he said finally.

"He's not back from Florida yet, but I'll leave a message on his answering machine," she said. She had tried to reach Court ever since Jimmy O'Brien had told her about Hunt's death. She hadn't called her in-laws' home in Florida, not wanting to tell anyone the news over the phone. *It's been eight years,* she thought. *What can one or two days more matter?*

She dialed Court's number, waited for the answering machine to come on, and left another message for Court to call as soon as he got back.

"I'm sure he will want to discuss the drawings with you," she assured Whit, re-rolling the papers, replacing them in the cardboard tube, and returning it to her bag. "I'll let you know as soon as I hear from him. Are you sure you won't have some lunch, Whit?"

He shook his head again. "Have you had time to think about what we talked about the last time I was here, Elayna?" he asked suddenly.

"I've thought about it," she hedged, using her search for casserole ingredients as an excuse not to meet his eyes. When she finished, she turned to find Whit looking out over the patio, waiting for her answer. She noticed the silver highlights in the thick black hair that waved slightly over his neck and forehead, the lean, firm body he kept in shape with jogging and regular workouts. He was a good-looking man, cultured, with a keen mind, someone she always had been proud to introduce as her escort.

How would I feel about introducing him as my husband? she wondered. She was free to think such thoughts now that Jimmy O'Brien had released her from her marriage vows with his news of Hunt's death. Whether or not her emotions were free was another story. But there always had been a spark between her and Whit. Did she want to see if it could grow into a full-fledged flame? Did she want to start a new life with him?

He turned to face her. "Will you let me—or Court, if you're more comfortable with that—begin the process to free you of Hunt's legal ties, Elayna?"

"Hunt's dead, Whit," she said flatly. "I've just learned that he died in a war in Afghanistan, of all places."

He absorbed the news. "Why, that's wonderful!" he said.

She wasn't sure she liked his response to the fact of her widowhood, but she understood what he meant.

"It just makes things easier," he explained, quick to pick up on her reaction. He took a step toward her and took both of her hands in his. "Oh, Elayna, I have such exciting things to share with you! The concepts are so beautiful! Once we get every cell in the Global Brain thinking positive thoughts at the same time, evil will be totally eliminated and peace will flow throughout the world. And you and I will. . ."

"Global Brain?" she interrupted. "Whit, I don't understand."

He took a deep breath, then smiled. "Of course you don't!" he said. "How could you? I'll have to take you with me to our next conference. I can't wait to share it all with you!"

"What are you talking about, Whit?"

"Elayna, every person on Earth is a cell in the Global Brain," he explained. "Put them all together, and we have God."

She stared at him. His dark eyes were lit with a feverish intensity she'd never seen in them before. She eased her hands from his and took a step back. Had this suave, sophisticated man, with whom she had spent so many pleasant evenings, suddenly lost his mind?

He walked over to lean against the bar, his hand touching the purse that hid the cardboard tube. "It will be so beautiful, Elayna," he said earnestly. "These drawings are just a hint! They have chosen Frankfort to be one of five learning centers across the nation because of its wonderful capitol, which will become a temple, surrounded by shrines of every major religion in the world. People will come here seeking spiritual enlightenment. And you and I, if you agree, will play an important part in it all. Say you'll marry me, Elayna! I promise you we will have an exciting life together."

"I don't know what to say, Whit. I just. . ." She laughed shakily. "I guess I was just too indoctrinated as a child to get that far away from my family's traditional beliefs."

"Don't you want to develop your own beliefs, Elayna? Man is a divine being hampered by traditional concepts. We must tap into our divine potential—the Force in us," he insisted. "Don't you want to become the divine entity you were always meant to be?"

"I don't understand, Whit," she repeated. "Are you saying we will all become gods of some kind? Is that what you believe?"

"I know these concepts are hard for you to grasp so quickly, sweetheart. I must remember that I've been easing into them for several months now. I've been to conferences and workshops and seminars. I've read books and magazines." He stopped and took a deep breath. "I realize I've taken you too far, too quickly, Elayna," he apologized. "Let me leave some literature with you."

Before she could protest, he had gone out to his car and come back with two magazines. "Look these over," he urged, dropping them on the kitchen table. "Tonight I'd like you to go with me to a meeting in Louisville. You will see that the people there are just as normal and just as weird as the rest of humanity, that there is no more to fear from these gatherings than there is from your local PTA. Will you come with me, Elayna?"

"Well, I suppose so," she answered, trying to keep her eyes off the magazines.

"Seven o'clock?" he prompted. "And don't eat. There will be a dinner."

She nodded. "I'll be ready." She locked the door behind him, relieved to see him go, for now.

No longer very hungry, she abandoned the idea of tuna casserole, fixed a small plate of crackers and sharp cheese, sliced a Granny Smith apple, and poured a glass of iced tea.

She sat down at the kitchen table and spread the first magazine beside her plate. She leafed through it as she ate, her uneasy feelings growing as she read about mantras, karma, reincarnation, channeling, spirit guides.

How long has Whit been into this Eastern religion? She had known he was involved in "saving the Earth" and "holistic health," but he'd never insisted on her joining him in it, and she hadn't paid it much attention. But he'd never mentioned a "global brain" before. Of course, he'd never asked her to marry him before, either. Maybe what she believed was just suddenly important to him.

She laid the first magazine aside and picked up the second. It contained articles on "ascended masters from Earth who have gone on to a higher life." There were stories about leaders of the world's various religions.

"Jesus did not die for anyone's sins," she read. "He simply came to show us the way and the possibilities of what we can become." *A sort of Jonathan Livingston Seagull*, she thought. "We all aspire," the article continued, "in our evolution through many lives, to reach that level of Christ consciousness that has been reached by only a few—Jesus Himself, Buddha, Krishna, Mohammed."

"Christ consciousness?" she muttered. "What does that mean?" Does it provide the kind of peace her grandmother had known as a believer in Jesus Christ, who had died for her sins and become her Savior and Lord? That belief had been the unshakable foundation of her grandmother's life, and even as she had faced death, she had had a calm assurance that God was in control and had her ultimate good in mind.

Elayna admitted that her own faith fell far short of Granny's. But, deep down, she knew she wanted more than some vague concept of "consciousness" or "global brain," as Whit called it. If she were going to trust in something outside herself, she thought, she wanted that something to be bigger and wiser than she knew herself to be.

She sighed and laid the magazines on the bar. If Whit was as adamant about this new religion of his as he seemed to be, could there be any real future for them together?

Chapter 51

Jayboy could feel the man standing over him. Looking down at him. He curled his spine as tight as he could around his body and cradled his head in his arm. Trembling. Waiting for the bullet to slam into him.

Then he heard the man move away. He heard him open a cupboard and rummage around inside. He guessed the man was looking for something to eat. Would he give him something? His stomach ached with emptiness. It had been so long since he'd had anything to eat.

He stretched out on the bunk. Why was he thinking about food? Food wasn't important compared to his dead hand and arm. Could he get the man to unchain it? He guessed it wouldn't be any good now. But the numbness was spreading up into his shoulder. Soon he would be dead all over! Like Mac. Like Shirleene. Like a big old wooden tree lying in the woods. Rotting. Nothing but a home for bugs and maggots.

He could feel the blackness creeping up. He whimpered. He rubbed his dead left hand with his right, but there was no feeling. It was dead, all right!

"Arm gone to sleep, Loony Toons?" the man asked. He came back to stand over him. Looking down with pale, cold eyes and an evil grin. Jayboy couldn't stand to look at him. He let his gaze slide down to the man's hands. He saw red scratches all over the left one, the one that had held the gun, the one the man used the most. And there was an angry-looking red bite on the back of it. Teeth marks. Red and puckered around the edges.

Jayboy shivered. He knew where the man had gotten those marks. Shirleene had fought when he killed her. He had seen her. She had clawed and bitten and kicked. And she had left cuts that bled. He covered his eyes with his right arm and whimpered.

He heard the chain rattle and a weight fell onto his chest. He peeked out from under his arm and saw his other arm and hand lying across him. Like a heavy piece of wood with no feeling. He picked them up with his good hand. The way Mac used to do after he had the stroke. They didn't feel like part of him anymore. They were dead. Like Mac's arm and leg that never got better. That stayed that way until the rest of him died.

"Rub it, Loony Toons!" the man said, laughing at him, going back to the cupboards. "Boy, Loony Toons is a good name for you!" he said. "You're a real cartoon!"

Jayboy rubbed the dead hand and arm. They didn't belong to him. They were just dead weight hanging from his shoulder. Flopping helplessly when he dropped them. He couldn't stand it! He had to get them off him! He screamed and screamed.

Chapter 52

As they headed west on I-64, in a steady rain, in Whit's black Mercedes, he talked about the spectacular colors of the foliage along the roadway and in the grassy median of the four-lane highway. He touched on the latest political complications in the state capital, and his planned campaign for governor. He told her how becoming her hunter green suit was, bringing out a hidden green in her gray-blue eyes. He even discussed the plots of a couple of movies they had seen recently.

Not once did he mention the topics that were on Elayna's mind, though she couldn't imagine they were not on his: his proposal of marriage and their destination this soggy autumn evening.

Finally, as they took the right lane into River Road that ran along the Ohio River, Elayna asked, "Where is this meeting tonight, Whit?"

He concentrated on making the right moves under the overpass and onto Third Street before he answered. "It's in the ballroom of the Galt House East Hotel. That's the only space that can accommodate several hundred people for dinner. It's probably a buffet. Hope you don't mind," he added. He turned right onto Muhammad Ali Boulevard, then took another right onto Fourth Street and into the parking lot under the hotel.

"No, that's fine," Elayna said. It wasn't the meal that concerned her, but the concepts she might be fed. Whit was an intelligent man, well-educated, astute, and he certainly had been convinced. Her faith wasn't very strong. Would she be able to withstand what she feared would be brainwashing in the values of this movement?

"Whit, I looked through your magazines. . . ," she began.

"I realize that the things you read in those publications are strange to you, Elayna," he interrupted. "They were to me not so long ago. I was feeling my way for months. You know I never mentioned them to you. I wanted to be sure. Just go to the meeting tonight with an open mind. The speaker is world famous, you know."

"How involved in this are you, Whit?" she asked, still hoping for some way to salvage a life for them together, without any demands for her to be a part of the strange concepts she had discovered in his magazines.

"My involvement has grown gradually over the months," he said, swinging the car into the first empty parking space and cutting the engine. "Now, I am totally committed to the cause. And my strong chances of being elected governor of Kentucky have given me a fast track to the top ranks of our movement. Having the governorship in our pockets, so to speak, will make our transition to power much easier."

Elayna's heart sank with her hopes, as she saw the obvious conviction that lit his eyes as he spoke. There would be no convincing Whit to return to a more normal way of life, not even for his chosen "perfect-for-the-part" mate.

He removed the keys from the ignition and turned to face her. "Please don't make judgments yet, Elayna," he urged. "Listen to what you hear tonight, go home and think about it, and we will discuss it later. In fact, that new supper club in Frankfort is open now. They say it is very elegant and that the food is excellent. I'd like to take you there tomorrow night and renew my proposal in an appropriate atmosphere. How about it?"

His intense dark eyes held hers. Finally, she nodded. "Sure, Whit," she answered. "But I wouldn't feel right if I didn't warn you that I have grave reservations about all of this."

He took both of her hands in his. "Please, Elayna, give me this one chance, at least. I promise not to try to force you into anything you really don't want to do. Just let me show you my new world."

Again, she nodded, though more reluctantly. "All right, Whit. I will try to keep an open mind. But you must realize that nothing could have induced me to be here tonight except my respect and admiration for you."

He squeezed her hands, then released them. "I know, sweetheart, and I do understand. Believe me, less than a year ago, I was exactly where you are now. Just try to relax and enjoy the evening. You don't have to accept anything you don't want to accept, and you don't have to make any decisions tonight."

Whit locked the car and they walked the easy distance to the lobby. Elayna had been involved in many meetings and exhibits at Al Sneader's unique hotel complex on the banks of the Ohio River, but she hadn't been to the Galt House East for several months. She was pleasantly surprised to find the improvements that long-awaited renovations had made.

New carpet, new or newly covered loveseats and chairs, new wallpaper and artwork judiciously placed amid the soaring wood gave the spacious lobby with its rising stairway an elegant air that had been missing. In fact, she and Leslie had joked that the hotel's owner surely had employed a blind decorator to choose the decor for his first and still-favorite hotel. Now, the lobby displayed a charm and grace to rival any of Louisville's historic properties.

As they climbed the single flight of stairs and headed down the long hallway to the ballroom, Elayna saw exhibit booths lining the right side of the hallway, displaying everything from literature to crystals and holistic medical supplies. Soothing strains of New Age music floated toward them from the ballroom. She glanced around, hoping none of her friends on the hotel staff would see her and think she was a part of all this.

Whit had asked her to keep an open mind, though, and she thought that was the least she could do in fairness to the man with whom she had spent so many pleasant evenings, the man who had honored her with his proposal of marriage not many hours ago.

Whit stopped to chat with a vendor selling crystals, a pretty, young girl with long dark hair and gold hoop earrings. He didn't introduce them, and Elayna wandered down the row of booths, stopping to examine some hand-made jewelry displayed by a petite blonde with a sweet smile.

"Are these supposed to have some special mystical powers like the crystals?" she asked cautiously, eyeing an unusual bracelet of brown and black stones on a silver elastic thread and a pair of earrings to match. The jewelry was attached to a printed card that identified it as "Wild Things by Jenni." The price seemed reasonable.

The blonde shook her head. "It's just jewelry," she answered with a grin. "No powers, except to make you look charming."

Elayna smiled back, then rummaged through her purse for money to pay for the set. For the first time since she had found it, she had left Shirleene's "evidence" behind, hidden in the orange juice carton in her refrigerator. She didn't think the killer would search her house again, but if he did, she was fairly certain he would not find the drawings there.

"How long have you been a part of this movement, Jenni?" she asked the blonde.

"Oh, I'm not!" the girl answered emphatically. "I'm just here to sell jewelry. This group seems to like the natural look of my pieces. I sold everything I brought last spring."

"Well, these will add the finishing touch to my new beige outfit," Elayna said. "Do you have a necklace to go with them?" When the girl pulled one out of a case beneath the table, Elayna bought that, too.

Pleased with her purchases, Elayna moved on down the row of booths, but everything else seemed too closely connected to the New Age beliefs to tempt her. About halfway down the hall, she glimpsed friends of hers from the George E. Fern Company, who had set up many booths for her in the past. Not wanting to explain why she was here, she turned and moved back to stand beside Whit, who still was engaged in conversation with the crystal vendor.

He turned to smile at Elayna. "Time to go in," he said, taking her arm as if he thought she might try to escape.

Elayna had hoped they would sit near the back, but Whit was motioned to one of the tables just in front of the platform, where two men in business suits and ties, two well-groomed women, and two men in jeans and T-shirts already were seated. Whit quickly introduced her, and they all went to join the line that stretched from the back doors down both sides of several laden buffet tables.

Carrying a plate of crisp, colorful salad offerings and one of hot vegetables and a slice of prime rib, Elayna returned to the table, already supplied with glasses of water and iced tea, along with empty coffee cups turned upside down in saucers. She sat down and spread her white cloth napkin across her lap.

"What's your sign, dear?" the large woman on her left asked, slathering butter on a roll.

"I beg your pardon?" Elayna said.

"She means your astrological sign, Elayna," Whit explained. "It's Libra," he answered for her. "This is her first meeting, and it's all a little confusing to her. You know how it is," he said with a charming smile all around.

The heavy woman answered around a mouthful of roll, "Can't say I do. I grew up on this stuff. My mother channeled and my grandmother was a whiz with the tarot."

Elayna realized she was staring and dropped her gaze to her plate.

"One of my earliest memories is of my grandfather giving psychic readings," the man on the other side of the woman commented, tucking his napkin into the neck of his long-sleeved white shirt.

The balding man across from Elayna leaned forward and smiled at her. "Pay them no mind, young lady," he said. "Helen and I attended our first seminar just a year ago last April." The gaunt, red-haired woman beside him confirmed that with a nod. "And your escort, here, our honorable governor-to-be," the man went on, "came in after that."

Whit laughed. "But I'm making up for lost time! I've been to six seminars in the past six months."

So that's why he's been traveling so much lately, Elayna thought. She cast a smile around the table and pretended to concentrate on her food.

"This food isn't bad, for a buffet," Whit commented.

"This spinach quiche is very good, isn't it, Harold?" the red-haired woman said uncertainly.

"It's all delicious!" the large woman slurred around a mouthful of something. "And I'm starved!"

"You're always starved, Stella," the man beside her growled. "Wipe the butter off your chin."

Elayna averted her eyes in disgust and focused on the two men in jeans and T-shirts who, so far, had not contributed to the conversation. They were staring into each other's eyes and had not yet touched their food.

Elayna finished eating and was sipping a hot cup of black

coffee when a woman arose, walked to the podium, and gave a short welcoming speech.

"I am sure that Marlowe Reed needs no introduction to most of you here tonight," the woman at the podium said. "But, just in case we have new ones among us, let me say that Dr. Reed is one of the most sought-after psychic readers in the world at the present time. He has published six books of automatic writings given him by his guide, Aldolpho, and was instrumental in establishing the New Age Publishing and Retail Alliance of over fifty publishing houses. Please help me welcome Dr. Marlowe Reed!"

The applause came in waves, as Elayna watched a short, lean gray-haired man take the woman's place at the podium. He held up both hands for silence. "Thank you, my friends and colleagues," he said. "You almost make me believe I deserve that enthusiastic welcome!"

He took the microphone from its stand and walked out to the edge of the platform, where Elayna could see that his perfectly fitting gray suit and dark red tie gave him the look of any CEO about to address his employees.

His talk, interrupted many times by applause, was laced with references to various things Elayna had encountered in Whit's magazines. When he spoke seriously of his encounters with UFOs manned by ascended masters, Elayna could not keep her eyebrows from raising skeptically, and she glanced at Whit to share an amused grin. But Whit was absorbed in what the man was saying. There was no trace of amusement on his face.

Have I followed Alice down the rabbit hole? Elayna wondered, looking around the table at her dinner companions. *I can't do this!* she thought, feeling a smothering panic rising within her. *I won't make a scene, but if we ever get out of here. . .*

Whit reached over and took her hand and held it under the tablecloth. His dark eyes sought hers, and he whispered, "Not yet, sweetheart! Don't say the things I see in your face just yet, please."

When the man had finished speaking and the woman who had introduced him had dismissed the meeting, Elayna let Whit lead her around the room, acknowledging his introductions politely, trying not to compare the people she met to singing flowers, pipe-smoking caterpillars, and Cheshire cats who disappeared leaving only their grins behind.

Finally, they were out of the hotel and in Whit's car, heading back toward Frankfort.

"Give it time, Elayna," Whit cautioned, before she could gather her thoughts enough to tell him what she thought about their evening. "My rational, analytical lawyer's mind rejected most of it at first. And there is room in the movement for all kinds of people, including some pretty weird characters, I'll admit. Unfortunately, they all seemed to be seated at our table tonight! Just give it some time, and we will discuss all of it openly and honestly tomorrow night," he assured her.

"All right, Whit," she agreed and began to tell him about the evidence against Jayboy and all her reasons for believing he was innocent of Shirleene's murder.

"I will defend Jayboy, Elayna," Whit repeated his earlier promise, as they pulled up in front of her house almost an hour later. "I really don't think he is guilty, but even if he were, I am a defense attorney, and sometimes we must defend the guilty. Either way, I promise you, sweetheart, that Jayboy Calvin will not see the inside of a prison."

He got out, opened the car door for her, and saw her safely inside the house. Elayna stood watching as he returned to the car and drove away, hoping with all her heart that he was right about Jay, wishing things could be right between her and this attractive man who had so much to offer, but who had placed a formidable barrier between them this evening.

Chapter 53

Shut up!" the man yelled. His slap jolted Jayboy's head sideways. He stopped screaming and lay there trembling. Waiting for the next slap. Waiting for the man to get his gun and blow him away. His heart pounded. His mouth was dry. He felt sick.

The man reached across him. Jayboy flinched and whimpered. He couldn't help it. He was so scared. But the man was only reaching for his dead hand. He picked it up and began to rub it between his hands. Hard. Fast.

Jayboy writhed on the bunk as the hand began to tingle. To ache. Like the time he had played in the snow until his feet were frostbitten and had no feeling. Mac had rubbed them in snow. And they had begun to tingle. To ache. Just like his hand and arm did now. He moaned and writhed with the pain.

The man dropped his hand. "Keep rubbing it, Loony Toons!" he ordered. He moved away, back to the cupboards.

Jayboy reached over with his right hand and began rubbing his left as the man had shown him. Rubbing. Shaking. Massaging. The left hand was coming back now. It wasn't dead after all! He wasn't going to be like Mac for the rest of his life. If he had any more life. If the man didn't shoot him.

"You need to go to the bathroom, Loony Toons?" the man asked.

He tried to say yes, but his voice wouldn't work. He nodded his head.

"Go ahead, then," the man said. He cocked his head toward the back of the boat.

Jayboy knew where the bathroom was. He knew there was just a toilet in the little closet back there. No wash basin. No tub or shower. He knew more about this boat than the ugly little man did. He knew more about this boat than anybody. Except 'Layna. And Court. He had been on it a million times. He was Captain Jayboy Calvin. Skipper of the 'Layna. He didn't say anything, though. He just got up and walked straight back to the bathroom.

"Hurry up, Loony Toons!" the man yelled before he was finished. He tried to hurry, but that just seemed to make it take longer.

When he came back, the man was sitting at the table. The gun was on the table in front of him. He was eating a sandwich. Jayboy couldn't tell what kind it was, but his mouth watered, anyway. And his stomach rumbled.

When the man saw him watching, he said, "Sorry, Loony Toons. I've only got one, and it's mine." He laughed and reached for a red and white can. He took a big drink. Jayboy knew it was beer. The kind that lizards and frogs used to drink on TV.

When the man finished his sandwich, there wasn't a crumb left. Jayboy could tell by the way he crumpled up the paper before he threw it in the trash. Then the man turned the beer can all the way upside down, drank the last drop, and licked his lips. He threw the empty can in the trash, too.

"It's you and me against the world tonight, Loony Toons," he said. "I'm not going back out there in this rain. And guess what, I get the lower bunk!" He studied Jayboy with a frown. "And I'm not gonna sit up all night to make sure you don't run away while I'm asleep, either." He came over to the bunk and picked up the chain.

Jayboy flinched. He couldn't stand it if the man chained him to the bunk again! His hand and arm would die! Maybe this time they wouldn't come back!

The man laughed. "Relax," he said. "I'm just gonna chain your feet together so you can't walk. You're not gonna get off this boat hopping. And if you fall in the river, with this heavy chain on, you'll sink to the bottom like a rock." The man threw back his head and laughed.

Jayboy climbed onto the upper bunk. He tried not to cry as the man wrapped the chain around his ankles, clicked the padlock shut, and put the key in his pocket.

Chapter 54

Elayna awoke the next morning feeling like her head was full of spiderwebs. She decided that a brisk walk through River View Park behind her house might be the best remedy. At the edge of the park, though, she found that the rising, debris-filled river had covered the walkway.

As she stood there, studying the encroaching water, wondering how long it would be before it reached her back patio, she noticed the markings painted in a dark red paint on the lower portions of the railroad bridge.

Until now, she had thought they were just graffiti, but after reading Whit's magazines, she recognized the pentagrams, scarabs, pyramids, and other signs as occult symbols. The word *park* had been marked through with an *x,* and an arrow pointed to the right. She turned to the right and saw more arrows marked on the floodwall, pointing straight toward her house.

Don't be ridiculous, she scolded herself. *It's just as likely they're pointing toward Liberty Hall and its gardens. But why?* she mused, as she turned and headed back toward her house.

Suddenly, she remembered the lights she had seen flickering back in the gardens the night the intruder had torn her back door from its hinges. Were there some kind of occult meetings going on at night in those dark gardens? She had seen no more flickering lights. Still, she had paid little attention, after deciding they were part of an innocent, one-time celebration.

Then the thought came to her that this might be something in which Whit was involved. Should she ask him about it?

The phone was ringing when she came into the house. She picked up the receiver and answered, "Elayna Evans."

"Elayna, you need to come to the shop," she heard Leslie's familiar husky voice say. "We've had a break-in. I can't tell yet if anything is missing, but some merchandise has been damaged and the place is a mess. I've called the police."

"I'm on my way as soon as I shower and change," Elayna promised, already kicking off her walking shoes and socks and peeling off her sweats.

In twenty minutes, she was entering the narrow gray-blue Italianate building on Lewis Street that housed Elayna Evans Imports. *This run-down three-story structure has come a long way since I bought it ten years ago for a warehouse,* she thought with satisfaction.

A city police car already was parked out front, lights flashing, and she was met at the door by Detective Dave Myers. An African-American policeman she did not know was bent over something on her desk in the corner.

"Looks like our boy has been busy since he escaped," Myers said. "Either you've got something Calvin wants real bad, or you've done something to make him awfully mad at you."

"Dave, it wasn't Jayboy," she insisted. "He's—"

She stopped in time to keep from blurting out that Jay was traveling down the river. "He's not here," she said. "He hasn't been home, hasn't contacted Doris or me. We don't know where he is."

"We'll find him," Myers vowed. "Calvin hasn't got the common sense to get very far. To breaking and entering and criminal trespass, we've added resisting arrest, assaulting an officer, and, of course, he's still our prime suspect in the Evans murder. I'm asking for an indictment for all of it."

Elayna walked past the detective, then stopped in dismay. Shipping boxes had been ripped open and their contents, much of it broken, lay scattered over the floor. Cabinets and file drawers gaped open. Papers were everywhere.

"We'll have to inventory before we know how much we've lost, Elayna," Leslie said, straightening up from behind a display case with a whisk broom in one hand and a dust pan filled with broken glass in the other. Styrofoam packing peanuts clung to the legs of her pants.

"We're through here," Myers said. "We have Leslie's statement, and Todd has fingerprinted everything."

Elayna glanced at the policeman at her desk. As he packed up his fingerprinting equipment, his eyes followed Leslie's every move. Elayna noted again how attractive the nearly forty-year-old woman was—soft black curls framing an oval face, a generous mouth, straight nose, and dark eyes with a hint of mischief sparkling just beneath the surface.

"There are at least three distinct sets of prints," Myers continued.

Elayna turned back to address the detective. "Mine, Leslie's, and Jayboy's. We all work here, Dave," she reminded him. "If there are only three sets, then the perpetrator must have worn gloves."

The detective ignored that. "It's the same MO as at your house, Elayna."

She nodded. "And there were no fingerprints that shouldn't have been there, either, remember? It wasn't Jay," she repeated. "He's so proud of the way he keeps this place, he'd never do this, Dave!"

He eyed her narrowly. "You do know the consequences of

aiding and abetting, don't you, Elayna? You would tell me if you knew where he was?"

"Of course." *Eventually*, she added silently. "Whit Yancey has agreed to defend him, Dave," she said.

"Our noted defense attorney has his work cut out for him this time," Myers predicted. "Calvin cut his hand when he broke the glass in the door to gain entry. He left a nice little blood sample for our DNA experts. Come on, Todd, let's get these samples and prints down to the lab," he said, motioning with his head for the other policeman, whose eyes still were on Leslie.

When they had shut the door behind them, Leslie grimaced and shook her head. "What a mess," she said.

"I'll get Doris to come in and help us clean up, Les," Elayna promised. "Unless you'd prefer to get that young policeman to help. I don't think he would be too hard to persuade."

Leslie gave her a cryptic look. "Since you're here, you might want to examine that latest shipment of jade from Hong Kong," she said, ignoring the teasing comment. She spread a piece of black velvet over the top of the display case and began placing samples of jade on it.

"I know the jeweler is recuperating from cataract surgery and these probably were done by an assistant. But these designs are far inferior to what we have come to expect from this supplier." She pointed out flaws in the craftsmanship and even in some of the stones themselves.

Elayna recalled how hard her assistant had worked to learn their trade, taking classes and workshops, reading everything she could find on related subjects. She now knew more than Elayna herself about gemstones, porcelain, silk, blown glass, tapestry. Her contributions to the business were invaluable. *One day soon*, she thought, *I will offer Leslie a partnership*.

Glancing at her watch, Elayna gasped. "It's nearly two o'clock.

No wonder I'm starving. Come on, Les, let's go get a bite to eat. I owe you lunch, anyway. You've done so much for me lately."

Leslie laughed, a throaty chuckle that seemed to come from somewhere down near her toes. "You don't owe me anything, Elayna," she protested. "If anything, I owe you, for giving me a job when I needed one so badly and had almost no skills."

It was Elayna's turn to laugh. "No skills? Woman, I don't know what on earth I'd do without you!"

"Oh, I suspect you'd manage," Leslie said dryly. "You did it for several years. But lunch sounds good. Let me put the CLOSED sign on the door and I'll be right there."

"We'll be closed until we get things back in order here," Elayna said. "Who do you think did it, Les?"

"I think whoever killed Shirleene thinks you have something he or she wants, Elayna. And as long as the police are convinced Jay's guilty, they aren't going to look for anyone else. I don't think you will be safe until the real murderer is caught."

Elayna was sure she was right. "Well, we know it wasn't Jay, and I'm just as sure it wasn't Court. So who does that leave as a suspect? Leslie, do you think it could have been C. J. Berryman?"

"I don't know, Elayna. I've heard that he was having an affair with Mrs. Evans, but that doesn't necessarily mean he killed her. I don't know the man well enough to make a judgment on whether or not he's capable of murder."

"I've known him all my life," Elayna answered. "He's an irritating little punk. And the mess we've found here today is just his style. But is he capable of murder? I don't know."

Chapter 55

When Jayboy woke up, he thought he smelled bacon. And eggs. And toast. He thought 'Layna must be on the boat fixing breakfast.

They would sit at the little table, and 'Layna would ladle scrambled eggs onto their plates. She would set a big brown platter of bacon in the middle of the table in front of them. And another plate of buttery toast made in the oven. And they would eat 'til they couldn't eat any more. Or until it was all gone. "Whichever comes first," Hunt used to say.

Then Hunt would offer to wash the dishes. And Jayboy would, too. But 'Layna would say, "You guys get the poles and the bait ready. It won't take me long here." 'Layna didn't much like to fish. And she hated the ugly night crawlers. She wouldn't even touch the bait can. But Hunt would bait her hook, and she would hold the pole for awhile. Then, if the fish weren't biting, she'd wander off to explore the riverbank. Or read a book.

Jayboy knew he had been dreaming. 'Layna wasn't on the boat. There was just him. And the ugly little man. With his back turned toward him. Cooking something in a skillet on the stove. He could smell coffee, too. From the pot on the back of the stove.

Would the man give him something to eat? He said he only had one sandwich last night. Did he have enough to share today?

Where's the gun? There it is! Lying on the counter. Looking as

233

innocent as the can opener lying beside it. But Jayboy knew. That gun wasn't innocent. It was a killer. Just like the man who owned it. Who had killed Shirleene.

Jayboy might be a murderer now, too, if the cop he knocked down had died. He groaned. He wished he knew. He hadn't meant to kill the cop. He had just wanted to get away. To keep from being taken inside that flat brown building. To keep from being locked up and tortured by the police. Like Shirleene had told him. Like he had seen on TV when he had to go through the front room while Doris was watching one of her shows. He hadn't meant to hurt anybody. He had just wanted to be free.

Suddenly, Jayboy realized he *was* free. The man was bending over him, unchaining his feet. Now he was reaching for his wrist to chain him to the bunk again.

Chapter 56

My car's still being repaired," Elayna explained as she and Leslie left the shop together, "but I'm sure we can find something to eat within easy walking distance."

They crossed the railroad tracks on Broadway and walked toward Serafini's, a restaurant that catered to downtown professionals and the usual courthouse crowd. The building's unique triangular entry was formed by the strategic placement of a column at the point where Broadway met St. Clair Street. Large brass letters above the doorway spelled out the name of the restaurant.

When Leslie realized where they were going, she said, "I'm afraid this place is too rich for my budget!"

"This is my treat, Les, remember?" Elayna said. "This place always brings back memories. The building originally held Serafini Drugs, and when I was a child, a couple of generations later, Vic Serafini and Sam Horn ran a pharmacy here. My grandfather and I often came here on errands for Granny." She stopped for a moment as the memories replayed in her mind.

"Then, as likely as not," she went on, "we would continue on down the street to Joe Luktemeier's hardware store, with its fascinating bins of merchandise lining the wooden floor all the way through the long, narrow shop, and spilling up the creaky wooden stairs. But old Mr. Luktemeier always knew exactly where to find whatever Grandad wanted."

"I didn't come to Frankfort until I married Bob," Leslie said. "I don't remember those places, but he told me that his mother said there used to be a bus station down on the corner that had three restrooms—one marked LADIES, one marked GENTLEMEN, and one marked COLORED."

"Oh, Les, how awful! I didn't know that!" Elayna said. "That building held Putt Benassi's restaurant when I was a child. I do have a very early memory, though, of Julia from Dr. Minish's office sitting on that long seat across the back of the bus in her white nurse's uniform instead of beside Granny and me, when we were all such friends at the doctor's office."

"I didn't encounter any of that," Leslie said. "Even the schools were integrated before I came along."

"Actually, desegregation was accomplished with little fuss here in Frankfort, maybe because the town was so used to change, with one government administration replacing another every four years," Elayna explained. "I remember that when the town was threatened with sit-ins like those of the deep South, one day we were sitting at a drugstore soda fountain sipping sodas, and the next, the long counter with its wonderful revolving stools no longer existed."

"I don't think we'll be sipping anything at Serafini's today," Leslie said, pointing to a sidewalk easel announcing that lunch was served from 11:00 A.M. to 2:00 P.M.

"It's already two!" Elayna wailed. "But I'm still starving. Where shall we go, Les?"

"Elayna, isn't that Senator Yancey?"

Elayna felt her heart jump, as she followed Leslie's gaze to the window of Serafini's private dining room where Whit and three other men were being served coffee by a hovering waitress. Whit had his back to her, and she was glad. She wasn't ready to talk with him. Quickly, she walked on down the street.

"Are you still seeing him?" Leslie asked, hurrying to catch up.

"Seeing him?" Elayna hedged. "Oh, we go to a movie, a play, to dinner now and then. How about the Kentucky Coffeetree Cafe?" she suggested. "The rush should be over."

"Sure," Leslie agreed. "It's one of my favorite places, with Poor Richard's Books on one side and the Completely Kentucky gift shop on the other. I could spend the afternoon there.

"By the way," she went on, "I was wondering if we shouldn't offer some more Kentucky crafts in our next catalog. They wouldn't be imported, but we already have Satian Leksrisawat's pottery from Louisville and those quilts from Appalachia, and both have been extremely popular. I thought maybe we could add some of those terrific animal carvings by that man from Glasgow that we saw at the craft show, or those exquisite copper leaf fountains by Andrew Skerchock up in Burlington. . . ."

"All excellent ideas, Les," Elayna said as they entered the cafe and stopped at the front counter to study the menu. *The girl is definitely partnership material,* she thought.

"I'll have the Southern chicken salad on wheat bread with a lemon-poppy seed muffin and the kiwi pear tea," Elayna said to the clerk.

"Kiwi pear tea?" Leslie repeated with a skeptical grin and raised brows. She turned to the clerk. "I want the plain old garden variety black tea, please," she ordered, "with pimento cheese on rye and a cinnamon muffin."

They walked under ancient ceiling fans suspended from a white-painted tin ceiling all the way to the back of the long, narrow room. They sat down at a small round table for two, flanked on two sides by book-filled shelves. Except for three women chatting animatedly three tables down and a lone man reading a newspaper across the aisle, they had the place to themselves.

"Now," Elayna said, "tell me why you wanted to know if I was still 'seeing' Whit. It's not like you to be nosy, Leslie. I know you had a reason."

"Oh, well, I. . .he's a nice-looking man," Leslie finished lamely, concentrating on receiving the flat basket containing her lunch from the waitress. She dipped a carrot stick into a small paper cup of dip. "I prefer these raw vegetables to the usual chips, and this is a good dip," she commented when the girl had gone.

"It isn't going to work, Les," Elayna said firmly. "If you know something about the Honorable Whitley Yancey that I don't, you must tell me. I promise not to be offended."

The woman's dark eyes met Elayna's. "I saw him at a rally the other day on the capitol steps," she said reluctantly. "I had to deliver those imported favors to the governor's office, and there was this transcendental meditation rally going on. Senator Yancey was there."

"He's at the capitol a lot, Les," Elayna said. "Maybe he just stopped by to see what was going on." She toyed with her sandwich, knowing without a doubt that Whit's attendance at the rally had been no accident.

Leslie shook her head. "He was leading it, Elayna."

Suddenly, Elayna wanted the woman's opinion of Whit's new religion, of the meeting she had attended the night before at the Galt House.

"He's into some New Age movement, Les," she admitted. "I went with him to a meeting in Louisville last night. It was. . . well, bizarre." She described the meeting and her dinner companions. "I felt like I had followed the White Rabbit straight down the rabbit hole to Wonderland!" she finished, laughing nervously.

"Elayna, I have no right to tell you what to do," Leslie began seriously, "but I have to warn you about getting involved in—"

"Leslie, Whit has asked me to marry him," Elayna interrupted. She looked away from the concern in her assistant's dark eyes. "And he's deeply committed to this movement. I'd have to be involved. I don't know what to do."

Leslie took both of Elayna's hands in hers. "Senator Yancey is a very attractive man, and I know his friendship has been comforting to you. I also know he is likely to be the next governor of the Commonwealth of Kentucky. But, Elayna, these insidious New Age beliefs are dangerous. They could lead to your soul's eternal damnation!"

Elayna looked away. "Aren't you ever lonely, Leslie?" she almost whispered. "Like me, you lost the two most precious things in your life—your husband and your child. You don't have any family left except those cousins in Colorado. Don't you ever just get hungry for someone to love, to love you back? Don't you ever long to be the most important thing in someone else's life again?"

"Once you are Real, you can't be unreal again!"

For a second, Elayna saw intense pain migrate across the other woman's face and settle in her eyes. Then it was replaced with a peace that Elayna envied with all her heart.

"The pastor and congregation of First Assembly of God church have become my family," Leslie said softly. "And, like the Bible says, Jesus Christ 'sticks closer than a brother.' When I get those moments of excruciating loneliness—and believe me, Elayna, there are times—I just begin to talk to Him, and He fills all the holes with His presence."

Elayna knew she had never known anything like what Leslie was describing and like her grandmother had known. She wanted to ask how she could get it. Instead, she asked, "Is your church. . . ?"

"African-American?" Leslie finished for her. "No. There are several of us who attend, but it's just. . .Christian. Pentecostal. I'm very comfortable there." She stood up and picked up her basket and empty plastic cup. "Thanks for lunch, Elayna," she said.

"I'll take you to dinner one night," Elayna promised, picking up her own basket and cup. "We'll go to Serafini's, or maybe to that new supper club Whit's been raving about, Mockingbird's I think it's called."

Leslie eyebrows rose. "Senator Yancey is raving about Mockingbird's?"

"Yes, he's taking me there tonight." As Leslie's face continued to register astonishment, Elayna asked, "Have you been there, Les? Is there something wrong with it? Whit says he has heard that the food is great and that the atmosphere is elegant."

"I'm sure it's all of that," Leslie agreed, an amused smile lingering on her lips. "I've heard. . .interesting things about it. I just didn't think it was the senator's kind of place."

"Whit's right at home in elegant places!" Elayna defended.

Leslie chuckled. "I hope he's at home at Mockingbird's. You'll have to tell me all about it later," she said. Still smiling, she headed across the street and back toward the shop, leaving Elayna frustrated and more confused than ever.

Chapter 57

The man reached across Jayboy with the chain in his hand. Jayboy smelled sweat and sour beer, mixed with some sickly sweet shaving lotion. He knew he could not let the man chain him up! He couldn't stand for his arm and hand to die again. He couldn't stand to be fastened up so he couldn't get loose. He always had to have one foot outside the blanket. Even in cold weather. He couldn't be tied down. He couldn't stand it! He couldn't!

Jayboy shoved with all of his might, driving his fists into the man's middle. Just like he had hit the policeman at the jail. He heard the man fall backward into the table and benches. But he knew he hadn't killed him. The man began to curse. A long string of ugly words. Words that would have made Doris wash his mouth out with soap just for hearing them. He almost gagged, remembering the burning, bitter taste of the soap.

Before the man could recover, Jayboy was out the door and across the deck. Down the slippery gangplank. Up the muddy bank to the top, only inches above the water now.

"Come back here, Loony Toons!" he heard the man shout. "I'll blow your brains out!" Then the man began to curse again.

Jayboy looked over his shoulder. The man was running across the deck. The ugly gun was in his hand! Jayboy cringed, expecting to feel the impact of a bullet any second. He ran up the hill, crouching low. Like the soldiers in the war movies Mac had watched. Keeping their heads down as they ran for cover. With enemy bullets exploding all around them.

He heard a spitting sound. A bullet crashed into the tree beside him, tearing out a chunk of bark and wood. He swerved.

"You Loony Toons!" the man yelled. "When I catch you, you're dead meat!"

Another bullet hit the tree in front of Jayboy. He ducked behind another tree. But he couldn't stop. He couldn't! He ran on. Dodging from tree to tree.

Then he saw the big white sycamore. Its trunk was hollowed out like a big empty room. He ducked inside and stood still. Panting. Trying to listen. Waiting for the man to come. Feeling the blackness behind him, breathing down his neck.

Chapter 58

As she turned left from Broadway onto the newly bricked St. Clair Mall, Elayna's mind went back to the days of her childhood, when there was no mall. People from the country had parked their cars here along St. Clair Street on Saturday nights to shop, or simply to sit watching the crowd flow up and down the wide street with its tall, Italianate buildings, shaded by ancient trees and lit by round, white globes hanging like fruit from tall iron posts.

Back then, families named Sullivan, Fitzgerald, Mucci, Serafini, and Benassi had operated the downtown restaurants, pharmacies, and banks, most of them sending their children to parochial school in neat navy blue uniforms that Elayna, in her ordinary skirts and sweaters, had envied.

Then, there were the Simons, the Krinskys, the Marcuses, the Gershmans, and the Rosensteins, who ran the jewelry, clothing, and furniture stores, which were closed on strange-sounding holidays like Hanukkah, Rosh Hashanah, and Yom Kippur.

Except for the huge clock on its tall green post outside the venerable Selbert's Jewelry store, little remained to remind her of the days when she and Granny had visited Lerman's and Miss Bertha Watson's hat shop, while her Grandad sought refuge across the street in "Frenchie" LaFontaine's establishment for men only.

Most of the old family businesses had fled to the suburban shopping centers, or gone out of business entirely. "Improvement committees" had removed many of the town's fine old trees and period lighting fixtures, while state government monstrosities had usurped the space of graceful pre-Civil War and early-1900s buildings.

The ground floors of the old buildings that remained now held lawyers, realtors, and small restaurants and specialty shops that catered to the daytime tourists who came to visit the Old Capitol at the north end of the mall or the ironically modern History Center that sprawled, prison-like, over a whole block of Broadway.

And now, except for a bar or two, the downtown stores close and the streets are rolled up at five P.M. She waved to the Scottow brothers, who ran Judd's Office Supply about where the Woolworth's and Newberry's five-and-dime stores had been. Judd's had been up on West Main Street when she, Granny, Doris, and Jayboy had bought school supplies there each fall. Afterward, they had gone down the street to Mucci's for black and white Bostons.

Sometimes she wished those pleasant days had been as eternal as she and Jay had envisioned in their Dandelion Kingdom. Back then, serious crime had been rare in the small-town capital. The good guys always wore white hats and she could tell who they were. Good always triumphed over evil, as it had on those Saturday afternoons when they paid their fifteen cents to sit inside the Grand Theater, eating five-cent popcorn from waxed-paper cones.

She had read in the paper that some group was trying to restore the old theater as a museum. *I'll have to contribute to that,* she thought. She turned left at the south end of the mall, passed Melanie's on Main and Marshall's restaurants, and entered Rodgers' Studio.

"My husband is out photographing a wedding," Joan Rodgers informed her, "but here are the pictures for your fall brochure. I think Bill has done a fabulous job with them, if I do say so myself." She laughed, then added, "I've got to have one of those Irish sweaters!"

They chatted a few minutes; then Elayna tucked the envelope containing the photographs into her bag and left the shop.

As she headed back down West Main toward home, she noticed bright orange flyers tucked under the windshield wipers of parked cars on both sides of the street. Curious, she took one.

"Psychic Fest This Weekend," she read. *In Frankfort?* she thought in amazement, scanning the page until she located an address, which she recognized as out in the country on the west side of town.

"Something for everyone!" she read. "Tarot. Psychic Readings. Holiestic Health. Yoga. Crystals. Runes. Books. Jewelry and Crafts. Food and Fun. Come find that missing piece in your life!"

Will Whit be going? she wondered. *Will he be leading it as— according to Leslie—he led the transcendental meditation rally at the capitol? Will he expect me to accompany him?*

"Honey, you don't want to go to that."

Elayna turned to find an elderly woman standing behind her, reading over her shoulder.

"Oh, I wasn't—" she began.

"No, dear," the woman continued, her head cocked sideways like a bright-eyed robin, her red-brown coat completing the picture. "Do you remember that story last year—it was in the paper, front page—where that young girl was found dead on that farm out there after one of these 'fests'? They said it was a drug overdose, but, honey, my cousin works in the coroner's office, and she says that girl's body was full of. . .oh, I forget the name. . .that drug they use to sedate their human sacrifices."

Elayna took a step backward away from the woman. *Human sacrifices?* She vaguely recalled the story. The girl's death had been ruled an accidental, self-administered drug overdose, if she remembered correctly.

The woman stabbed a bony finger at Elayna's chest to emphasize her words. "That girl was murdered, as sure as we're standing here, and it was all hushed up. They were afraid to dig too deep, if you get my drift. Nobody wants to take on the supernatural. No telling what may happen out there this year. You don't want to go!" she repeated.

"No, ma'am, I won't," Elayna promised, backing up again, then turning to walk quickly away. When she looked back, the woman was removing the flyers from car windshields and crumpling them up.

She took a deep breath. *It must be my week for "rabbit hole" adventures!* she thought, folding the flyer and putting it in her bag to discuss with Whit.

As she passed the real estate office of Berryman and Son near the corner of West Main and Washington Streets, she could see C. J. talking on the phone at the big desk that once had been her father's.

She had unpleasant memories of C. J. as an obnoxious child, jumping out at her from dark corners of the narrow two-story building, whispering vulgar, unfunny jokes into her ear when their fathers weren't watching, shooting her with soggy paper wads from a rubber band. Once she had told her father about his harassment, and C. J. had retaliated viciously for weeks.

She stood there watching C. J. through the slats of wooden blinds as he transferred the phone to his right hand and began to scribble notes on a scratch pad with his left. *What on earth did Shirleene ever see in that pathetic little weasel with his pockmarked face and small, pale eyes?* she wondered. After she had been around C.J., she always felt like she needed a good bath. It made her sick to see him sitting there behind her father's desk as though it belonged to him.

It does belong to him, she reminded herself, feeling the old bitterness rise sourly into her mouth. *Mother sold Dad's half of the business—lock, stock, and barrel, as they say—to C. J.'s father before the funeral was over.* C. J., eventually, had inherited it all.

She had to admit he had done well with the business, well enough to enable him to live in a luxurious condo, to belong to the best clubs, to drive the best cars, and to provide that red Porsche for Shirleene. She supposed it was the money that had attracted Shirleene, or the power that always comes with money.

She had expected C. J. to run for some government office, but Court said his image was too soiled by shady business deals and unsavory political connections. She knew he often acted as a lobbyist for certain dubious interests during sessions of the Kentucky General Assembly.

She recalled one session when C. J. had used his handpicked representative to sneak a piece of legislation through the House at the last minute by attaching it to an unrelated bill. Only Whit's astute reaction in the Senate had stopped it. Still, he and Whit had remained friends, at least on a casual basis. She thought that was odd, because C. J. had taken Court's opposing votes on the city commission so personally that he had sought revenge through an affair with Shirleene.

Elayna remembered the policeman's comment, from the night Shirleene was murdered, that it was "a crime of passion—of intense hatred or vengeance." She peered at C.J., still talking into the phone and scribbling. He was known as a vengeful man. Had he taken a kitchen knife in that left hand and spilled his former lover's blood all over the Gypsy Tearoom floor?

She hadn't heard if the police had determined whether the

killer was left-handed or right-handed. *On* Law and Order *they always know those things,* she thought wryly. *They figure it out from the angle of the wounds or something.* If the killer was left-handed, that meant it couldn't have been Jayboy, who was decidedly right-handed. She had to find out, for Jay's sake.

If the killer was left-handed and he turned out to be C. J., then it was this despicable little man who had trashed her house and her shop looking for the drawings she had found in Shirleene's refrigerator. But why would C. J. want those drawings so badly? It was possible that they were a realtor's layout of properties, but were they worth a murder, and all the subsequent risks the killer had taken to find them?

As C. J. hung up the phone and tore some pages from the pad, Elayna's cell phone rang. She quickly moved away from the window and around the corner.

Chapter 59

The man stood right below his hiding place. Jayboy could hear him talking on his telephone.

"I can't find that stupid Loony Toons anywhere! He must have turned into a real loon and flew away." The man laughed bitterly. Jayboy heard the phone crackle and he almost laughed out loud. He had watched the man hunting for him with the gun in his hand. Behind rocks. In the woods. Inside hollow trees. Even inside the big white sycamore. But he hadn't discovered the secret room high up inside the big hollow limb. It had a knothole in it, just like a little window, that let him look right down on the boat. Only he couldn't see much right now, because the fog had once again settled over the water.

The phone crackled again. Jayboy couldn't hear what the other person was saying, but the man answered, "He said what? They're in her purse? Well, that figures! I've looked everywhere else. Some places twice! Look, I'm coming to town, anyway. I need to pick up some things. I'll take care of it."

The phone crackled. Then the man said, "No, I brought the car this time. But I need to get back here and finish things up. This river's rising fast, and I want Loony Toons on this boat when it goes! Dear Miz Evans knows too much, too. Maybe she can be persuaded to take a little trip with her loony friend." The man laughed, shut off the phone, and shoved it into his pocket. Then he climbed the hill and disappeared into the fog.

Jayboy knew that "Loony Toons" meant him. But what did he mean by "when it goes"? Was the boat going somewhere? And why did the man want him on it? Did he want him to steer the *'Layna*? He knew he could. "Miz Evans" must be 'Layna. The only other Miz Evans around here was Shirleene, and she was dead. Was the man going to bring 'Layna to the boat? Jayboy felt his heart skip at the thought of seeing her. But the man wanted her to "take a little trip," too. He had said she "knew too much." *That means he wants to kill her, too! Layna's smart, though. She'll know it's a trap. She won't be fooled. Will she?*

Jayboy's thoughts shifted to his present predicament. Should he climb down now? Should he try to get away while the man was gone? Should he try to get home to warn 'Layna?

Even if the man wasn't out there, though, the blackness was. He could feel it gathering. Whispering. Waiting for its chance. Jayboy whimpered and covered his eyes.

Chapter 60

Elayna fished the phone out of her bag and answered it.

"Elayna?" It was Leslie. "Court's house has been ransacked, too," she said. "The cleaning lady went in, found the mess, and called the police. Detective Myers is trying to reach Court, but he already has left his parents' house and is on his way back from Florida. Do you have a cell phone number for him?"

"I do," Elayna said. "Les, it has to be the same person who wrecked my place and the shop, still looking for Shirleene's 'evidence.'" Instinctively, she moved her bag up under her arm and held it tightly. Then she remembered that she had taken the papers out of the bag and hidden them in her refrigerator.

"I'll call Court and ask him to call Dave, Les," she promised. "By the way, do you want me to get Doris to help with the mess there at the shop?"

"Nope. I already called her and she should be here in an hour," Leslie said. "With her help, I think we can get the front room back in order pretty quickly, but it will take days to sort out the scramble of papers from the files. But if we can at least get everything back in the file drawers, we can be open for business tomorrow."

"Let's just stay closed until Monday," Elayna said. "And thanks, Les. As I've said before—"

"I know. You don't know what you'd do without me. Just hold that thought, boss," Leslie said, laughing as she hung up the phone.

Unable to remember Court's cell phone number, which she seldom used, Elayna quickly covered the block and a half to her house.

As she opened her front storm door, she noticed an envelope from the print shop taped to the inside door. *Betty must have finished my brochure earlier than she thought*, she mused, removing the envelope and carrying it inside.

She went straight to the telephone, looked up the number, and dialed. She was relieved to hear Court's strong voice answer immediately.

"Court, it's Elayna," she said.

"Elayna!" he exclaimed. "It's good to hear your voice. Are you all right?"

"I'm fine, Court, but Dave Myers is trying to reach you." She hesitated, reluctant to tell him the bad news, then plunged on. "Your house has been ransacked, Court. So has my shop. Jayboy has been arrested and has escaped. The police are convinced he killed Shirleene and have quit looking for the real killer. . . ."

"Whoa, Elayna!" he broke into her recital. "I'm not taking in all of this. Slow down, back up, and tell me, from the beginning, what's happened since I left Frankfort."

She took a deep breath, trying to sort out the events that happened before he left from what had occurred since. "It seems Shirleene had some papers the murderer wants, and he thinks she left them with me. Since he searched my house and shop without finding them, he must have thought they were at your place, and—"

"What papers, Elayna?" he interrupted again. "I don't know anything about any papers."

"I have the papers, Court," she said. "They were in Shir-leene's orange juice carton in the refrigerator at the tearoom. They appear to be an architect's detailed drawings of downtown Frankfort, completely flooded by the river. Whit wanted me to give them to him to return to someone he thinks they belong to, but I want you to see them first."

"Elayna, what in the world is this all about?" he asked.

"I don't know," she said. "Court, what should I do? Should I turn them over to Dave Myers? Should I let Whit take them? If there's any way they could help clear Jayboy. . ."

"Just hang on to them, Elayna," he said. "I'm crossing into Georgia now. If I don't get caught in one of their speed traps, I should be home in a few hours. Then we'll decide what to do. Call Dave and tell him I'm on my way. See you soon, kid." He broke the connection.

Elayna hung up, then picked up the receiver again and dialed the police station.

"Dave," she said without preamble when Detective Myers came on the line, "was Shirleene's killer right- or left-handed?"

"Elayna?" he said quizzically. When she confirmed her iden-tity, he said, "I don't know. I'd have to check the coroner's re-port. Why?"

"Well, if the killer was right-handed, that would clear all left-handers, and vice versa, wouldn't it?"

He chuckled. "I get it! You think this information will sup-port your conviction that old Calvin is innocent. But, Elayna, if the killer was right-handed, that just places him in the category with almost everybody else. Yes, it would eliminate the lefties, but if your buddy is right-handed—"

"Dave, please humor me, just this once," she begged. "Oh, and the other reason I called. . .Court said to tell you he's on his way home. Do you need me over at his house?"

"Thanks, but that won't be necessary. Just tell Court to contact me as soon as he gets back. And, by the way, I've just been informed that the medical examiner found a trace of someone else's blood on Shirleene's hand and some skin under her fingernails. All we need are samples from old Calvin, and we can wrap up this case."

"I wish we could find him, Dave," she answered, "and prove to you—and to the world—that he is innocent."

The detective chuckled. "I'll check that report and get back with you, Elayna," he promised. She could hear him still chuckling as he hung up the phone.

Elayna didn't know how she could come up with a blood sample with Jayboy gone, but she thought it was worth a call to Doris. She picked up the phone again and dialed the Calvins' number, hoping that she hadn't left yet to help Leslie at the gift shop. When she heard the woman's familiar voice on the other end of the line, she said, "Doris, this is Elayna. I need your help. The police have a blood sample, probably from Shirleene's killer. If we could provide one from Jay, we could prove his innocence," she explained, knowing the woman had watched enough police shows on TV to understand what she meant.

"I saw on *Law and Order* once where the cops got a blood sample from a Band-Aid in a man's trash," Doris offered. "Hold on. I'll check Jay's trash can and the one in the bathroom."

When she came back on the phone, she said, "I'm sorry, Elayna. The trash has been emptied since he's been gone." Elayna thought she heard a catch in the woman's voice. "Where do you think he is, Elayna? I reckon he's too scared to come home. Poor baby!"

"Just hang in there, Doris," she said. "And let me know if you hear from him. I'll do the same for you." Then she added, "Doris, this is extremely important. Call me if you hear from him, not the police! I need to talk with Jay first."

"The police were here," Doris said. " 'Course, I hadn't seen him, so I had nothing to tell them. But, Elayna, the police believe he murdered Shirleene! They say he had her pin, and that there was blood on his shoe. You don't think he's guilty, do you?" It was a plea, more than a question.

"Of course not!" Elayna assured her. "Jay's not capable of the act that took Shirleene's life. You know that, Doris! He's gentle and loving, just like a child."

"Well, I don't think he could have done it," Doris answered. "But you know how strange he is sometimes. He wouldn't hurt anything on purpose. But he's always been so afraid of Shirleene. You don't think—?"

"Doris, no!" Elayna interrupted. "Get that thought out of your mind!"

"He's all I've got, Elayna," Doris said, and this time Elayna definitely heard tears in her voice. "My fifty-five-year-old baby. I've often wondered what would become of him when I'm gone. What's gonna become of him now, Elayna? He has no family but me."

"Doris, you know I will always make sure that Jay is taken care of," she promised. "And Whit Yancey has assured me that he will represent him in any legal proceedings he has to face, without charge."

"Pro bono," Doris said. "Thank Senator Yancey for me, for us, Elayna. And thank you, for being his friend all these years. You're the only friend he's ever had."

Elayna felt tears gathering and her throat begin to tighten. "We're going to get Jay out of this mess some way, Doris," she promised.

She broke the connection, then immediately dialed the number of the shop. When Leslie answered, she explained what she was after, mentioning Doris's tip about the Band-Aid.

"Elayna!" Leslie responded excitedly. "He cut his hand on the box cutter last week! And you know how Jay loves Band-Aids! Just like any kid. I always keep the printed ones here for him. You know, the Scooby Doos, the Tiggers. Road Runner is his favorite. He must have used a dozen on that one little cut, putting one on, taking it off, replacing it with a fresh one. Let me check the trash cans, Elayna, and I'll call you right back."

When Elayna answered the phone a few minutes later, there was disappointment in Leslie's voice. "The trash has already been hauled away by the city garbage collectors," she reported. "I'm sorry, Elayna."

"Oh, well, it was worth a try," Elayna said. "If you think of anything else, let me know."

She hung up the phone. *What do I do now? If only I could find him!*

The day stretched before her, until it was time to get ready to go to Mockingbird's with Whit. She had plenty of time to hunt for Jayboy, but she didn't know where to begin. He had left on the *Elayna*. He could be anywhere along the river by now, still trying to navigate the wild current, tied up at some landing, crashed into the rocks. There had been no report from the media of a boat crash, though, so it was likely that Jay was still alive, still trying to escape the mess in which he found himself.

Poor Jay! she thought. *He must be as confused and scared as any eight year old.* She wished she could comfort him, but until he was found, there was absolutely nothing she could do.

She hated those words! They were what the experts had said when meningitis claimed little Carrie Hunter, when Granny's stroke left her paralyzed, when Hunt disappeared. She prided herself on being able to solve problems, on being in control, on taking care of herself and everything around her. Being helpless like this was extremely frustrating.

The phone rang. It was Dave Myers. "I've looked at the report, Elayna. Our killer seems to have used both hands, but mostly the left," he admitted.

"Oh, thank you, Dave!" she exclaimed. "Jay is decidedly right-handed. He can't do anything with his left." Then she remembered. Although Jayboy always used his right hand to do any kind of work or to laboriously sign his name as she had taught him, he often picked up his fork and ate with his left. She didn't mention this, though. "Dave, if we just had blood and skin samples to compare with that found on Shirleene's hand and under her fingernails, I know Jay would be exonerated."

He grunted noncommittally. "You tell me how we're gonna get a blood sample from a chicken who has flown the coop," he said. "Look, Elayna, I don't hold a grudge against old Calvin. I know he knocked me down because he was scared and wanted to get away. There was nothing personal in it. But all the evidence points straight to him. If he's innocent, I'll be the first to congratulate him. If he's guilty, I'll be the first to try to get him locked up."

"I understand, Dave," she said. "Thanks."

She hung up again, still frustrated, still at a loss for what to do next. She wished Jayboy would contact her or Doris. She would find some way to help him. She would not give up her belief in his innocence, no matter how much circumstantial evidence piled up against him.

The fact that he sometimes used his left hand when he ate did not mean he had used both hands to kill Shirleene. If she had fought back, as the skin under her fingernails indicated, the killer might have switched hands instinctively, to protect the hand she was hurting. She knew the DNA of the skin and blood samples would clear Jayboy. But how could she provide them if she could not find him?

Chapter 61

Jayboy listened. All he could hear was the roaring of the river and the rustling of the leaves in the wind. The man still had not come back. He might, though, at any minute. Jayboy's stomach grumbled. Did he have time to get back to the boat to try to find something to eat?

He could see the dark water swirling by down below. Tugging at the boat. Making it pull against its rope. Slapping at the gangplank. Washing over it. Could he walk that wet, slippery plank in his slick Sunday shoes? Maybe he could take them off and walk barefoot.

He never had liked going barefoot. Not since the time he had stepped on a big old locust thorn and run it right into the side of his foot. It had hurt so bad! He had pulled it out, but he couldn't walk on that foot for weeks. Until Mac had heated his knife in the fire and poked a hole in the red, swollen place and let out all the poison. Doris had put salve and a clean bandage on it every night. Not a Band-Aid. A big bandage wrapped all around his foot. Finally it had healed. But he still had the scar. Right there under his ankle. And he never went barefoot after that. Not even on the soft grass of Liberty Hall's gardens.

Then he had a new thought. If he got on the boat, maybe he could start it. Maybe he could take it home to the landing below 'Layna's house. But then he realized that the river was running too fast. He couldn't take the 'Layna back upstream. The current was too strong. He would be carried away downstream to some far-off place.

Mac had taken him to Carrollton once to show him where the Kentucky River poured into the Ohio. Mac had told him the water would travel all the way down the Ohio to the Mississippi, then down the Mississippi to the Gulf of Mexico.

That's what would happen to him if he tried to take the boat back up river. The current would carry him all the way to Mexico. He shuddered to think what would happen to him then.

Chapter 62

Granny's clock struck five o'clock, followed, as always, by the chimes from the Presbyterian church. Elayna supposed she should proof the brochure before she had to get ready for Whit at 7:30. Then she could get it and Bill's fantastic pictures to the print shop first thing in the morning.

She kicked off her shoes, fixed a glass of ice water, and sat down at the kitchen table. She pulled the paste-up from its envelope, quickly proofed the cover, and then opened the brochure. As Elayna tried to read, her mind began to wander and the neat Bookman type marching starkly across the white page blurred into an image of Whit's burning dark eyes as he was telling her about his new religion.

Have I overreacted to his involvement in this New Age movement? she wondered. *Could we still find happiness together by agreeing to disagree about this one subject? Could I just continue to go to services across the street when I feel the urge, and let him go his own way?* She thought she could, but she didn't think that was what Whit had in mind. She felt sure he wanted more from her than passive acceptance. He would expect her to "grow toward godhood" with him.

Sighing, she refolded the brochure and laid it aside. She simply could not concentrate.

What are you going to tell Whit tonight? she asked herself. The thought of marrying him and becoming a part of the crowd she met at the Galt House appalled her. She could just imagine the two of them, through the years, attending meetings like that one, sharing the information they might have gained from dolphins or from ascended masters flying around in UFOs.

She reached for the magazines. If she was going to discuss this with Whit tonight, she needed to be sure she knew what she was talking about. She needed to be able to recognize the terms, and to understand the concepts.

First, she read an article by a leader of public education, extolling the virtues of the New-Age-oriented "confluent education" that was "sweeping the country." *Whatever that is,* she thought. The writer didn't explain. He went on to give a glowing report on the success of "values clarification" in schools across the nation.

She had read about that in the newspaper, where it had been labeled everything from "an insidious secular humanistic philosophy" to "the greatest thing since sliced bread." Task forces and committees had wrestled with guidelines for it ever since the Kentucky school system had been declared unconstitutional and the Kentucky Education Reform Act had been adopted by the legislature in 1990.

The way she understood it, students studying values clarification were taught to throw out traditional moral absolutes, such as the teachings of the Bible, and to trust their own feelings about right and wrong, to decide their own moral guidelines regarding truth or untruth. She had had no idea, though, how invasive it had become in the public schools—from kindergarten through high school—or that it was considered by New Agers as a first subtle step toward the spiritual humanism they espoused, the belief that man is his own god.

In one of the magazines, she discovered a statement by a former assistant secretary general of the United Nations that urged, "We must join our Hindu brethren and call henceforth our planet Brahma or the Planet of God." A footnote explained that "Brahma" was a major pantheistic Hindu deity.

As Alice said, "This is getting curiouser and curiouser." She continued reading about pantheistic nature worship of such things as the Sun, stars, trees, animals, the "Earth-mother," and the "Sky-father." Then she read a report about "world peace meditations" that sought to bring peace to the planet through gatherings much like the "harmonic convergence" events she remembered from the late 1980s, when hundreds of people formed huge circles, holding hands, and chanting "ohm" to bring the planets back into alignment and balance.

As she continued to leaf through the magazines, she imagined attending seminars and training sessions with Whit and Fortune 500 company and government employees, having their "right brains recharged," "their alpha waves enhanced," "their paradigms shifted," and, all in all, learning to "activate New Age higher consciousness." Or maybe she and Whit would be leading seminars, teaching less enlightened ones to "open up to their higher selves," to "become godlike through creative visualization," to practice Yoga techniques to "awaken the serpent power that lies dormant at the base of the spine."

She could envision her future catalogs featuring things advertised in the magazines—crystals, pyramids, ankhs, scarabs, ouija boards, magic potions, subliminal recordings to assist transcendental meditation, aids to mystical out-of-body experiences. *Witches' brooms,* she thought. *Shaman's fetishes.*

She could imagine herself as the wife of the governor of Kentucky, presiding over state functions in the capitol-turned-temple, leading the citizens of the Commonwealth away from their traditional religions in an enlightened "quest to become one with the cosmic god force," as Whit put it. It wasn't a role that appealed to her.

According to the magazines, though, she would have well-known company. Many articles in the publications were by or about famous personalities who had espoused New Age philosophies: Tina Turner, Linda Evans, Helen Reddy, John Denver, Marsha Mason, Shirley MacLaine, of course, and many others. They spoke readily of having spirit guides, of channeling, of automatic writing.

An article on the world-renowned Carl Jung, recognized as "a founding father of modern day psychologies," claimed that Jung admitted he was taught by a spirit named "Philemon," who walked and talked with him in his garden.

Elayna could see herself as a reluctant participant in some eternal occult croquet game, while the Red Guru yelled, "Off with her head!" For she was convinced that she never could accept these concepts that Whit was so eager to share with her. She always would be an outsider, resisting with all that was in her these Eastern philosophies that were so foreign to everything she had been taught to believe all her life.

Yet the thought of never seeing Whit again, of going through the years as a lonely widow without even the low-key relationship she had known with him, was equally unattractive. She had enjoyed their times together these past years—the ballets, the concerts, the plays, the dinners. She had been proud to be seen with the attractive senator, to be introduced as his friend. She had enjoyed their quiet times together. She knew she was not "in love" with him, the way she had been with Hunt, but she felt that they could have developed a deeply satisfying relationship, given time.

If only he had not become involved in this New Age movement! she thought with regret, laying the magazines aside.

She wished she had someone to advise her. Leslie would tell her to talk to God, or Jesus, about it. "We're not on a first-name basis, Les," she said aloud, "and it's too personal a subject to discuss with a casual acquaintance."

She wished things were different, but after all these years of trusting no one but herself, it was hard to reach out to someone else, even God. *Especially God,* she thought, as she rummaged through her closet to find something to wear to Mockingbird's.

She guessed she still held some long-buried resentment of a God who would allow Carrie and Hunt to be taken away from her. If God had loved her, REALLY loved her, He wouldn't have let those terrible things happen. He would have provided her with a "happily-ever-after" ending. She found that hard to forgive.

"What a friend we have in Jesus," she remembered Granny singing.

"I'm just not like you, Granny," she whispered. "I don't know God the way you do, or Leslie—or the way Court and Jimmy O'Brien know him. Maybe if I did, things would be different. But I'm out here on my own."

I'll just have to "play it by ear" tonight, she decided, gathering clean underwear and heading for the shower.

Chapter 63

Jayboy didn't know what time it was, but it was getting late. He knew he had to do something before the man came back. Maybe he could climb up the hill like the man had done. There must be a road up there somewhere. The man had said he had a car. Maybe he could find the road and get a ride with somebody back to town.

He knew how to hitch a ride. He and 'Layna had seen a movie once. At the theater down in the middle of town where they used to go every Saturday afternoon. The man had hitched rides all over the country. He would stand by the road and stick out his thumb. And somebody would stop their car, or their truck, and pick him up. Once, he got a ride in the back of a wagon with sheep in it. It was a funny movie.

Then he had seen another movie where a boy stood beside the road holding out his thumb. And a man in a big truck stopped and picked him up. He had acted friendly. Talking. Laughing. Offering the boy a drink out of his Thermos. Then he took the boy into the woods and killed him with a knife. Like the man had killed Shirleene. And he had left the boy out there alone in the woods. Dead. 'Layna said the man got caught and put in jail. But he hadn't watched any more of that movie. Because of the killing and the blood.

This was a lonely place. He was afraid to catch a ride with

some stranger. Anyway, there might not be many cars on the road. Maybe he would just walk. It might take days and days. He had no idea where he was, or how far it was back to town. He would have blisters on his heels from wearing his Sunday shoes. But it would be better than waiting here until he starved to death. Or until the man came back and shot him.

Jayboy climbed the hill and came out of the trees into a cornfield. *Corn! I love corn!* In the summer, Doris would buy it at the farmers' market at the edge of River View Park. She would get him to shuck it, and she would boil it on the cob. Then they would eat it with melting butter dripping down their chins. He reached eagerly for an ear left dangling from a stalk. He stripped the husks away and bit into the kernels. *Hard as a rock.* He threw the ear on the ground. Tears welled in his eyes. He was so hungry. And he had thought the corn would taste so good.

He stumbled out of the cornfield and into the remains of a garden, abandoned now to weeds and frost. If only he could find something the farmer had not harvested, something still good to eat.

Suddenly, Jayboy recognized the green tops of turnips growing in the very last row. *Mac used to raise turnip*s. He would pull them and store them in the shed where he kept his tools. Sometimes he would bring a mess of them to the house for Doris to cook. Jayboy made a face. He didn't like cooked turnips. But he loved the cool, crisp taste of raw turnip when Mac would slice off the top and scrape off a mouthful of the white vegetable for him with his pocket knife.

He pulled a turnip from the ground and wiped the clinging dirt off on his pants. He sliced the top off with his knife and scraped a bite into his mouth. It tasted so good! Cool. Moist. But scraping it took too long. He peeled the turnip, sliced it, and stuffed the whole thing into his mouth, slice by slice. Then he gathered all the turnips he could carry and took them back to his hiding place. He forgot to listen for the man to come back. He forgot his plan to find the road and follow it home. He was too busy feasting on raw turnips.

Chapter 64

I've always loved this old house," Elayna said, as Whit maneuvered the Mercedes into one of two vacant parking spaces beside a three-story brick mansion a few blocks from her house. "I knew somebody was restoring it, but I didn't know they were turning it into a restaurant."

Whit came around to open her door, and she got out, admiring a handsome black and white sign bearing a tall gray bird dressed in a green tuxedo that matched the deep hunter green of the shutters and front door. "Wonder why they called it Mockingbird's?" she mused.

"I have no idea," Whit answered, opening the green door and ushering her inside. A man wearing a tuxedo similar to the one on the sign came toward them.

"Do you think we're under-dressed, Whit?" she murmured, wishing she were carrying her silver evening bag instead of the oversized black leather purse she had chosen to hold Whit's magazines until she was ready to return them later tonight.

He looked her over, from her plain, street-length black silk dress and matching jacket to her three-inch black heels. "You look lovely," he said sincerely, "but I'm not sure about me!"

Elayna scrutinized his dark suit, white shirt, and printed red silk tie. "You look lovely, too," she said with a mischievous grin.

"Welcome to Mockingbird's," the man said. "Right this way."

Relieved to see that most of the other patrons were dressed much as she and Whit were, Elayna followed the maitre d', her heels sinking into the deep pile of a carpet in the same rich green as the front door. She took the upholstered chair he pulled out for her at a table draped in white linen in front of a window where green velvet drapes framed a view of the swollen river in the moonlight.

Past the protection of the earthen floodwall, she could see the muddy water already lapping at the restaurant's stone foundation. If the river didn't crest soon, it surely would invade the building. She shuddered to think of all the stinking yellow mud it would leave behind when it receded. *The owner might have been better advised to use hardwood or tile flooring,* she thought. It still would be a mess, but there would be more chance of salvage.

"Well," Whit broke into her thoughts, "is this place elegant enough?" His dark eyes gleamed in the light from white candles in pewter holders on either side of a pewter pot of violets.

Elayna dropped her purse beside her chair and picked up a green leather menu embossed with a silver mockingbird. "I'm starved!" she said, scanning the offerings inside, not yet ready to face Whit's reason for bringing her to this "elegant place."

Whit grinned. "I get the message: Eat first and talk later." He opened his menu. "What would you like, madame? The filet mignon? The prime rib? The lamb in mint sauce?" He stopped, and Elayna glanced up to see a frown between his eyes. She followed his gaze to the lower edge of the menu.

Trust in the Lord with all your heart, and lean not to your own understanding. In all your ways acknowledge him, and he shall direct your paths. Proverbs 3:5 and 6, she read silently.

Then a spotlight drew her attention to a small platform in the corner, where a woman in a silver lamé evening gown was seated at a small piano. She began to play a medley of soft background music that left plenty of room for conversation.

"Good evening," a white-coated waiter said. "Are you ready to order? The lamb is especially good tonight."

Elayna ordered the filet, with a salad and baked potato.

Whit sighed. "Ah, prime rib, thy name is cholesterol!" he said regretfully. "I'll have the lamb, and could I see the wine list?"

"I'm sorry, sir," the waiter said, "but we don't have a wine list. Mockingbird's serves coffee, tea, sodas, lemonade, and sparkling apple juice. May I get you one of those?"

"I'd like the apple juice," Elayna said quickly, noting the deepening scowl on Whit's face.

"Coffee. Black," Whit muttered.

The pianist continued to play as they sipped their drinks. Elayna sometimes thought she recognized a hymn, but the woman expertly swept tunes in and out of the medley too quickly for her to be sure.

A bearded man in evening attire joined the woman on the platform. "Good evening, ladies and gentlemen," he said into a handheld microphone. "Welcome to Mockingbird's. You may be wondering about the name of our little supper club. So let me introduce you to the man responsible, the owner of Mocking-bird's, Mr. Jimmy O'Brien!"

Elayna's sip of apple juice went down the wrong way. Surely she had misunderstood! But, no, the red-haired preacher, the former eighteen-wheeler driver she had thought of as an "old jeans and leather patches" kind of guy, was mounting the plat-form, looking very comfortable in his tuxedo. His grin buried freckles as he took the mike from the bearded man.

"If you're from around here, folks, you probably are familiar with our mockingbird," he began, as the pianist played softly in the background. "No doubt you've heard his 'poor-johnny-one-note' songs without paying them much attention. His song is monotonous, unappealing—until he somehow connects with the melody of a master singer like the wild canary. Then he becomes a virtuoso whose trills rival those of the canary itself."

Elayna stole a glance at Whit, but he was absorbed in the Irish preacher's lyrical story.

"Friends, like the mockingbird, you and I each have a song to sing," Jimmy O'Brien went on, "but it's only when our spirit connects with the Spirit of the Master, through the reconciliation provided by His Son, Jesus Christ, that our lives become the symphony of praise and worship we were meant to sing. Only then can we experience the 'exquisite pleasure of His eternal presence in our lives.'" He looked out over the crowd. "If anyone would like to discuss this with me, just tell your waiter, and I will meet with you in private," he invited. "Now," he finished with a freckle-swallowing grin, "enjoy your visit to Mockingbird's!" He handed the mike back to the bearded man and left the stage.

The bearded man began to sing, in a pleasant baritone voice, about an old violin being auctioned for a few dollars until the master violinist tuned and played it.

Elayna looked at Whit. He was watching the singer, his expression noncommittal, except for a small frown set between his eyes. He caught her watching him and smiled wryly. "I'm sorry," he said. "I had no idea we would be subjected to propaganda here. Do you want to leave?"

She shook her head. "As I said, I'm starved, and here come our salads."

"All right," he agreed reluctantly, as the waiter set frosted plates heaped with greens and colorful vegetables before them.

Engrossed in eating, Elayna didn't see Jimmy O'Brien making his way among the tables until he stopped beside her.

"Well, good evening, Elayna Evans!" he said.

"Good evening," she answered. "You. . .ah. . ."

". . .clean up pretty good?" he finished for her, his grin widening. "How are you, sir?" he said to Whit, extending his hand. "Jimmy O'Brien."

Whit stood to shake hands. "Whitley Yancey," he responded.

"I'm sorry!" Elayna apologized for not introducing them. "I just wasn't. . ."

A waiter appeared. "Could you come to the kitchen, Mr. O'Brien?" he asked. "We have a problem."

"Of course," he said. He turned back to Elayna and Whit. "Excuse me, please. Maybe I'll see you later, depending on the severity of the crisis brewing in the kitchen."

"The river's still rising, and we need to. . ." she heard the waiter say before they disappeared through an arch to the left of the stage.

"You obviously know our host," Whit said. His expression was puzzled. "He looked familiar, but I can't think where I've seen him."

"He preached Shirleene's funeral," she reminded him.

His expression cleared. "Oh, yes, the self-righteous preacher who said we all must. . ." He stopped while the waiter served their food. Then he abandoned the topic, as he cut and tasted the lamb, chewing slowly, evaluating. He nodded, gave her a wink of approval, and they ate in silence for several minutes.

"Elizabeth Moore has an art exhibit at the capitol," he said. "Maybe we can go sometime this weekend. There's a unique view of the old railroad tunnel, and some watercolor night scenes I know you'll like."

She smiled noncommittally. Whit knew she was a big Elizabeth Moore fan, but she wasn't sure how he would feel about taking her anywhere after tonight.

He finished the lamb and pushed his plate aside. "Dessert?"

She shook her head. "I'm going to have to go on a diet, if you keep feeding me this way!" she said, laughing. Then she wondered sadly if they ever would share another evening like this.

He looked her over approvingly. "You're perfect, Elayna," he said, taking both of her hands in his. "Which brings me to my proposal. Have you thought about it?"

She looked down at their hands together on the table, hers small and fine-boned, his pleasantly strong. *Could we build a satisfying life together?* she wondered wistfully. She would so love to have someone to share things with again. Then she remembered the magazines tucked away in her purse. She drew her hands away from his and folded them in her lap. Whit's smile faded as he realized the significance of the move.

"Whit, I have the greatest admiration and respect for you," she began hesitantly. "I think I could love you, but. . ."

"What is it, Elayna?" His dark eyes studied hers. "We've spent many pleasant hours together. And I promise you, I'll do everything in my power to make you happy."

She nodded, glad he could not see the nervous twisting of her fingers beneath the overhanging tablecloth. "I believe you would, Whit. It's just. . ." She took a deep breath. "I read your magazines," she said, reaching into her purse and drawing them out. The flyer she had taken from the car windshield fell onto the table.

Whit looked at it, then at her. His expression was guarded.

"Are you involved in this 'psychic fest,' Whit?" she asked, laying the magazines on the table, with the flyer on top of them.

He shook his head and dropped his gaze. "No, Elayna, I don't attend these celebrations, though I have given the group legal advice on occasion. But I keep a low profile locally."

"I understand that you were leading a transcendental meditation rally on the capitol steps not long ago," she said. "That's pretty high profile!"

He smiled. "Everybody's into TM. All the major corporations, even the federal government requires employees to attend such seminars periodically."

She ignored that. "Did you give these 'psychic fest' people legal advice when that celebrant was found dead of mysterious causes last year?"

"I believe that girl's so-called death was ruled accidental," he said evenly.

"Someone told me she was a sacrifice, Whit," she insisted. "If that's true, it was murder or at least suicide. And apparently it was more than a 'so-called' death. She is dead, isn't she?"

He shrugged his shoulders. "Death is an illusion, Elayna, merely a transition from one stage of life to another. That girl's soul may have known she needed that death experience to advance her karma, and so she became, either consciously or subconsciously, a willing sacrifice. Or perhaps in some past life, she had murdered someone, so that she had to be murdered in a subsequent life to balance the karma."

Elayna stared at him in disbelief. *Do people actually believe this stuff?* Obviously, Whit did. His dark eyes burned with conviction.

"Don't you understand, Elayna, that the soul is immortal?" he explained patiently. "Therefore, it can never die. It just keeps reincarnating. So there really is no such thing as 'death.'"

She broke the magnetic hold of his eyes and looked down at the magazines she had dropped on the table between them, where moments ago their hands had rested together. "'I am evolving into the god I was always meant to be'?" she quoted. "I'm sorry, Whit, I just can't accept all that."

He leaned across the table. "Elayna, we will create a perfect world."

Vaguely, she was aware that the bearded man had returned to the platform to sing softly about an old rugged cross.

Whit's lip curled. "When we reach the planetary pentecost, we will have no need of the Christian's angry God who demands blood sacrifices for inherited sin," he said. "Those who are incapable of understanding the god concept as we do will be removed."

Elayna shivered involuntarily. " 'Removed'?" she asked. "How?"

He smiled reassuringly. "We are not a violent group, Elayna, or the New World Order would be no better than the present one, would it? No, the purging will be done by a series of spiritually controlled cosmic changes," he explained.

She hugged herself, suddenly cold. "How many are in your movement, Whit?"

"Thousands," he answered with satisfaction. "But the entire world is being prepared to accept the concepts. Everything from cartoons to prime-time movies are full of magic, witchcraft, mysticism, reincarnation, encounters with the spirit world, quantum leaps. Hardly a man, woman, or child in America does not know and use the terminology. Even kindergartners are being taught transcendental meditation and how to follow spirit guides. When we are ready, the people will be ready to make that quantum leap."

"I'm so sorry, Whit," she said with real regret, "but there's just no way that I can be a part of all that."

He stared at her for several seconds. "I had to be sure, Elayna," he said finally. His voice was controlled, but a deep sadness shadowed his eyes in the candlelight.

He summoned their waiter, paid the bill, and, with a hand under her elbow, led her out of the restaurant. He opened the car door for her, went around to the driver's side, got in, and drove her home in silence. He saw her to her front door and unlocked it for her.

"Tell Court I'd like to go over those papers with him, when you hear from him," he said impersonally.

She watched him walk back to the car, her mind a whirling

kaleidoscope of relief and regret. Whit was the only man who had stirred a spark in her since Hunt had disappeared. Now she had shattered whatever they might have had, and he had stepped over the pieces and walked out of her life.

It's not too late! she thought. *I can say I'm sorry, that I want to try!* Surely their years of pleasant companionship would earn her another chance. But, somehow, she couldn't do it. The differences between them were just too great. Still, it seemed that she should say something.

"Thanks for dinner," she called as he opened the car door. "I'll try to make the art exhibit." Then she felt her face flush. What a stupid thing to say, after what they'd just been through.

"Please do," he answered coldly. He got into the car and was gone before she could think of anything else to say.

Chapter 65

Before he could make up his mind what to do, Jayboy heard the man coming back. He slid down the bank, crossed the deck of the boat, and went into the cabin.

Now he could see the man through the broken window, sitting under the light at the table with a brown paper package in front of him. Where he and 'Layna and Hunt and little Carrie Hunter had sat. Eating pizza. Or hotdogs. Or scrambled eggs and bacon. Playing Monopoly. Playing checkers. Telling stories. Where he and Court and 'Layna and Annie had sat playing chess.

He liked chess. He didn't really understand all the rules and the moves. But he liked the knights. He was a knight. Well, not just any old knight. He was the special knight that protected the Princess of the Kingdom of Dandelion. Her favorite. 'Layna had said so. She had told him to kneel in front of her. And she had touched him on both shoulders with a branch from the boxwoods. Then she had said, "I name thee Knight of the Golden Scepter." And she had made him a knight's hat. And a sword.

The man took some sticks and wires out of the brown paper package. He laid them on the table. Then he took a knife out of his pocket and began to cut and splice. Like he had seen Mac do many times. But never with dynamite!

He knew it was dynamite. Or something like it. Just like in

277

the cowboy movies Mac had watched. Where the robbers blew up the railroad tracks to stop the train. Or the miners blew a passage through the rock to get to the gold.

The man had made three bundles of sticks and wires. Was he going to blow up the *'Layna?* Why would he blow up a perfectly good boat? Then he knew. The man had said he wanted him on the boat! He was the one he wanted to blow up! That's why he kept looking for him. He wanted 'Layna, too.

He saw the man get up and pick up one bundle. He went toward the back of the boat where Jayboy could not see him. Then he came back without the dynamite. He picked up another bundle and carried it out of sight. Then he came back for the last bundle. The biggest. He carried it to the front of the boat and attached it to something inside a cabinet.

Jayboy wished he knew what the man was going to do. He wished he could get the man's phone and call 'Layna. Tell her something awful was about to happen to her boat. To her knight. She would know what to do. The Princess of Dandelion always knew what to do.

Chapter 66

Knowing she would not be able to sleep after Whit left, Elayna changed into her favorite faded blue sweatsuit and went back to the kitchen. She might as well finish proofing the paste-up and have it ready to go back to the print shop in the morning.

She opened a cabinet, rejected Whit's Irish Creme coffee, and chose Jimmy O'Brien's Earl Grey tea. She emptied a packet of Sweet 'n' Low into a mug and waited for the water to boil.

Then, with her tea and the brochure, she sat down at the table. Quickly, she proofed the cover and opened the pamphlet.

She read through the first column again, then the second. As she began the final column, the doorbell shrilled its tinny signal.

Elayna glanced at her watch and saw that it was after eleven. Should she just ignore the bell? But, surely, at this time of night, the summons must be important.

Then the thought struck her that it might be Whit, and her heart skipped. Had he changed his mind about. . .about what? He certainly wasn't going to give up his religion. And she wasn't going to share it. So they would be right back where they had left things earlier this evening. Did she want to see him? Strangely, she realized that she did, in spite of everything.

She was halfway down the hall before she remembered Shirleene's murderer. Then she laughed. "Do murderers ring doorbells?" She supposed he might, to trick her into opening the door. "Who's there?" she called cautiously.

"It's me, Elayna!" a muffled voice answered. "Jimmy O'Brien."

She unlocked the door, half relieved it wasn't the killer or Whit, half aggravated at the preacher's late-night intrusion.

"I'm sorry," he apologized with a freckle-swallowing grin as the door swung open. "I know I should have called first. But you left these in the restaurant, and I wanted to talk with you about them."

Elayna saw that he held Whit's magazines in his hand. Whit must have left them lying on the table where she had dropped them. In their preoccupation, neither of them had noticed.

"I didn't know if you'd still be up, but when I saw your light on, I figured I wouldn't be disturbing you too much," he finished lamely. "May I come in for just a moment?"

Elayna opened the storm door and motioned him in with her other hand, letting her lack of verbal welcome convey her irritation.

He walked down the hall ahead of her and stopped by the bar between the kitchen and the keeping room. He dropped the magazines on the bar.

"New Age," he said. "It sounds exciting, enlightened, doesn't it? What people don't realize is that it isn't new at all. It's the same old lie Satan used to deceive Eve in the Garden of Eden."

"It is?" Elayna said, feeling incredibly stupid.

He nodded. " 'Has God said you will surely die if you eat of the fruit of this tree? You won't die! You will become as gods, knowing good and evil,' " he quoted sarcastically. He flicked the cover of the top magazine with his fingernail. "Same old lie."

"The magazines belong to a friend," she explained. "I guess he's trying to convert me." She tried to laugh. Then, suddenly exhausted with the emotional strains of the evening, she snapped,

"But I really don't see that it's your concern whose they are or what I think about them."

He held up one hand to ward off her anger. "You're right, of course," he agreed quickly. "I just wanted to warn you to be careful. The philosophies are very persuasive: 'We are all seeking the same thing. Only the narrow-minded Christians stand in the way of true ecumenism, insisting their way is the only one.' "

"You sound just like Whit!" she exclaimed, chilled by the similarity of his sarcastic words to Whit's almost fanatical ones.

"But Jesus said, in John 14, 'I am the way, the truth, and the life. No one comes to the Father except through me,' " he reminded her. "And we come to him on an individual basis, not as a cell in some universal brain, or whatever they call it." He threw a derisive glance at the magazines.

She raised both hands. "I surrender!" she said, finally able to laugh. She was relieved to see that he laughed with her. "I assure you, I have no interest in these magazines. Whit insisted that I read them. I attempted to return them tonight, but he wasn't very happy with me when we left your restaurant, and I suppose he forgot them."

"By the way, how did you like Mockingbird's?" he asked eagerly.

"It's a lovely place, and the food was delicious."

"And the 'food for thought'?" His eyes studied hers.

"The pianist was exceptionally good," she hedged, "and the baritone has a pleasant voice."

"It's been a dream of mine for a long time. It came to me one evening as I was driving my rig down I-75. I would open a quality restaurant where, as people's physical appetites were fed, I could also feed their souls, or at least plant a seed that would make them think about their need for a personal relationship with their Creator."

Suddenly uncomfortable, Elayna moved to place the bar between them.

"So many people live out their lives, as I was doing a few years ago, with some vague idea that there is a God," he continued earnestly. "Often they even believe, on some superficial level, that God sent His Son to be the Savior of the world. But they have no consciousness of the fact that they need to accept that salvation on a personal level, that Jesus Christ did not suffer and die for the world in general, but for each person in it, on an individual basis." He stopped and stood looking at her, as if waiting for some response.

" 'A blood sacrifice for inherited sin,' " she repeated Whit's words of a few moments ago.

Jimmy O'Brien looked at her sharply. "Hebrews 9:22 says that 'without the shedding of blood there is no forgiveness.' But it's not 'inherited sin,' Elayna," he corrected. "It's the inherent tendency to sin, to rebel against our Creator and become our own gods. We're all guilty of it in one way or another."

I'm not! she thought defensively. Then she knew it wasn't true. She had no desire to be God up there somewhere ruling the universe, but she did like being in control of her own life. She guessed she hadn't done such a great job of it, though.

"Well, thanks for bringing the magazines by. I'll see that Whit gets them," she said, hoping he would take the hint and leave.

"I never really thought about a personal relationship with my Creator until that day in Afghanistan," he said, his thoughts obviously miles—as well as years—away from her curt dismissal. "But when Doc. . ." He shook his head, as though to clear it. "I'm sorry, Elayna. I didn't mean to open old wounds for you." He took a step, as if to go.

Elayna held out a hand to stop him, wanting to hear more

about Hunt's last days. She had loved him so! And she had spent so many weary years wondering what had happened to him. She let her thoughts drift back to those last days they had spent together, seeing again his anguish over Carrie Hunter.

"It was the death of our only child that destroyed him," she said softly.

"And that saved him," Jimmy O'Brien said.

She looked up at him. "Saved him? What do you mean? He's dead, isn't he?" She recalled Whit's reference to the girl's "so-called death."

"Physically, yes. But he came to identify greatly with a God who had suffered as he watched his only child die."

"But he was so bitter toward God!" she broke in. "What changed his mind?"

The preacher pulled out a bar stool and perched on it. "We had a sort of self-appointed chaplain who held services for the men when there was a lull in the fighting," he continued. "There being little else to do, we attended, Doc and I. One day, the chaplain spoke very graphically of God's suffering as He watched His only Son die for our sins. I could see that his words were having a tremendous impact on Doc. After the service, he borrowed a little New Testament from somebody and nearly read the print off of it."

"And that changed him?" She couldn't believe it. Hunt had loved and respected Granny, but he had refused all her efforts to comfort him. He had left his wife, his profession, his friends, and his family to wallow in his bitterness. And now Jimmy O'Brien was sitting there telling her that the words of a total stranger and some ink on a page had been able to reach him?

" 'God hurt when He watched His only Son die on that cross for me, Jimmy-O,' " he told me. We had two Jimmy's in our company, and he always called me 'Jimmy-O,' " he explained, with a grin. Then his face grew grave. "The raw pain exposed in Doc's eyes was terrible," he went on. "I was relieved when he covered them with his hands."

Elayna nodded. How well she remembered the pain in Hunt's eyes!

" 'Oh, God, it hurt so bad!' he cried," Jimmy O'Brien continued, "and I knew he was no longer speaking in the abstract, but out of the very depths of his own soul. 'The trust in my baby's eyes that I would make her better,' he agonized. 'The knife that twisted inside of me as I stood there, powerless. The unbelief in Elayna's eyes when I failed.' "

"I never blamed him. But he could not forgive himself," Elayna said sadly.

"He made a great effort to gain control then," the red-haired preacher went on. " 'I watched my child die, just as God watched Jesus on that cross,' he said. 'I know what it cost Him. How can we escape, Jimmy-O, if we ignore a salvation bought at so great a price?' He left me then to go talk with the chaplain. When he came back, he said, 'I'm going home, Jimmy-O! I've got to share all this with Elayna.' "

Jimmy O'Brien looked down at his clenched hands, then spread them on the counter. "It just didn't work out that way," he said. "There was a new offensive, with so much to do, so many wounded." He sat there, lost in his memories.

Elayna fixed him a cup of tea and set it in front of him. "It's Earl Grey. With cream and sugar."

He looked up at her, and for a moment she was afraid he was going to cry. He took the cup, closed his eyes, and drank. When he raised his head again, his eyes were tear-free. He glanced at the clock, drained the cup, and set it on the bar.

"It's nearly midnight, Elayna. I'll get out of here. I'm sorry to barge in so late. It's just that when I found those magazines on your table, at your place actually. . ."

"I'm not into Whit's Eastern religions," she broke in, "if that's what you mean. In fact, that's what. . ." She stopped. It was none of Jimmy O'Brien's concern what her rejection of Whit's beliefs had cost her.

She wasn't completely convinced it had been worth the price. She and Whit probably could have had a good life together, if she hadn't been so bent on defending traditional religion. *And what has it ever done for me?* she thought bitterly. She had sought desperately for answers, for peace when Carrie Hunter died and when Hunt left. Granny had said she would find peace when she stopped running, surrendered it all to God, and just rested in Him. But, somehow, she hadn't been able to accept Granny's simple solution.

Finally, like an oyster building a pearl around a painful grain of sand, she had developed a numbness that allowed her to function somewhere outside her grief. But she had no real peace, any more than Hunt had, not as her grandmother or Leslie knew it. *In fact, I have nothing,* she thought resentfully. Even her role as the wife of the absent Dr. Hunter Evans had been taken away by Jimmy O'Brien's news of his death.

News? she scoffed silently. The "news" was eight years old—stale, like the taste in her mouth. "I'm afraid I'm not very good company tonight," she apologized. "I'm just. . ." She hesitated.

"Are you all right?" he asked, a warm concern in his eyes.

Suddenly she longed to break open her tightly controlled, self-reliant shell, and expose the bleak emptiness inside. Like little Carrie begging for a kiss on a scraped knee, she wanted this Irish preacher to "make it all better." The temptation to reach out for whatever comfort he could offer her was so great that she reeled with its impact and reached out to the bar to steady herself.

"Elayna, what's wrong?" he asked immediately. "Are you ill?"

She steeled herself against her longing to sink down into the soft warmth of his concern, to let someone carry her for awhile, as Carrie had sunk into sleep in the car, secure in the knowledge that her father would carry her safely to her bed when they reached home. *I can take care of myself,* she thought. She could face the world and make it back down, without human or divine help. Hadn't she done it for more than ten years now?

"I'm fine," she assured him. "It's been a long day, filled with momentous decisions. I'm just. . ." She faked a yawn. "Exhausted."

"And here I am keeping you up," he apologized again. "I'm so sorry. I need to get back to the restaurant, anyway. We're moving everything to the second floor, just in case. We're even taking up the carpet. I hear this river mud stains and stinks forever."

He headed for the door, then turned back. "Are you sure you're all right?" An uncertain frown creased his brow.

"I'm fine," she repeated, forcing a smile.

"If you need me. . ." he began.

"I'll call you," she promised. "Thanks."

When he had gone, she sat down on the stool where he had sat, laid her head on her arms, and wept.

Chapter 67

The man was rummaging through 'Layna's cupboards again. He put a pan on the stove, then opened a can and dumped something from it into the pan. He opened drawers until he found a big spoon to stir what he had put in the pan.

Then Jayboy could smell what the man was cooking. It was. . . He took a deep breath. Spaghetti and meatballs. He was sure of it. Sometimes 'Layna would fix spaghetti and meatballs when they came out on the boat at this time of year. The air would get cool, and the hot food would warm them up as they traveled home in the early dark.

Jayboy's empty stomach growled. He whimpered. He was so hungry! He could almost taste the tangy tomato sauce. He could feel the strings of spaghetti sliding down his throat, making his stomach feel warm and full. Not like the cold, hard turnips.

He'd been so happy to find the turnips sticking up through the weeds in somebody's garden. He'd eaten all that he had been able to stuff in his pockets. Before the man came back and he'd had to hide again. They had filled the empty space in his stomach for awhile. He even had wished for more. Until they gave him a stomachache. Now, just to remember them made him sick.

He could see the man dipping the food into one of 'Layna's heavy brown bowls. He opened the spoon drawer again and took out a small spoon this time. He put it in the bowl and then walked out on deck, carrying 'Layna's bowl by the handle with his right hand and holding a flashlight with his left. He shone the light on the bowl filled with spaghetti and meatballs.

"Hey, Loony Toons!" he called. "Want some supper?"

Jayboy swallowed hard. His stomach growled again. He started down out of the tree. Then he knew. It was a trick to get him back on the boat. Where the man could shoot him. Or blow him up! He shifted his position, but he stayed in the tree. Watching.

The man set the bowl down on the deck. He shone the light over it again. Then he went back inside, taking the light.

Jayboy still could see the bowl in the light from the cabin doorway. He couldn't take his eyes off it! His stomach begged for it. His mouth watered. He felt sick with emptiness.

Then the boat heaved and the bowl slid across the deck! What if it slid off into the muddy water lapping greedily at the boat? The boat heaved again and the bowl slid back toward the cabin. Jayboy sighed in relief. But he knew the bowl would slide again.

He had to have that food! He was starving! His mind raced. How could he get that bowl without the man seeing him?

Chapter 68

With the radio for company, Elayna spent Friday morning trying to bring some order back to her office upstairs. That done, she picked up her cleaning supplies and reached to turn off the radio, then stopped, as a news bulletin came on.

"The latest development in the case of the Dandelion Killer is the ransacking of City Commissioner Courtney Evans's home," the announcer said. "The husband of murder victim Shirleene Evans, the commissioner was in Florida at his parents' home when the break-in occurred. Because of new incriminating evidence discovered in the investigation of the break-in, according to reliable sources at the police department, Evans has been asked by police to return immediately to Frankfort. He is, however, reported to be traveling under his own recognizance. No other information is available at this time. Stay turned to this station for further develop—"

Angrily, Elayna snapped off the radio. *What new incriminating evidence?* Court had answered the police's questions, and never, to her knowledge, had he actually been a suspect in Shirleene's murder. He had talked with Dave Myers before leaving for Florida, and been given his blessing. And he hadn't been "asked to return." He was on his way home before he even knew Myers was trying to contact him.

What could have been found at Court's house that has the police wanting to question him? The murder weapon had been found beside Shirleene's body. There never had been any doubt that her attacker had used one of the kitchen knives from the tearoom. What could have been found in Court's home that would link him to the crime?

She picked up the phone, dialed the police station, and asked for Detective Myers. "Dave, it's Elayna," she said. "What's this about Court being asked to return to Frankfort because of 'new incriminating evidence'?"

"I can't discuss that, Elayna," he replied. "There are just a couple of questions we need to ask. I'm sure Court can explain it all. Anyway, I don't want that story out until I can talk with Court."

"Dave, I just heard it on the radio," she informed him, "attributed to 'reliable sources at the police department.'"

He swore. "I'm gonna clean a few clocks around here when I find out who leaked it," he vowed. "That's supposed to be strictly confidential. Did they identify the evidence?"

"No," she answered. "They suggested that we stay tuned."

Myers swore again. "I might as well tell you before you hear it on the evening news. We found the missing earring Shirleene was wearing that night," he said. "It was in Court's coat pocket."

Elayna gasped. "Are you saying that Court is now a suspect? You know him, Dave. Do you think he's capable of doing what the murderer did to Shirleene?"

"Most of us are capable of doing about anything, Elayna, given the right circumstances," he answered cynically. "He could have surprised her with Berryman, or somebody else. You know there were many candidates. . . ."

"But, Dave, Court had known about Shirleene's infidelities

for years," she interrupted. "I don't understand it, but he still loved her. Deeply."

"He could have just lost it, Elayna. It obviously was a crime of intense passion."

"I can no more believe Court did this terrible thing than I can believe Jayboy did it. Be looking for someone else to accuse of Shirleene's murder, Dave. C. J. Berryman, for instance. He's left-handed. Did you know that?" she added.

He grunted. "Every time I get a suspect you try to prove he's not guilty!" Myers said. "Will you please let me wrap up this case?" He laughed, then said seriously, "I don't believe Court is our killer, Elayna, but I have to ask the questions. It's my job."

She hung up, feeling better knowing that the story had not come from Myers, but still angry at whoever had shared it with the media. She was sure Court could explain the earring in his coat pocket, but it was one more embarrassment for him.

She picked up the phone again, dialed Court's cell phone, and got a busy signal. She waited a few minutes, then dialed again.

"Elayna!" Court said when he heard her voice. "I just talked with Dave. He says they found Shirleene's earring in my coat pocket. I remember picking it up that night at the tearoom. It was lying on top of the wall telephone. You know how she always took off that right earring when she talked on the phone? She must have made a phone call just before she was attacked. Maybe she was confronted by the killer before she could put the earring on again. Anyway, I picked it up just as Dave called us. With the excitement of following the footprints, I forgot about it. Then with the funeral and leaving for Florida, I never thought of it again until Dave told me they had found it."

"I remember seeing you pick up something, Court," she said, "just before Myers yelled for us. But I never saw what it was, and with all that happened afterward, I, too, forgot it. Anyway," she went on, "doesn't that explain the earring in your pocket?"

"If they believe me," he answered. "Dave seemed a little skeptical."

"Where are you now?" she asked, hearing the tiredness in his voice.

"About an hour and a half from Knoxville. I should be home in five or six hours," he said. "I may take a short break. I'm getting pretty tired, and a cup of coffee might help. If it doesn't, I may spend the night somewhere."

"Please do that, Court. I'll see you when you get here. And I'll vouch for your story, though I think Myers has begun to doubt everything I say. He says I'm trying to deny him suspects."

She could hear Court's tired chuckle as she broke the connection. She sighed, wishing there was some way she could settle all this for Court, for Jay.

She wondered if there was anything else at the tearoom that might clear both Court and Jayboy. Was there some as-yet-undetected clue to the murderer's identity? She still had the key Court had given her on the night of the murder. She could go back to the tearoom to search.

She put on the gray jacket from the hook by the keeping room door, got the key to the tearoom from her purse, and put it in her pocket. She unlocked the keeping room door and was reminded that she would have to stain the unfinished wood of the new door frame soon. She locked the door behind her and dropped that key in her other pocket.

The air was crisp with a distinct smell of autumn, stirred by a breeze that encouraged her to zip the jacket from bottom to top and stuff her hands in the pockets. She turned left at the end of the Bar Center wall, walked quickly down Sutterlin Lane to the intersection with Broadway, and turned right. Another half block, and she was standing in front of the Gypsy Tearoom.

There was a busy hum of traffic behind her, a couple of blocks away down near the Capital Plaza Hotel and state office buildings. A car came down Wilkinson and passed under the railroad trestle, without a glance her way from its occupants. Halfway down the next block of Broadway, a woman led two children hurriedly toward town. An old man shuffled up Wilkinson toward West Main. A cat napped on the sidewalk in front of the antique store across the street. None of them showed the least interest in a woman standing in front of the scene of a recent murder, with a key in her hand.

Elayna stepped over the sagging yellow police tape, unlocked the tearoom door, pushed it open, and went inside. Again, her senses were assaulted by the sharp, bitter smell of charred wood and cloth, the incredible sight of broken glass and mutilated furnishings. She flipped the light switch beside the door, but the low-hanging wooden chandeliers remained dark. She assumed that, after the fire, the electrical service had been shut off.

The late afternoon sunlight from the kitchen window where Whit had raised the blind the other day was the only light in the building. In the dimness, she stared at the eerie chalked outline that marked the spot where Shirleene's mutilated body had fallen.

What am I doing here? she asked herself silently. *The police have thoroughly searched this place.* The murder weapon had been wiped clean of fingerprints, and everything else in the room bore too many prints to be helpful. Court had the missing earring. The police had the dandelion pin they had taken from Jayboy. She had the papers Shirleene had hidden in the refrigerator. *What else can there be?*

Suddenly, she sensed something behind her. She whirled around, but there was nothing there. *Nothing visible, anyway,* she thought, shivering in the dim light that barely penetrated the tearoom's dark interior.

Somewhere she had read that the restless spirit of a murder victim sometimes hovered near the place where the crime had occurred until the killer was brought to justice. Did Shirleene's troubled spirit haunt this spot, waiting for someone to avenge her violent death?

"Shirleene?" she whispered. She didn't really believe the dead woman's spirit was here, but in the tearoom's ghostly atmosphere, anything seemed possible.

"Don't be ridiculous!" she scolded herself aloud, heading for the door, feeling the cold breath of evil on the back of her neck. She slammed the door, locked it, and, to avoid the isolation of Sutterlin Lane, fled down Wilkinson Boulevard.

What a fool I am, running like a kid from a haunted house, or like Jayboy from his dreaded blackness, Elayna thought, as she let herself in her back door. It felt good, though, to be back home, away from the scene of her sister-in-law's murder.

She showered and dressed in clean jeans and a denim shirt, slipped her feet into comfortable loafers, and fixed a grilled cheese sandwich and a bowl of tomato soup. With a glass of iced tea, she sat down at the table where she had left the brochure half proofed the night before, when she had been interrupted by Jimmy O'Brien ringing her doorbell.

He's a strange one, full of contradictions, this Irishman who drinks English tea, she mused. She could see why he and Hunt had become friends in Afghanistan, but his almost intimate knowledge of her, gained through that friendship, made her feel at a disadvantage.

She wondered what Hunt would have thought of her interaction with this man he had influenced so strongly. What would he have thought of Jimmy O'Brien's blunt declaration, "I guess I fell in love long ago with another man's wife, or with the image his words created."

Resolutely, she pushed away thoughts of the red-haired preacher and tried to focus her attention on the brochure and her supper, but it was no use. She simply wasn't in the mood for either. Again, she laid the brochure aside, got up, threw the remaining half of her sandwich in the garbage, and poured the rest of the soup down the drain. Carrying her glass of tea, she moved restlessly to the keeping room window.

It was dark outside now. Beyond the patio, the thin light of a cantaloupe-slice moon glinted on the muddy water lapping at the edge of her back yard. The house had never flooded, but the water was closer than she had ever seen it. Should she start moving things upstairs?

A faint swirling of mist hung over the water, and there were almost no stars. *Another perfect night for hauntings,* she thought, *but if there's a shadow out there tonight, I have no hopes left that it might be Hunt.*

She left the keeping room and went to look out the living-room window, over toward Liberty Hall. All she could see of the tall Georgian mansion was a vague gray outline against the black sky. No light fell from Laura's windows onto the street below. She turned toward the gardens. They were as black as the inside of a cave.

All at once, she felt the isolation of the lonely house between the floodwall and the reaching river. For company, she turned on the television and watched Fox News awhile. Then she began to watch a rerun of a favorite Agatha Christie movie, but she could not concentrate on it. She heard Granny's clock and then the church bells chime eleven o'clock.

Again, she looked out the keeping room window, then moved to the living room and peered over toward the gardens. The moon had disappeared, but flickering lights moved in the darkness.

Another nighttime celebration? What's going on over there? Suddenly, she had to know.

She reached for her gray jacket, then thinking it might be better if she wore something darker that would merge with the shadows, she took a hooded navy blue raincoat from the closet. Slipping it on, she put her flashlight in one pocket and her cell phone in the other.

Remembering the intruder who had entered her house last time, she double-checked the front door and found it locked and bolted. She went out the newly repaired back door, locked it, and dropped the key into her pocket with the phone.

Elayna moved silently around the back corner of the house and across the yard. From the end of the white plank fence, she could see candle flames moving in the back corner of the gardens. *They must be carried by figures dressed in black to blend with the night.* All she could see were the candles and some disembodied faces and hands.

Quickly, she moved away from the white fence and into the edge of the trees. Skirting the encroaching water, she edged from tree to tree until she stood behind a huge dark trunk that she thought would hide her completely from sight.

Now she could see that a young girl sat on a wooden bench that had been moved to the side from its usual place at the end of the gardens. Her black jogging suit was outlined clearly against the white bench. A dozen or more figures holding the candles milled around her.

Suddenly, the small figure on the bench slumped, then straightened, and a deep male voice came from her mouth. The others quickly gathered in front of the bench.

"O great king of the Assyrians, come back to lead the select of humanity into the ancient mysteries, we of the Council are counting on you to bring in enough people with higher consciousness to soon meet the requirements for intervention on earth," the voice growled. "You will no more be called Whitley Yancey, but Abyrion, for your followers into the kingdom will be as numberless as the drops of water in this swollen river beside us."

There was a murmur of voices, and Elayna saw one figure fall to its knees before the bench and bow toward the ground.

"Albeit, mighty Abyrion," the voice continued, "you have failed with one, and that one must be accounted for—brought into the fold or eliminated. This one is unprotected. You will know what you must do."

There was another murmur from the group, and all of them fell to their knees with their heads touching the ground. A strong wind blew over them, extinguishing the candles and rustling the trees. It swirled the muddy waters, circled the tree where she hid, then moved on through the dark gardens. Trees and shrubs bowed in its wake. Elayna could have sworn she heard the echo of laughter.

She glanced at the figure on the bench and saw that she was slumped over, as though in a deep sleep. Then she sat up, and Elayna saw the one she knew must be Whit get up and go to help her. One by one, the dark figures left the gardens.

Finally, there was no one left but her. *And whatever spirit may be loose here,* she thought, feeling the threat of evil at her back as she fled through the trees and across her yard. Hurriedly, she unlocked the back door and slammed it shut behind her. She locked the door, wedged a chair-back under it, and leaned against the raw wood of the door frame, struggling for breath.

Now I'm not just the target of Shirleene's murderer, she thought, terror wrapping itself around her, *I have been marked for destruction by some demonic spirit, probably the same superhuman force that ripped my door from its hinges the other night. What protection do chairs and locks offer against that?*

Chapter 69

It was daylight. The fog had lifted some. Jayboy could see the bowl on the deck, sliding one way, then another when the river current made the boat yank against its rope. Was there any food left in the bowl? It didn't look as full as it had last night. Some of it must have slopped out onto the deck or into the river.

He needed a drink even more than he needed food. His mouth was so dry that his tongue stuck to the top of it. His throat felt like it was full of dust. And there below him was all that water.

He could see that the muddy river had backed up into the creek that poured into it below where the boat was tied. It had pushed the creek over its banks, causing it to spread into the fields on each side. Cornfields. He could see the stalks sticking up through the water. Just like the dandelion stems 'Layna hated to see sticking up through the snow.

He knew he would probably catch some awful disease if he drank that water. Doris had told him never to drink out of the river. "Even when it's not muddy, it's full of germs," she had said. "Filthy!"

There was clean water on the boat. It probably had been there since Court had last used the boat. But even if it tasted stale, it was a lot cleaner than the river.

He was going down there! Even if the man caught him. He was going to walk across that gangplank. Climb right onto the deck. And he was going to grab that bowl. . . .

Suddenly, the current jerked the gangplank loose and carried it around the boat into the middle of the river. Tears stung Jayboy's eyes as he watched it. Whirling. Bobbing. Diving under the water. Then shooting into the air and disappearing around the bend.

There had to be a way to get onto the boat even without the gangplank. If only one of the trees along the river had a limb he could use to run out over the boat and jump down onto it! Old Spider-Man could handle that. He could climb the trees in Liberty Hall's gardens. He could climb the trees along the river-bank below 'Layna's house. He could jump from one tree to another, just like a squirrel. If the limbs were close enough.

He could climb the Bar Center Wall and the drainpipe to his porch roof. 'Layna said he could climb anything. Just like Spider-Man. But there wasn't anything here to climb close to the boat. Anyway, he wasn't sure he could climb without his sneakers. He hadn't been able to climb the wall behind 'Layna's house in these slick Sunday shoes. And that policeman had caught him and pulled him down onto the ground.

He stared at the boat. He guessed he would have to eat turnips. Again.

Chapter 70

After a sleepless night and a morning spent trying to make up for it, Elayna got up and made a fresh pot of coffee. She poured a cup and drank it black.

What did I see and hear last night in Liberty Hall's gardens? she wondered again. Surely it had been a nightmare! But she knew it hadn't. Was it all some elaborate game? She knew that wasn't true, either. Just the memory of that chilling voice and that forceful wind convinced her that, whatever it was, it had all been very real.

She had read about channeling in Whit's magazines, but this was the first time she had seen it with her own eyes. Something supernatural had spoken to Whit through that girl, and Whit instantly had fallen to his knees in a kind of worship. She supposed that indicated his blind acceptance of the message, of his new name as a leader in the cult, of his assignment to "bring into the fold or eliminate" the one with whom he had failed.

A chill goose-walked her skin. There was no doubt in her mind that the "one" with whom he had failed was her. He had tried and failed to bring her into the movement, and now she knew too much and must be eliminated. *So much for a nonviolent New World Order.*

What should I do? she agonized, as she had done often during the night. *Am I truly in danger from this demonic spirit? Is*

Whit really a threat to me?

She felt like she was living out some weird episode from *The Twilight Zone* or *The X Files*. Two nights ago, she had dined in a luxurious restaurant with this man. She had talked with him about becoming his wife. To now accept that he was out to kill her was incredible.

She wished Court were here. He should be home by now, if he hadn't spent the night at some motel along the road. She picked up the phone to call him, then put it down. How could she ever make him believe this wild tale about his friend and mentor? He probably didn't even believe such things were possible. She had been a skeptic herself—until last night.

In a desperate effort to clear her head, she took a cold shower. Hunting for something comfortable to wear, her gaze fell on a black sweatsuit. Suddenly, she could see the black-clad figures moving around in the gardens, holding their candles. She shuddered and grabbed a green one instead.

As she came out of the bedroom, she heard a mower start up across the way, and knew it was the meticulous Liberty Hall gardener mowing the gardens one last time before winter. The everyday sound brought her some sense of stability, of normalcy.

Her head had begun to throb, though, with the pain of sleep deprivation. She swallowed three Bufferin tablets with a glass of water, looking out the keeping room window at the muddy water that appeared to have moved a few inches closer to the house during the night. She knew she should begin moving things upstairs.

She fixed a couple of pieces of wheat toast, spread them with grape jelly, and sat down at the table with a fresh cup of coffee. The shower and the Bufferin were beginning to take effect, along with the food, and she reached for her long-neglected brochure.

It's time to get this paste-up proofed and back to Betty, with these wonderful outdoor photos Bill has done, so we can launch the fall line of Irish sweaters before Christmas, she told herself firmly.

She had reached the last column before she noticed a black box around some bold type that did not match the Bookman font she had ordered. Then she gasped as she read:

> *Leave the papers taped behind the case that holds the latest set of First Lady dolls at the capitol before 5:00 P.M. Friday, and you will be told where to find Loony Toons and your boat unharmed.*
>
> *Otherwise—*

A chill slid down Elayna's spine. She had thought Jayboy had taken the boat downriver to the farm. But, obviously, somebody had him—and the boat—which explained why she hadn't found them at the landing. But who? And why? And what should she do about it? She had missed the prescribed deadline by almost a day!

She noticed a loose corner to the box, stuck a fingernail under it, and removed the entire box. Underneath, unharmed, were the words of her original brochure. She had no doubt that the message was authentic, but how had it gotten into her brochure? Certainly, Betty wouldn't have put it there. But who else had had access to it? Had Betty farmed the job out to someone because she was so busy right now? She had said they had hired some temporary help.

Elayna picked up the phone and called the print shop. The phone rang and rang, but apparently they were already gone for the day.

Again, she wished Court were here, but when she dialed his number, the answering machine came on.

Should she call the police, let them try to find Jayboy? But what if something went wrong? What would happen to him then? And was he now in greater danger because she had missed the deadline?

Poor Jay! she thought. *How frightened he must be!* Then her heart sank as she realized that he could identify the man who held him, who must be Shirleene's murderer. Why should he keep Jay alive? Or was Jay already dead, and the message in her brochure a lie, like it so often was in kidnappings?

She refused to let her mind dwell on that possibility, forcing her thoughts back to what to do about the papers. She glanced at her watch. This was Saturday. The capitol was open to visitors until three o'clock, and it was 1:30 already! She had no car. Could she do what they had asked of her in time to save Jay?

She supposed she should copy the papers. The copier at the shop did color. But she would have to give back the originals, or they—whoever they were—would figure out what she had done. Until she could rescue Jayboy, she would have to play the game their way.

Was there an advantage to having the original papers if Court decided they should be turned over to the police? she wondered. She needed advice, but to whom could she turn? She was unable to reach Court. Obviously, she couldn't call Whit.

Suddenly a boyish freckled face came into her mind. But the preacher unnerved her almost as much as Whit, maybe more so. And what could he know about murderers and architectural designs? Of course, he had been a mercenary in Afghanistan, driven an eighteen-wheeler, and now ran a supper club. Who knew what hidden talents the man possessed. And Jayboy was in grave danger.

She grabbed the phone book, looked up Jimmy O'Brien's number, and dialed. She let the phone ring several times, but there was no answer, not even an answering machine. *So much for that*, she thought. She would just have to make her decisions alone, as usual.

She dressed quickly in a yellow sateen suit. Then, remembering that she would have to make the journey to the capitol on foot, she debated whether to wear the matching yellow sling pumps or her frumpy white walking shoes that would do nothing for the outfit, but certainly would be easier on her feet. Still, she was used to wearing heels, and there was no telling whom she might run into at the capitol with the art exhibit there.

"Vanity, thy name is Elayna!" she said aloud, laughing as she slipped her feet into the pumps. Then she wondered if, subconsciously, she was hoping to run into Whit. "Forget it!" she told herself firmly. "It's over!" *Before it really had a chance to begin,* she thought sadly. Then, remembering the channeled message last night, she knew Whit was the last person she wanted to see.

She threw a yellow wool coat around her shoulders, took the papers from the refrigerator, put them in her purse with the brochure, and was leaving the house when she heard the phone ringing. Thinking it might be Court, she went back to answer it.

"Your car needs a computer for the fuel injection system, and I've got one ordered," a male voice said, "but it won't be in for a week. If you want to drive it 'til then, it may do okay. Sometimes it sticks, sometimes it doesn't. I've put in new plugs and changed the fuel filter."

"Frank, you're a life saver!" she exclaimed. "You must have known how badly I need a car right now!"

He laughed. "Only thing is, there's nobody here but me. Can you come get it?"

She'd already exhausted her resources trying to find someone to accompany her to the capitol. How could she get to the service station? But surely there was somebody who would give her a lift. "I'll do my best, Frank," she promised.

She ran upstairs and looked out the window. Laura's Honda was parked across the street from her apartment, and behind it sat Toni's Cadillac. She picked up the phone again.

A few minutes later, she, Laura, and Toni were on their way in Laura's Honda, Toni holding a huge stainless steel pot in the front seat, and Elayna balancing two giant urns of coffee in the back.

"We'll just drop off this chili and coffee for the Bellepoint rescue workers, then swing on out to the west end to pick up your car," Laura explained, starting the car.

The radio came on. "The river is now out of its banks at the lower end of Wilkinson Boulevard, and Kentucky Avenue in the Bellepoint area is totally closed," the announcer said. "We have been asked to remind our listeners that former governor Amos Sheldon is providing boats to evacuate any whose home is threatened by the flood waters," he continued. "If you need help, call—"

Laura switched off the radio. "If I have to listen to one more promotion for our dear former governor, I think I'll croak."

"He's going to run for governor, again, as sure as we're breathing," Toni said.

"Well, I'm voting for that good-looking Senator Yancey," Laura declared. "They say he's going to announce any minute."

Elayna said nothing. She wondered what the girls would say if she told them about her experience last night and Whit's role in it. She knew Laura's apartment had no windows overlooking the gardens, so she probably had not been aware of the black-garbed candle bearers.

"What do you think, Elayna?" Toni prompted.

With difficulty, Elayna brought her mind back to the conversation. "Oh, he is good-looking," she agreed.

They all laughed, then Toni said, "What I want to know is do you think he'll be a good governor? Of course, I guess anything would be better than Sheldon."

"Well, I. . ." Elayna began.

"Of course she does!" Laura teased. "I hear she has been seen out with the senator more than once."

"Look out, Laura!" Toni shouted. "That idiot pulled right in front of us!"

"Wasn't that C. J. Berryman?" Laura asked. "It looked just like that red Porsche he gave Shirleene Evans. Guess he's got it back now that she's dead." She glanced sideways at Elayna. "I'm sorry!" she said quickly. "I didn't—"

"It's okay," Elayna assured her. "We all knew about Shirleene and C. J., even Court. She wasn't trying to keep it a secret."

"I wouldn't be surprised if that rascal killed her," Laura said, "though I know some people think it was Mr. Evans, and the police are convinced it was Jayboy Calvin, who never hurt a fly in his life! Poor old fellow."

"Who do you think killed her, Elayna?" Toni asked.

"All I could swear to is that it wasn't Court, and it wasn't Jayboy. But I'm afraid there is a lot of circumstantial evidence against Jay. Whit Yancey is going to defend him, though."

"That's certainly in his favor!" Laura declared, crossing the railroad tracks and pulling the car over to the side of the road where a half dozen or so men and women in rain slickers and boots stood around a small camp stove, warming their hands. Traffic lights at the intersection cast an eerie glow through the fog.

As the girls left the car to carry the chili and coffee to the workers, Elayna saw that the river and Benson Creek lapped at the edges of the road just beyond them, and two motorboats were moored where no boat normally could go. She hoped Jimmy O'Brien's supper club still was dry, but she was afraid there wasn't much chance of it.

Back in the car, Laura said, "That floodwall has been a blessing to Wilkinson Boulevard, but it surely hasn't helped old Bellepoint any!"

Now headed south, they crossed the Singing Bridge, where the water swirled by just inches below the bridge's metal grids. Laura turned right on Second Street.

"Without the South Frankfort floodwall, Second Street would be a river itself," Toni remarked. "Remember how it used to get up to the second story of Second Street School?"

"Let's change the subject to something more pleasant," Laura suggested. "When's your new catalog coming out, Elayna? I keep hoping that gorgeous Thai pottery by the guy with the unpronounceable name will go on sale—at about ninety percent off."

"Satian Leksrisawat," Elayna supplied. "He's a transported Thai who married an American girl and is now located in Louisville. He won first place with that new flower design at the St. James Art Fair. It's my favorite of everything in the catalog."

"Mine, too," Laura agreed. "I just can't afford it."

"It isn't cheap," Elayna agreed, "but my prices are lower than Bloomingdale's, and they can't keep in it. So it isn't going on sale anytime soon."

"Oh, well. Story of my life," Laura sighed, swinging the car smoothly into a space beside Elayna's blue two-door LeBaron in the service station parking lot.

Laura brushed away Elayna's offer to pay for gas with a wave of her hand. "We were coming over on this side of town to shop, anyway," she said.

"Then we're going back and see if we can help out in Bellepoint," Toni added with a wave.

Elayna made a mental note to see that Laura got one of Satian's exquisite blue vases for her trouble tonight. And she wouldn't forget Toni's loan of her car the other day, either.

She let Frank fill the gas tank, then headed downtown. The car ran like nothing ever had been wrong with it.

From Louisville Hill, rooftops and autumn-colored trees seemed to float above the town, their bases totally obliterated by the thickening fog. To her right, the dome of the capitol glowed eerily in the mist, like a mythical temple lit by some supernatural presence.

She laughed at her imaginings. Whit's mysterious words had set her up for that. It was just the lighted dome of one of the nation's most beautiful capitols, surrounded by fog.

This surely has been the foggiest October on record, she thought, as she parked the car on Lewis Street in front of the tall, narrow old house painted with the gray-blue trademark color of Elayna Evans Imports. *November usually is the month for fogs.* She got out of the car, unlocked the front door, and went inside.

She crossed the main showroom between illuminated glass showcases displaying exotic items on velvet draping. Leslie had everything looking wonderful again, she noted on her way to the copier. She hoped the water didn't ruin it all. The river never had spread this far, but one never knew what that old river might do.

She made two copies of the drawings, put the originals back in the tube, and looked around for a hiding place for the copies. Her gaze fell on her favorite Monet print of poppies in a field. She removed the print's backing, placed one set behind it, replaced the backing, and returned it to its hanger.

The killer's not likely to search here again, she thought. *But, as Granny always said, it's better to be safe than sorry.*

She folded the other set of copies, sealed it inside a manila envelope, and addressed it to Court. She ran the envelope through the postage meter and placed it in her purse, along with the cardboard tube and a roll of strong mailing tape.

Elayna left the shop and drove toward the mail drop at Franklin Square. Lower Wilkinson Boulevard, where the post office was located, was already closed by the muddy water, according to the radio. *Jimmy O'Brien's supper club must be flooded,* she thought.

She dropped the envelope into the mail slot, then headed the car back down to South Frankfort and her appointment with the miniature First Ladies at the capitol.

Chapter 71

Jayboy shifted his weight. His legs were growing numb from his cramped position in the limb of the sycamore tree. The river was still climbing. He couldn't see much now with the fog and the growing darkness. But he could hear the angry water lapping. Almost to the top of the bank now. Sucking at the roots of the tree just below him. And he could hear the boat. Straining against its rope. Trying to break free. To go whirling off downstream like the gangplank. Riding on the river far away from here.

He wanted to get away, too, but he was afraid. Of the ugly swirling water. Of trying to find his way home down some strange road in the dark. Of the ugly little man with the gun.

The man had left the light on in the cabin, but Jayboy could not see the food. It had moved out of the light. But he knew it was there on the deck. If it hadn't spilled out of the bowl into the water. Would the spaghetti and meatballs still be good? Doris always told him not to eat food that sat outside the refrigerator for a long time.

His stomach growled. He was so hungry! Even if the food had spilled or spoiled, he knew there was more food on the boat. But how could he get on it with the gangplank gone? With nothing to climb?

The light from the boat lay in a golden path across the water.

Like a bridge. He could almost believe he could walk on it. He knew better, though. That bridge of light was a trap. Once he stepped out on it, it would fold up and dump him into the cold, black water. And the water would close over him. Like a grave. He shivered.

To get to the food, he would have to take off his shoes. Then lower himself into the water and grab that rope that held the boat to the willow tree. And walk his hands across it to the boat. Then he could climb up the side and onto the deck.

The current was slower between the boat and the bank. But it had carried off the gangplank like it was no more than a straw or a matchstick.

He shuddered at the thought of getting into the swirling black water. What if he lost his grip on the rope? Or what if one of those frayed pieces snapped and dumped him into the water? He would go under. Maybe all the way to the bottom. And settle into the stinking, black mud. He would never be able to breathe again. The blackness would have him. Forever.

Chapter 72

As she drove up Capital Avenue, Elayna could see the tall columns of Kentucky's current capitol, its elaborately carved pediment and lighted dome rising like a Greek temple out of the fog. *It's lovely enough to be the capitol of the world,* she thought, recalling Whit's statement that Frankfort would be one of five "centers of learning" for his New World Order.

She circled the building, noting that Whit's black Mercedes occupied one of the reserved spaces by the east doors. Then she stared in amazement. Was that C. J. Berryman's red Porsche in the end slot, the one Shirleene had driven? Was C. J. here, too, or had he chosen some new love interest to drive the car?

She parked her LeBaron on the street just past the governor's mansion, got out, and locked the doors. She climbed the series of steps to the capitol's front entrance, pushed open one of the heavy wooden doors, and crossed the lobby and the hallway to the rotunda, her heels clicking loudly against the marble floor.

Although it was past visiting time, a Boy Scout troop was just finishing a tour, and people still milled through the marble corridors. Elayna decided to wait to deposit her package until the halls emptied.

She entered the rotunda, resisting the urge to try to touch the gleaming toe of the copper statue of Abraham Lincoln, aged to the dull bronze of an old penny except for this one spot that was kept polished by the hands of people who rubbed the toe of the great man's left shoe for luck. *Why do people rub only the left foot?* she wondered. And, of all the marble statues of famous men displayed here, why seek luck from the ill-fated Kentucky-born president whose luck had surely run out when he encountered John Wilkes Booth?

Still, I need all the luck I can get, she thought wryly, reaching up and across the velvet rope to rub Lincoln's toe before she crossed the rotunda and turned left down the hallway in front of the closed door of the governor's office, hoping to find the art exhibit.

Suddenly she stopped, backed up, and read the nameplate on a desk inside a small office: Jamie Madison. Whit had said the girl worked here. Then she remembered the red Porsche outside. Was Jamie the one driving C. J.'s car now?

Elayna's eyes swept over the desk, noting the usual dictionary and *Secretary's Handbook.* She surveyed the room's contents—file cabinets, a computer, a printer, and a fax machine. A paper showing samples of various typestyles hung from a clipboard beside the computer. Whipping her brochure out of her purse, she walked over and compared typestyles. Courier Bold matched perfectly the one used in the threatening message.

A movement in the office behind the desk warned her of someone's presence, and she hurried back to the hallway and around the corner. Questions tumbled through her mind as she walked down the corridor. Was Jamie Madison responsible for the message in her brochure? If so, how had she managed to get it in there? Did she moonlight in desktop publishing for the print shop? And who was behind the threatening message? Was Shirleene's killer actually holding Jayboy prisoner? But she found no answers to her questions.

She located the art exhibit in the lobby and hallways of the east wing and forced herself to concentrate on the paintings. Mostly watercolors, they were reminiscent of Paul Sawyier, but done with Elizabeth Moore's own unique style. She found herself wishing Whit were there to share them with her. She knew he would like this one particularly haunting night scene.

There was no sign of him, but he could be anywhere in the building. He could even have left the car here while he went somewhere with someone else. Or he could be out for his evening jog through the neighborhood. She knew he was a dedicated jogger. In fact, he was a holistic health devotee. After reading his magazines, she was beginning to understand that it was all part of his commitment to his religion, which now had ordered him to "eliminate" her. Would he be committed to that, too?

As she retraced her steps to the front of the capitol, she found that the building was nearly empty now. She ducked into the restroom and attached tape to each end of the cardboard tube, using her manicure scissors to clip it from the roll.

She took the left corridor from the front of the rotunda, turned right, and walked between the glass cases holding dolls dressed in miniature replicas of the gowns Kentucky's First Ladies had worn to their inaugural balls. She quickly taped the cardboard tube to the back of the case that held the newest additions.

Elayna turned and recrossed the lobby to the front doors. Relieved that the job was done, she turned the brass knob, but the heavy door was locked! She tried the doors to the left, and then to the right. All three sets were locked, and there was no one in sight.

I've waited too late! I'm locked in this mausoleum alone for the night! she thought, feeling an unreasoning panic rising within her. She forced herself to calm down. *Surely some exit is still open,* she told herself as she ran down the hall to the east doors, nearest the governor's mansion and her car. But they, too, were locked, as were the ones on the west end.

The only other exit she remembered from her days of working in the annex, back before she married Hunt, was in the basement, through a tunnel that connected the capitol and the annex that held more government offices and a cafeteria.

Her memory served her well, and she quickly located and entered the tunnel, hoping she was not too late to find an exit still unlocked.

Suddenly, the lights went out. Elayna gasped and stopped dead still as the tunnel plunged into unrelieved blackness. She literally could not see her hand in front of her face. What could have caused the lights to go out? Was it a power outage? It was foggy outside, but there had been no storm. She knew the lights were not turned off here at night. There were maintenance and janitorial crews here in the evenings, and she had seen several offices going strong far past the usual closing hour of 4:30.

At least the tunnel is straight, she thought, groping for the wall and guiding herself by running her hand along the cool squares of tile as she inched forward. Eventually she would come to the double doors leading into the annex basement.

Her clicking heels drummed against the hollow silence of the tunnel. Then she became aware of an echoing set of footsteps, a faint rustling of clothing. She stopped again, straining to hear in the blackness.

"Hello?" she called softly. "Is someone there?" Her voice reverberated down the long expanse, deepening the silence that followed. Elayna felt her heart begin to race.

Don't be ridiculous, she scolded herself silently. It had to be someone in the same predicament as she. *Or my imagination,* she thought, moving forward again.

She stopped. *There!* Three echoing footsteps betrayed the presence of someone caught unaware by her sudden stop. The sound had come from back down the tunnel some distance behind her, she calculated, because she could not hear anyone breathing.

"Is—?" she began, then stopped, the hair rising on the back of her neck as the single word bounced off the walls, then fell and was lost in the silence. Elayna quickened her steps, almost to a run, guiding herself by her right hand along the wall, holding her left in front of her to ward off a headlong crash into the doors somewhere ahead of her.

The footsteps behind her picked up their tempo, too, abandoning any effort at secrecy. They seemed to thunder in her ears, as she felt the doors in front of her at last and pushed frantically against them. They opened, spilling her from the tunnel into a second set of doors, and then into an almost equally black corridor.

The lights must be off all over both buildings. She hesitated, letting the last set of doors swing shut behind her. Her nose picked up a trace of the day's luncheon pizza from the cafeteria straight ahead. Was there an exit that way?

Forcing her mind to slow down, to think rationally, she tried to recall the layout of the building. The hallways ran in predictable intersecting hollow squares, she remembered, with. . .

The doors behind her flew open, smashing her into the wall. She bit her lip at the pain, but managed to control all sound. Beside her, she could hear heavy breathing. Her pursuer stood inches away, struggling to regain his breath. Was he straining for some clue to her whereabouts? She held her breath, pressing into the wall, certain that he could hear the pounding of her heart. At last, she heard him moving away from her, past the cafeteria.

Elayna reached down and removed first one shoe, then the other. Carrying them by the straps, she edged down the corridor to her left on silent stocking feet.

Suddenly, a beam of light hit her directly in the face. Her heart stopped, then began to pound again.

"Lady, what in tarnation are you doing in here in the dark?" an exasperated male voice asked.

Elayna grabbed the flashlight and swung its beam over the silver identification badge and black and white uniform of a state security guard. She laughed weakly. "I. . .I got locked in," she answered. "Can you get me out of here?"

He chuckled. "Yes, ma'am!" He took hold of her left upper arm. "Come with me." Following the beam of his flashlight, he led her down a hallway. She had no idea where they were by now. He stopped. "Do you have a car? Where is it?"

Elayna hesitated. Where was her erstwhile pursuer? Had he given up? Had it all been a mistake? Or did only the presence of this blessed security guard stand between her and unimaginable horror? How much should she say here in the echoing blackness?

"I need to get to the east side of the capitol," she hedged.

The guard moved on, pulling her along with him, back down the hallway, through the tunnel where she had known such terror only moments before. *That small yellow beam of light and his hand on my arm make all the difference,* she thought gratefully.

"We've had some kind of power shutdown," he explained. "I was on my way to try to find the problem when I heard you stumbling around in the dark."

"Thank you," was all she could think of to say, but he surely could hear in her voice how heartfelt it was.

The guard led her through the double doors back into the capitol and up a flight of stairs to the east doors, where he let her out into the parking area.

She was relieved to see that, apparently, the blackout involved only the state's lighting system at the capitol. The streetlights were on along Capital Avenue, though they provided little illumination against the fog.

"I'll watch you into your car," the guard assured her.

"Thank you," she repeated fervently. Then she slipped the yellow sling pumps back on her feet and fled down the drive to her car.

Chapter 73

Jayboy knew he was going to die. And there wasn't anything he could do about it. He was going to starve to death. Right here in this hollow tree. He felt weak already. And a little sick. How long would it take to starve?

He remembered seeing pictures on TV of starving children in some far-off place. Little girls with big hungry eyes. Little boys with stick arms and legs. And fat stomachs. Only they weren't fat, Doris said. Their stomachs were swollen because they had nothing to eat. And they never smiled. Then some movie star would beg for money. "Just a few cents a day will feed a hungry child," they would finish, looking as sad as the children.

Once, he had asked Doris if he could feed one. Out of the money 'Layna gave her for his work down at the shop that mostly just sat in the bank. But Doris had said, "No, son. We can't be sure the money ever gets to those children. Some fat man is probably spending most of it on sports cars and trashy women."

He still felt bad about it, though. If the stomachs of those scrawny little kids hurt like his did. . .

How bad would it hurt to starve completely to death? It was bound to get worse. And worse. Until. . . His stomach knotted. He had to get that food!

Slowly he slid down the inside of the hollow tree. He took

off his hard-soled Sunday shoes. He pulled off his socks and stuffed them into the shoes. He set them carefully inside the tree, where nobody could see them.

He shivered as the cold, slick mud touched his feet. But he had to go. He started down the bank. Then he stopped. What was that? Back up in the hay field? He peered through the fog, but he couldn't see anything. He listened. Was somebody coming? Was it the ugly little man with the gun?

He could feel the blackness slipping closer. Reaching out. Jayboy turned and scrambled back up the bank and into the hollow tree. He wasn't going to get the food. He was going to starve. And no one would ever know what happened to him or where he was. He would rot away until there was nothing left but a skeleton that would clack and rattle in the wind. Like that skeleton in the haunted house 'Layna had taken him to one Halloween.

Doris would worry and get sick. She might even die. Just from worrying about him. And 'Layna would have to carry on the Dandelion Kingdom without her trusty knight. She wouldn't have anybody down at the shop, either. To keep the floors so shiny she could skate on them. Or to keep the windows so clean the birds would try to fly through them.

He stifled a sob. He wished 'Layna would come and take him home.

Chapter 74

In the fog, the street-lights were fuzzy blurs that did little to illuminate the dark cavern that Capital Avenue had become. She locked the car doors and leaned her head back against the headrest, exhausted.

Had she imagined the terror that had stalked her through the tunnel? Had it been the guard's footsteps she had heard? She didn't think he had come from that direction, but she had been so scared and so confused, she really didn't know. He just seemed to materialize there in front of her. And was she glad that he had! She might still be wandering around down there if he hadn't rescued her.

Or I might be dead at the hands of Shirleene's killer, she thought. Then she rejected the idea. Why would anyone want to kill her? She had done exactly as they had asked with the papers. Surely they had no other quarrel with her. She had seen the papers, though. They made absolutely no sense to her, but they might not know that. If they wanted them badly enough to commit murder and kidnapping for them, there must be more to the drawings than she could decipher.

She wondered if her pursuer had been Whit, following the orders of his demonic spirit. But she chased that thought away and started the car.

Slowly, she drove down Capital Avenue, again wishing Court

were here. Somehow she felt that he would know what to do. Anyway, it was his decision to make. The papers had been in his wife's possession. They may have been the reason she was killed. If so, her own escape in the capitol a few minutes ago had been from more than a figment of her imagination.

She turned left onto Second Street. Should she go straight to the police station, tell them about the drawings, and give them the threatening brochure? But they were convinced that Jayboy was the killer. She felt that it would take more than an obscure drawing and a childish threat to make them believe otherwise.

She turned right at the stoplight, marveling that, with the river so high, Second and Bridge Streets still were dry and navigable. She crossed the Singing Bridge, the familiar hum of her tires on its grids a friendly sound in the fog-wrapped silence.

Suddenly the car coughed and died. Startled, Elayna threw the transmission into park, turned the ignition key, and swallowed her rising panic as the engine caught. She put the car in gear, eased left onto Wapping Street, and drove past the Paul Sawyier Library and Good Shepherd School.

It was hard to tell in this fog how high the water was on this side of the river, but, as the fog swirled and drifted in her headlights, she thought she caught a glimpse of it halfway up the parking lot between the library and the Vest-Lindsey office building on the corner.

Should she be seriously concerned about her house just around the river's bend? What a mess of stinking mud and debris people had cleaned up after the last flood, when the floodgates at Dix Dam had been opened all at once to prevent the dam from breaking. Her house had not been flooded then, but it had sat like an island surrounded by water. With the new floodwall on the other side to push the water this way, who knew what might happen? Still, there was little she could do except move furniture to the upper floor and hope for the best.

As she applied the brake for the four-way stop at the Washington Street intersection, the car coughed and died again. This time, she could not get it started. It sounded like it was out of gas, but Frank had filled the tank only this evening. That was the way it had been acting, though, with the erratic fuel system computer.

She looked out the windshield into the fog. She was a little more than three blocks from home, she calculated. After her experience in the gardens last night and at the capitol tonight, did she have the nerve to cover it on foot?

She tried to see the dial of the dashboard clock, but it had gone off when the car died. She peered at her watch in the dim light of the streetlight. She thought it said 7:35. There would be nothing open at this hour, except a couple of bars down on the Mall, farther away than her house. *The streets of downtown Frankfort are rolled up at five P.M.*, she reminded herself grimly, getting out of the car and locking the doors.

She looked around. Buildings that had been familiar for a lifetime were barely recognizable in the fog. Resolutely, she began to walk. She covered the first block, felt for the curb with her foot, stepped down, and crossed the street. She stepped up and started down the next block, the clicking of her heels a lonely sound.

She paused at the next corner, then crossed the street again, this time stepping up onto the brick sidewalk that ran the block from Orlando Brown House to Liberty Hall.

She was halfway down the block before she realized that the off-rhythm sound of her heels on the uneven surface had been joined by a whispery padding behind her. She stopped to listen, hardly daring to breathe. *The whole area is as silent as a tomb*, she thought, grimacing at her unfortunate choice of imagery.

Elayna glanced over her shoulder, but the street behind her was impenetrably dark. She took a few steps, then stopped again. The whispery padding echoed briefly behind her. A chill slid down her spine.

She moved on, and the ghostly footsteps moved with her. *If I believed in ghosts,* she thought, *I would think the Gray Lady had left the rooms of Liberty Hall to walk the streets tonight.* But she was sure that whoever was following her was alive and part of the twenty-first century.

She looked around. The fuzzy glow of the floodlights behind the front plank fence of the two-hundred-year-old Georgian house were as useless against the fog as the streetlights. The windows along the street were dark. Many of the houses in the historic area had been turned into offices, now closed for the day. Unless Laura was in her apartment at the back of Liberty Hall, Elayna knew she was likely alone down here.

Suddenly Shirleene's white face as she had glimpsed it on the stretcher that awful night came into her mind. Was it Shirleene's vicious killer that now stalked her down this lonely street? Was it Whit?

She stepped off the brick sidewalk onto the smooth surface of the street, where her heels clicked out a telltale staccato rhythm. She reached down and removed the sling strap from each foot, and, again carrying her shoes by the straps, moved around the corner of Liberty Hall.

She peered into the fog, straining to see a light leaking onto the street from Laura's shuttered windows. Apparently, she wasn't at home. *Even if she were,* Elayna thought, *it would be almost impossible to get her attention before. . .*

She pushed away the image that came into her mind, and broke into a run down the street toward her driveway, the padding of her stocking feet barely audible, but the pounding of her heart so loud she couldn't hear any footsteps that might be following. Could she make it to her front door, get the key into the lock, open the door, then slam and lock it behind her before the killer struck?

She slipped under the chain across the driveway. She could hear running footsteps behind her now. She couldn't possibly get inside in time. Desperately, she dived behind the floodwall between her house and the Bar Center.

The footsteps paused, and she could hear ragged breathing. Then she heard the clink of the low chain as someone passed under or over it. She could make out a faint shape just beyond her now, and knew that, if he looked her way, her bright yellow coat and suit would target her against the wall. The shape hesitated, then moved on toward her front door.

Elayna stood and began to edge along the wall back the way she had come, holding her breath, willing him not to turn around. She eased the chain up so she could pass under it, but there was one small clink. She heard a low curse before her feet took wing down the street.

Chapter 75

It must have been an animal he had heard. The man still had not come back. Was he coming? Jayboy strained to hear above the river's roaring and the noise of the boat pulling against the rope. But the night was silent, except for an old screech owl calling again from back in the woods. Then a dog howled from somewhere beyond the hay field. And another one answered from farther down the river.

Jayboy shivered. His jeans and sweat jacket were damp. He was so cold! So hungry!

He could see it in his mind. Soft, pink ham on white bread. Cut in half. With lettuce and a little mayo. Lying on a thick white plate. With chips beside it. And a long, thick slice of dill pickle that neither he nor 'Layna would eat.

There would be a tall glass filled with crushed ice. And Coke from the fountain. He would sip it slowly through a thin straw until it made that slurping noise when it was all gone. "Behave yourself, Jayboy!" Doris would say, frowning at him across the table. He and 'Layna would giggle—and slurp just one more time. Then 'Layna's granny would say, "Elayna, don't be rude." And they would look at each other and put their hands over their mouths to keep from giggling. And the nice lady would come in her black dress and little white apron. She would take their glasses and fill them up again.

It would be warm outside. And the paddle fans overhead would be humming. . . .

But it wasn't warm. It was cold. And there were no paddle fans. Just the roar of the river. And the cold fog that made his clothes soggy. He began to shiver and he could not stop. His teeth began to chatter. "Oh, Princess," he stammered. "I need you!"

They had taken a vow. Back in Liberty Hall's gardens. That the Knight of the Golden Scepter would always be there if the Princess needed him. And the Princess would come to his rescue if he needed her. 'Layna had wanted to seal the vow by cutting their fingers and letting their blood join together. Then she remembered his fear of blood. And they had sealed it with their little fingers crooked and joined together like two links of a chain. 'Layna had said she liked that better after all.

'Layna would come to him. He knew she would. If she knew he needed her. If she knew where he was. She never would find him here, though. He laid his head against the tree and began to cry.

Chapter 76

Elayna veered to the right, crossed the brick walk, and entered Liberty Hall's gardens, hoping her pursuer was not close enough to hear the faint creak of the ball and chain that swung the gate. She eased the gate shut behind her, padded down the brick walk inside, then onto the freshly mown grass. She felt a chill begin at her dew-wet stocking feet and travel upward.

She peered into the lower recesses of the gardens, remembering what she had seen and heard there on the previous evening. The gardens were dark and unreadable—and, at the moment, her dread of her pursuer was greater than her fear of whatever else the darkness might conceal.

She stopped behind the brick toolhouse, catching her breath, straining to hear the sound of footsteps in the darkness. The deep silence was unbroken. Then she heard the creak of the gate and a bump as it closed against its post. He was in the gardens! She shrank against the rough brick, listening in terror to the muffled padding of feet in rubber-soled shoes coming down the brick walk.

A double creak betrayed the lifting of the halves of the divided wooden welltop. She had hidden in the dry, shallow well too many times playing kick the can not to recognize the sound. A faint glow appeared against the darkness, and she knew he must be shining a flashlight into the well. *Thank goodness I'm not in there,* she thought. It was a great place to hide, but, once discovered, there was no escape.

A soft double thud told Elayna her pursuer had dropped the welltop back into place. The padding steps retreated to the walk, hesitated, then turned right. He was coming her way. Her heart began to thud against her chest. Surely he would spot her here against the toolhouse. But, no, he turned left into the maze of boxwood. She could see the pinpoint of light flicking in and out of the leafy tunnels. She let out her breath in silent relief.

Then the beam of light was reflected back from water, which she knew meant that the river had spilled into the lower part of the gardens and her back yard. Her pursuer would have to turn back this way soon, and when he did, his light would pin her to the brick like a mounted yellow butterfly. She had to find a better hiding place.

He had already looked inside the well. Surely he would not look there again. If he did, she would be trapped, but what choice did she have, what other refuge was there from the probing flashlight? She took a deep breath, crept from the shelter of the toolhouse, passed in front of it, and around to its other side.

Elayna felt for the first stone step with her toes, mounted it, then guided herself up the second one. She groped for the wooden knobs of the welltop, raised the cover, and laid it back against its support.

The well was an unfathomable black hole. Gingerly, she lowered herself into it, three or four feet before her wet stocking feet sank into the soft dirt at the bottom. She pulled the top, holding it with both hands until it eased into place above her, hoping her stalker was still too far away to hear the small protest of the ancient hinges.

She crouched in the dark, then squatted on her heels in the cramped space. She stretched out her arms and touched the familiar rough brick walls that surrounded her.

Poor claustrophobic Jay had never been able to hide in the well, she remembered. But it was a perfect hiding place, so long as one didn't get caught. She shivered, only partly from the coldness of the dirt beneath her wet stockings.

From inside the well, she could no longer see the flashlight's glow, nor could she hear the padding footsteps. All she could do was wait and hope he did not find her, hope that Laura would come home, and she could call to her to get the police. What if the killer attacked Laura, though? She didn't want to endanger the girl's life to save her own.

If Toni was with Laura, would the killer attack, or would he wait until they went inside and then come for her again? If she cried out, would he attack them all, or would he run? Even if she made the girls understand, by the time they got inside, made the call, and help arrived, would it be too late for her?

He had used a kitchen knife on Shirleene. Would he use a knife on her? Would it be horribly painful, or would there be the one sharp thrust, and then. . . ? Then what? she wondered suddenly. Would she simply cease to exist? Or would she awaken in some strange place where she would be judged for her life on earth and sentenced for eternity?

Eternity. She had heard the term all her life. She had given it a lot of thought when Carrie died, but the idea was incomprehensible to a mortal whose every breath was measured by the ticking of a clock. *Or, in these gardens, by the silent shadow on a sundial,* she thought.

Jimmy O'Brien had said the doctrine of his church was simply John 3:16. She had memorized the verse a lifetime ago in the summer Vacation Bible Schools she had attended. How did it go? "For God so loved the world that he gave his only Son that whoever believes in him shall not perish, but have eternal life."

I believe that Jesus of Nazareth existed two thousand years ago, she comforted herself. But Jimmy O'Brien had said, at Shirleene's funeral, that mere belief in His physical existence was not enough, that demons believed and trembled.

Could she go a step further? Could she believe that the Creator of the universe loved her so much that He had sent His Son to die for her sins, for the sins of others like her? If so, it meant that she would be spared because of the death of another, just as she had thought earlier about Laura. If she admitted that, she would have to acknowledge that her life belonged to Him.

The concepts had been around her all her life, as surely as the brick walls of the well surrounded her now. But she realized that she never had claimed the promise of John 3:16 for her own, as Granny, Court, Leslie, and Jimmy O'Brien had. The ceremony she had gone through as a child at Vacation Bible School had been a childish game. It had meant nothing to her adult life.

"I'm not ready!" she whispered. But what if the assassin's knife took away her options, as it had Shirleene's? What if he sent her headlong into eternity unprepared? What if. . .

She caught her breath and held it. She was sure she had heard footsteps, and they had stopped right there below the well. He must be standing where the walk to the house branched off to the gate or to the well, trying to decide which way she had gone. The silence inside the well was so deep she could hear her heart beating. Could he?

"Elayna?" The whispery voice startled her, but she managed to swallow her gasp. "Elayna, it's okay. He's gone."

It was impossible to identify the voice based on a whisper. Was this a trick to lure her from her hiding place?

Suddenly a car came down the street and stopped. She heard a door slam, then another, and the girls' laughter preceded them to the gate.

"Good evening, ladies," a voice said pleasantly, as the ball and chain gave its familiar creak.

"You nearly scared me out of my wits," she heard a girl's voice respond. "What are you doing down here on a night like this?"

"Looking for Elayna," the male voice answered. It was familiar, but she couldn't place it. The acoustics were terrible inside the well! She raised the welltop an inch or so.

"I saw her car parked down the street, but she wasn't in it. She's not at home, either. I'm a little concerned, with all that's been going on," he said.

It was Whit! Her pursuer must have fled when he appeared, she thought, weak with relief. But what was Whit doing down here? He had been quite finished with her on Thursday night, and last night he had bowed in worship to a demonic spirit that surely had ordered her death. How hard it was to believe that Whit wanted to kill her! She had one advantage, though. She didn't think he knew she had been hidden in the gardens last night.

"With a murderer on the loose, it's time to be concerned!" she heard Laura agree. "Where could she be?"

"I knew we shouldn't have taken her to pick up her car before Frank got the computer fixed!" Toni said. "She should have borrowed my car again."

"But why would she be here in the gardens at this time of night?" Laura asked.

"I don't know," Whit answered. "I thought I heard something in here. In this fog, I couldn't be sure where or what it was."

"The murderer!" Toni gasped. "Laura, I told you—"

"I didn't see anybody as I drove down the street," Laura broke in, "but he could have run down toward Elayna's."

"I'm calling the police!" Toni said. "What if he's killed her and left her lying somewhere in this garden?"

Elayna pushed up on the welltop. "Girls! Whit! I'm over here!" she called.

Whit came toward her, his dark jogging suit blending into the shadows, giving his face and hands the eerie, disembodied look they had had last night. He helped her out of the well, and, with one hand under her elbow, guided her back to the brick walk where the girls waited, their white shorts and sweatshirts bearing the name of a volleyball team plainly visible in the beam from his flashlight.

Quickly, Elayna told them about her pursuer and her desperate efforts to hide. The girls' obvious concern gave her a warm feeling, in spite of her shivering from the damp cold of the well and her wet stockings.

"At least you're all right," Whit broke in finally, "and whoever it was is surely far from here by now."

Elayna tried to study him in the flashlight's beam. Surely he was no threat to her!

"I still think we should call the police," Laura said. "The murderer may be lurking around here, and I'd feel better if I knew the area had been thoroughly searched."

"I'd feel better if both of you just came home with me," Toni urged. "That river's rising awfully fast. We could get cut off down here."

"There's some time left, I would guess," Whit said. "I'll see Elayna safely home for now. We'll be there, if the police want to ask questions," he added.

Elayna had questions of her own. Why had Whit come looking for her? Did he still care about her, or did he want to kill her? Who had just stalked her through these gardens? And why? Was it truly the murderer? Or was it Whit?

Reluctantly, she let Whit take her by the arm and lead her through the gate and toward her house in its isolated spot behind the floodwall.

Chapter 77

Someone's coming! Jayboy straightened up and stretched his cramped muscles. He had left the hollow limb. Now he sat inside the shell of the lower part of the tree, leaning against its back. He strained to hear over the roar of the river.

He didn't care anymore. If the man came with the gun, he would jump out of the tree and give himself up. Maybe the man would feed him. And let him wrap up in a blanket. Or warm himself by the oven on 'Layna's stove. Before he shot him. Or blew up the boat.

But it wasn't the man. It was a deer. He had heard that whuffling snort before. Mac had made him go hunting with him once. He had hidden his eyes when Mac shot the deer. And he'd never look at the deer's head when Mac brought it home stuffed and mounted on a piece of wood. Mac had hung it on the wall.

Mac liked to hunt. Usually he just skinned the animals he killed. Rabbits. Squirrels. Woodchucks. And brought them to Doris to cook. Jayboy could eat them if he didn't see them before she cooked them. But he didn't like wild game much. And he never went hunting with Mac after the deer.

When Mac died, Jayboy had taken the deer's head and thrown it in the river. Then he had felt bad about it. Mac had been proud of that old deer's head. Finally, he had told Doris what he'd done. She hadn't scolded. She had looked at him with that look in her blue eyes that told him she loved him. She hadn't liked the deer's head, either. And she knew how he felt about dead things.

This deer wasn't dead, though. He could hear it moving down the hillside through the trees. It stopped once to give that strange whuffling sound. Probably when it smelled his scent. He guessed it had come for water. He would stay in the tree until it was gone. Try not to frighten it. He knew the water would taste good.

He waited until the deer got its drink and left. Then he came out of the hollow tree. His mouth was so dry! His lips stuck together and his throat felt awful. But there was no water here except in the muddy river. And Doris had told him not to drink out of it.

"I have to, Doris! I've got to have some water!"

He followed the water up the creek to where he could see the line of green water joining the muddy river. Just like he might have drawn it with his crayons. The green one and the brown one right together in a kind of crooked double line.

He knelt down in the mud and drank right out of the creek. Just like a dog would do. Only he didn't lap the water with his tongue, he just slurped it up. The water tasted awful, but it eased his thirst. He stood up and rubbed at the mud on the knees of his jeans. His stomach was full of water, but he was still hungry.

He turned and climbed the hill behind him, then followed the road through the hay field. Then through the cornfield. To the turnip patch. He pulled up half a dozen hard turnips and carried them down to the creek to wash. Then he took them back to the hollow tree, pulled out his pocketknife, and peeled and ate them. Every one.

Jayboy whimpered. He knew that better food was waiting for

him down there on the boat. But it was guarded by the deep, dark water. Like moats had guarded the castles in the stories 'Layna used to tell him. With a dark dragon hidden underneath that would rise up out of the water and swallow him up.

It didn't matter. Jayboy knew he had to go back. Whether the man came back or not. He had to have water. And food. And warmth. He couldn't stand it any longer out here in the cold, hungry darkness.

Chapter 78

Back in the keeping room, Elayna studied Whit's black jogging outfit. A black outfit was not good to keep a jogger from getting hit by a car in the darkness, but it was perfect for following someone secretly through the shadows. And now that he had her alone down here behind the floodwall, what would he do?

"I was out jogging and saw your stalled car," he began.

"Why, Whit?" she interrupted. "I thought we were friends. What have I done to make you want to—"

She stopped. She had spent dozens of pleasant evenings with this man. It was incredible to think that he wanted to kill her. She knew he was following orders, but still she found it hard to believe. "What have I done to put me on your hate list?" she asked, unable to keep the hurt out of her voice.

"Hate list? I wanted to marry you." A sadness grew in his eyes. "We could be happy, Elayna. We really could."

"People refuse to marry people every day. Is that any reason to try to kill me?"

"Kill you?" he echoed. "What on earth are you talking about?"

She caught her breath. He seemed genuinely puzzled. Could she be wrong? But if it wasn't Whit, who was it? And why? She had delivered the papers. They had no reason to want any more from her. *Except my silence,* she thought, *and the best way to ensure that is to kill me.* Still, demonic orders or not, she simply could not picture Whit in the role of murderer.

"You didn't kill Shirleene." It was a statement, not a question.

He raised one eyebrow. "Elayna! How could you think—?"

"But you did stalk me down the street and through Liberty Hall's gardens." The methodical, determined stalking she had just experienced was altogether different from the intense passion that had inspired Shirleene's murder. Then she remembered her earlier experience. "And you did follow me through the capitol annex."

He was shaking his head in denial. "Elayna. . ."

His protest was cut short by the ringing of the doorbell. She hesitated, unsure what he would do if she attempted to leave the room. The tinny sound shrilled through the house again.

"Aren't you going to answer the door?" he asked. "It's probably the police."

Elayna found it impossible to read the expression in his dark eyes. What would he do if she ran out the door, yelling for the police to help her? As she approached the front door, she noticed the flashing lights down at the end of the driveway.

She unlocked and opened the door, expecting to find a police officer on her stoop. "Frank!" she said in amazement. "How did you know I needed you?" With the door open now, she could see her blue LeBaron attached to Frank's tow truck, which was parked—lights flashing on top of the cab—behind the chain that blocked the driveway.

"Toni called me. Your car was out of gas. I put some in, and it kicked right off. You must have been doing some tall driving in the last couple of hours. I filled that tank just before you left the station."

"Frank, that's impossible! I drove less than twenty miles before it stalled. Would the faulty computer make it do that?"

As she spoke, her mind was searching for a way to communicate to him that she needed help with more than her car. Should she just run out and beg him to take her to the police station? She hadn't even been able to convince Dave Myers that Jayboy was innocent. How would she ever convince him that the upstanding Senator Whitley Yancey was planning to kill her?

"The computer might make the car act like it was out of gas," Frank said, "but the gas would still be in the tank. Your tank was dry as a bone. Somebody must have drained it. Probably some hot-rodding kid who needed gas. They don't want to work for it anymore." He grinned. "Anyway, it's running fine now. You'll need to add some gas, though. I only put in a couple of gallons. By the way, did you know you left your key in the ignition?" He held it up for her to see. It was still attached to the plastic tag from Frank's Service Station. "Once I got the door open, using the Slim Jim, it made it real convenient."

Even more flustered now, Elayna said, "Wait while I get my purse so I can pay you for the service call and the gas." She headed back to the kitchen, reached into her purse for her billfold, then took out her checkbook instead. Quickly, she wrote out a check. Across the top of it, she printed in bold, desperate letters: "Call 9-1-1. Get Detective Myers here. Quick!" She tore the check out of the book, took it back to the front door, and handed it to Frank.

"Thanks," she said, trying to signal him with her eyes to read the message, but he wasn't looking at her. "I really appreciate your coming down here after hours, and even before I called! That's real service."

"No problem," he said, folding the check in half and sticking it in his shirt pocket. Then, with a grin and a wave, he walked down the driveway, stepped over the chain, and climbed into the truck. Elayna's heart sank as she watched him back down the driveway out of sight. He might not look at that check for hours!

Was her imagination simply working overtime? Had it been some hot-rodding kid, as Frank had suggested, who had drained her gas tank while the car sat at the capitol? Or had someone drained the tank to make sure he would find her alone and on foot in the fog? She hugged herself against the chilling thought. Then she realized that it wasn't only the thought that was chilling.

"I'm going to change into something dry," she called to Whit, heading for the bedroom. "My feet and legs are soaking wet from dew."

As she stripped off the ruined hose and threw them into the trash, she noticed that they were peppered with small pieces of freshly mown grass. If Whit had been the one stalking her through the gardens, his shoes and pant legs would also be peppered with grass.

She pulled on a pair of faded blue jeans and a gray-blue sweatshirt bearing her company logo, and went back to the keeping room, dreading to test her theory. With relief, she saw that Whit's shoes and pants were clean.

"It wasn't you following me, was it, Whit?" she said.

He shook his head. "I tried to tell you."

Suddenly she was tired of playing games. "Whit, I believe our relationship over the years entitles me to some answers," she said. "Obviously, you know something about those drawings. What do they mean, and why am I suddenly a target, if not for you, then for somebody?"

"Elayna, I swear I have no idea what you are talking about—stalkings and targets! But I suppose I do owe you some explanations," he conceded. "It won't matter now. Without the papers, no one would believe the story. I wish I had the papers here to support my words," he went on, "but I will have to rely on your memory for that."

"I remember them very well," she assured him. "I just don't understand them. It seemed to me that most of North Frankfort and all of South Frankfort except the capitol and the area directly behind it were totally covered by water in that painting."

"You have a good memory, Elayna," he said.

"But how? And what does it all mean?"

He smiled. "The *how* is simple. Recent word from the ascended masters is that there will soon be many climatic and cosmic changes. The fault in Dix's Dam is increasing. With the right cosmic conditions, at the least pressure from rising water, the dam will burst. Tons of water will descend upon Frankfort. The major floods of past years will seem like puddles from a summer shower."

She stared at him in disbelief. Had he lost his mind? She had learned that he was mixed up in some weird things, but this was insane.

"With the locks in place and Dix's Dam gone, the flood will not recede as in the past," he went on. "The town's natural bowl shape and the judicious reconstruction of roads will make Frankfort a perfect basin to hold the lake you saw in the painting."

Elayna felt like she had fallen down the rabbit hole again. "Won't the water gradually seep out through the lower areas, through creeks and roads?" she asked. "And what about the floodwall?"

He laughed. "It will be several feet under water."

She considered that. "But how can you dam up a whole town without anyone knowing what you are doing?"

"Only Court has noticed anything so far," he said, "and I've been able to convince him that everything is legitimate, all ordered by a legislative committee and done by the state's engineers. There are only a handful of holes left to close now, and there will be a couple of bridges to finish later. Until then, we will use boats and a ferry. Government offices will be relocated around the cliffs, all connected by the elevated bypass roads recently constructed."

"But why, Whit? What good will it do your cause—whatever it is—to destroy Frankfort?"

"Destroy it? Elayna, we will make Frankfort the most beautiful place in America! It will be breathtaking, with the temple rising above the lake."

It's breathtaking, all right, she thought, *the whole insane idea.* "What about all those people who live in North and South Frankfort? Doesn't your group care that many will lose their homes, and others will lose valuable property, much of it on the National Historic Register?"

"Can't you understand, Elayna, that the individual does not matter in the global scheme of things? The combined good is all that counts."

"That's what Hitler said. And Mussolini. And Stalin," she countered.

He waved one hand as if to dismiss her comparisons. "The lake is important to our spiritual completion. A river is always restless, constantly moving, seeking. But a lake signifies arrival, fulfillment, peace," he explained.

"Those who own homes in the flood zone will be relocated, of course," he went on patiently. "Property owners will be reimbursed by insurance companies or the federal government. Until the government is replaced with a higher order, we will use it."

"And the property that will replace the downtown area will all be for sale by members of the consortium," she said, suddenly understanding the implications of Court's discovery that the consortium now owned most of the property on the cliffs and hills surrounding Frankfort. *There's a lot of money to be made,* she realized. *Millions of dollars. That must be how Whit's group has been able to convince people, even government officials, to buy into their mad scheme.*

Whit studied her. "Sometimes concessions and compromises must be made, for the larger good of the cause," he answered finally. "But I've kept my name clear of the consortium. I suppose Court has stumbled onto something?"

"Does that mean Court will have to be eliminated, too?" she asked scornfully.

"Our movement is peaceful, Elayna. Can't you understand that? We are not a violent people, but the signs of imminent cosmic change are increasing almost daily." He sighed again. "Our movement has waited a long time. Now we are nearly ready. I assure you it will be beautiful, Elayna. I wish you could be convinced to join us."

She thought of the beautiful old homes and churches, the public buildings, Liberty Hall, and her own house here on the riverbank—all at the bottom of Whit's lake.

The phone's abrupt ring cut off her thoughts. She glanced at Whit. Would he let her answer it? On the third ring, she answered, then handed the receiver to him.

He frowned. "Nobody knows I'm here." Then into the receiver he said, "Whit Yancey." As he listened, Elayna saw an angry flush mount his face. "I warned him!" he said angrily. "I told him no more violence! I ought to let the creep serve that murder one!" He listened again. "There's little doubt that he was at the Gypsy Tearoom that night," he said. "He had the pin and the blood on his shoe. C. J. may think Calvin saw him."

"What's going on, Whit?" Elayna interrupted. "What about Jay?"

He placed one hand over the mouthpiece. "C. J. Berryman's got him on your boat, tied up at some landing."

"But I went to our landing earlier. The boat wasn't there. Where could they be? And what will C. J. do to Jay, Whit?"

His frown deepened. "I don't know, Elayna. If C. J. thinks

Calvin saw him that night, who knows what he'll do?"

A chill slid down her spine. Whit was saying C. J. Berryman had killed Shirleene! And he had Jay! "Whit," she begged, "I've got to go to Jay, and my car's not dependable right now. Could you. . . ?"

"Jamie," he said into the phone, "could you get my car down here right away? I left it at the capitol when I went jogging. Thanks, sweetheart." He hung up and turned to Elayna. "It's. . ."

The phone's ring cut off his words. Elayna snatched it up.

"If you want to see Loony Toons alive, you'd better do exactly as I say!" a man's voice growled in her ear.

"What do you want?" she almost whispered. "Is Jay all right?"

The man began to swear. "That Loony Toons! You'd better be quick if you want to see him again!"

"Where—?" she began, but her mouth went dry and she couldn't speak. She swallowed. "Where are you?" she finally managed to say. She knew it was C. J.

"The landing just below the Evans place," he said. "And you'd better get here ASAP, or I'm gonna blow that Loony Toons to smithereens!"

"No! Please!" she cried, but the phone clicked and she heard the burr of the dial tone.

Chapter 79

The man had come back. Before Jayboy could get out of the tree and back on the boat. He could hear him talking on the phone, just below his hiding place in the hollow tree.

"She had that bag with her, but I never could get close enough," he said. He listened. Then swore. Jayboy covered his ears. "So you already had her leave the papers, and I've been traipsing around after her all night for nothing?" He swore again. Then he listened some more. "He's bringing her with him?" he asked. "You saw them get in the car? Is Whit *with* us then? Is he willing to bring our little lamb to the slaughter? I thought he was sweet on her."

Whit? Were they talking about 'Layna's friend? The senator? Jayboy knew he wouldn't be "with" this evil man. 'Layna liked him. The senator would never do anything to hurt 'Layna.

"Well, I don't care what he wants," the man almost shouted. "No, I still can't find Loony Toons." Jayboy cringed and covered his ears as the man swore. "I think he'll come to her, though." The man laughed, and the nasty sound of it was worse than his swearing.

"What am I gonna do with 'em? Well, babe, I learned a few useful things in 'Nam. How to search and destroy. How to use a gun. How to use a knife. And I became a demolitions expert."

The man listened for a moment, then said angrily, "Yeah, I guess I should have used those skills on the tearoom, but I thought a fire would look more like an accident. So I made a mistake, but I won't make one this time. This boat is wired, babe. All I have to do is set it adrift. When this wild current carries it into the cliffs around the bend, it'll blow to smithereens!"

He listened again. "I'm telling you, it will look like an accident, Jamie!" he said loudly. "She got away from me at the capitol and down there in the gardens, but if I can get her on this boat, you will read in the morning papers about the tragic accident that claimed the lives of one of Frankfort's prominent businesswomen and her Loony Toons friend."

His voice softened. "It will be so sad. She came to try to talk him into confessing his crime, promising to help him if he surrendered to the police. But before they could get off the boat, the flood carried it away. Or maybe they were trying to escape down the river together. Or maybe Calvin held her hostage as he tried to escape. The speculations of the media won't make any difference. One Elayna Evans and one Jayboy Calvin, who both knew too much, will be no more!" He laughed, turned off the phone, and pushed down the antenna.

Jayboy's head throbbed. He tried to think. 'Layna was coming. But the man was planning to kill her!

He could feel the blackness out there. Gathering. Only this time it was after his Princess, too! He had to save her! But what could he do?

Chapter 80

Elayna caught her breath as the Mercedes slipped onto the shoulder of the winding, narrow road, then bounced back onto the pavement. She glanced at Whit. He was gripping the steering wheel, frowning as he concentrated on piloting the car through the fog that swirled around them like strands of cotton, absorbing the light from the headlamps before it could reach the road.

"What we need here is a jeep!" Whit muttered.

Elayna leaned back against the headrest, letting her mind replay the events of the last few days that had brought them to this moment. Shirleene's murder. Jayboy's arrest. His escape. The threatening instructions in her brochure. Her ordeal at the capitol. Her terrifying flight through the fog down Wilkinson Street and in Liberty Hall's gardens.

Inevitably, she came back to the same questions: Who had followed her and why? Was it C. J. Berryman? Was he trying to kill her because he thought she knew he had murdered Shirleene? Or had someone hired him to kill her because she knew about the plans to flood Frankfort?—and that brought her back to Whit.

If Whit was behind all this, she supposed she had played right into his hands by coming with him to some isolated spot along this lonely road. She sighed. There was little chance that Court would get the architect's drawings she had mailed him or the message she had left on his answering machine in time to help.

She wondered if Frank had discovered her written plea on the check he had tucked away in his pocket. But even if he had seen it and called the police, they would have no idea where to find her. It could take days to follow whatever trail they might pick up, and by then it would be much too late to do her or Jayboy any good.

Poor Jay! she thought. *He surely must be terrified, if he's still alive.*

"If we follow the road a little farther toward Henry County, will we come to the next landing beyond the Evans's farm?" Whit broke into her thoughts.

"I don't know, Whit," she answered uncertainly, peering ahead into the impenetrable white cavern of fog.

"I remember driving out here a couple of times when Court invited me to some gathering or other," he said. "We once had a small political meeting on the boat."

Elayna recalled one time when Whit had joined them for a cookout on the boat. He had been delayed by a courtroom trial, and they had gone downriver to the landing without him. About dark, he had driven out to have supper with them. It was two or three years after Hunt's disappearance, and she had suspected that Court was playing matchmaker. She had been uncomfortable all evening. Later, though, when they had gone out on their own, she had found that she enjoyed Whit's company.

She studied his handsome profile in the dim light from the dash. Was he just a religious fanatic, or had he gone completely insane? He definitely was involved in the incredible plans to turn Frankfort into a lake and the state capitol into some pagan temple. Would he help her rescue Jayboy, or should she fear for her own life, as well as that of her lifelong friend?

Oh, Jay, she thought, *am I coming to save you from C. J., or leading someone to you who will give orders to kill us both to further his fanatical cause?*

Her thoughts returned to those she'd had in the gardens. If she were killed, what would be her eternal destiny? What was it Jimmy O'Brien had told her Hunt had said? Something like, "How shall we escape if we neglect a salvation bought at so great a price?"

The words hit her with new impact. She, too, knew the excruciating pain of watching a child die. If God had deliberately endured that for her, how insulting to ignore His pain, to casually reject the offered sacrifice. What a mockery to answer, "My Son died for you," with an arrogant "So?" "God will not be mocked," Court had said the night Shirleene was killed.

And what about Jayboy? Surely God would not hold him accountable for concepts he could not understand. But she knew Jay could understand if she explained them to him. She had been his doorway to the world's great literature, and he had understood all the basic, important things. She even had shared with him some of the stories she learned at Vacation Bible School, though he never would go with her for fear that the other children would make fun of him, as they had in school.

In spite of all the times she had sat in church, hearing God's plan explained; in spite of Granny's and Court's and Jimmy O'Brien's gentle urgings, until now, she had never grasped the enormity of rejecting the personal relationship that God offered through the reconciliation provided by His Son's sacrifice. And she had never tried to make Jay understand it.

To plead ignorance was no excuse, she knew, for she had been given every opportunity to overcome that ignorance. But Jay had not. Was it now too late for him?

"I'm so sorry, Jay," she whispered. "Oh, God," she prayed silently, "please don't let it be too late for Jay. Please help me save him from C. J. Berryman. Please give Jay and me another chance, and I promise to. . ."

She stopped. Was she ready to commit her life to God? Was she ready to surrender her independence, her will to His? She didn't want to be someone's slave, not even God's.

"You shall know the truth and the truth shall set you free!" The words were from some long-forgotten sermon, she supposed. She knew they were from the Bible. *Is it possible to know God that way?* she wondered. *To communicate with Him in a true freedom of united thought and will?* Like Granny had. Like Jimmy O'Brien apparently did?

"If you will give Jay and me another chance," she prayed, "I promise to. . ."

Again, she hesitated.

". . .to seek You until I truly find You," she finished honestly. "No more 'business as usual.' No more games," she vowed.

Suddenly the fog opened, and she saw that they were at the top of a long, steep hill. Just ahead, if she remembered correctly, would be Jimmy O'Brien's church, with its quaint parsonage with woodbine climbing the chimney and Earl Grey tea waiting on the shelf.

Why hadn't she thought to call Jimmy before they left the house? She recalled the preacher's words that day at the church: "I guess I fell in love long ago with another man's wife." She hadn't wanted to pursue the thought then, but she knew Hunt was that other man, and she was that wife. She wasn't sure how she felt about that, but she was sure of one thing. Jimmy O'Brien would come to her rescue if he knew she needed him.

As the Mercedes eased down the hill, back into the eerie mist, Elayna thought she could see a faint glow where she assumed the church would be. Then, as they passed the mailbox out at the roadside, she was able to make out the shape of the ancient black pickup truck parked in the driveway. *Sure enough,* she thought. *There's a light on in the parsonage.* She turned to look back longingly as the fog closed rapidly behind them. She wished she could think of some reason to ask Whit to stop. Or should she just open the car door and jump out? But she couldn't leave Jayboy to their mercy.

Mercy? she thought, as they passed what she felt sure was the road to the Evans's landing. *Shirleene certainly was shown no mercy. Why should I expect any for Jay or me? Unless we receive it from God, there will be no mercy for either of us on this dank, foggy night.*

"There's another road," Whit said, swinging the car into a rutted lane that put even the Mercedes' refined suspension to the test. Finally, he pulled off the road and parked.

"I'm sorry, Elayna," he said, reaching into the glove compartment and taking out a flashlight. "I guess it's shank's mare from here to the river. Better get out on the driver's side, though. Who knows what that tangled vegetation hides over there."

Shank's mare. She hadn't heard that term for going somewhere on foot since her grandfather's death many years ago. Somehow, the familiar phrase from her childhood lessened her fears. She slid to the driver's side and out of the car.

Whit clicked on the flashlight and began to walk into the gloom. Elayna fell into step behind him, peering into the forest on either side of the so-called road. She could see no farther than the line of trees at the road's edge. Then cornstalks replaced the trees on either side. Soon they were passing through a hay field, its grasses overgrown and neglected, the road through them barely discernible in the fog.

Elayna shivered and reached for the back of Whit's coat. Even if she were being led like the proverbial lamb to the slaughter, Whit's presence was comforting in the lonely, fogged-in wilderness.

Chapter 81

Somebody else was coming over the top of the bank. Then Jayboy could see 'Layna in the light of a flashlight in the hand of someone behind her. *That must be the senator. 'Layna's friend.*

He liked the senator. He always shook his hand when they met. And talked with him a few minutes about things that were going on. Just like he was regular people. Just like he could vote for him in the next election. But the senator knew that he couldn't vote. He wasn't signed up for it. 'Layna had talked to him about that once. Then she had agreed. It was better if she just voted for both of them. She always talked with him, though, about what she called "the issues." And he always told her exactly what he thought.

They stopped at the edge of the water where the gangplank had been. The senator whistled, and the man on the boat appeared in the cabin doorway.

"You'll have to jump," he yelled. "The plank washed away. And, if you ask me, this boat's not gonna be here much longer." He crossed the deck like he was ready to jump ashore.

"I didn't ask you," the senator said calmly. "Where's Calvin?"

"Loony Toons? He's not here," the man on the boat said. And he began to swear, a long string of ugly words. Jayboy put his hands over his ears.

"Stand back, Berryman," the senator ordered. "We're coming aboard."

He gave 'Layna a little nudge. She jumped and landed on the deck. Then she fell to her knees. The senator jumped. His rubber-soled shoes squeaked on the wooden deck, but he kept his balance. He reached a hand down to Elayna, but Berryman grabbed her wrist, yanked her to her feet, and pulled her with him inside the cabin.

Jayboy knew he had to do something. But how could he get on the boat without the men hearing him? If he jumped, his feet would hit the deck with a loud thump. And the ugly little man was just waiting for a chance to shoot him.

He knew he had to get on the boat, though. He didn't know what he would do once he was on there. He only knew he had to try. To help 'Layna.

Easing himself out of the tree, he padded barefoot over the cold, slick mud to the water's edge. He would have to lower himself into the water, grab onto that rope, and walk his hands across it to the boat—without making any noise.

Fear rose up in his throat, smothering his breath. He turned away. He just couldn't do it! He could not put himself into that ugly water. Then he cocked his ear. Was that 'Layna calling his name?

Instinctively, he saluted. "It is impossible. But if the princess is in danger, I will do it!" he recited quietly to himself. Lines from the games they had played in the Dandelion Kingdom. But this was no game. 'Layna really, truly was in danger. And there was nobody to help. Except her trusty knight.

"I'm coming, princess!" he whispered. He grasped the root of the willow tree and lowered himself into the water. He grabbed the rope and held on for dear life.

The angry water licked at his face. Like a friendly dog. Only it wasn't friendly. It was cold. And he could feel it trying to pull him down to where the blackness waited.

Jayboy pulled his face above the water. He took a deep breath, pushing the air past the smothery place in his throat. Then he began to inch his way, hand over hand, toward the boat.

Chapter 82

Elayna winced at the memories the small cabin evoked: Hunt at the table drinking coffee from a brown pottery mug; Hunt filleting fish with a surgeon's deft moves at the stainless steel sink; Hunt leaning over the lower bunk to drop a kiss on the cheek of a sleeping Carrie Hunter. Carrie sitting in the corner of the bench, crooning softly to P. B. Bear or one of her dolls; Carrie bending over the table drawing pictures with her colored pencils, her flyaway hair falling around her face. Hunt. Carrie. Hunt. She closed her eyes against the flashing images.

"Tired, Elayna?" Whit asked solicitously. He led her over to the bunk and helped her sit down on it.

The boat was crowded, with the living and the dead, she thought, but shouldn't there be one more person in the tiny cabin? Had C. J. already killed Jayboy and dumped his body in the river?

Whit echoed her thoughts. "Where's Calvin?"

C. J. swore. "Ol' Loony Toons got away. I've searched these woods from creek to river, but I couldn't find him. But he's got to be out there somewhere. He's too stupid to find his way home. I thought getting his friend down here might coax him back to the boat, where I can take care of him for good."

"Berryman, when you told me what had happened at the

355

tearoom and begged me not to turn you in, you promised me there would be no more violence. Nobody's going to believe Calvin's story, any more than they would have believed Shirleene's without the drawings. We have those now, and I want him found and released."

"And I told you I can't find him," C. J.'s voice rose. "You want him, Mr. Senator, you find him. That water's rising faster by the minute. I'd say the dam's already busted loose. And I don't aim to be on this boat when it goes."

Whit stared at him. "If that dam goes before we're ready, we'll have our hands full, finishing barriers to hold that lake, getting our emergency governing bodies in place. This will be our one big chance. I hope the dam won't go until I'm governor."

"And I'm telling you I think it's already gone," C. J. shouted. "Look at that water boiling by out there."

"Shut up, Berryman," Whit ordered. "Just shut up and let me think."

Elayna saw C. J.'s fist clench at his side. He licked his lips nervously. "You don't understand, Senator. I've wired this boat. Any major impact and she'll blow to kingdom come!"

Suddenly the boat began to shudder. It stopped, and then began again.

"It's going!" C. J. cried. "We'll smash into those cliffs at the turn and blow to smithereens!"

Whit made an impatient gesture for him to be quiet. "Somebody's trying to board," he hissed, easing behind the right side of the cabin door and motioning C. J. into place on the left.

The boat rocked violently and Elayna heard a small thud somewhere on deck. The boat resumed its rhythmic tugging against the tether. Then she saw a shadow move amid the other shadows outside the window.

She gasped as Jayboy appeared in the doorway, barefoot,

breathing heavily, with water dripping from his clothes and hair. *He had to have come through the water, but how?* she wondered. *He can't swim, and he's terrified of deep water, much less the boiling cauldron out there.*

His eyes, bulging with a mixture of fear and determination, came to rest on Elayna. "Princess!" he cried. "Are you hurt?"

"I'm all right, Jayboy," she assured him, forcing her voice to a calm she didn't feel. She glanced at Whit, then motioned for Jay to come to her. He came and knelt beside her, whimpering.

C. J. began to curse again. "You Loony Toons! I've spent hours looking for you!" He pulled a gun from his pocket and pointed it at Jayboy with his left hand. "I'll blow you to—"

Elayna threw herself across Jay's trembling body, just as Whit stepped in front of them. Was he trying to protect her, after all? He had seemed concerned about her being tired earlier, too. Hope grew inside her.

"Put it down, Berryman," Whit ordered coldly. "I told you there will be no more violence! It's bunglers like you who are dangerous to the cause."

"The cause! The cause! I'm sick of hearing about the cause," C. J. yelled. "It could be the 'cause' of me serving a murder one rap."

"Shirleene's death was unnecessary, if you had completed your assignment as planned. Without the drawings, no one would have believed her wild tale. But you let your personal feelings take over. Then you bungled your attempt to destroy the evidence. I ought to have you arrested for murder, Berryman. You deserve to serve that murder one! But I can't risk a trial that would unearth things not yet ready to be revealed."

"Well, I aim for Loony Toons here to take the blame," C. J. said. "And there won't be any trial."

"Just how do you expect to accomplish that?" Whit asked.

"It's simple," C. J. said. "Loony Toons here killed Shirleene. The police already believe that." He laughed. "Then he escaped from the police, took his best friend off down the river on the boat, and both of them met their tragic deaths when he crashed into the cliffs and the boat exploded." C. J. folded his arms in a gesture of smug finality.

Elayna shivered, knowing full well that C. J. intended for her to die, along with Jayboy. It was a clever plan. The police would believe that Jay was Shirleene's murderer, and the case would be closed.

"And our lady here is going to confirm it with a phone call to our esteemed city commissioner," C. J. added, extending the antenna on his portable phone and holding it out to Elayna. When she hesitated to take it, he began to swear.

"Court's still on his way back from Florida," Whit said. "We tried to reach him earlier, but only got his answering machine."

C. J. chuckled. "So much the better. It'll be on tape." He held out the phone again.

Elayna took it, trying desperately to think of some way she could warn Court without C. J. knowing what she was doing. Then she thought she knew what she could say to make Court realize something was wrong. She punched in the numbers.

"Court, it's Elayna," she said when the answering machine clicked on. "You know how much I've enjoyed being on the boat lately, how much peace it brings me. So I've decided to take Jayboy downriver on it to give me some time to think, to decide how to help him."

She handed the phone back to C. J., praying that Court would come in soon, and that he would remember how she had avoided the boat ever since Hunt's disappearance and realize something was wrong with that message. Still, there was almost no chance that Court would get her message or be able to respond to it in time to help them.

C. J. really didn't plan to shoot them, though, so there was no point in crouching here on the floor, she decided. She got up and sat back down on the bunk behind Jay. Whit still stood between Jay and C. J.'s gun.

Suddenly Jay lunged, butting Whit in the small of the back with his head, sending him crashing into C. J. Elayna heard the gun spit as Jayboy grabbed her hand and pulled her toward the doorway. She looked back and saw the gun sliding across the cabin, and Whit and C. J. in a tangled heap on the floor.

Then Jay was propelling her out the door, across the deck, and over the side of the boat. She gasped at the shock of the cold water that closed over her head. Instinctively, she began to push against it with her arms and legs. Surfacing, she realized that Jayboy still had her by the hand. She knew panic would cause him to grab her and drown them both. She spun him around, grabbed him in a chest hold, and began to sidestroke toward the boat's rope.

With the boat creating a bulwark between the river and the bank, the current wasn't overwhelming, but it took all her strength to keep from being towed around the hull and into the mainstream. She lunged for the rope, grasped it, then felt it break. She grabbed desperately for the end of the rope that dangled from the tree root.

She whirled Jayboy around again and planted his hands on the root. She was relieved to see him begin to scramble up the bank like a monkey. Then he turned, and seeing her still dangling from the frayed rope, came back to hold out his hand for her. She grasped it, let go of the rope, and let him pull her to safety beside him on the bank.

Elayna turned back to the river and saw the boat whirling around and around in the current, traveling downriver at a rapid pace. She saw a shape stagger across the doorway, then disappear back into the cabin. She couldn't tell if it was Whit or C. J.

She watched in horror as the water picked up the boat and flung it into the cliffs. The explosion was immediate and terrible.

"Kingdom come." She repeated C. J.'s prediction, watching the flames shoot into the sky, carrying pieces of burning wood that fell back to be extinguished in the water. The would-be trapper had been caught in his own trap. Shirleene's death had been avenged.

Then she thought about Whit and she was numb. So much had happened so fast that she didn't know how she felt about his death. For a moment she was transfixed by the irony that both her husband and the only other man she had ever considered marrying had met death in much the same way.

She noticed that she was shivering and then she realized that a cold wind was plastering her wet clothing to her body. She turned her thoughts to how to get Jayboy and herself out of this remote location and to warmth before they suffered hypothermia. Pushing Jay ahead of her, she maneuvered the slippery riverbank and came, panting, into the flat cornfield above.

"C'mon, Jay, we've gotta get out of here," she said as she began to jog down the rutted lane toward the main road. Without a word, Jayboy began trotting along beside her.

Suddenly, a light swept through the trees, and she heard a motor coming toward them.

Jamie Madison is the only one who knows where we are, she remembered, and a new fear crept over her. Had Jamie come herself or sent someone else to make sure the plan was completed?

Before she could decide whether to hide or stay put, she and Jay were pinned to the road by the headlights of a truck. She saw a dark figure jump down from the cab and come toward her in the light. Her breath caught on a sob. Then she began to run.

Chapter 83

Jayboy scooted back on the carpet away from the heat of the crackling fire. Jimmy O'Brien's jeans and sweater were a little too big for him, but they were dry. He had been so cold that his teeth had chattered. And he shook all over. But he was beginning to get warm again.

It felt so good sitting here by the fire. Holding a steaming mug of chocolate between his hands. He took another sip, then stirred the marshmallows with the spoon. He let them melt a little, making white designs in the brown liquid. Then he took another sip and leaned back against the couch, where 'Layna and the preacher sat. He could hear them talking just behind him, but it seemed like they were way off in another room. Maybe even in another world.

"I heard the explosion and knew something terrible had happened," the preacher said.

"It was awful!" Elayna agreed. "The boat just disintegrated. There was nothing left."

Her words wove in and out of the images playing across Jayboy's mind. That awful journey through the dark water. The gun pointed right at him. Butting the senator with his head. Knocking him into the man with the gun. Grabbing 'Layna's hand. Pulling her out of the cabin and over the side of the boat. Falling from the broken rope. Grasping the tree root. Helping 'Layna up the bank. Just as the boat came apart and flew into the sky.

Jayboy became aware of a long silence behind him. Then the preacher said, "After all these years of searching, then finding you at last, I shudder to think how close I came to losing you."

There was another long silence. But Jayboy had seen enough of Doris's TV shows to know. The preacher was kissing 'Layna. He'd bet his Spider-Man shirt on it. That was okay, though. 'Layna liked this red-haired preacher. He could tell. When he had jumped out of the truck, she had run straight into his arms. Now she had that shiny look in her eyes. Like she had when Hunt first started coming around. He hadn't seen that look for a long time.

He wanted 'Layna to be happy. He loved her. *Not that mushy, kissing kind of love. Yuk!* But he loved her. She had been his best friend ever since he first met her. And she had taught him so much. Things like how to see inside books and understand the stories. Even though he couldn't read the words.

She had taught him how to write his name. Just Jayboy. Not Calvin. But he could write it. On his puzzles. On his Lego boxes. On his crayons. And he could carve it in trees. Just like the other kids did. Inside a big heart. And put it on all his pictures. Right up in the top corner of the page. Where everybody who saw it would know that he—Jayboy—had colored that picture.

Best of all, she had taught him about the dandelions. And she had made him the Knight of the Golden Scepter. The most important knight in the Dandelion Kingdom. The knight sworn to protect her. And he had. He had gone into the dark water for her—twice! He had faced the blackness for her.

He knew she loved him, too. She had saved him from drowning. She had fought other kids for him when they made fun of him. She had fought Shirleene. And, just tonight, she had thrown herself between him and the gun when the man wanted to shoot him. They would always be there for each other. They were very special friends. The Princess of Dandelion and her trusty knight.

The blackness still was out there. Waiting. But it wouldn't come after him here in this warm, happy place.

Jayboy sighed. He leaned his head back against the couch and closed his eyes.

Chapter 84

Whit had said, "You're perfect for the part," Elayna recalled, and, "We'll be good together." But never once had he said, "I love you." It had been a long time since she had heard those words that Jimmy O'Brien kept whispering in her ear.

She wasn't sure how she felt about it. Could she find that tree-top feeling she had known with Hunt with this red-haired Irish preacher? Could the realness that the Skin Horse insisted was "for always" be hers again without the pain she had suffered by losing the ones who had made her Real in the first place? She didn't know, and she was too exhausted to try to sort it all out right now.

Still, she couldn't remember when she had felt so content as she felt here by the fireplace in this old brick parsonage, wrapped up in Jimmy O'Brien's oversized bathrobe, with her head cradled in the hollow of his shoulder.

She supposed she had every right to be here, now that she knew Hunt was dead. But where was Hunt? Had he found peace at last? Did he still exist in some beautiful place, as Jimmy O'Brien believed? Or had that bomb in the mountains of Afghanistan blown him into nothingness? *But if that were true,* she thought, *then little Carrie Hunter no longer exists, or Granny, or Leslie's husband and son.*

"A penny for your thoughts," Jimmy O'Brien offered, shifting position so he could look into her eyes.

"Oh, I was just thinking about life and death, about eternity," she answered with a deprecating laugh.

"All the simple, easy questions." His grin buried his freckles.

She sighed. "There's a peace that emanates from you, Jimmy O'Brien," she said. "My granny had it. So does Court. So does Leslie, my assistant down at the shop. I guess I envy all of you that peace."

He took her hand in his. "It's the peace of God, sweetheart," he said. "It comes from totally surrendering our lives to Him. Haven't you ever done that, Elayna?"

She shook her head. "No. I. . ." She stopped. She had started to say she had never felt the need, but all at once she knew that wasn't true. Even underneath the happiness she had known with Hunt and Carrie Hunter, she had always had a hunger for the feeling she had first experienced as a child that day in her swing when the presence of God had filled all of her cold, empty places with warmth and joy.

Suddenly she remembered her prayer as she and Whit had driven along the road to the landing. She had promised God, if He would give Jayboy and her another chance, that she would seek Him until she truly found Him.

"You can have that peace, you know," the preacher assured her. "All you have to do is confess that you are a sinner—like all the rest of us—and ask for the forgiveness provided through the substitutionary death of His Son, Jesus Christ, and tell Him you want Him to be the very center of your life."

"I. . . ," she began hesitantly.

The knocking at the front door didn't penetrate her consciousness until Jimmy O'Brien sighed heavily and got up from the couch. "I suppose I'll have to answer it," he said reluctantly.

"There you are!" Elayna heard Laura exclaim, as she and Toni appeared in the doorway, followed by her brother-in-law, Dave Myers, and Danny Butler. She got up and went to meet them.

"We've been worried to death about you," Toni said.

She saw surprise register on their faces as they took in her bathrobe and the fire, and then incredulity as they became aware of Jayboy leaning against the couch. Elayna began to laugh.

A faint smile touched Court's lips, but his eyes held a puzzled look. "I found the drawings and your note in the mail. Then I listened to your messages on my answering machine," he said, apparently trying to bring some order into the proceedings. "I knew something was wrong when you mentioned how much you enjoyed being on the boat lately. You haven't been on that boat more than twice since Hunt left."

He gave her another puzzled look, but she couldn't stop laughing.

"Anyway, I headed straight for your place, ran into the girls and Dave and Danny, and we all came out to the farm together."

"Frank called me when he read your SOS on the check you gave him," Detective Myers explained, eyeing Jayboy's new hiding place behind the couch. "When Court told me you likely were out here somewhere, I realized it was out of my jurisdiction, but I figured I could call the troopers in later, if we needed them."

"Not finding you at the boat landing, we wandered on down this way," Court added. "Seeing all the lights on over here, we took a chance on. . . What's so funny?" he finally asked.

"You are a little late, Court," she managed to gasp. "As usual."

He ignored her comment. "It was C. J. Berryman, wasn't it?" he said. "He killed Shirleene. He wanted those drawings back for the consortium, for Sheldon."

She shook her head no. "You were right about the consortium and the property they were buying. But it was Whit who wanted the papers."

"Whit?" he repeated.

She laid her hand on his arm. "It was Whit, Court. He was using Sheldon, C. J.—all of you—in a scheme to support an unbelievable cause. His ambitions to be governor were all bound up in that cause. He even tried to get me to marry him because I fit some image of what he thought the next governor's wife should be." She realized that she hoped that wasn't Whit's only reason for proposing marriage to her, but it was the most obvious one.

"Over my dead body," Jimmy O'Brien muttered, and Elayna saw Toni and Laura exchange enlightened glances.

Court sank down on the arm of a wingback chair. "Whit?" he repeated. Then he shook his head in denial. "Whit didn't kill Shirleene, Elayna. I can't believe that, not unless he tells me with his own mouth."

"He's dead, Court, he and C. J. both." She saw the shock in his eyes, but went on with her explanation. "C. J. killed Shirleene. But Whit sent him to get those papers from her. He planned to be the grand poobah or guru or something of some weird religious organization that would have one of its main headquarters in Frankfort. They were going to make a temple out of the state capitol, and. . ." She stopped, realizing how incredible it all must sound to her listeners, and she hadn't even told them about the bizarre events in the gardens. She couldn't believe it herself.

"Whit," Court said again.

"I'll put on the coffeepot and the teakettle," Jimmy O'Brien said resignedly, retreating to the kitchen as Elayna began to relate the entire story for the second time that night.

Several minutes later, she finished her retelling of the convoluted plot: ". . .and that's why he had C. J. try to get the drawings back from Shirleene and, when that didn't work, ransack my house, the shop, and your place. Whit knew that, once you saw those drawings, you would figure out what they intended to do, even if you didn't know the whys and wherefores of the religious concepts behind the plot," she concluded.

She looked up and saw that pain had darkened Court's eyes. "It's hard to believe Whit would order Shirleene's death," he said, shaking his head. "He was my friend."

"Whit didn't order C. J. to kill Shirleene, Court," Elayna said. "I think C. J. lost control when she wouldn't cooperate. He was into the consortium strictly for the money, not for the cause. He had no commitment to 'love and peace,' as Whit did, though his was somewhat warped." *Would he have killed her in obedience to the demon's orders?* she wondered. She supposed she would never know.

Jimmy O'Brien came back into the room with a tray holding empty cups, a sugar bowl, and a pitcher of cream. He set them on a table and went back for the coffeepot and the teapot.

While the others busied themselves with pouring and passing, Court moved closer to Elayna. "Jimmy O'Brien told me about Hunt's death," he said quietly. "He said you already know about it."

"Oh, Court, I wanted to tell you myself, and Vivian and Cliff. I just didn't want to do it over the telephone, and there hasn't been another opportunity. I've only known it for a couple of days."

Court shook his head. "I think you've known it for a long time, Elayna. We all have. We just didn't want to admit it. Now we can put my brother to rest, along with all the questions about what happened to him. Thank God Jimmy was able to tell us the whole story."

She nodded. "You're right. And it is better to know than to wonder, to keep expecting him to turn up somewhere, someday. I'll always love him, Court. He was a very special part of my life, ever since I first saw him in eighth grade."

"He was a very special part of my life, too," he said. "My bratty little brother, always wanting to wrestle, always wanting to go somewhere with me, always ready to tattletale to Mom if I wouldn't let him, and always there with a hug or a gentle punch in the stomach when I needed one."

For a moment, Elayna glimpsed tears in his eyes, then his iron will resumed control. He chuckled. "Like most big brothers, I guess, I used to give him quarters to leave Shirleene and me alone when we were dating."

She smiled. "And he spent them on strawberry sodas for us at the drug store down the street—one soda with two straws."

He laughed aloud this time. "I'm sorry, Elayna! I should have paid him more so you could have had your own soda."

"You know that wasn't the point, Court," she said. "It was the two straws in one glass, bringing our heads so close they were almost touching. I would look up into those Evans blue eyes and forget all about the soda." She blinked away the tears this time, and Court put an arm around her and gave her a brotherly hug.

"Come on out from behind that couch, Calvin," she heard Dave Myers order, as he fixed himself a second cup of coffee, with cream and lots of sugar. "You're in the clear, and I will apologize for trying to put you in jail, if you will apologize for putting me in the hospital."

Elayna saw Jayboy peeking out around the couch, and motioned for him to come to her. "Are you dropping all charges, Dave?" she asked.

Myers grinned, then nodded. "Obviously, he's not guilty of anything but knocking me down. Guess I owe you an apology, too, Elayna," he admitted. "And a thank you. You just wouldn't let me wrap up the case. 'Course, I was trying to put it in the wrong package." He chuckled.

Danny Butler, who had not said a word since he arrived, gave her a broad smile, asked Jimmy O'Brien where the bathroom was, and disappeared into the back of the house.

"What can we do about the consortium, Dave?" Elayna said. "Court and I both have copies of those drawings that prove they intended to turn Frankfort into a lake, even though Jamie Madison may be the only one left who really knows why."

"Well, we can conduct an investigation," Myers offered. "If that turns up nothing that can be connected with anyone specifically, we can 'leak' the drawings—no pun intended—and enough of the story to the media to at least cause them to drop their plans to flood Frankfort. We have somebody in the police department who is experienced at leaking news to the media," he added wryly. "Maybe I can trap him—or her—by planting this flood story."

"The flood!" Toni broke in. "Elayna, your house must be under water by now. Liberty Hall's lower gardens are totally submerged."

"What?" Elayna said stupidly. *Granny's house? The nooks and crannies that hold all my memories?* She felt Jimmy O'Brien's arm slip around her shoulders.

"They say the fault in Dix's Dam compelled them to open the gates to prevent a massive failure," Court explained. "That sent tons of water rushing down upon Frankfort, faster than any flood we've ever seen. It may be that the South Frankfort floodwall pushed the water higher than usual into North Frankfort. Anyway, several buildings are completely gone, Elayna, and we won't know what it has done to your place until the river crests and begins to drop."

Her head was spinning. She couldn't grasp it all. "Liberty Hall? The Bar Center?" she managed to ask.

"The Center's own floodwall seems to have protected it," Court said, "and Liberty Hall is dry, so far."

"Some of the lower streets are flooded, though," Laura added. "I don't know how long I'll be able to get to my apartment. I'm going home with Toni until the river crests."

Elayna didn't know what to say. Except for a few photos and trinkets at the shop, everything of personal value to her was in that house. When the waters receded, would there be anything left of her past, of her life?

She looked up and caught tears in Toni's big blue eyes. Laura turned quickly and began to gather up dirty cups.

"You're welcome to stay at my place," Court said, "though with Annie in Florida, I suppose the gossips would have a field day with that. But I don't care, if you don't."

"I'm not going to do that to your political career," she assured him, still a little dazed by the news she had just absorbed.

"You can stay with us at my house," Toni offered.

"Thanks," she said, "but I have an empty, furnished apartment over the shop. I'll be okay." Then she gasped. "It didn't get the shop, too, did it?"

"I don't think the water came that far," Court said. "The Wilkinson Street floodwall seems to be holding, but the water from above it has spread out over the area. I don't know if we can get to the shop right now. You can all just stay with me until morning," he added. "I'm all alone in that big house."

"That's a great temporary solution," Jimmy O'Brien agreed, "but I have a better long-term one in mind."

Elayna felt a blush creep over her face. He certainly knew how to unnerve her. "Are my clothes dry?" she asked him. "I need. . ."

". . .to bury your dead," he finished for her again, as he headed back to the clothes dryer.

Yes, bury my dead past. Get my "temporary" present in order. And then, like Scarlett O'Hara, I will think about tomorrow, she decided, taking the dry clothes he handed her. She gave him a tired smile and went into the bathroom to pull on dryer-warm jeans, sweatshirt, socks, and shoes.

Tomorrow, she promised herself, *I will deal with the future, with questions of eternity, with the strange emotions this red-haired preacher stirs in me. But, for tonight, I have coped with more than enough.*

Chapter 85

Jayboy stood behind the Bar Center's floodwall watching the mist rise above the water. The river was green again. And almost back inside its banks. But he could see the muddy mark where it had climbed the wall nearly to the top. It hadn't spilled over, though.

He would miss his safe place under 'Layna's porch. He would miss knowing she was there behind his and Doris's house. But he would see her at the shop. She was living there for now. Just a few blocks away. If he needed her, he could be there in no time. Or if she needed him.

There was no porch at the shop that he could crawl under. And the flood had damaged the leafy boxwood caves he and 'Layna had played under in the gardens of Liberty Hall. The gardener was taking out some of them and making low hedges out of the rest. All his safe places were gone. But maybe he didn't need a safe place anymore, now that the blackness had gone away.

He sighed. Most of his life, the blackness had waited for him. And there had been that empty space inside him. Waiting for the blackness to fill it. To swirl over him and gobble him up until there would be nothing left of him. Only the blackness.

Jimmy O'Brien said everybody had an empty space inside. "A God-shaped space," he called it. "That can't be filled by anything less." That's what he had said in the service last Sunday when

'Layna had taken him and Doris out to that tall brick church in the country. And he had done what the preacher said about asking Jesus to forgive him for all the bad things he had done.

He knew he had done a lot of bad things. Like hiding Doris's class ring in his coffee can and letting her think she had lost it. And once he had looked at some naked girls in a magazine he found in somebody's trash. And he had sacrificed Hunt and Shirleene to the blackness. And he had been happy when Shirleene really was dead. Not when she was being killed. That was awful! But knowing she couldn't torment him anymore had felt good. And he had hit the policeman in the stomach with his head and run away. Oh, he had done lots of bad things!

Jayboy smiled. He wouldn't be doing those things anymore. Now that Jesus was living right there inside of him.

He had gone down to the altar first. Before 'Layna. Then she had followed. He didn't know what had happened inside her. But God and Jesus had filled up all his empty space. There was no room for the blackness. And it had gone away.

He stretched and wiggled his toes in the new red sneakers Doris had bought him. He felt really good. Like when the first dandelions appeared in the spring. Bestrowed across the lawn like golden jewels.

A sadness crossed his mind. He wished they had let him keep the dandelion pin. He could have kept it in his new coffee can that Doris had given him. And he could have taken it out whenever he wanted to brighten up a dark winter day. When the dandelions were gone.

At least they had quit calling him the Dandelion Killer. Now that was what they called the man on the boat. Who had blown up like a ripe dandelion bursting into the sky. Then he had been swallowed up by the blackness. And he—Jayboy Calvin—hadn't had anything to do with it. But the Dandelion Killer was gone.

And he wouldn't be back.

Neither would 'Layna's friend. The senator. He was a little sad about that because 'Layna and Court were. And he had liked him, too.

The dandelions would come back, though. Nothing could kill a dandelion. He had heard Mac say that. And Mac had tried. But dandelions were eternal. Just like 'Layna always said. They might be buried in the ground for awhile. But when it was time, the wind would whisper to them. The sun would beckon. And the dandelions would appear. Like magic.

He had tried to tell Brother Jimmy about the Dandelion Kingdom. But he said the dandelions were just a small part of the kingdom of God. And the "magic" was the power of the Holy Spirit using the dandelions to show a picture of Jesus being buried and raised up again. And he said the dandelion seeds were like the word of God scattering everywhere to spread God's kingdom.

That was all right. The preacher could say it any way he wanted to. But Jayboy knew. 'Layna would always be the Princess of Dandelion. And he would always be her trusty knight.

He watched the fog gathering over the luminous surface of the water. It swirled and thickened, reaching for the space where the small brick cottage had stood. But he wasn't afraid anymore. It was just an autumn mist. It was time now for autumn mists. And bright-colored leaves. As bright as the colors in his crayon box. With the black one broken and thrown away.

Chapter 86

Elayna sat at her antique walnut teacher's desk in the bay window of her third-floor apartment in the building that housed Elayna Evans Imports. It wasn't Granny's desk. That was gone with the flood that had taken her house. It was very similar, though. She had been lucky to find it in the antique store down the street.

She looked around the big room with its sloped ceiling and ancient wood moldings, its walnut and marble fireplace—that worked! Already the four-room apartment, which she had kept for business visitors, reflected the personality of its new occupant—the Monets on the wall, the richly patterned carpets from Damascus, the books, the jade cat she had rescued from the debris of the break-in. *The chip out of its side doesn't show at all placed on the mantel that way*, she thought with satisfaction.

She was very comfortable here, except for the long winding staircase she had to climb to reach it, but she knew that added to the building's charm. *I'm just glad I still have good knees*, she thought wryly.

She had not decided whether she would build another house on her lot behind the Bar Center. Without a floodwall, it would be foolish to rebuild there. It wouldn't be the same anyway. It would never be the house her ancestors had converted from a stable. It would not have the lingering smell of old horse sweat mingled with the carnation scent of the powder her grandmother had worn. It would not have the floors, the woodwork, the cabinets blessed by the loving touch of her grandfather's tools.

Maybe she would just sell the lot to the Bar Center. Or maybe she would donate it to the city to add to River View Park, with the stipulation that they put up a plaque in memory of her grandparents, who had made her childhood so happy there. Then she would just stay here in this apartment over her shop. *At least until my knees go,* she thought. *Or maybe by then I will be able to afford an elevator.*

She needn't worry about that yet, though, and she had other things to think about right now. She had promised Jimmy O'Brien she would be at the reopening of Mockingbird's tonight, and she was looking forward to it. He claimed the restaurant was as elegant as ever, now that the aftermath of the flood had been eradicated and the luxurious green carpet brought back downstairs and reinstalled.

The red-haired Irish preacher still unnerved her a bit, with his insistence that God had brought them together, and his suggestions that she not rebuild her house, but marry him and share his. She was growing fond of Jimmy O'Brien, but she wasn't ready yet to make that commitment.

Suddenly, Elayna felt the need for a brisk walk. She glanced at her watch. Granny's clock had been destroyed in the flood, and she could barely hear the church bells from here. But she had a couple of hours before she was due at Mockingbird's. Deciding that the green wool slacks and sweater she was wearing would be all right for a stroll through town, she replaced her loafers with black walking shoes and left the apartment.

Standing on the sidewalk, she breathed in the mellow scent of ripening leaves, mixed with a hint of wood smoke from some nearby fireplace. The sun was staining the western sky as it sank quickly down the horizon.

Leslie had closed the shop and gone home. Most of the other downtown business owners had done the same. Elayna quickly covered the short distance to the deserted mall. At its southern end, she turned right onto West Main and automatically headed toward her old home. But she had already visited the devastated site where her grandparents' house had stood, and she didn't want to go back there now.

She paused in front of C. J. Berryman's real estate office, remembering the last time she had stood there watching him take down a phone message with his left hand, the first real clue that he might have been Shirleene's killer. He had been a terrible man, and he had met a terrible end. She supposed Whit would have said that evened out his karma.

She moved on down the street, covering the next few blocks as if she had known all along that she would end up in Liberty Hall's gardens, the scene of her happiest childhood days, and of her greatest nighttime horror.

Entering the gardens, she walked down the brick walk, then across the lawn, where she stood looking down at the green patina of the ancient sundial that, moment by moment, hour by hour, marked the relentless passing of time.

Margaretta Brown had taught Sunday school in these gardens, she remembered. Had she ever encountered anything supernatural here? Or had the demonic spirit she had seen and heard the other night come in recent days, at the request of its New Age seekers?

There was a definite chill to the air. She shivered as she looked toward the river. Then, as she watched, a mist swirled through the open space of the lower gardens. The leaves on the trees and shrubs began to tremble. She looked around her. The leaves in this part of the garden were still. There was no breeze here. Only in the part of the gardens where she had heard the demonic spirit speak to Whit did some force disturb. Would the force that had commanded him to "eliminate" her attack her now itself?

Jimmy O'Brien was convinced that Christians were protected from demonic spirits by the name and by the power of the blood of Jesus Christ. She had called on that name last Sunday, when she and Jayboy had walked the aisle to the altar. Afterward, she had told the preacher about her terrifying experience in the gardens. That was when he had told her that, although demons might harass Christians, they could not do them any real harm. He had even told her what to say if she ever faced that kind of situation again.

Slowly, she began to walk down the wide path between Margaretta's flower beds, keeping her eyes focused on the lower gardens. The trees and shrubs below her began to flail to and fro. She glanced behind her. The leaves of the upper gardens were still. Elayna's heart pounded. She tried to swallow, but there was no saliva in her mouth.

"In the name of Jesus Christ, the Son of the Living God...," she began, but she was too scared to remember the rest of the words. She stopped behind the hedge between her and the lower gardens. Covering her head with her hands and arms, she stood there, repeating aloud, "In the name of Jesus Christ, the Son of the Living God..."

The branches of the trees and shrubs around the open space tossed in a frenzy. The leaves on the hedge trembled. Then, as though the wind had hit a wall of glass, the hedge was still, as still as the leaves of the garden behind her. With a whooshing sound, the wind moved toward the river. Down past her landing, she saw a small cabin cruiser whirl around twice, then stop, rocking in the wake of the force that had passed. The trees along the river's path tossed, then were still, as the wind moved on around the bend.

Elayna took a deep breath. Her knees felt weak. Had she really seen what she thought she had just seen? Had her imagination simply run wild there for a few moments? She wanted to talk it over with Jimmy O'Brien, but she wasn't sure she could put it all into words.

She turned and walked back toward the gate, thinking of all the things that had happened, of all the changes in her life over the past few days and nights.

My past is so much flotsam swept away by the angry river. My present, at best, is temporary. But isn't everybody's past just so much debris, carried along by the river of time? Isn't the present always transient? And who knows what the future holds, for any of us. All she knew was that it was time to move on with her life.

She left the gardens, hearing the clink of the chain as the heavy ball pulled the gate shut behind her.

About the Author

Wanda Luttrell was born and raised in Franklin County, Kentucky, where she lives with her husband, John. She is the mother of five grown children and was employed for nearly thirty years by the Kentucky Association of School Administrators.

Wanda's writing has appeared in various Christian and general publications. Her interest in local Kentucky history eventually led her to write several books with themes from the Bluegrass State, including *The Legacy of Drennan's Crossing* (Tyndale House), *In the Shadow of the White Rose* (Tyndale House), and the *Sarah's Journey* series (Chariot-Victor Publishing).

Would you like to offer feedback on this novel?
Interested in starting a book discussion group?

Check out:

www.barbourbooks.com

for a reader survey and book club questions.

If you liked this book, here are other
BARBOUR BOOKS
fiction titles that will interest you. . .

Face Value
by Andrew Snaden and Rosey Dow
ISBN 1-58660-589-5

A cosmetic surgeon finds himself playing amateur detective after being framed for a killing.

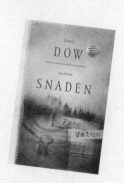

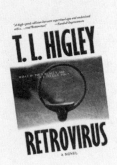

Retrovirus by T. L. Higley
ISBN 1-58660-697-2

Are Christians the guinea pigs
in sinister DNA research?

A Treasure Deep by Alton Gansky
ISBN 1-58660-673-5

Booby traps—and a murderer—protect a
world-changing treasure.

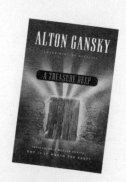

Available wherever books are sold.